The Long Reach Back

– P. J. PATERSON –

Printed and bound in England by www.printondemand-worldwide.com

http://www.fast-print.net/bookshop

The Long Reach Back

ISBN: 978-178456-498-8

A catalogue record for this book is available from the British Library

First published 2017 by
FASTPRINT PUBLISHING
Peterborough, England.

The Long Reach Back

P. J. Paterson

Contents

Acknowledgements 7

Prologue 9

Chapter 1 – The Thin Line: July 11

Chapter 2 – A Dusty Ghost 17

Chapter 3 – The Tablecloth: September 24

Chapter 4 – The Hole: October 27

Chapter 5 – Miss Busy Knickers: November 33

Chapter 6 – The Secret Dress: Early December 43

Chapter 7 – Mixed Emotions: The Following Day 46

Chapter 8 – Knickers in a Twist 49

Chapter 9 – Madame Renard 53

Chapter 10 – You Wouldn't Want to Know 62

Chapter 11 – From the Ground Up 65

Chapter 12 – Reincarnate 69

Chapter 13 – The Understudy 77

Chapter 14 – The Catalyst 82

Chapter 15 – The Skeleton 87

Chapter 16 – The Long Reach Back 96

Chapter 17 – The Sisters 103

Chapter 18 – Christmas Come Early: February 110

Chapter 19 – The Mexican Wave 122

Chapter 20 – Cause and Effect... 128

Chapter 21 – The Man with No Name 134

Chapter 22 – Achilles Heel 145

Chapter 23 – The Photograph 157

Chapter 24 – The Commitment.. 168

Chapter 25 – The Tourist: Day One...................................... 182

Chapter 26 – Gift of Good Fortune...................................... 194

Chapter 27 – The Tourist: Day Two...................................... 207

Chapter 28 – Distant Glow.. 224

Chapter 29 – The Showdown: Day Three.............................. 247

Chapter 30 – A lesson in Morality: Day Three 274

Chapter 31 – The Land of his Birth 288

Chapter 32 – Something Borrowed 311

Chapter 33 – Stepping Stones 318

Chapter 34 – Secrets and Truths.. 328

Epilogue – Three Weeks Later.. 354

About the Author.. 355

Connect with the Author 355

Note from the author:

The Long Reach Back was written, produced and edited in the UK where spellings and word usage can vary from U.S. English. The use of quotes in dialogue and other punctuation can also differ.

Acknowledgements

To Emily, and all the children of the
world who have succumbed to illness.

To Kimberley, editor and fellow biker – thank you.

To the Bard, for his undeniable and
exceptional contribution to English literature
and language worldwide.

Prologue

"One last thing, Sam . . . I love you with all my being, and I sure as hell know you love me. Ask me to marry you again, please? Please . . . I won't mess up again, I promise. I'm spent. I can't do any more." She held her breath, waiting, watching his every expression as he gently stroked her face with the back of his hand.

He could see she was worn out – she didn't have to tell him – so with a loving smile he pulled her to him and gazed into her beautiful hazel eyes. He then took a breath and held it, a breath that would change their lives forever.

"So, where do you want to go on honeymoon?" he asked, with the smile she had come to love.

Absorbing those words into her whole heart and soul, she smiled right back and said, "Niagara Falls, sweetheart, *and don't forget the roses . . .*"

Sam opened the bedroom door for them to leave, and then closed it again with a puzzled frown on his face.

"This is no good, no good at all. We can't spend the rest of our lives together, knowing you never said yes." He reached for her hands, gazing into her sparkling eyes, still moist from tears of joy from moments before.

"Marry me . . . please?"

She smiled at him, a confident smile. This time she wouldn't have any trouble saying the word, the word that in the past she'd either regretted saying – when she said it to Toby – or couldn't say at all when Sam first asked her.

"Yes, Sam . . . my darling Sam. Yes, yes. . .!"

Chapter 1

The Thin Line

July

"Bugger, who could that be?" Penny muttered, reaching across the bed to grab her phone.

"Archie, sweetheart, this is a bit early for you. It's only 8 o'clock. What's up?" she asked, knowing that Archie Goodmann was the proverbial night owl, and when he did eventually rise from his luxurious slumber, the sun was well on its way to its azimuth, sometimes even passed it.

"I'm sorry, sweetie," he said apologetically. Despite his nocturnal habits, Archie had something important to tell her that couldn't wait, and important enough for him to prematurely leave the comfort of his sumptuous Egyptian cotton sheets. "Is Farmer with you?" he asked.

From the first time Penny introduced them to each other Sam and Archie had become great friends, and Archie would always insist on addressing Sam by his surname. 'Oh, it's got to be Farmer, sweetie, that's a strong man's name,' he'd told her.

"Yes, Arch, he is," she replied with a saucy giggle. "I'm sprawled across him. Say hello to Archie, sweetheart."

Archie gave a little shiver of excitement in response to the picture she'd drawn for him, wishing it was he, and not her in Sam's arms.

Archie knew Penny had finally found the man of her dreams, and all *he* could do was dream, realising his fantasy was just that . . . but knowing Penny was blissfully happy and having Sam as his close and dear friend placated him.

"You're teasing me! Oh, you lucky girl," he replied. Then his excitable, boyish tone changed to one of business-like seriousness as he added, "Will both of you join me for lunch, there are a couple of things I wish to discuss?"

Penny sat up to talk to Sam, and saw him nod in agreement – he'd heard what Archie had said.

"I'm on Belinda's chat show at eleven, Arch, where do you fancy . . .?"

Sam may now be her fiancé, but when it came to being ready to leave the house on time, she still kept him and the car that would take them to the television studios waiting.

"Sorry, sweetheart," she said, watching Sam open the front door for her. "You don't want your future misses going out looking like she's not long been out of bed, now do you?" She ended her words with a kiss.

He laughed, knowing that apart from a quick shower, a mug of coffee and a mouthful of marmalade-coated toast, she hadn't been out of bed very long at all.

"Thank you for coming with me, Sam. I'd like people to meet the man who has given me this beautiful ring." She added another kiss to his lips.

"Miss McCain. How lovely to see you again," chirped the voice of Trudy, a tall, leggy woman in her late twenties. Her crisply spoken English had been practiced in the mirror hour after hour to mask her North Country origins - and a past life that few were aware of. The tight-fitting, lime-coloured cropped trousers (which were slightly garish), topped off with a flowery chiffon blouse were all donned to distract and seduce the senses of any red-blooded male.

Chapter 1

"Down boy," Penny whispered, pulling on Sam's hand as they watched this colourful vision teeter towards them, her six-inch heels giving her the posture of a woman who walked as if she was in need of a pee!

Penny politely returned her smile, aware that Trudy's employer, Belinda Carson, wasn't only known for her sharp-pointed interview technique, but also for her style and elegance, and she would *never* consider employing anyone, let alone a personal assistant who would win over her on points in the sophistication stakes.

"I'll get you signed in and then to make-up," she said, turning to Sam, her alluring gaze not lost on Penny.

"This is my fiancé, Sam Farmer," Penny said, with emphasis on the word *my*.

"Oh yes, you're the 'foot spa man'. Miss Carson is looking forward to meeting you," Trudy said, seeing Sam break into a broad smile as he remembered when and why he got that name.

Having had her face powdered and rouged and made up, Penny allowed Sam to kiss her gently on the cheek - not their usual unrestrained way of showing affection for each other, but even he knew that to kiss her wanting lips would result in her having to recoat them, and there wasn't time.

Trudy was eagerly waiting to show Penny onto the set. Once she had left the hospitality lounge, the green room, and with a cappuccino in hand, Sam ensconced himself onto the deep-cushioned sofa to watch the large plasma television. She reappeared on the set, which was comprised of fake marble (topless) pillars separated by screens that displayed various backdrops of London, with pictures of Penny, captured in time, playing Katherine on the stage.

The show's host, Belinda, greeted her with her arms outstretched for the customary hug and air cheek to cheek kisses, and then Penny turned to acknowledge the studio audience with a fingery wave as they clapped their greeting, orchestrated and prompted by one of the show's studio producers, mimicking the actions of a seal in a water park.

Penny settled onto one of the modern, but not-so-comfortable steel-framed leather chairs, combing her hands through her long brown hair. Its natural auburn tints were highlighted by the glare of the studio lights. Smiling and relaxed, she readied herself for the friendly but probing interview from a girlfriend of many years, knowing that to some degree that meant absolutely nothing.

The theatre stage was where Penny excelled and had few equals; Belinda's stage was the TV studio. But the difference was that when Penny became Katherine she operated within the constraints of her character. Belinda Carson didn't have those constraints and Penny knew that; Belinda could probe and tease as she pleased.

As with previous shows she'd appeared on, they had discussed how her time in front of the cameras would be sequenced with preprepared questions and any pictures or props being shown at the appropriate time. But there was one snippet – a teasing reminder of how one night Penny had showed her friends for the first time just how a new man in her life had become more than just a casual acquaintance – that Belinda Carson had no intention of forewarning her about, or what she had planned prior to the show going out live.

The thirty-five-year-old attractive brunette knew her guest and friend had had her fair share of ups and downs, particularly when it came to men, and was more than aware that Penny's happiness with Sam came at a cost: that of the betrayal and humiliation by her ex-boyfriend Toby, whose self-destruction with drugs was masked only by his boyish charisma. But Sam was different, and Belinda knew and respected that, so she had drawn herself a line that she would not cross . . . but it was a very tenuous line.

She began with her customary small talk, congratulating Penny on her triumph in the new version of Shakespeare's *Taming of the Shrew* that was playing to packed audiences in the West End.

Sam watched and listened with interest as the two women laughed and reminisced, with the audience's non-prompted ovations and laughter setting the scene for what was to come.

"Tell you what, Pen," Belinda said, fidgeting, acting out her part. "These chairs aren't very comfortable, are they?" Her concerned gaze, masked the fact that those words were the cue for a two-seater settee to be brought on to the set directly in front of the audience, accompanied by two foot spas.

"Oh my god . . . no!" Penny declared, as a flush appeared on her face, more than a little surprised at what her crafty friend had conjured up.

The predominately female studio audience followed with polite bemusement, as yet not realising the significance of the gate-crashing studio props. Penny did though and quickly responded to the rouse her host had laid.

Without any prompting, she slipped off her silvery sling-back sandals and walked barefoot a few paces to the crimson settee, hitching up her blue polka dot dress to her knees as she settled herself down. She dipped her feet into the warm water of the foot spa as Belinda sat beside her to continue the now jocular interview.

She described to her captivated audience, how one evening during a girly night at Penny's home, her four pals were shown a gift from a new friend, and how the fondue set and chocolate fountain were soon abandoned for the opportunity to soak their tortured feet.

While the two women chatted about that night with fondness, paddling their toes in the water, Penny knew Belinda could have mentioned that Sam was a widower who had lost his wife a few months before they'd met, or the fact that, at the time, she was engaged to another man . . . but she didn't . . . that would have put her perilously close to crossing her line. She knew that that should remain private, but at the same time she had a job to do – which was to titillate her audience's interest in her guest. Also at the back of her mind, Belinda knew there was a wedding in the offing, and she hoped she had a foot through the church door, but knowing Penny as she did . . . cross that line and she would have that door slammed firmly in her face.

Their friendly banter continued as Belinda posed questions she already knew the answers to, but those were purely for the benefit of her audience.

"So, tell us, hun," she asked, glancing into a camera, engaging her viewers. "This man of yours, does he still give you gifts?" Her eyes were now wide, eager for Penny's reply.

"Oh yes, he sure does," Penny answered, her eyes moist with unfettered joy. She raised her left hand to show Belinda's audience the rose-pink solitaire diamond engagement ring. "His name is Sam . . . and I'm going to marry him."

Chapter 2

A Dusty Ghost

"Oh hello, dear," Auntie June exclaimed at the surprise visit from her niece.

Penny entered the lounge, normally relaxed and joyous on visiting her aunties, but not this time, no, not this time.

"I thought I heard June talking to someone," said her sister May, as she re-entered the lounge after a quick U-turn – she'd been making her way up the stairs for her after lunch nap. "Is Sam with you, dear?" she asked, knowing that if he was, he would surely require a cup of tea – or in Sam's case a mug – and, as it was the last Friday of the month, one of the saffron buns she'd started baking for their bridge night.

"Yes, he is, he's chatting to Harry outside, but to tell you the truth I wanted to talk to the two of you on my own first," Penny replied. She stared across the room, a frown crumpling her expression.

"Oh. Yes, dear. Why is that?" May enquired.

The reaction of the two elderly ladies was one of cautious smiles, wondering if she had found out what they had done.

"We had lunch with Archie today," Penny said, endeavouring to be calm and concise as she sat herself down on one of the two settees. Her aunties settled themselves onto the one opposite. Both had their hands resting on their laps, waiting for the emotional questioning which was surely imminent.

The Long Reach Back

Penny gazed at her aunties, holding back tears at having to recount the conversation she and Sam had had with Archie.

As the rays of the afternoon sun danced through the still air, it couldn't brighten the darkened atmosphere that filled the room. Penny was acutely aware that what her aunties had intended to do had sprung purely out of the love they felt in their hearts for her and Sam, but it pained her to know that it wasn't the first time they had done it.

"I've been informed by Archie that you recently had a visit from Bertie Matthews, the Book Man," she said, and then paused. Her aunties could see the tears begin to trickle down her face. Penny then moved and knelt in front of them, reaching out her hands to hold theirs. "Archie told us how you had sold part of your cherished book collection to Bertie to pay towards my university fees all those years ago, and how his mother found out and bought them and gave them back to you."

Penny leant forward to hug the two ladies, who were now concerned as they could see their niece was in a state of flux.

"You silly cows," she continued. "Now you've nearly gone and done it again, and you don't have to . . ."

"But we wanted to, dear, just like we wanted to the first time," May replied, her fingertips soothing away the tears from Penny's cheeks.

"Everything . . . all this . . . is as much yours *now* as when we're gone," she said, trying to explain their motives with an animated movement of her head. Her tone of voice was gentle, but unapologetic. If anything, she spoke with conviction, not being in any way swayed by what she thought was her niece's misplaced reaction to the situation. "When you came to live with us as a child, you changed me . . . you changed us from two self-centred spinsters to two mums! That's why we intend to contribute towards the wedding of our darling angel."

Penny experienced a pain in her heart, a truthful stab, knowing the words May had spoken were exactly that: heartfelt.

The sisters looked up to see Sam had entered the room quietly, observing the three women, not intending to interrupt. He knew that although Penny's future was planned around him, her past was deeply rooted with these two endearing, yet at times troublesome, ladies she was holding onto.

"Tell her, Sam. Tell her that's what parents do, isn't it? If you love your child, you do anything for them, don't you, dear?" June implored, her tone of voice desperate as she prised herself to her feet, using Penny's shoulder as a support, and then stiffly made her way over to Sam. He at least was pleased to see them, and had his arms ready for a friendly hug and a kiss on the cheek from June.

She could see in his eyes he was deep in thought, though, pondering her words, an almost un-focussed stare on his face. He was thinking of his two beautiful daughters, Daddy's girls Maggie and Estelle, and knew all too well that June was right. He couldn't think of a single thing he wouldn't do for them, as yet unaware that there would come a time when his daughters would reciprocate his un-flinching love for them and risk everything for him, even their lives.

"Time for a cuppa, dear?" June asked, slipping her arm through Sam's, aware that if there was anything to quench an atmosphere of tension, you couldn't beat a good, hot pot of tea.

Penny moved to sit next to May, her fingers searching in her bag for her requisite tissues, knowing once again her aunties had driven her to tearful distraction. They heard the distinctive sound of china and the rattle of teaspoons, and it broke into the stilled atmosphere. Sam wheeled in the tea trolley – a gift from him, and a godsend to the two elderly ladies – and they prepared themselves with bated breath, knowing their niece hadn't just turned up to chastise . . . she wouldn't just leave it at that.

They were right, and Penny hoped that what she said next

would at least be a bridge for her aunties' desire to sell their rare and coveted books, but she also had to tell them a truth, a truth that hadn't been deliberately hidden or suppressed, but had simply been buried with time.

"Archie wants to contribute towards the wedding . . ." she ventured. "And no, not because of your antics, but because he's family . . . isn't he?"

The look that passed between the sisters was as pointed as a spear, a turn of their heads and a gaze that momentarily left them without words to reply. June breathed in, and the air of acceptance filled her as a suspicion held for many years by them was finally going to be realised.

"Yes, we believe he is, dear. Archie's possibly our half-brother," June replied.

She felt Sam's hand squeeze hers, and his strong yet comforting touch stilled her emotional tremors.

May then continued, picking up June's verbal batten – it was a sisterly trait of theirs that without prompting they could pre-empt each other's thoughts and put them into words, and as accomplished actresses, they instinctively knew when the spotlight had turned on them.

"How long has Archie known?" May asked.

"Oh, only recently. Which was due to Maggie . . . well, sort of," Penny replied.

"What do you mean, 'due to Maggie'? She couldn't have known, surely, and she doesn't strike me of the sort of person who would tell tales?" May said.

"No, you're right, she isn't and she didn't," Sam interjected. "Archie confided in her that his father, Lord Malcombe, had died from a rare genetic disorder and said that in most cases the gene is passed to your offspring." His look settled on Penny; they both knew the friendship between his daughter and Archie was in some ways similar to their own, but would never be more than a deep, platonic friendship bound by their love of horses and a zest for enjoying each other's company. "Archie couldn't bring himself to get tested for the gene, to put it bluntly, because he was scared to. But he made an error of judgement: he confided in Maggie, thinking she would just hold his hand and let it be. He was wrong totally wrong. She made all the arrangements, quietly and without any fuss, and persuaded him to have the test." Sam stopped talking, putting his mug of tea to his thirsty lips. Again, his eyes sought out Penny, aware that like her aunties she also knew when the spotlight had fallen on her. He knew that the answers to the questions the elderly ladies were bound to ask would be better coming from her lips.

"Did you never ask yourselves why Archie tolerated you both, with your cajoling and at times emotional bullying of him . . . well, did you?" As Penny uttered those words, the harshness of them resonated in her auntie's eyes, and a realisation that yet again they had been blinkered to his feelings manifested itself in their expressions. "Don't bother to answer that," she continued. "It's because he loves you both, like a brother would love his sisters. Arch said that ever since he was a child he felt an energetic connection to you both, and was mystified as to why that was."

She ended, sharing her gaze between her aunties, and then witnessed something few people had seen or heard before: a complete breakdown of communication and timing between the two of them!

"Why? Why in hell didn't he tell us?" May cried.

"Why? What? What else has he told you?" June demanded.

The two spontaneous questions became an amalgam of words woven into a muddlement of sound, a jumble of whys and whats, sounding more like 'whywhatinhellelsetellhasheustoldyou?'

The sisters then fell silent, seeing the caring looks on both Sam and Penny's faces; they didn't have to repeat themselves.

Sam was first to respond to their simultaneous questions.

The Long Reach Back

"When Archie called recently to see you both, he removed samples of hair from your hair brushes and had them DNA tested. To cure an itch he had, so to speak."

"Oh . . . did he now?!" May responded.

He laughed. "It's hard to imagine, isn't it?" he mused. "The old dapper tip-toeing around upstairs, supposedly going for a pee, and all the time he was sleuthing." He looked down at June's hands as they repetitively moved up and down her thighs, causing her floral-patterned dress to ripple and ruck under the pressure of her fingers, disfigured with arthritis.

Penny then confirmed her aunties' suspicions: "The test results for the disease thankfully came back as negative, but your DNA match tests proved positive . . ."

Then a silence fell, for only a few seconds, but long enough for all of them to realise that a page had been turned on a suspicion that had now become indisputable fact.

June let out a sigh of resignation, knowing that another dusty ghost was about to appear: an admission, a poignant verse that had lain hidden in the pages of the past, was about to be told.

"*I have entered another man's orchard and left my seed to grow and flourish,*" she uttered.

"After Father was promoted to glory, as we like to say," June continued, "we read through his journals, having in mind to write a biography of him, but were soon enlightened about his many infidelities. The sentence, 'I have entered' was later followed by another insertion, the following year, with a reference to the Gregorian calendar: 'a bissextile year' – a leap year to you and me, dears."

Again, June passed the batten to May. It was *their* father after all whom they were verbally reincarnating, and together they squared the circle on a puzzle from long ago.

"It was the 29th of February . . . the day and year Archie was born," May said.

Chapter 2

"So why didn't you ever tell the poor sod, for Christ's sake?"

"Why? Because we couldn't be totally sure, that's why — until now," June said, replying to Penny's tersely delivered question.

"Well, you can tell him yourself tomorrow, because he's coming around to see his sisters," Penny frowned, glancing at her wristwatch, aware it was time to leave.

"You would have liked our father, Sam, he was a lovely man . . . a philanderer but still a lovely man," May said, uttering the last few words in a sincere, but remorseful tone.

Chapter 3

The Tablecloth

September

"Any chance of another slice of your wonderful strawberry cheesecake, please?" Maggie pleaded. Her dark brown eyes lured the attention of the waiter as he served the ladies their afternoon tea.

The young man was tall and slim, and his white, cotton gloved hands and shirt were a lovely contrast against the blackness of his bibbed apron. He smiled politely as he replenished Maggie's plate with another wedge of calorie-laden delight.

"'Ansom," she replied, preparing herself for her task ahead with a sip of tea from the finest of bone china.

Estelle and Penny looked on in quiet amusement. They were resting after enjoying an afternoon shopping beyond the black lacquered doors of the Parisian-styled tearoom, away from the frenetic goings on as hordes of people shopped or just soaked up the atmosphere of London's iconic streets.

Unknown to Penny, the sisters had not only chosen the tearoom for its fine sustenance, and to rest their tired and aching feet – 'tootsies' as Estelle affectionately called them – but they also hoped to show her the type of fabric her wedding dress could be made from.

Dabbing her lips with a napkin, Maggie briefly glanced in the direction of Estelle as she broached the subject on their minds.

Chapter 3

"How are you getting on finding a wedding dress, Pen? I expect with the play an' all, you probably haven't had that much time to think about it, have you?"

"No, to tell you the truth I haven't. I've flicked through a few magazines, like you do, but I haven't found anything that 'floats my boat', as your dad would say."

They all giggled at that remark.

"Have you thought about having it made from lace - French lace to be exact?" Estelle asked, and then flipped open one of the side pockets of her bamboo-handled bag.

She passed over a photograph of a woman on her wedding day, arm in arm with her new husband, smiling effortlessly as they embarked on their life together. Looking at the picture, Penny's mouth fell open, but her smile was tinged with the knowledge that that life had come to a sad and premature end for this beautiful couple.

"God, your mum looks so, so beautiful . . . so happy," Penny said.

"Yeah, that was before Maggie was came along," Estelle quipped, looking at her sister, who didn't bother to reply as she filled her mouth with another piece of strawberry cheesecake.

Penny was transfixed by the photograph of Sam and his late wife Annie, realising that apart from a passport-sized picture he'd shown her from his wallet when they first met, it was the first time she had seen a picture of them together.

"'Ansom bugger, wasn't he?" Maggie said, taking another sip of tea to make more room for more cheesecake.

"Oh, he still is, sweetheart," Penny replied. Then followed that Eureka! moment, as she added: "Wow . . . what a wonderful dress she's wearing." Her eyes were then distracted as Maggie and Estelle gave each other a high-five, celebrating that their surreptitious plan had stirred Penny's interest in the picture, but moreover, the wedding dress.

"OK, what have I missed?" Penny asked, her eyes squinting suspiciously as she looked at the two grinning, pleased-with-themselves sisters.

"That's exactly the point, Pen, you haven't," Estelle replied. "It is a beautiful wedding gown, isn't it? It was made by two of the finest lace makers in France, grand-mère and her sister Madame Renard. It's a family tradition that the elders make the dress for the bride-to-be."

"Mother loved butterflies, so she had a design of them woven into the dress using the finest of gold braid. It makes her seem like she's being carried along by them, don't it . . ." Maggie said, laying her spoon and fork to rest on her now redundant plate. "Mmmm, that was scrummy."

Penny couldn't help but crack a smile at Maggie's sincere words, and not only because of the eagerness in which she said them, but the way she said them: Maggie's way, and to hell with the poor grammar!

"Feel this," Estelle said, tip-toeing her fingertips across the white lace tablecloth with designs of prancing figurines around the delicate, scalloped edge. "It's a reproduction of Normandy lace, where Mother's family are from. Lovely, isn't it?"

Their presentation had the desired effect, arousing Penny's imagination as thoughts of incorporating fine lace into her dress design formed in her mind. Again, she could see the sisters poised ready to respond to their future stepmother's curiosity.

"Go on . . . put me out of my misery, you're scheming, I know it. So, what is it?"

They broke into spontaneous laughter – laughter that demonstrated the deep and sincere friendship between the three of them.

Chapter 4

The Hole

October

"Bugger," Penny muttered unhappily, placing her phone precariously back on the corner of the bath as her shoulders slipped beneath the relaxing water. She wished, as always when Sam was away, that he was there sitting on the edge, washing her hair, his strong fingers soothing her scalp, sending her mind and body to places only he was capable of. Instead she felt disappointed that he'd had to cancel his plans to be with her this weekend and stay at the cottage in Devon.

"Hi, Harry," she called out, as she later walked down the cobbled cul-de-sac towards her aunties' mews house. She looked down at his pair of khaki-clad legs, this time visually severed from the rest of his body by an old 1950s car. Sadly, it now only journeyed ten feet before being pushed back into its garage, powerless to do otherwise.

"Hello, angel. So, where's my mate, then? You haven't dumped him, have you?" he joked, groaning to his feet. He pointed his rust-dusty face in her direction, pouting his lips to give her a welcoming kiss.

"He's had to stay at the cottage. It seems a hole has appeared in our life and he has to deal with it."

"Oh," he replied, gazing over the rim of his grease-smeared glasses, not quite sure how to respond to her hazy answer.

"Got to go, Harry, we're having our first meeting to plan the wedding. No doubt the old ladies will tell Betty all about it," she said, leaving a rouge lip-shaped print on his aged face.

Penny hung her coat on a hook in the hallway, and breathed in the heady essence of black pepper with a hint of musk – a cologne she instinctively recognised. She smiled. Archie was here.

"Come and sit down, dear, we've been waiting for you," May said, as Archie rose to his feet to pull out a dining chair for his belatedly acquired niece. Not even the aroma of the freshly ground coffee that hung in the air could compete with the sense of excitement around the table.

"I'm looking forward to this, sweetie," he said, placing a tender peck on her cheek.

"God knows why, Arch, it's mostly your money we're spending," Penny said with a cheeky grin. But behind the jovial reply, she already knew that he and Sam had talked in detail about the wedding and who would pay for what – and it was the 'what' that Archie was insistent about paying the lion's share of.

As a well as being a highly-respected theatre critic - who happened to cloak himself in the façade of an exorbitant lifestyle – the real Archie was a shrewd and an intelligent businessman who found little room for trust. With Sam, though, he found it hard not to trust him; if he held any person in high regard, it was him. Archie knew Sam was a proud and resourceful man. He'd had to be in order to dig his way out of the financial chasm he'd found himself in many years before – the result of the actions of his own traitorous elder brother, a situation which culminated in the premature death of his twin sister Ruth. The memory of her dying in his arms still haunted Sam, Archie knew that, and family and responsibility weighed heavily on his shoulders, drummed into him by his father after the sacrifice of another man a generation before.

And so, Sam and Archie had agreed to share the costs. In their eyes that was what close friends and future family do. There was also, however, a special something that Penny had planned, something that could only take place with Archie's connections, influence and, of course, his money.

"Well, as it's my wedding, I'll get the ball rolling, shall I?" Penny smiled. She then took a deep breath, and prepared to plan for the day she could hardly wait for.

"Just before we start, dear, Sam phoned earlier and talked about a hole or something?" June said, seeing Penny shake her head in polite refusal of a fresh croissant.

"It's a disused mineshaft to be exact," Penny replied.

Her cup of coffee then took temporary precedence over Archie and her two aunties, who eagerly waited for her to enlighten them as to why Sam was still in Devon. She gazed at the two elderly ladies, her dear aunts, two world-renowned actresses who had instilled a passion for theatre, and above all, Shakespeare, in her from such a young age.

"I remember how you both would say to me that sometimes you felt Shakespeare had been hijacked by the posh people, but that his plays were for the masses not just the privileged," she said. She then looked stern as a determined frown covered her brow. "Well, I'm going to do something to address that. I'm . . . we . . . Archie and I are going to put on a production of *Katherine* in the village 'for the masses'. A one-nighter for the locals!"

"Bravo, dear! What an excellent idea. Good on you," May responded, clasping her hands together as a gesture of solidarity with her niece.

June, however, looked on, wondering what the play had to do with the hole in the ground. "That's wonderful, dear, really. I think it's a commendable idea, but ...what has that got to do with the hole, or shaft or whatever you called it?" she asked.

"It's in the same field we want to erect the marquee for the wedding reception and stage," Penny replied. "The farmer, Mr Hunkin, has given us permission – which is very useful as it's right behind the pub – but it's not that simple. The council have been around to inspect the site for a licence for temporary change of use. They've laid out a list of requirements, one being care of the old, exposed mineshaft because *bats* live in it, or down it, or whatever.

"Sam was told it goes down hundreds and hundreds of feet. Apparently, locals have been known to dump old fridges and TVs down there, and that if you wait long enough when you throw something down it, you'll hear the splash at the bottom."

"Oh, it sounds as if Sam has got his hands full, the poor dear, buying the cottage next door and all the building work he's doing, plus running his company," May said, with pen and paper at the ready. (She liked to jot down anything important enough not to be forgotten as her memory was not as sharp as it used to be.)

Penny leant forward to rest her elbows on the table, her hands clasping her face. "Yes, it's not fair on him, is it? He has to deal with all the hassle on his own – and just because I want to get married in the village – while I'm up here twiddling my thumbs," she said, sitting back into her chair. (She remembered that as a child her aunties would constantly remind her: 'Don't slouch, chin up, shoulders back.')

"Do you remember Trudy?" she asked. "She used to work for Archie, but is now Belinda's PA."

Archie's eyes talked long before a word was uttered from his lips; they rolled, making his eyelids flutter, trance-like. "*Miss busy knickers*, I call her . . . she's a bloody workaholic," he blustered. "She'd never turn off or slow down. Always on the go. I tell you, Trudy wore me out just watching her, but she's a darling of a girl."

"Well, that's good to know, because Belinda said that if I need a good organiser, I could borrow the services of *Miss busy knickers*, as you call her, Arch."

"Yes, I remember her now, dear, the Yorkshire lass, you'll

get your pound of flesh from her. But hasn't she got a bit of a sketchy past or something?" June asked, as her gaze then sought out Archie, hoping her inquisitive remark would tease further facts from him about her to bolster the tentative few she already knew!

"You're not going to get Archie on that one, June, we're on to you both now, so stop prying into her past! You know the trouble you caused getting your facts wrong about Sam's," Penny scowled.

"Sorry, dear, force of habit . . . you know how it is with us."

Only too well, she thought.

"OK, shall we get on?" Penny said, once again taking the lead.

They then spent some time going through item after item, discussing in detail her planned nuptials.

"Right, that's almost it, but just a couple of other things," she then said, aware that she was about to turn her back on the gifted opportunity that had been handed to her, literally on a proverbial plate.

"I've told Angie I'm leaving the play when my contract comes to an end in April, and that I don't want her to find any future work for me, other than the odd day or two . . ."

"I bet she jumped for joy on hearing that," June replied sarcastically, aware that her agent, Angie, was also her close friend and who had, when Penny's acting career looked doomed to flounder over the years, never, ever given up on her.

"To tell you the truth, she wasn't that surprised. She's known me too long. Anyway, I'm not going to retire, I just want the chance to be myself with Sam, rather than having to become someone else all the time."

Penny's profound words brought caring smiles to the faces of Archie and her aunties, and they looked at the woman whose hazel eyes now shone with child-like excitement as she began to tease them with information about her special dress: "My wedding gown. I'm not going to go into any detail . . . other than it's going to be the most beautiful dress a woman could ever wish to wear."

Penny saw the knowing grin on Archie's face, shielded from her aunties' glare by his hand. Unlike them, he knew of Maggie's and Estelle's plan.

"The gown's being made for me in France, by the House of Renard," she added.

She could see the elderly ladies were just itching to glean more information from her, unaware of what the House of Renard really was, but sensing by the now enigmatic expression on their niece's face that that was all they were going to get . . . for the time being.

Chapter 5

Miss Busy Knickers

November

The deep, bellowing throb from the Harley Davidson's exhausts drew Sam's eyes as he peered through his lounge window; the engine's slow rhythmic beat resonated against the glass. He walked out into the November gloom – the air still damp from a downpour of rain that passed over an hour before – and gazed curiously at the red-leather clad figure. Tassels draped from the arms of the jacket and they moved in the breeze as the motorcycle, with its metallic red paintwork and copious amounts of chrome, were angled over to rest heavily on its stand.

With her crash helmet removed, the expected visitor stretched, cork screwing her torso after the arduous ride down from London.

"Hi, Sam! Trudy reporting for duty!" she said with a self-assured grin, stepping forward to accept a welcoming peck on her cheek. "Are you a biker?" she asked, unzipping her jacket to pass it to Sam, whose gaze was immediately distracted by a faded black t-shirt bearing the print of a naked female riding a penis-shaped motorcycle. It was worn over a pink long-sleeved fleecy top.

"No, not with Dartmoor on my doorstep. I walk a lot. But Estelle my youngest daughter is, or was. When she studied in London, she would go everywhere on her scooter."

"Oh, you can't beat a bike, Sam. There's nothing better than having throbbing horsepower between your legs, believe me."

"I'll take your word on that," he replied, smiling politely as he led her in the direction of the settee, upon which she effortlessly slumped down. "Tea? Coffee?"

"No thanks. I only ever drink water. Warm water will do me fine. Thank you."

Sam returned with a glass of water.

"That was delicious. Ta," she said after gulping thirstily.

"It's good of Belinda to volunteer your services. I'm sure you're busy enough without having to add our wedding to your workload."

"You've got Archie to thank for that, Sam. He gave her a call. Not that she minds . . . nor me for that matter. I'm glad to help. It's what I'm good at, organising events and things. Ask Archie, he'll tell you."

Why am I not surprised that Archie's behind this? Sam thought, knowing all too well that Archie may love Penny dearly, but when it came to spending his money, he wouldn't just hand it over to her in wads. He realised that this was another reason why Trudy was here.

"So how did you come to work for him?" he asked.

She didn't reply straight away, but stared at Sam, her eyes slightly squinted: she was studying him.

"How well do you think you know Archie, Sam?"

The tone and delivery of her question made him realise that it wasn't only an enquiry, it was also a test. How she responded was dependant on *his* reply.

"Well enough to know that if you take him at face value, you're a fool. Does that answer your question?"

He watched as her studious look returned to a casual, relaxed smile, but then, as she told her tale, that calm persona dissipated and was replaced with a stare he recognised: a mirrored reflection of how *he* looked when his painful memories of the past were shown the light of day.

"I first met Archie late one night in one of the side streets off Soho, about ten, no, nearly twelve years ago, now. He was trying to get into a private club with a party of friends, but the guy on the door wouldn't let him in. Big Russian bloke he was. Archie kept trying to tell him that he was a part owner of the club, but the idiot wasn't listening. He kept on insulting Arch, calling him a faggot and using all sorts of expletives, so I thought I could help – I speak a bit of Russian, you see. Eventually Archie was let in and I went on my way." Then she suddenly changed the subject, getting to her feet to stand in front of the open, but un-lit fire. "No wonder Miss McCain loves it here. I bet when the fire is alight it gets proper toasty."

"It's Penny. You can dump the McCain," he told her, sensing that she was prevaricating, but wondering why. "You were saying?"

"Yes, sorry. Where was I? Yes. Archie. He sent one of his friends outside to find me, but the Russian guy found me first. I guess he wanted his wallet back. I'd stolen it. All I remember is waking up in a private hospital with my jaw all wired up and tubes coming out of every orifice."

Trudy paused for a moment to wipe her nose with the small, pink-chequered handkerchief she had plucked from the sleeve of her pink top. She felt strangely accommodating, as if it was necessary for Sam to know everything.

"When I came to, Archie was holding my hand," she continued. "He didn't look best pleased with me. I remember the first words he spoke were: 'You can work for me and turn your life around, but if you ever betray me, I'll throw you back into the gutter where I found you last night'."

She then rolled up the sleeve of her left arm, showing Sam fading scars; puncture marks of her drug-controlled past.

"The truth is, Sam, I was in the gutter long before Archie found me. As with most addicts, I was prescribed Methadone to counter withdrawal symptoms, and then, after I left hospital, complete with new teeth, Archie sent me off to Ireland to straighten myself out. I didn't see him again for almost a year."

Sam walked to the kitchen, retuning with another glass of warm water for her. Trudy smiled, acknowledging his thoughtful gesture. Sam didn't need to ask her any questions as she continued her story unprompted.

"Archie said you're a trusted friend, but I know it's rare for him to trust anyone. You might not be aware, but I thought that you should anyway, that I'm also HIV positive. That's one reason I only drink water now. The only drugs that pass my lips are the ones that keep me alive. I owe Archie everything . . . for giving me my life back . . . and that's why I willingly work my arse off for him." She laughed thinking of her nickname.

"Ha! He always calls me Miss Busy Knickers! Did you know that? But it's a darn sight better than being called a junkie, don't you think?"

"So why don't you work for him now?"

Trudy was being open and frank with him, and it put both of them at ease with each other, but he did feel he needed to ask her that.

"In a way, Sam, I still do, that's why I'm here, but he recognised I needed a change. So now I'm Belinda's PA. It's good. I like her."

Sam showed Trudy around the cottage and the extension he was building. He joked with her that it was because he needed another bathroom, as 'Madame', as he affectionately called Penny, loved to soak in the Jacuzzi bath for what seemed like ages while others waited patiently outside to use the loo.

After their tour of the cottage, he drove her to the pub where she would be staying, her Harley safely locked away in his garage.

The bad weather from earlier in the day returned with a vengeance by the time Sam made his way home – leaving Trudy in the bar chatting to a few of the locals, enjoying a relaxing weekend drink and a gossip – and the blustery south-westerly wind was driving the rain relentlessly against the cottage windows. Winter was on the rampage.

He glanced at the clock on the kitchen wall, anticipating a phone call from Penny. With a matinee and an evening performance, Saturdays, like her Wednesdays, were long days and he knew exactly what Penny would do when she arrived home: pour a glass of her favourite wine, Merlot rosé from the Bordeaux/Bergerac border, and savour it while soaking in the bath. He wished he was there talking to her as he sponged her body, stealing sensual kisses. He then sighed as reality returned to him. *Next week, Sam, you can sponge her body . . . next week.*

Sam had barely removed those thoughts from his mind when his phone rang. He instinctively patted the pockets of his jeans for the phone, and then cussed himself for wasting time, his hearing directing his eyes to the kitchen table behind him.

The following morning, he made his way back to the pub, to be greeted by his friend Dave, the landlord, and his chirpy young son, Martin, who sneaked out from behind the bar.

"Hi, Uncle Sam. If you're looking for Trudy, she's gone to church with Mummy and that silly sister of mine."

"Ha! That's quick work for an eight-year-old! First name terms with an older woman, eh? You, cool dude, you!" he said, giving the boy a sideways smile.

"Oh no, Sam, she told me to . . . honest. She's hell of a funny!" Martin said, blurting out the words with excitement. "We've been in the field helping her. She was telling us jokes about sheep, but Clare didn't get them. Sisters . . . who'd have 'em?" he said, regally gesturing the flats of his hand in exasperation, mimicking a maturity beyond his years.

"So, what were you lot up to in the field, then?" Sam asked.

"Gizmoing," said the boy, making it sound like it was so obvious.

"Ah Sam, just the man I've been looking for!" Trudy called. She walked over to him, hand in hand with Martin's younger sister.

"I hear you've been to church?" he asked.

"Yes, but I had to cross myself a few times," she replied – her words sounding like an admission of a guilty action – "I'm a Catholic, you see."

"Ooops! Does that mean you'll be excommunicated for entering a *Protestant* house of God?"

"Nah . . . I can live with it. Besides, I wanted to see inside the lovely church, and introduced myself to Rick the Vic, as you locals call him. He gives a cracking sermon."

Sam became aware as he listened to her that he was in the company of another Trudy, a different Trudy. The first time they'd met, she was the PA who'd organised Penny's appearance on Belinda's chat show, and her foxy attire hadn't been chosen purely to arouse, but as a deliberate, flamboyant rouse to avoid being stereotyped as a dour, downtrodden employee of a chat show diva.

Then yesterday, Sam mused, she'd arrived at his cottage not in a girly Mercedes or a BMW, no, this was another Trudy: leather-clad queen of the highway on her motorcycle. But not just any bike, not a machine whose engine made less noise than the zip on her red leather jacket, it had to be a Harley Davidson, providing more muscle between her legs than even Arnold Schwarzenegger could conjure up! Then a short while later, as they'd talked on his settee, she again showed another side to her: how she'd rebuilt her life from the ground up . . . from the gutter up. Yes, with the helping hand of his friend Archie, but Sam knew that for Trudy to succeed in turning her life around, it had taken more mental horsepower than the brute of a bike she lovingly called, although abstractly, her 'physical mantra'.

He found himself intrigued by her, even slightly entranced. And here she was, yet again, another Trudy. Her stylish Sunday dress and sweet essence of perfume all adding to her air of self-assured maturity. Her lightly applied make-up and short black bobbed hair, highlighted by a mother of pearl hair clip set to one side, was so stylish. She was a woman whose multi-faceted personality was attacking his senses from all points of the compass.

"How the hell did you get all this wardrobe of yours in your bike's saddlebags?" he asked, watching her give a hearty laugh in reply. But it was then that he noticed the tell-tale marks on her face that brought him back down to earth with an uncompromising jolt. There were two scars on her cheek, to the right of her top lip. Not big scars, but scars he knew were most likely caused by her face being either brutally kicked or punched, and which had resulted in her teeth cutting through her own flesh.

"Come on, I'll treat you to a Sunday roast in the pub restaurant!" he told her. "By the way . . . what's gizmoing?"

After lunch, and hoping to dodge the intermittent rain showers, Trudy returned to the field, this time with Sam to help her complete her gizmoing and see for herself the dangerous, disused mineshaft that was proving problematic to Sam and Penny's wedding plans.

She wandered off.

"I wouldn't go any closer," Sam warned, watching her pick her way along an overgrown path towards the disused mineshaft. The jumbled mass of brambles and blackthorn patiently waited for a victim to be scratched and snagged. "Come back, please?" he pleaded. "If you slip and fall in, you'll be gone for good."

She turned to take hold of his out stretched hand, seeing the look of concern etched on his face. "Sorry Sam, you are right of course . . . silly of me, sorry."

"The farmer will have stripped away the undergrowth by the time you come back again. You can see the mineshaft then. There's a concrete plinth around it, but it's very slippery at the moment with all the rain we're having," he said. Then he looked up at the sky, seeing the dark, rain-filled clouds looming in the distance. "Come on, you'd better get your gizmo out if you want to finish mapping the field."

"That's it, we're all done gizmoing, Sam," Trudy laughed.

As they walked back towards the pub, Trudy held on to his arm, and then broached a question concerning a young lady whom he dearly missed: "After we left the church, Sam, Sue showed me where her eldest daughter Emily's ashes are placed. I've seen the pictures of her and Penny hung behind the bar. Sue said you were both very kind to their daughter."

He stopped to face her, his feelings of sorrow clear to see in his eyes.

"It's odd, I was married to my late wife Annie for almost thirty years," he said with a strained, thoughtful frown. "I know this must sound terrible, but I don't miss her any more. Probably because of Penny, but I'm not sure. All I do know is that I miss that little angel of a girl every day, and Penny does too. It makes her sad to think Emily won't be coming to our wedding."

Trudy wiped tears from her cheeks, visibly moved by Sam's admission. She turned away from him to look around the field they had just come from. Her expression of sadness was suddenly replaced by a confident grin. *Who said she can't come to the wedding?* she thought.

"You remind me of her," Sam then said.

"Why? Is it because, like her, I have something in my body I can't do anything about?"

Her questioning tone left Sam in no doubt that she wanted a reason for his statement. He stopped and turned to face her, seeing the searching look in her eyes. She was definitely waiting for his reply.

"No. Not because of what you have – in spite of it – and that's the similarity between you both" He reached for her hand, damp from the light rain that had started to fall. "With Emily, she accepted she had a limited time left – long before us adults could face up to the reality ourselves – and within her tenuous sphere of health, she just enjoyed herself."

He chuckled out loud as fond memories of her came rushing back.

"Ha!" he continued. "She would wear lovely party frocks, mostly with pretty red shoes. Then, just to amuse herself, she would wear red wellington boots instead. Once I remember she came into the bar with the most outrageous wig on imaginable; she looked like a miniature country and western singer. She never stopped having fun, right to the end." He noticed that as he spoke, not once did Trudy alter her gaze on him. "Like Emily, you like to be like a chameleon, for fun, so that people around you don't know whether you're Trudy the Biker, Trudy the Alluring PA, or Miss Busy Knickers."

He watched as she cracked a smile, gesturing with her eyes, an admission he was right.

"So, who am I now, Sam?"

"Now?" he asked. "Now you're someone who's getting wet, that's who you are now! Come on. Let's get you dried off!"

Sam stood in his porch to keep out of the rain as Trudy prepared herself for the ride home. The pulsing throb from the Harley Davidson's engine reverberated around them, restrained before being unleashed into a thunderous mile-consuming beast.

"I'll text you when I get back, Sam," Trudy said. Then she kissed him on his lips – not an overpowering kiss, but she enjoyed it. "Do you think Penny would let me have that one?" she asked . . . again she had done something unexpected.

"No, she wouldn't, but I'll let you, just this once!"

He then watched as she rode off, and the tranquil surroundings of his cottage were once more restored to normality.

Chapter 6

The Secret Dress

Early December

The din of the audience shuffling along the rows of the now emptied seats as they made their way to the exits became fainter as Penny walked back to her dressing room at the end of another evening's performance. She counted down in her mind to the time when she would have to stand on that stage for the very last time and take her final bow. Acting, and particularly acting in the theatre, was all she ever cared for; but that was before she met and fell in love with Sam. Now her focus was beyond the stage doors. Becoming Mrs Penny Elizabeth Farmer was her future desire. She knew like any bride-to-be that before she could stand in front of the altar with her beloved Sam, there was that obligatory "to do" list to get through, and at the top of hers was her dress . . . her secret dress.

"Oh yes. What's all this then? Am I interrupting you both?" Penny asked on entering her dressing room and finding Sam with another woman in his arms. The look on her face wasn't anger; she was too exhausted to pretend to act out the role of a jealous fiancée, besides, the glint of tears around Mavis's eyes told her that the embrace was due to the gratitude she felt towards Sam and Penny, and for what she knew they had planned for her after Penny left the play.

"Hi, sweetheart," Sam replied as Penny quickly pursed her lips for an impatient kiss; her mouth was dry from talking on stage under the glare of the spotlights.

"It's a good job you're staying at my aunties. They'll keep an eye on you while I'm in France. Otherwise I'd think you'll be carrying on, where you left off with this old tart" said Penny endearingly. She turned around to be unzipped by Mavis, her dresser, and then stepped out of the red and white polka dot dress, a copy of the one she wore on her first date with Sam, now her trademark costume for the play's final scene. Penny sat at her dressing table wrapped in her bathrobe as she removed her stage makeup while talking to Sam.

Mavis stayed in the background. She had a wealth of knowledge regarding the etiquette of the theatre that she had learned over many years. As a young girl, straight from school, she had first trained as a seamstress and eventually became a sought-after and respected dresser, whom many high-profile actors were fortunate enough to have had in their dressing room. That knowledge had taught her to become discrete when company was present, and to only appear at the appropriate times.

Penny smiled into the mirror at the reflection of Mavis as she held her clothes ready to be put on.

"I may as well just keep my robe on, Mavis. That lot isn't going to stay on too long once Sam and I get home," she said, giving the elderly lady in the mirror a wink of her eye and a gaze that needed no explanation.

Sam sat on the edge of the bath, keeping the promise he had made to himself a few days before. He was sponging Penny's body, but that was as good as it got. It wasn't long before they could hear laughing and general pandemonium coming from downstairs: Maggie and Estelle had arrived at Penny's house, ready for their trip to France to introduce her to Madame Renard.

"Well, there goes my sex life," Penny muttered.

He then petted the side of her neck. She arched her back to feast on the sensual pleasure of his lips on her skin.

"Never mind, sweetheart," he whispered, "you're only going for three days. Then we can spend the rest of your week off at the cottage, alone."

"Come on, Dad, out of here! I'm busting for a pee!" came the desperate plea from Maggie, doing an on-the-spot jig, barely able to contain herself.

He walked out of the bathroom to be met by Estelle also hastily making her way up the stairs.

"Hello, sweetheart!"

"Hi, Dad," she replied, blowing him a kiss as she shimmied past him on the landing. "Must dash, can't stop!" she blurted, disappearing into the bathroom. Penny's laugh was lost over din of his daughters.

"Come on, sis, chop, chop!" Estelle cried.

"Hold yer horses, maid!" Maggie responded loudly.

That's it now, you'll not see them for hours, Sam thought, not sure if he felt bemused or dejected, or was that ejected?

Chapter 7

Mixed Emotions

The Following Day

As Penny waited for the ferry to dock, mixed emotions filled her thoughts. Even after an eight-hour journey by sea from Portsmouth to the small port in Brittany, she was still pondering whether if it was, after all, a good idea to agree to have her wedding dress made by Maggie and Estelle's late mother's relatives, whom she intriguingly named, 'The House of Renard'.

Penny knew that Maggie and Estelle, whom she loved dearly, had no doubts whatsoever that it was a beautiful gesture, not only on her part to agree, but also for the Renards. Would they . . . *could* they accept her as she so dearly hoped into *their* family?

Penny looked out over the miles of golden sandy beach that seemingly had no end. She still wasn't sure.

"You get a fantastic view of the beach from here. It's wonderful, isn't it?" Estelle exclaimed, looping her arm through Penny's.

They stood together on the deck waiting for Maggie to join them after her breakfast. Penny had little appetite, and Estelle sensed why, so she kept her company. The salty sea breeze intermingled with the exhaust fumes from the ship's funnel set the scene for what Estelle was about to say next.

"This is where it all began, you know – D-Day, the 6th of June 1944. The Normandy landings," Estelle said. Her stretched out arm with fingers spread apart in a fanning motion directed

Penny's gaze towards the west to tell of a day, an historic moment in time, that unbeknown to Penny was the catalyst as to why Sam was Sam, in more ways than one.

"From here at Ouistreham, right around to Arromanches," Estelle continued, "is where the British and Canadians came ashore. Oh, and not forgetting the Free French Forces, of course." She halted the history lesson for a moment to cast her gaze far beyond where the eye could see. "Miles further down coast were the Americans on Omaha and Utah beaches." Her tone of voice was now subdued and mournful in respect for that fateful day. "Granddad Farmer would describe to us how it was shear carnage . . ."

"Your dad never told me his father took part in it?"

"That's because he didn't," Estelle replied, wanting to correct the possible misunderstanding "But—"

"Come on, you two, the ferry's getting in. We'd better go to our cabin and collect our gear," Maggie interrupted breathlessly, holding a half-eaten croissant between her fingers.

The three women made their way to the cabin.

"There's MP, the old codger," Maggie said, hastily wheeling her small suitcase behind her; it rumbled across the pot-holed car park in the direction of a stout, elderly man who stood beside an equally ancient-looking car.

"Who's MP?" Penny asked, watching Maggie race ahead.

"Monsieur Paul, Madame Renard's eldest son," Estelle replied. "Mags always calls him that. Thick as thieves they are."

Penny waited patiently in turn to be greeted by Monsieur Paul. She watched as first Maggie and then Estelle were given an embracing hug and then kissed on each cheek, their heads turning almost metronomic in movement. For Penny, it was a gentle handshake as she gave him a nervous smile in return. His light blue eyes, pale within his rugged face, were honed by a lifetime of working the land. Both sisters instinctively now spoke in French, as if a switch had been flicked. Their fluency and ease as they conversed reminded her of what Maggie had once said: at home their mother had insisted they spoke French at meal times; no French, no food . . . and Maggie loved her food.

Maggie sat in the front with Monsieur Paul, clearly pleased and excited to be back in France.

"Don't be put off by old MP here, being all sullen and grumpy looking," Maggie said, turning around to talk to Penny. "He's a shy old sod, but lovely once you get to know him. It's because of him I wanted to become a vet," she added, and then leant over to give him a lingering kiss on the side of his face as he endeavoured to concentrate on his driving.

"Huh, my cows can kiss better than that," he muttered in a huffy tone. He then glanced into the rear-view mirror at Penny, his reflected smile now making her feel slightly at ease, but only slightly.

I haven't met your mother yet . . . she thought.

Chapter 8

Knickers in a Twist

"We're here!" Estelle chirped, her excited tone blotting out the sound of the car's tyres at they came to a crunching halt on the gravel-laid driveway.

The farmhouse, as the sisters had described it to Penny, had given her the impression that it was just a larger version of their father's cottage back in Devon, the difference being bare rendered walls and quaint shuttered windows.

"So, this is what you call a farmhouse, is it?" Penny asked. Her eyes scanned the building in front of her, contradicting all her ideas of what a farmer's home set in the picturesque Normandy countryside would look like. "It's a bloody chateau, you buggers!" she exclaimed, and then scowled at them, but once again finding it hard not to see the funny side of another of their harmless deceptions.

"Yes, well, I suppose you could call it that, but we've always known it as The Farmhouse. Nice, isn't it?" Estelle replied, waving at two ladies standing outside the entrance to the grand building.

Penny gazed at the impressive, so-called '*farmhouse*', imagining how the French windows would dwarf the relatively small sashes in the cottage at home. The façade, with its stone coins and lintels, appeared orderly alongside a tower that seemed to have bulged out from a side elevation. Its round, rugged medieval appearance contrasted with the chateau's steeply pitched slate roof.

"Come on, maid. Come and meet the rest of the family," said Maggie, taking Penny's arm in hers as they walked up the four baroque-style steps towards the two waiting ladies.

"Don't worry about your bags, MP will bring them in," Estelle said, following up behind.

Yvette, Monsieur Paul's sister, stepped forward with reached out arms to embrace Penny into the family fold. Penny was glad of the heavy winter coat she'd put on, which gave her some protection from the winter chill blowing in from the northeast.

"*Bonjour*! Welcome to our home!" Yvette said.

"We've been so looking forward to this, haven't we, mother?" added her daughter Sophie, a rather buxom young lady whose tone of voice bordered on an excited babble at meeting her cousins' future stepmother.

"Paul, we've put Penny in the burgundy room. Take all the bags to their rooms for them, will you?" Yvette ordered.

"*Je suis son esclave sanglante* (I'm her bloody slave)," he muttered, once again glancing at Penny with another of his reassuring winks. His arms bulged with the bags he carried, and the suitcase in tow, as he politely waited for the ladies to lead the way inside.

"You see, Pen," Estelle whispered, "there's been no need to get yourself worried. By the time we leave they'll love you as much as Mags and I do."

Estelle's rapturous tone and the warm welcome from her hosts did ease her anxieties a little, but she still hadn't been introduced to Madame Renard.

Penny entered the grand entrance hall, an impressive space with large black and white floor tiles that added a sense of dimension to the robust carved oak staircase. It was designed to dominate and impress all those who entered, its balustrade sweeping her sight up to the first floor with its landings that led off to the east and west wings of the château.

Sophie took hold of Penny's hand and led her to a door to one side of the staircase.

"We mostly only live in the west wing now," she explained, as they entered the enormous kitchen – to be greeted by the sights and atmosphere of an area that Penny perceived to be the hub of the household. Taking up a great deal of the floor area was the large kitchen table made from solid pine planks, with six unyielding legs that would hold up a house, let alone the centre piece of the kitchen! "You must meet Monsieur Johnny, our chef. He bakes the most wonderful pastries!"

Penny let slip a surreptitious grin as she realised why Sophie had such a comforting waistline and, to some extent, Maggie too.

"*Bonjour, Mademoiselle*!" Johnny greeted, his floury hand offering Penny a polite welcome.

The contrast between the chef and Sophie wasn't lost on her. There he was, a man in his forties whom, according to Sophie, produced the most delicious gastronomic delights imaginable, yet he was tall – very tall – and very skinny!

"You must be starving?" Sophie suggested.

"I am," Maggie interceded.

Like Sophie and Maggie, Penny soon succumbed to Monsieur Johnny's culinary delights, and found his crusty bread rolls hard to resist when smothered with homemade blackcurrant jam, and then washed down with a bowl of delicious freshly made coffee.

"When you're ready, I'm sure the girls will want to show you around, and then I'll introduce you to ma mère," Yvette said, but she then sensed a slight look of trepidation in Penny's eyes. She smiled at her, placing a reassuring hand gently on her shoulder. Her voice was kindly and sincere. "Ma mère is going to make the most wonderful wedding gown for you. You are family now."

Penny's expression became strained as her eyes glazed with tears. The delivery of those words stirred her emotions. She then realised Estelle was right: she needn't have got her knickers in a twist after all.

Chapter 9

Madame Renard

Penny's desire to lose a few pounds in weight before her wedding was well and truly hijacked by the chef and his tasty baking, so although a little tired from her journey, the prospect of a guided tour of the chateau to walk off the calories was most timely.

Sophie led the way back into the grand entrance hall to stand in front of a pair of imposing doors that reached endlessly up to the ornate ceiling. The faded gold leaf inlay on the handcrafted panels, like the chipped powder-blue lacquer, told of an opulence that was diminishing with time. Sophie swung the doors apart, the eerie creaking sound from the hinges setting a surreal scene as Penny entered the once magnificent ballroom.

She found herself surrounded by headless torsos, impaled on chrome poles.

"Huh! Naked mannequins!" Penny gasped.

"Grand-mère and my mother have turned the chateau into a craft school and museum of the history of Normandy lace," said an informative Sophie.

Maggie put her arm around Penny's waist, giving her a light squeeze, and said, "As you can see, the chateau is closed for the winter now and everything is put away, but when they reopen in the spring, this is where most of the beautiful exhibits of clothes and anything made of lace are displayed. Even mother's wedding dress is displayed in here." She then paused for a moment, before adding, "One day yours will be in here also, so future generations can marvel at another wonderful gown made by the finest lace makers in all of France."

Penny kissed her on the cheek – an impulsive response to the sincere words that she knew would be echoed throughout time by those who would gaze in wonder at the famous Renard lace.

"Come in here!" Estelle called out, standing at the entrance to another room. "This is where your dress is going to be made."

Her excited tone of voice focused their thoughts on the reason why Penny was there. They stood in front of a large rectangular cutting table, covered over with a white dustsheet. The room was fitted out with storage cupboards and shelves, all of which were full of materials and implements for lace and garment making. Three sewing machine tables and even more mannequins stood idly by waiting to be brought back into use - and soon they would be: within days the dust sheets would be removed to bring shape and form to a gown that was still only in Penny's imagination.

"Ah, there you all are," came the resonating voice of Yvette. (Even a whisper in the grand hall was amplified like a prayer in a cathedral.) She paused at the bottom of the stairs, a tray held firmly in her hands with two cups of coffee, one black and one with cream. There was also a single shot glass half filled with a transparent liquid, the vapours of which were not instinctively recognisable to Penny. (It was *Obstler,* a variety of Schnapps from the Alsace region of France, and Madame Renard's tipple before lunch.) "Shall we meet ma mère?" Yvette asked; her gentle smile told Penny it was time.

"Don't worry, Pen," Estelle said reassuringly, linking her arm with her sister's in a gesture of solace, as if their friend was going to a fate worse than death. "We'll come up in ten minutes or so to rescue you. All you've got to remember is: don't look into her eyes, she'll turn you into stone else!"

"Oh be quiet you two, and that goes for you, too, Sophie," Yvette retorted. "Ignore them, dear. It's they who should be guarded. Ma mère doesn't take kindly to foolhardiness!"

Penny turned to climb the stairs, glancing briefly over her shoulder to look at the two sisters; she shot them an expression as if to say: you're not going to fool me this time.

"Does your mother spend a lot of her time in her room?" Penny enquired, intrigued to know why the elderly lady seemed to keep herself to herself.

"If only she did . . ." Yvette muttered. "At eighty-six she does far too much. Every day she's out at the crack of dawn, and in all weathers, too, helping Paul and my husband Andrea with milking the cows – and she still drives bloody Millie around even at her age."

"Millie?" Penny asked.

"Oh, Millie! Millie's her tractor and it's almost as old as she is! Like ma mare, the thing just keeps on going!" Yvette let out a nonchalant laugh thinking about her stubborn mother. "Mmm, I think . . . I think she enjoys the challenge of keeping Millie working. If ma mère can, then so can the old lump that's only held together with rusty nut and bolts."

The stair runner, with its red and gold celestial pattern, distracted Penny's eyes, but not her thoughts, which were firmly on Madame Renard as she listened to Yvette speak of her. Within moments they were standing outside her rooms, and again a pair of impressive sculptured double doors stood in front of them. Their matching engraved escutcheons and delicately scrolled porcelain handles added to their air of importance.

"Be a love and open the door for us," asked the tray-carrying Yvette.

Penny felt a thumping sensation in her chest, an untimely awareness of nerves as her knuckles sounded a polite *tap, tap* – and then her hand pushed down and forward on the door handle. She then saw the barrier that separated herself from a woman she had travelled to France to meet, swing serenely open.

"Mother. Coffee, dear?" Yvette called out quietly as they

entered Madame Renard's private lounge. She placed the tray on a small table that was appropriately set between two cushioned art deco chairs. "She must be in her bedroom. She'll not be long, I'm sure. Ma mère doesn't like her coffee cold."

"What a wonderful view!" Penny exclaimed, taking in the gorgeous aspect of the garden and surrounding countryside from one of the lounge's two impressive French windows. The expansive lawns and flowerbeds were segmented into symmetrical shapes by ornately designed boxed hedges. Her observations provided her with a welcome distraction, *though still not a patch on Dartmoor, though*, she decided. Then a voice broke into her distant thoughts of home.

"In the spring, it's laden with colour, like Monet's palette!" came the poetic words from the far end of the room.

Penny turned to her right to see a lady approach her, wringing her hands together to absorb moisturiser she had applied moments before. Like her smile, the tone of her voice was soft and welcoming.

She reached out to Penny's hands to greet her with a light kiss on each cheek. Penny's eyes sparkled with genuine pleasure at finding herself, at last, in the company of Madame Renard, her nervousness suddenly gone.

Her host gestured with her right hand, a low swinging motion in the direction of the two chairs and their waiting drinks, the high-octane vapours of the *Obstler* competing with the aroma of the freshly ground coffee.

Yvette stood next to her now seated mother, with a hand resting lightly on her shoulder. She then spoke to Penny, the words accompanied by a sympathetic gaze that left Penny in no doubt that, by marrying Sam, she would inherit an onerous responsibility.

"I've got lunch to prepare. I'll keep those future step daughters of *yours* at bay for a while."

"Thank you!" was the slightly breathless response, accompanied by a small laugh.

Madame Renard, however, reacted with a knowing look, intuitively aware that the sisters had, without any qualms, already accepted Penny into their family as their soon-to-be stepmother, and above all, their friend. She briefly glanced up at her daughter, and then fixed her stare firmly back on Penny.

"You can tell Sophie to stop behaving like a silly school girl now. You would think this young woman was a rock star!"

Again, Penny laughed as Yvette left the room; the analogy of a rock star sounded far more impressive than being just an actor – *unless it was one of her aunties*, she thought.

"Would you like a drop?" Madame Renard asked, offering Penny a share of her morning tipple.

Penny slowly shook her head to politely decline, and then observed as the spirit disappeared between the elderly lady's lips with a quick swig; an expression of having thoroughly savoured the moment fleetingly appeared in her eyes as the *Obstler* hit the desired spot.

As she sipped her coffee, Penny detected a trace of Madame Renard's moisturiser on her skin; *L'occitane,* she thought, remembering how she gave each of her aunties the quality skincare product for a Christmas gift – and that they would only use it sparingly. It was with her aunties in mind that she realised that once again she'd been had, duped, kidded, all the analogies she could think of, *and* by the two young ladies she'd left in the grand hall. The words 'You won't fool me again' rang in her ears.

It wasn't just that the sisters had misled her by making her think the so-called 'farmhouse' wasn't a great deal larger than their father's cottage, this time they had done the opposite: they had said very little about the person opposite her, letting Penny come to her own imaginative conclusions.

Even before they had met, she had made comparisons between

Madame Renard and her aunties. Both May and June, who were in their seventies, were riddled with arthritis; June was waiting for her second hip replacement and was in constant discomfort, while May had the early signs of the onset of Alzheimer's. Penny naturally concluded that Madame Renard, who was at least a decade older than them, would also be wizened with age, the joints in her fingers ravaged with pain as a result of a lifetime of making lace – but they weren't. Then there was the tractor-driving milkmaid side of her that Penny was unaware of until moments before they finally met! That revelation had caused her mind's eye to swing like a pendulum as she envisaged a portly-looking woman whose hands would be strong enough to crack a walnut!

The truth was that she was totally wrong on both concepts. In front of her sat a slim, elegant woman who wasn't hunched with age, but sat up straight, shoulders back, confident in posture. Her long brown hair was put up into a bun with not a single hint of grey to be seen. She wore black denim jeans, but not those purchased from one of the street market traders in Bayeux, hers were designer-cut and fitted her like a glove; she looked very good in them. (And there Penny was, feeling tired and dishevelled in her company!) Penny also noticed her perfectly manicured nails and eyebrows, and not done after a bath sitting on the edge of the bed, no, this lady had been to a beauty parlour to be pampered, fussed over and indulged. This was an elderly woman whose healthy appearance defied her age, and confounded those who thought that because she had wrinkles, she should wear paisley patterned dresses and fluffy slippers.

"I've heard those nieces of mine have been up to their playful games again, this time about our farmhouse," Madame Renard smiled.

"Oh yes, they have," Penny confirmed. Her eyelashes fluttered and she grinned, a grin that displayed her acceptance and acknowledgement – not only to Madame Renard, but also to herself – how cerebrally clever they both were. "It must be the French in them," she added.

Her host didn't respond in words to her honest repos, she didn't have to; the reactive stiffening of her shoulders and pointed but checked smile, like a lady taking in a fragrance that was pleasing but wasn't quite what she expected, was her reply.

Penny detected an air of management about the age-defying lady. She knew it was normal in such families that the elder was the head of the household – and Madame Renard was certainly that – but she also had a presence, a mystique . . . after all, she was a lace-making, cow-milking, tractor-driving style-setter!

Any notion of apprehension Penny had had about meeting Madame Renard dissipated like the morning mist as she then explained why the chateau was known as the farmhouse.

"There *was* a farmhouse here once, way back in the sixteenth century, but then the chateau was built." Madame Renard turned her head slightly to the left to gaze past and beyond Penny; her thoughts and view were of the grand garden. "It was during the German occupation that the chateau became known as the farmhouse."

Penny turned in her seat, curious to see why Madame Renard's stare had become so profound.

"There used to be a pole out there, and an enormous red Nazi flag with a hideous swastika that fluttered from it," Madame Renard continued. "My sister Monika – Maggie and Estelle's grand-mère – and I were just young girls at the time, and our father was the Renard's accountant.

"The chateau was commandeered and became a brothel for the German officers . . . if these walls could only talk!" She let out a sigh as thoughts of those dark days stirred up memories of how the chateau played its part in defeating their occupiers.

"Unbeknown to the Germans, the walls had ears, and just about every word of pillow talk that may had been of any significance was secretly documented and passed to the allies via the local French resistance, and their code word for the chateau was *the farmhouse*."

Penny listened with captivated interest as tales of the two young sisters who ran errands for the resistance were told. She was so absorbed by her thoughts, and pictures in her mind of how difficult life must have been for them, that she was almost oblivious to the sound of knuckles *tap-tapping* on the doors of Madame Renard's boudoir. Then a sense of sadness filled her, aware that their private tête-à-tête had been brought to an end as the three young ladies entered, freed from the watchful eyes of Yvette.

Maggie and Estelle stood quietly next to Penny, respectfully poised as they shimmied along to take it in turns to be welcomed by their great aunt. So different, Penny thought, to the times they would bound up to her aunties with a joyous hug and a lipstick-smearing kiss on the side of their faces. She observed the sisters lightly kiss Madame Renard's outstretched hand, a gesture not in the realms of adulation as a cardinal would kiss the hand of the Pope or like a member of La Costa Nostra affirming obedience to his Don, but simply to show their love and respect to this elderly woman, their great aunt.

"I've been hearing all about the shenanigans that went on at the chateau during the occupation, or should that be *the farmhouse*," Penny said, her smile and slightly narrowed eyes directed specifically at the sisters.

"Oh, did grand-mère also tell you the story of the sailor and the airman? It was very sad," Sophie asked. Her unchecked words, blurted out without consideration, instantly chilled the atmosphere. Memories of that fateful time, especially those of which Sophie spoke, were deeply personal to Maggie and Estelle and should have been remembered with reverence and sadness, not asked in a matter-of-fact way.

If Madame Renard did possess the ability to turn a person to stone with her eyes, the cold stare that she now fixed on Sophie certainly endeavoured to do so.

Sophie turned to face her cousins, realising her foolish error, and tears of remorse trickled down her face as she spoke again, her child-like tone adding to her sincerity. "I'm so sorry, I forgot, please forgive me."

Penny sat there like a spectator, not engaging but wondering quietly to herself what that tale had to do with the sisters and ultimately with their family? Her inquisitive nature tempted her to ask, but she felt deep inside her that if it involved a tragedy caused by the war, some questions were best not asked.

"Don't do your head in maid, it was a long time ago," Maggie said as she wrapped her arms around her young cousin's shoulders. She hoped her comforting hug and settling tone would bring the fractious situation to an end.

Madame Renard's cold stare slightly softened, and within the tightness of her face was the hint of understanding that the girl was truly sorry.

"We've been told to tell you lunch is ready, Pen," came the timely words from Estelle, the expressive movement of her head indicating it was time to make a tactical retreat.

Almost instantly Penny rose to her feet to take her leave, but Madame Renard gestured with the flat of her hand for her to remain seated.

"Sophie, tell your mother that Mademoiselle McCain will lunch with me." She then glanced up at the two sisters who were looking unsure of what to do next. (*Did she also mean them?* they thought.) "Yes, yes, and you two as well," she added.

With her stern gaze, diluted by the chink of a smile, Madame Renard in those short moments had, in her indomitable way, put the air of calm control firmly back in her grasp.

Well, I've made it to lunchtime, Penny thought, *so far so good*.

Chapter 10

You Wouldn't Want to Know

The sensation of her duvet being pulled lightly across her body alerted Penny to the possibility that she wasn't alone in her bed. She turned over to see a smiling face with beautiful pale green eyes staring back at her.

"Morning, sweetheart," was her sleepy, whispered response, now dozily aware that Estelle had climbed in beside her.

"Come on, maid, rise and shine," said an unmistakable voice.

Penny pulled herself up, plumping her pillows to gaze across at the hazy shape of Maggie standing at the end of her bed. She was silhouetted against the glare of the morning sun that shone through the window behind her.

"Sleep well, did we? Some bed, ain't it!" she asked, seeing Penny taking in the bed's colourful canopy of burgundy satin with a lace overlay that, when untied from the four corner posts, would hang like a veil to give privacy to any lovers within.

"I reckon it's the sexiest bed ever," said Estelle.

"Rumour has it that Marie Antoinette had a shag or two in this bed!"

"Really? Well, I must admit that it's lovely and snug. Is this the bed your dad sleeps in when he comes over?"

"Dad hasn't been over since Mum died," Estelle replied.

Penny detected an air of sadness in her tone as if she'd wished he had.

"It isn't that he's not welcome, he knows that," she continued. "I think Dad just feels there's nothing to compel him to visit now Mum has gone and we've grown up. Besides, when he did come, all he ever did was to help keep this place working - always sorting out the plumbing or the electrics. If it wasn't the electrics, it was something else."

Penny remembered when she'd first introduced their father to her aunties, and how within moments he'd had the cold water tap in their kitchen in pieces to repair.

"That's your father through and through, isn't it, sweetheart? Family and friends – especially family – they're very important to him. He once described it to me as an obligation."

"God, don't *we* know it!" Estelle said, and her look of resignation broke into a forlorn smile.

(Neither Maggie nor Estelle could ever have imagined how that word – *obligation* – would, before too long, dominate their lives in a manner that would test the bond between them and their father. It would ultimately put a question mark over whether Penny would even ever get to wear her wedding dress and marry Sam.)

"Anyway, what have you been up to?" Penny asked Maggie, noticing she was dressed and looking rather windswept.

"I've been down on the farm with MP being shown two boy calves that were born a couple of days ago; lovely little fellas they are. Come the spring, they'll be ready to be steered."

"Steered? What, like steering Millie the tractor around you mean? Sorry, you know me . . . I'm a city girl. Well, used to be," Penny said, her half-awake smile showing her longing for Devon and the sprawling ruggedness of Dartmoor, a world away from the metropolis of London she no longer thought of as home.

"No," Maggie replied with a kindly, un-demeaning laugh. "Steering is castrating young calves. Back home we use a rubber band, but over here they still use a knife; a quick flick of the wrist and their balls are in the bucket!"

"Oh, please tell me you haven't done it like that . . . have you?" Penny asked, her eyes peeping out from between fanned fingers that she hoped shielded her look of horror.

Maggie shrugged her shoulders, her expression an acknowledgment that being a livestock vet wasn't as mundane as treating a little boy's pet dog who had swallowed a piece of his master's Lego.

"You wouldn't want to know what I have to do at times. It'd put you off your breakfast!" she laughed.

"Ah yes, breakfast. That reminds me!" Estelle blurted, her interruption purposely timed to change the conversation to more pleasant thoughts. "Message from on high: when you're ready – after breakfast – they'll get started on that dress of yours."

"And our maids of honour dresses, of course," Maggie said.

"They're going to need a fair bit of fabric for yours, Mags," came the pithy response from her sister.

Penny listened to the playful banter which ensued between them, which only confirmed to her that as individuals they were more than able to give as good as they got - and watch out anyone who came between them!

Chapter 11

From the Ground Up

"Oh come on, slow coach!" said an impatient Estelle, arm in arm with Penny as they waited for her sister on the landing.

"OK, OK," Maggie puffed, plodding her way up the stairs as she nibbled away at yet another croissant; she had eaten a veritable feast compared to Penny and Estelle's bowls of oatmeal.

Maggie always described herself as 'built for comfort', her waistline not as well defined as her sister's. And Estelle and Penny's shapely, proportioned figures were a testament to moderation – a discipline she applauded, but had not practiced.

"Grand-mère is winding Mother up again," whispered the cautious-sounding Sophie, tasked with returning the bones of her grandmother's breakfast to the kitchen: the crusty remnants of a baguette and an empty glass that once contained freshly squeezed oranges, the bits of which lined the inside like shattered fragments.

I wonder if she's had her tipple yet? Penny thought, suppressing the urge to smile.

The tray in Sophie's hands gave the appearance of levitating as she stood by Madame Renard's lounge doors. Her foot wedged one of them open as the sound of voices from inside the room were heard.

"Mother, let the girls do that when they come up, please," said an exasperated Yvette, trying and failing to stop her mother from moving furniture around her lounge in preparation for Penny's first fitting.

"Oh, don't fuss so. Now go and tell Penny and the girls we're ready."

"No need," Estelle called out, poking her head around the door, her chirpy, higher-than-normal vocal tone cheerfully announcing that the trio had arrived.

This time there was no polite taking it in turns to greet the elderly lady, more of a free for all as peck followed peck with giggles and jovial banter from the two maids of honour and the bride-to-be.

"Come on, young lady. Get your derrière off that. You've got things to do," Yvette ordered, her pointed smile aimed at Maggie who had ensconced herself on the chaise longue, her head back, arms akimbo, embodying the once bourgeoisie attitude of centuries-past occupants of the chateau.

Penny went to sit with Madame Renard at her dining table. Like the lady herself, it had an air of sophisticated chic. Its pastel-grey painted frame and cabriole-shaped legs – the tops curved like those of an animal, outwards like a knee and then curved inwards – gave the veneered rosewood table top a sense of proportion. They studied sketches that Estelle had drawn – interpretations of Penny's dream wedding dress that they had discussed over lunch the day before – and she felt herself shudder; an uncontrollable response to the tingle that passed through her whole being, a wave of realisation that, from then on, her fantasy wedding gown – that was once held within her private thoughts – was no longer hers alone.

"Wow, they're pretty good, aren't they?" she whispered faintly, and then swept her fingertips under her eyes as tears overcame her.

"This will do for starters . . . something to work with," said the lady, whose hand had reassuringly rested on Penny's.

Chapter 11

Madame Renard was aware that, as an actor, Penny had no difficulty portraying a character's emotions – it was a craft she had mastered – but it was her own emotions that, at times, she couldn't control.

Penny returned her smile, trusting her and knowing that not only did Madame Renard have her hand in hers, but she also knew that an important part of the happiest day of her life was also in her hands.

"Bugger me, sis, your fingers ain't half cold," Maggie gasped. She was standing arms apart, scarecrow-ish, in only her bra and knickers, while Estelle took her sister's vital statistics. "Eh! I hope this dress of mine ain't gonna hide my baps! If you've got tits, flaunt them - that's my philosophy!"

"Oh stop gassing, Mags," Estelle retorted, as she endeavoured to relay her sister's measurements to Yvette, who was sat at the coffee table with sheets of lined writing paper at the ready for every detail to be meticulously noted – as Penny was soon to find out.

"When you are ready, Mademoiselle Penny," said the calm voice of Yvette.

Penny turned her head to see Yvette beckoning her over, as if to say: "The journey to your desires starts here." An immediate but brief feeling of motionless filled her; unable to move a muscle, her heart thumped, and then she became focused and composed. In that split second, Madame Renard and Yvette had, to all intents and purposes, become her directors. She would be guided by them, like other directors she had worked with in the theatre, to labour towards a creation that would not only take *her* breath away, but all those who set their eyes upon it.

"Come on, maid, get your kit off! Oh, I see . . . I get Miss Frozen Fingers to measure me, but Penny doesn't. Talk about a pecking order!" Maggie blustered with a sly smile across her face.

With the measuring tape draped between her fingers, the

elderly lady mused thoughtfully at Penny and then gently pressed the flat of her hand onto her abdomen.

"What's she doing that for?" Penny asked.

The sisters sheepishly slipped a grin to each other; they knew all too well why she did that.

"She's feeling your tummy to see if you're pregnant," Maggie replied. "I wouldn't worry about it, maid, she does it to us all the time, especially to Estelle, don't she Est?"

Estelle showed Penny a mischievous, toothy grin, raising her shoulders in response.

"The last thing she wants is to make a beautiful wedding gown that will fit you like a glove, only to realise you're up the duff," laughed Estelle.

"Well I'm *not!*" Penny answered, directing the fact to Madame Renard.

"Yeah, but that's not to say you won't be one day, eh? Dad's still got plenty of bullets left, I bet." Maggie replied, her cheeks billowing out, restraining herself from a hearty laugh.

Madame Renard gazed deeply into Penny's eyes; a searching look that many a matriarch possessed, aware that Penny was daydreaming. From the ground up, Penny was measured every which way – even the distance she covered between steps. The height and style of her shoes was also given consideration.

"We can't have you being taller than the groom, now can we," insisted her directors.

Estelle at five foot ten inches was as tall as her father, so she became the yard stick to Penny's five foot eight. Then there was the fabric to complement the lace. Everything was decided; *nothing* was left to chance.

Chapter 12

Reincarnate

"Would you like some more soup, Mademoiselle?"

"No, no more for me, Monsieur Johnny, thank you," Penny replied, puffing out her cheeks as she sat back in her seat after another irresistibly sumptuous feast. "I've never tasted such delicious onion soup in all my life. I think the melted Camembert on the crusty bread did it for me."

"Well, it's a good job all that measuring lark was done before lunch, Pen, coz like you, I'm buggered," Estelle remarked, and then sipped at her glass of Pinot Gris. ('The perfect wine to complement their lunch,' Yvette had advised.)

Estelle then held the almost empty bottle of wine up against the light and peered into it.

"Time for another, I think," she said.

Relaxed, and at that moment without a care in the world, Penny could do nothing more than smile. She felt favoured to be in the company of people who had an infectious desire to immerse themselves in the very French tradition of enjoying their every meal, no matter how long it took - in stark contrast to how she had once described having lunch 'on the hoof' to Sam: a quick snack, snatched in between scenes when she was filming on location!

"MP has to run an errand for the old lady and drive into Bayeux later, so sis and I thought we could all go and show you around. Fancy it?" Estelle asked.

"Oh yes! And also . . ." blurted the now grinning Maggie, her eyes flaring with excited thoughts and impatient to tell what else was planned. She filled her mouth with the remains of her wine, swallowed with a satisfying gulp, and uttered a word, a description that was pure Maggie: "'Ansom!" she announced. "We're going to stop at a racehorse stables on the way," she continued. "The owner is a very dear friend of ours, and there's a pregnant mare I'd like to say hello to. I was there when she was born and now it's her turn to be a mummy."

Penny realised that when it came to animals, Maggie could be very emotionally contradictive: one moment very matter of fact about castrating a young calf, and then almost gushing in her enthusiasm for the equine mother to be.

"That would be lovely," she replied.

Monsieur Paul drove along the thickly hedged country lanes in the direction of the stables, a distance of about three miles from the chateau, before turning into a driveway to come to halt at two large, robust security gates.

"It's like getting into Fort Knox," Maggie explained, peering out at one of the many surveillance cameras that watched timelessly at all the comings and goings in and around the stable compound. "Mind you," she continued, "some of the beautiful beasts in there are worth a king's ransom, especially my pal Fanny."

MP spoke into an intercom, a rust-streaked innocuous box that was fixed onto a post at almost the same height as his car window. The tinny, barely audible sound of a man's voice was heard, and he returned an acknowledging acceptance to proceed. The gates then juddered apart for them to continue along a well-ordered gravel driveway with fenced-off paddocks on either side. Three horses corralled within them gazed with curiosity, their quilted winter coats not only keeping the windy chill at bay, but setting them apart: their arrogance of stature as much as their colourful attire affirmed that they were more than your average horse: they were thoroughbreds.

Chapter 12

They drove up to the stable's entrance. An imposing red brick archway loomed upon them, lofted high above the single-storey structures that branched off east and west, each with equally spaced cottage-sized windows. Their white-painted woodwork was in contrast to the edifice that gave an air of triumphalism as they entered the quadrangle.

Maggie and Estelle dived out of the car – seemingly before MP had brought it to a halt only metres away from a man in a wheelchair. He waited patiently to greet them, his green tartan blanket tucked firmly around his legs, shielding him against the cold and overcast afternoon, but his brown trilby hat and gloves concealed more than a balding head or offer protection against the weather. The sisters then crouched down either side of him like two obedient pets, gently kissing a face that was disfigured with scars from burns inflicted years before. Penny could see that there was no hiding their affection for him, and he gazed at her as she walked up to him, his watery eyes glistening with boyish delight as the sisters held his hands tenderly in their own.

All those who knew him, and especially Maggie and Estelle, were more than aware of his charming, candid approach with women, a charisma that even then, in his waning years, didn't desert him. With silkily spoken words he welcomed Penny - who sent him an acknowledging grin, aware of a compelling desire, like the sisters, to kiss him.

"You are even more beautiful than I imagined, Mademoiselle. Sam is indeed a fortunate man to now have *three* delightful fillies in his stable."

"Oh my god, you're at it already! And we haven't even introduced you yet, you bugger, you!" said Maggie, feigning an exasperated tone which was brimmed with affection for the amiable man.

"This naughty old Frenchman, Pen," Estelle said, as she reached up for Penny's hand to help her to her feet, "is Monsieur

Raymond Goss, racehorse trainer extraordinaire. But we all call him Papa Goss, coz he's like a father to everyone."

"Tell you what, Pen," Maggie then said, "would you mind if we stayed here and MP picked us up on his way back?"

Penny could see the look on her face; she desperately wanted her to say yes.

"No, not at all. I'd like to stay and look around, besides, you want to show me your pregnant horse."

"Good, that's decided then," Papa Goss announced, gesturing with his gloved hand at Estelle – he wanted her to be his driver and wheel him back into his apartment.

As I am in the company of three beautiful women, Papa Goss joyfully thought, *champagne will be in order . . . yes, definitely champagne.*

MP continued on his errand for Madame Renard while Maggie took Penny on a guided tour around the stables. They hadn't walked far when Maggie paused by a small flowerbed that was laid out with winter bedding plants. It encircled a life-sized bronze statue of a young woman holding a bucket in each hand, who posed as if she was running towards the stable blocks.

Penny stood silently observing Maggie, who gazed forlornly at the figure, and then placed kissed fingers on the bronzed face. It was then that Penny realised that it wasn't only a beautiful work of art, it was a monument to someone - someone who Maggie may have once known. Maggie instinctively glanced down at her hand. She could see Penny's fingers lace into hers, a gesture of wanting to be by her side, caring for her friend whose eyes spoke of a lost soul.

"Who is she, sweetheart?" Penny then asked.

Maggie's reply wasn't immediate, and when she did speak she didn't divert her gaze from the sculpture. She then spoke with clarity and purpose, showing the importance of the memory of this person: "Her name is Sabine. She was my dearest friend, and Papa Goss's much-loved daughter." Maggie turned to look towards the rectangular paddock surrounded by stable blocks on three sides, pointing with her finger and directing Penny's sight to one particular area. "It's all been rebuilt now, but over there in the far left stable, a fire started. It was horrendous. The blaze got into the connecting roof spaces and with all the hay around, the flames quickly spread. Everyone was desperately trying to get the horses out, not least Sabine."

Maggie returned her gaze to the statue of her friend. Her tone had become fraught, reliving that desperate time.

"Sabine was seen running into the burning stables with two buckets of water, and Papa Goss went in to find her. It was said that when he came out with her slumped in his arms, their clothes were on fire. She's buried here. Papa Goss says her spirit now keeps a watchful eye over the stables. Poor man. He misses her so much . . . we all do . . . *I do.*" Her voice was cracked with emotion.

Penny reached into her coat pocket and handed Maggie the always-useful tissue to dab away the tears of sad memories that hung like glass beads on her mascara.

"Oh God, please don't tell old Gossy that I cried, he forbids it. He says Sabine's life should be celebrated, not mourned . . . but I know for a fact that *he* cries for her."

Maggie's tone then became agitated, worried what the future may hold for the stables.

"Now she's gone," she said, "her half-brother Bernard, from Papa Goss's first marriage, has muscled in to help run all this. It's not the same. Bernard hasn't got the vision that Papa Goss has for this beautiful place. I reckon once the old man dies, he'll close it and sell the land off to developers."

They stood quietly together for a few moments so that Maggie could compose herself, but as for Penny, she felt her own sadness for Maggie and Estelle, not only for the tragic loss of Sabine. She thought of the time when their father had confided in her how their Aunty Ruth had committed suicide, her sanity pushed over a mental cliff by her elder brother Sidney as a result of defrauding her and Sam in a joint business venture. *That alone would test anyone's strength of character*, Penny thought, *and then to also lose your own mother to cancer.* She wondered if the sisters may have imagined that their friendships and family were being dismantled by untimely deaths.

"Come on, maid," Maggie said, her enthusiastic manner returning to her. "Let's go and see my pal Fanny."

Penny was then shown a glimpse of horse husbandry, the day-to-day running of busy racing stables, a walking, talking insight around the complex, whilst stopping to chat to stable maids and lads who were either mucking out or dedicating their energies to pampering and caring for the equine equivalent of Grand Prix racing cars. Maggie was now in her element, enlightening Penny of the various features of the muscular thoroughbreds with their chiselled heads, and eyes that were dark and alert, yet soulful.

They left the main stabling quadrangle and walked towards a large, recently constructed single-storey steel and timber barn. Its expansive canopy extended out from the gable entrance, and drew them towards two barn doors that were decoratively clad in teak planking set to a herringbone design.

"Wow! This is different," Penny commented as they entered.

"Brilliant, isn't it! It was Sabine's idea. It is all state-of-the-art, the equine version of the Ritz Hotel and a computer controls all the lighting and heating, even mood music. Ha! My new flat isn't even this cosy!" Maggie enthused. Her gaze settled on two horses as they inquisitively peered out from their stalls, then another and another, each in turn. "Ah, here she is!" her voice now a mixture of relief and excitement, thrilled to see her pregnant, four-legged friend again.

The mare, like Maggie, also made it clear that she was happy, and her ears pricked up in recognition of a familiar face. She made a faint nicking sound as if to say "Good to see you again!"

"So, this is Fanny! She's beautiful!" Penny remarked.

"Oh, that's not her correct name. Her full name is Tryphana – meaning delicate, soft. It's Macedonian-Greek, or something like that, you'll have to ask Sab…"

Maggie paused; she knew that for a fleeting moment fond memories of her friend had made her forget the realities of the present time. "Fanny is Sabine's horse," she then said. "She's seventh-generation Normandy Trotter. They're renowned for their speed and agility, and Sabine trained her for show jumping and dressage." Maggie's tears had returned to her. "Please don't think it daft, but to me this gorgeous chestnut . . . *is* Sabine. Delicate and soft, yes, but also disciplined and true, and like Sabine, dedicated to her task."

Pushing aside her sorrow, within moments Maggie had opened the stable door.

"Now let's have a shoofty at you," Maggie whispered as she entered the stall, her tender, inquisitive tone needing no explanation; Maggie had to satisfy herself that her equine friend was in good health, regardless of the fact she was being constantly monitored.

"Come on, preggers, move out the way," she quietly ordered, gently easing the mare further back into her stall. She then put on her proverbial veterinary hat to cast an eager eye over the animal from ears to tail.

"So, when is Fanny due?" Penny asked, observing Maggie, whose hands were running across the mare's abdomen down to her teats.

"Horses have an eleven-month gestation period. She's five-months-gone now, and she's due to drop in early May – only a couple of weeks before your wedding, in fact."

The manner of Maggie's reply, although polite and courteous, told Penny that nothing was more important to her at that moment in time than the welfare of Sabine's cherished horse.

"She very compliant, letting you handle her like that. I always thought horses could be cantankerous."

"Ha! You'd better believe it!" Maggie laughed, directing a pointed, wry smile at the horse. "One time, Sabine and I were back in the stables after a run out on the gallops, when I heard this almighty yelp. I ran over to see what all the commotion was about, to find Sabine sitting on the hay rubbing her backside. This bugger here only went and bit her arse. Christ, you should have seen the size of her bruise – it was as big as a melon!"

Strangely on cue, the mare raised her head defiantly and neighed.

"Yes, you know we're talking about you, don't you!" Maggie responded, and then patted hard on the horse's muscular neck to say her goodbyes. "We'd better get back, Pen. Knowing Papa Goss, he'll have a bottle or two of champagne waiting for us!"

Chapter 13

The Understudy

"Ah, there you are," Yvette called out to Sophie, intercepting her daughter as she made her way down the grand staircase towards her mother. The urgency of her hurried steps was getting her ever closer, she hoped, to the kitchen for her mid-morning food-fix . . . but Yvette had other plans for her. "I need you to take this tray of glasses into the sewing room ready for Penny's little farewell get-together," she continued. "And talking of Penny - where is she and those cousins of yours? I haven't seen them since breakfast."

"They're all upstairs, Mother, packing their bags," she huffed.

(Her disgruntled breath of disappointment that duties had barred her from her sustenance wasn't lost on her mother.)

"Good. And when you've done that you can go and get them . . . and don't tell Penny anything, is that understood" Yvette insisted, looking at Sophie and doubting that she would be able adhere to that request.

"Did either of you have any missed calls from your dad last night?" Penny enquired.

She couldn't hide the guilty look of child-like naughtiness as Maggie and Estelle lazed on Penny's bed while she packed her bags, remembering how Papa Goss got the three of them so intoxicated on champagne the day before that she had crashed out, missing two calls from their father.

"Yep, I did, but I used the usual excuse: 'Sorry my phone

battery went dead' when I texted him this morning," Maggie replied.

"Oh shit, really? So did I!" Penny admitted.

"Me too!" Estelle added.

Their sudden laughter coincided with Sophie's polite knock on the bedroom door.

"Mother would like to see you all in the sewing room," said Sophie, passing on the message as ordered, and then winked at her cousins, her mellow brown eyes radiating a mischievous glare at them.

"Ah! I bet I know what that's all about!" Estelle guessed. "It's fun! And Mum had to do the same thing when her dress was being made. It's a little *family ritual* you have to do before we leave."

Penny began to ponder; her curiosity aroused by Estelle's teasing statement . . . then even more so as she saw Sophie press a finger against her pursed lips! And Sophie's gesture left her in no doubt that whatever the ritual was, the young lady had learnt her lesson about unwittingly blurting out secrets. That meant Penny would have to go downstairs to find out.

"Go on, Pen, after you. Brides-to-be first and all that," Estelle insisted.

Penny then felt Estelle's hand on the small of her back as she gently coaxed her into the sewing room. She entered the room and was dazzled by the bright lights that hung on wire chains from the ornately plastered ceiling. The brightness of the room couldn't have been more of a contrast to the dark, gloomy weather outside, framed by the French windows.

"Ah good, you're here, Mademoiselle," said Yvette, beckoning her over to stand by her and her mother. Near to them were three dressmaker's mannequins, positioned in the shape of a triangle. One of them was slightly elevated and appeared to have more prominence than the other two. Madame Renard noted how

Penny's eyes rounded on her, as if to ask 'what's all this about?' She reached for Penny's hand with a grasp that was firm and reassuring, a touch that vanished all of Penny's nervousness.

The matriarch then enlightened her as to why she had been brought to the room, speaking with reverence of past generations of brides-to-be like Penny who had had their wedding gowns devotedly made by various members of the Renard family clan all dedicated to one purpose: tradition.

"It's been part of our family custom for many years that the mannequin we'll use in the making of your gown should be given a name," Madame Renard said, and then let out a little chuckle; she wondered what name Penny would choose. Who would she compare the mannequin to? "You could liken it to an understudy you have in the theatre," she added.

Again, Penny felt a multitude of emotions, and was humbled by the sincerity of the words. She then concentrated her thoughts on an appropriate name - while Maggie and Estelle wasted no time in making straight for the glasses of red wine and delicious looking canapés on a silver platter! Sophie was waiting to serve them, salivating, as she never did manage to get her food-fix from the kitchen.

"Go on, maid, give her a good 'un. I'm naming mine Boudicca!" Maggie declared.

Penny let out an impromptu laugh. The contrast between Maggie and the Queen of the British tribe in Roman times wasn't lost on her.

"Gosh, it's a bit like naming a ship . . . not that I've done that either," Penny stated. Her eyes then became soulful, almost tearful, as a name came to her - a name she spoke with much emotion. "Megan," she said. "I'll name her Megan, after my sister. If she were alive now, there would be four of us. So, this way, she is here, isn't she?" Penny concluded, a soft smile on her face.

Estelle kissed her on the cheek. "That's perfect," she said, slipping a glass of wine into Penny's hand.

"So, what name have you chosen for yours?" Penny asked Estelle, turning to raise her glass to Megan.

"Joan of Arc, Pen. She'll beat the pants off Mags' Boudi-what's-her-face any day!"

A short while later, MP and André appeared to join in and toast Penny on her future happiness with Sam. *Monsieur* Johnny brought in another platter of canapés. He knew all too well that with the *one for you, two for me* Sophie serving them, a constant supply would be in order. (The men had waited until after the mannequins were given names before they'd entered. Not because of tradition though; Madame Renard ordered them not to.)

"Mademoiselle McCain, may I take . . . moment of time, in private?" Monsieur Johnny asked, his white-knuckled hands wringing the life out of his tea towel.

They moved away from any interruptions and the chatter of Maggie and Estelle who were saying their goodbyes to Sophie. The look of nervousness on his face, coupled with fleeting anxious smiles, reminded her of how she must have seemed when she begged Sam to propose to her again.

"I wondering if . . ." he began, and then his voice cracked and he paused to clear the tense dryness from his throat. Another uneasy smile appeared as he endeavoured to continue in his broken English: "I know you busy Lady Mademoiselle, and need to plan every detail of your wedding. So maybe you already have . . . done this . . . but I wondering . . . is anyone, do you have someone, who is to make your wedding cake for you?"

It hadn't taken Penny long to realise that Monsieur Johnny's culinary skills surpassed those of an ordinary run-of-the-mill chef. His passion in creating fine cuisine spoke volumes - as opposed to speaking his thoughts, which he found difficult to relay.

Penny stepped forward, noticing his nervous expression, and

then raised herself up on her toes to plant a long, tender kiss on the tall man's face.

"Yes, I have," she replied gazing at him, her eyes ablaze with unsuppressed pleasure. "You are, Monsieur Johnny. You are to make my cake . . . would you? Please?"

He said nothing in reply, his pose stiffening to that of standing to attention, and the accepting nod of his head was akin to acknowledging an order, but he was clearly overjoyed to be assigned a task, a creation that she could see in his eyes he had already started to plan. He scurried off back to the kitchen, his studio, the place of his heart to work his artistry, his magic, to make Penny a wedding cake that he knew would complement, even rival, her dress.

"Why do you look so sad, maid?" Maggie asked, as they later stood by the car waiting for MP to take them to the ferry.

"I love it here. Not quite as much as the cottage. But it comes a very close second," Penny replied.

Chapter 14

The Catalyst

Nothing could have been more straightforward, Sam thought – easy in fact. He had left Penny's aunts' house in Knightsbridge earlier than planned, so he knew he had plenty of time to spare. (He had been staying there doing a bit of decorating for them while Penny was in France.) She'd texted him the night before asking if he would pop back to her house to pick up a few clothes, and after that he was going to drive the two hours to the ferry terminal, dropping Maggie and Estelle off at the train station, before taking Penny down to Devon to the cottage for a couple of days before she had to be back in London. 'Oh, there is one other thing, sweetheart. I need you to pop in and see Cissy' Penny had added to her text. He was not to know that this one favour would become the catalyst that would later embroil him in a chain of events that would open a Pandora's box of evil beyond his comprehension . . .

"Hello, Sam. Come in, dear," said Cissy, Penny's elderly next-door neighbour.

She moved aside allowing him into her hallway. He positioned himself so that she couldn't close her door behind him, aware to his cost that in the past, like others before him, he would run the risk of being held captive, given half a chance, as Cissy reminisced about her thirty-plus years as a traffic warden. Her tales, although interesting and, in many cases, witty, did run on a bit . . . so having a clear exit was always advisable.

"Don't tell me, Sam. Penny's gone off to France with your front door key and you need the spare?" she said, slightly surprised but pleased to see him. She stood with a debilitating stoop and required the aid of a stick to move around, a poor posture which she put down to a lifetime of peering through countless windscreens and at parking meters.

"Not quite, Cissy. But Madame," he added, "sends her apologies for not leaving you the money for the window cleaner." Sam reached into his Northface winter jacket to retrieve his wallet.

"That silly, silly girl, she needn't have worried. Penny can settle up when she comes back . . ." Cissy's words seemed to tail off, her thoughts and gaze distracted by something or someone outside in the street. "Sam, come in and close the door, would you please." Her eyes, like her plea, were stern and unfaltering.

A thought entered Sam's puzzled mind – *why the sudden need to close the door? Is this how you dealt with drivers who parked on double yellows? The No-nonsense Move It Now approach!*

Cissy led Sam into her lounge, and the musty, stagnant air of the room filled his nostrils. He watched her stand to one side of the large bay window – which was spotlessly clean as she liked to spend hours gazing through it – out of sight of whoever was in the street, but near enough for her to see through the yellowing net curtains to observe.

"They're back," Cissy hissed. She then moved into the alcove, gesturing with a beckoning motion of her hand for Sam to come closer to her. Her whispered tone added to the drama. "Try not to be seen, Sam, but if you look across the road to your left, you'll see a black Volvo four by four parked up. Notice the driver and passenger. They're looking over at your Range Rover and at Penny's house."

"They're probably autograph hunters. Penny has had her fair share of them. Some are a pain in the arse, you know that."

He turned to look at Cissy, but she was having none of it, and looked frustrated at his dismissive reply.

"No, Sam, you're wrong. I haven't been her neighbour for all these years not to recognise suspicious individuals. Sit down and I'll tell you why."

Again, her Do It Now attitude resurfaced. She pointed to the settee with her walking stick, making it blatantly clear to him where the ex-traffic warden wanted his bottom parked. Sam reluctantly obliged, glancing at his watch, his timetable for meeting Penny on his mind, but the searing look of urgency in Cissy's eyes rendered that endeavour secondary.

She loomed over him to speak, using her indispensable walking stick, a trusted prop, to steady her. "I realise you must think me paranoid. An old lady who hasn't got anything better to do than peer through her curtains day in, day out. But one thing I learnt, Sam, as I went about my job, was to be observant. Like when I caught a young man double-parked using the excuse that he had to get something from the chemist to settle his pregnant girlfriend's tummy, and noticed that all he had in his hand was a packet of condoms!"

Sam smiled in polite response to her anecdote, but the seriousness of each and every word she spoke brushed aside any notion that Cissy would lose herself in *fond* memories. "In those days," she continued, "we got to know a good many of the Bobbies on the beat. Not like nowadays. All they do is race around in *poncy* cars. But back then they would rely on the meter maids, as they called us, to keep an eye out for any vehicles or people that were of interest. There wasn't a video camera on every street corner like there are now . . ." Then she paused for a moment, and gave him a thoughtful smile. "Like a cup of tea, dear?"

"Not for me, thank you, Cissy. You were saying?" replied Sam, his curiosity now aroused about the car parked outside and aware that, although he still had plenty of time in hand, Cissy was verbally eating into it.

"Sorry, Sam. I don't want to hold you up any more than necessary. Now, where was I? Oh yes, Bobbies on the beat. One of those young constables went on to become a detective chief inspector. He's retired now, of course. We still keep in touch with birthday and Christmas cards, and the odd letter now and again."

Cissy then hobbled over to sit in a rustic-looking armchair next to Sam. Its two back legs were wedged up on blocks of wood, tilting it forward to make it easier for her to get up. She let out a huff of relief as she dropped on to the faded black velvet cushion, her stick still firmly held in her hand for support. "His name is Harry . . . Harry Topp. I wrote to him after I had no response from the local police about that car out there and its comings and goings. I knew Harry still had a few contacts in the police force, and as they say, once a detective, always a detective."

She leant forward to move closer, the stick preventing her from slipping off the cushion to become a crumpled heap on the rug. Sam had a certain amount of sympathy for Cissy. Her lifetime spent in contact with the general public as a traffic warden was not what one would call an endearing job, but she'd loved it. Now she was practically a prisoner in her own home. The only highlight of the week beyond the confines of her four walls was going to bingo every Tuesday in the local pub just around the corner.

"To my utter surprise," Cissy continued, "Harry turned up on my doorstep a couple of days ago. At first I thought it most odd that he should bother to call, but he said he wanted to tell me what he'd found out in person." Sam remained mostly silent as she spoke, with only the odd polite "Really" or "OK, I see" passing his lips so that she could hopefully shed some light on the mysterious car. "Harry told me who they were. They're German. Oh sod it, I've forgotten their names! Get that book from on top of my sideboard, will you? And my reading classes."

Sam obliged, handing her a small black notebook, a well-used memento of her days when she would jot down details of vehicles parked next to an overrun meter.

"Yes, here they are," she said, the fine tremor of her forefinger weaving across the page. "Peter Faber. That's him. And the woman is his wife, Mila. Apparently, they're investigative journalists based here in London. According to Harry, they like digging into people's private lives to see if any skeletons appear."

Penny's got one or two of those, particularly that tosser Toby, Sam thought, a brief reminder of her not so distant past coming to mind. He noticed how Cissy's initial warm welcome had been replaced by a hard stare.

"It occurred to me, Sam, after Harry had left, that they've had plenty of opportunities to approach Penny in the street or they could have knocked on her door . . . but they haven't. And I realise now, it's not her they're waiting for . . . it's you. Why is that do you think?"

Sam walked back to the window to peer at the two Germans. He knew that people like that didn't sit in cars hour after hour if there wasn't the chance of a juicy story in it for them. They wait like hunters for their prey. If he tried to evade them, he may succeed – but for how long? And where would they eventually snare him?

"Well, I'd better go out and see if your assumption is correct, hadn't I Cissy? Maybe they've found out I've got a parking ticket I haven't paid," he joked.

She offered her cold, frail hand for him to hold, and the next words she spoke made him aware she was concerned for him. "You've made Penny so happy Sam," she said, "after that horrible Toby. The arguments they had. It was awful to see and hear. Now her life has changed for the better, thanks to you."

Sam wondered whether she may question him now, but she made no effort to discover why Sam had found himself to be the centre of interest. She just ended with words of caution, whispering, "Tread carefully."

Chapter 15

The Skeleton

With Penny's clothes already packed in the boot of his Range Rover, Sam was ready to leave. But first he stood outside Cissy's house for a moment, intentionally looking directly across at the parked black Volvo. He wanted to give her time to hobble back to her net curtains, to peer and speculate about what may be about to unfold in this street of unassuming Edwardian terraced houses.

The traffic was light: just a London taxi and two cars passed before the unexpected happened. Sam thought Peter Faber would be the one to make contact with him while his wife stayed in their car, or both of them would approach him, but he didn't reckon on Mila walking over to meet him alone. The hood of her sage-green Parker coat made it difficult for Sam to see her face – until she stood directly in front of him. Even then, because her sheepskin mittens clasped the bottom trim of the fur lined-hood, all he could clearly see were her eyes – blue, bright, and alluring as an ocean; beautiful eyes which could distract and cajole any red-blooded male who didn't have his wits about him.

Mila introduced herself to Sam in a polite, unrushed and charming manner – again, not what he was expecting. *Maybe you're too polite . . . too charming?* He put his doubts about Mila's friendly persona down to her particular line of work: journalism. Sam was aware that since Penny announced their engagement, she'd had magazine editors and pushy journalists clamouring for the exclusivity of their forthcoming nuptials and, particularly, pictures of her wedding dress. *Who is the House of Renard?* was the question on people's lips. By approaching him, Sam guessed it was another ploy to find out.

"Mr Farmer, is it?" Mila enquired.

Sam said nothing, just nodded to confirm.

"Good to meet you, at last. My name is Mila Faber. May I please talk to you? It *is* important," she asked; her quietly spoken and courteous English had only a slight hint of her native German accent, and certainly not as guttural as Sam might have imagined.

His focus moved from her eyes to her hands, noticing how she kept her hood in place, especially over her mouth, and he wondered why that was. Although it wasn't the warmest of mornings, it was neither cold nor windy enough to grasp it so firmly.

"Remove your hood, would you?" he asked, not so politely, making it a prerequisite to any dealings with her.

"Why must I? I'm cold." Mila's questioning and slightly obstinate reply only further convinced Sam that there was more in her hood than a pretty head.

"You heard me. Or I'll leave," Sam declared. He watched her turn and glance over her shoulder towards the Volvo. She then reluctantly pulled down the offending hood to let her naturally blonde hair fall free.

"There. Happy now?" She hoped her spiky riposte would distract Sam from the fact that she had stepped away from him and cocked her head slightly to the left; Sam did notice and let out a breath of frustration at her devious manoeuvre. He leant forward to speak into her ear, making her instinctively twist further away – which was exactly what Sam expected her to do.

"What are you hiding? Is it a microphone or something? So that hubby can listen in and instruct you?" he demanded.

Chapter 15

The answer to his question was almost immediate as the Volvo-man suddenly appeared from the car to stand cautiously on the other side of the road, ready to cross to his wife's aid in an instance.

"I already know who you both are, so let's end this time-wasting shall we? Tell me what you want?"

The look of puzzlement on Mila's face was obvious for Sam to see, her awareness that not only had he figured out that her husband was listening in on their conversation, brief though it was, but also that Sam apparently knew so much about them.

Mila scowled at Sam, seething that her softly-softly feminine approach had failed. She didn't like the feeling that someone had got the better of her, and felt that there was only one option left open to her: retaliate! Retaliate with a question that only required a simple yes or no. But there was a man's name she was about to raise within her enquiry that Mila knew would score a direct hit on what she perceived was Sam's contemptuous manner. "Is Miss McCain aware that you have a brother called Sidney? And that he is wanted by the British police for importing and distributing Class A drugs, mainly heroin and cocaine . . . well, is she?" Mila scornfully asked, her bad-tempered expression replaced by a self-satisfied smirk.

Like the stagnant air in Cissy's lounge, Sam hardly moved a muscle when Mila broached her question, except that his eyes registered that a nerve had been touched. Behind them his mind raced into overdrive as memories, locked behind mental barriers that were forced open, re-entered his conscious thoughts. Places and people he had wished to forget, like Penny's skeletons, no longer relevant in their future together - or so he had hoped. One skeleton in particular rattled Sam, a person whom he had once trusted and above all, loved: his estranged brother Sidney.

Mila waited for what she anticipated would be an outburst of annoyance and denials. Instead, Sam stayed silent and gazed directly into her leering eyes. He wasn't lost for words but lost in thoughts, thoughts of Sidney, the name of a man who had betrayed his family almost to destruction.

Sam glanced down at his shoes to ponder for a moment on Mila's question. He realised she had deliberately used his relationship with Penny as a conduit to reincarnate his brother into the present; the reason he could only surmise – Mila was an investigative journalist after all. Nevertheless, he felt her question warranted an answer that was more than just a 'yes or no'. An answer that would also make him understand why. Why for the first time, in a long time, was he not consumed with anger when Sidney's name was uttered?

"In answer to your question, Frau Faber, regarding Penny's knowledge of this – are you familiar with the quote 'truth will out'? It's Shakespeare. From the *Merchant of Venice* to be exact."

"Sorry, no, I'm not aware of that phrase," replied Mila; her look of curiosity softened her spiky persona and she even sounded engaging.

"To me," he continued, "it says to be up front and honest with the ones you love, because the truth will always come out sooner or later." He shot her a look as if to say *there lies your answer.*

Mila allowed herself to smile, aware she had failed for the second time; firstly, when Sam saw through her feminine ruse and secondly, refused to be intimidated by her spiteful outburst.

"I apologise Mr Farmer. I think, as you English say, we 'got off on the wrong foot'."

"Yes, I think we did," Sam replied, and then reached out to her mittened hand in a gesture of accord.

"Let's call it a draw, shall we? England one; Germany one."

Sam's subtle reminder of their two countries' footballing rivalry struck a chord with Mila. She showed him an unpretentious smile, and those sparkling blue eyes of hers once again beamed at him. While they had been talking, although distracted by the mention of his brother's name, Sam was aware that time was getting short and he had to leave sooner rather than later. "Look, I don't want to sound rude, but I really have to go."

Mila responded to his tone of urgency by turning and waving across at her waiting husband, gesturing for him to join them.

God, who do you remind me of? Sam thought, shaking the hand of Peter Faber. There was a sense of familiarity about him. Mila had married a man at least ten years her senior - much like Penny was going to do, except that in her case there was a twenty-year difference in their ages. Another thing he noticed was his handshake: it was firm and with purpose, much like his own, and he looked him straight in the eyes – a trait that in Sam's book told a lot about a person. He studied the man before him who was in his early forties, and slightly taller than himself. The tan on his face and hands suggested he'd either been somewhere a great deal warmer than England in December – or vainly spent his time in a solarium. On the other hand, Mila was, in contrast to her husband, a picture of natural health, with no sign of a tan. So, if he had been to warmer climes recently, he had left the misses at home, Sam surmised.

"I'm sorry for all the deception, Mr Farmer. Mila didn't reckon on you being so attentive. She thought that being approached by an attractive woman wouldn't make you feel intimidated or suspicious."

"I think the word you're looking for is gullible," Sam replied, resisting the urge to tell him that it was his wife's beautiful eyes that he found intimidating. "Unfortunately for your wife, I have three women in my life who at various times try the same ploy, and it doesn't work for them either . . . well, not always," Sam said, engaging in a little banter.

"Excuse me," said Mila quietly, interrupting the two men as they spoke. She gestured with her head towards Cissy's bay window. They could just make out the faint outline of her standing behind the net curtains, observing the street theatre that was unfolding right outside her front door. "Do you think she'll let me use her bathroom?" she asked, showing Sam a look of urgency, in unison with a jig-like wiggle.

"Yes, for sure, but be careful, she'll make your ears bleed!" Sam replied, as he waved a finger at Cissy pointing towards her front door.

"What do you mean, bleed?" asked Mila with concern, unaware of the term used to describe someone who talked a great deal.

"You'll find out."

The two men watched as Mila disappeared into the clutches of Cissy. *Oh God, the door has closed behind her. He'll not see his wife for years now* . . . Sam laughed, silently. He then turned his attention back to her husband, who may have thought that Sam was at ease with the two strangers.

"OK, so what's all this about? Are you trying to dish the dirt on me, to embarrass Miss McCain?" Sam asked, his direct business-like tone manifesting itself in an eye-straining glare at the German.

Peter slowly shook his head, aware that Sam had the physical ability to punch him between the eyes if that was indeed their intention. He slowly pulled down the zip on his black ski jacket to reach inside for a photograph that he then handed to Sam; a picture he knew could trigger a hand grenade of memories for him. "Recognise him, Mr Farmer?" he said. "It was taken three weeks ago in Jakarta, Indonesia. Over the last twenty years – since you saw him – he's moved around from country to country, always staying one step ahead of those who seek him."

Sam peered at the picture with a stone-hard gaze. It was a snapshot of a face, a face that prompted the distant memory of a man he had once proudly called his brother. It was taken in a restaurant with two other men; one casually dressed and the other in a uniform. At a glance, he could be mistaken for a high-ranking military officer, but he wasn't, and Sam knew all too well what he was.

"Sidney looks a lot thinner, and obviously older than I remember him, but I'm not so young myself now, am I? It has been a long time . . ." Sam calmly remarked, offering the photograph back to him.

"You can keep it, if you wish," Peter obligingly suggested. His command of the English language enabled him to be concise and clearly understood – and he needed to be for what he was about to say: he was about to change the dynamics regarding the reason why Sam had been approached and handed the picture in the first place. On the face of it, it was just a picture of his brother, reminding Sam of what took place some twenty years before, but the information Peter would now reveal would transport Sam back another thirteen years prior to that time.

"We want you to know . . ." he said, but then quickly paused to ask, "Please may I call you Sam?"

"I can't see why not, sure," Sam replied with an accepting nod.

"That's good. Sam, it is. Then you shall call me Peter, yes? But I must continue," he said, sensing that Sam's patience was wearing thin.

"Your brother Sidney is not our main focus of interest and, although he is a vital link, Mila and I have no intention to, as you say, dish the dirt on you. Please believe me when I say that." He hoped his frank words would mollify any desire Sam had to punch his lights out.

"So, if that's the case," Sam replied sternly, "then why the hell did you show me that photograph of Sidney?"

"Because Sam, it's the two other men with your brother *we're* interested in. Both of them, I believe, crossed your path more than thirty years ago, when you were in Indonesia as a young merchant seaman."

Sam only had one memory of that time and, if Peter had put his hand on Sam's chest, he would have felt his heart pound hard against flesh and muscle that had been mutilated, a memento of trying to defend himself all those years ago. His eyes closed in on Peter – who for a fleeting moment thought he was going to be floored by a clenched fist that appeared to be straining at an invisible leash.

"Are you telling me that that podgy-looking policeman and the other man with him are who I think they are?" Sam questioned.

For the first time since he engaged in conversation with the Fabers, he felt he had been punched below the belt, and his mind stalled for a moment because of what he'd just heard; such a contradiction compared to when Mila had endeavoured to provoke him about his wayward brother. He remembered that as he spoke the words 'truth will out', he became conscious that he had finally released himself from the burden of guilt he had carried for all these years, shouldering the blame like a mental scar for not knowing his brother was a drug-dealing thief until it was too late. His physical scars could never be explained away like that. They belonged to him, and they would be his companions for eternity. An unforgiving desire began to flow from the depths of his soul and it filled him. A desire that had lain almost dormant, simmering quietly for decades, buried because he felt powerless, powerless to find and confront the man who disfigured him. *Now, just maybe, what goes around will come around after all,* he concluded.

Sam then wanted to know everything as questions formed rapidly in his mind: who exactly were the two men? Why was Peter Faber interested in them? But top of his asks was: what was his brother doing in Indonesia talking to two men who may be the ones who had put Sam through hell? He closed his eyes to shut out the world for a fleeting moment, only to be distracted by the sound of Cissy's voice. Her instantly recognisable cackle of laughter heralded the release of Mila from her incarceration!

"Can Mila drive?" Sam asked, forming a clandestine idea that would enable the two men to continue to talk. "What say you get your wife to drive you around the corner – out of the prying eyes of you know who – and wait for me to pick you up?"

Peter acknowledged the wily plan and knew Sam wasn't just going to listen to all that he had to say. Sam would search and pry into every corner for clues, and draw out of him every morsel of knowledge he possessed regarding the other two men, one of whom had, a lifetime before, practiced his sadistic gratifications on Sam's body…

Chapter 16

The Long Reach Back

The gentle click of the passenger seatbelt as it engaged into its latch was the signal for Sam to be on his way. He glanced into the rear-view mirror to check that Mila was following on behind in the Volvo. Getting in and out of London was, at times, akin to driving in molasses, and just when you thought the road ahead was clear, you became stuck in gridlock.

"You wouldn't be so kind as to pass me the bottle of water from your door pocket, could you please?" Sam politely asked.

He had no intension of allowing his traveling companion to journey with him any further than was necessary, so what time they would have together wouldn't be spent in silent contemplation or listening to downloads of Mantovani on his car stereo. They were there to continue where they had left off. But first Sam had to quench the gravel-like thirst that threatened to divert his focus from the man sitting in the passenger seat beside him. The idea that he would relive the nightmare he'd found himself in all those years before would have been an anathema to him. Now those memories would be front and centre. He offered the bottle to his new acquaintance – who declined with a polite, "Nein danke," and then Sam drew in a deep breath to ready himself for the long reach back.

"Well, now we're all cosy, maybe you should enlighten me as to why *you're* so interested in those men with my brother and, more importantly, how can I get my hands on them."

It seemed a while before he heard Peter's reply, a reply that was considered and well thought through. Peter Faber was normally the one who asked the questions for others to answer, but to get the answers *he* sought, he realised that with Sam it would be: you answer mine, and then I'll answer yours.

"I've no doubt you, being an educated man Sam, have heard the quote *'Power tends to corrupt, and absolute power corrupts absolutely'.*"

Sam turned his head from concentrating on his driving to briefly have eye contact with him. "Yes, many times, and you can add to that: *'Great men are almost always bad men'.*"

Peter Faber acknowledged his counter with the look of a man who knew that not only could Sam cite quotations by the historian Lord Acton, but also, veiled within his reply, was an understanding of the sort of people Peter was possibly engaging with.

"I take it," Sam continued, "with what you have implied absolute power corrupting, and that more than just a few of the police over there are corrupt, and all powerful. Believe me, I should know. Is that why you're interested in my, possible past acquaintance, Mr Chubby Pig, the police chief, if that's what he is now?"

"Chubby Pig!" Peter replied, but then paused, thus preventing being drawn into descriptive characterisation, a trait he knew the British had a fondness for. "He's Sohaed Kazemi, and yes, you're right, he's the senior deputy commissioner of police. Mila has researched the meaning of his name. They all have a meaning over there, as you probably know? It translates to 'One who controls his anger'. But that is not in this man's DNA. As you found to your cost, he is a brutal and ruthless man."

"Nothing new there then, just your run of the mill servant of the people . . ." Sam nonchalantly replied, his eyes not straying from the road ahead as he continued to negotiate the seemingly habitual roadworks that spawned tailbacks of heavy traffic.

Sam may have tried to give his companion the impression of being indifferent to what he heard, but Peter Faber saw through it. He wasn't a man who neglected to find out all he could about him, and one fact he knew was Sam's ability to deal with tension and stress when others could not. Being irritated by having complete strangers approach you in the street was one thing, but to cope with painful memories, physical and mental, and then have to relive them, and at the same time maintain perceptive to what lay ahead, was completely different. Sam obviously cloaked such pressures by a perceived cold, out of context wit, bordering on sarcasm, a defence mechanism that in time would be tested beyond any of his nightmarish memories.

"Kazemi," Peter answered, "was, I believe, the man who arrested you. He was just a junior officer back then, and it was he who put you in the cell with the three other men."

"Ha, that's a joke!" Sam retorted, and this time he did briefly turn his head to glare. "It wasn't a cell, it was a cage with bars on all four sides, and the floor was filthy dirty with urine and vomit. I remember Kazemi – if that's who it was. He was goading two of them: 'Fuck him, fuck him' he kept repeating over and over again. It doesn't matter what language it's spoken in, it means the same thing." But there was no place for jest in Sam's words now. He knew that what he had just spoken of was only a small insight into what had followed, and could never be passed off as a scene of comedy. "So, what else do you know?" Sam asked, his mannered, yet straight to the point questions setting the tone.

"I know that you were set upon by a bunch of local youths on the way back to your ship, that the shipmate you were with ran off, and that the police then blamed you for the fight."

"Yes, it was something like that . . . At bloody last!" Sam cried, showing his relief at the sight of an open road ahead. "It's a good job Maggie, one of my daughters, isn't driving. She'd be sitting on the horn, pushing all the traffic along. That's the French in her for you."

"Ha!" Peter laughed. "That sounds a lot like Mila, also! But please don't tell her I said that!" His admission added a moment of light respite, but it wasn't to last. "You were saying about the fight?" he continued; like Sam, he too preferred the direct approach.

"Yes, the fight. According to the police it was my fault, and by the time I got home to Blighty–"

"Blighty?" Peter interrupted, confused as he hadn't heard the word before.

"Oh, Blighty! It's the name sailors call England."

"Ah, I see now, it's what you call slang, yes?"

"Yes, it is slang," Sam said. "Anyway, by the time I arrived home, after spending two months hidden away in a shit pit of an army hospital, it had all but been brushed under the carpet so to speak. Mum and Dad went berserk, of course, but the British police and Foreign Office did bugger all. Then the official report came out from the Indonesian authorities. It stated that they had eyewitness statements that implied that I had a brawl with a Russian sailor in a bar, and that he attacked me with a knife. Also, apparently, I was violent towards the police." He groaned loudly. "They did me up like a kipper, as the saying goes. The Indonesians don't like to admit that their people break the law, do they?" Sam then waved his hand across his rear-view mirror to attract Mila's attention. "Your misses is still with us," he confirmed, seeing her reply with a flash of her car's headlamps.

"So, do you also know the identity of the other man in the photograph, the bastard you've implied was the one who cut me up?" Sam asked.

"Yes and no," Peter answered. He wondered how Sam would react to finally being given the name of the man who had disfigured him a lifetime before. He wasn't sure. "The two Indonesian men in the cell with you I know little about, other than they're dead," Peter added. "But the one who, as you say, cut you up is referred to as the Barber. I know he's not Indonesian – he's possibly South American – and I was hoping you could shed some light on the man."

Sam frowned across at him, and blustered, "You've got to be having a laugh, haven't you? Not only was it over thirty-odd years ago, I was too busy trying to stop the two Indonesians from sticking their dicks up my backside. Then the Barber – if that's who you think he is – gestured to the two men to hold me down. One of them sat on my face while that sadistic bastard had his own fun with me." Sam paused to silently remember that moment, and then let out what may have been seen as an inappropriate laugh, saying, "Ha! The one who tried to smother me with his shitty arse - I bit into his bollocks and held on for dear life! You should have heard him scream. He didn't reckon on foreplay like that. Then it was all over." Sam then sighed. "C'est la vie."

A certain tension appeared across his face as his mind relived the physical sensation of his flesh being sliced and flayed by the Barber.

Peter hesitated to probe further, but he knew he needed to. "It wasn't a knife he used on you, was it?" he queried, hoping Sam's reply would confirm without a doubt that his torturer was the Barber.

"No, you're right, it wasn't, he used a cut-throat razor on me, but not the type I had ever come across before. It had an evil-looking flat blade . . . and then he wiped it across my lips to make me taste my own blood." Sam glanced at the clock on the dashboard and then signalled to pull into a layby. "We're making good time. I'd like to stop for a minute, if it's OK with you?" Sam asked.

He drank from the bottle of water that he had positioned between their seats and felt the refreshing winter air that filled the cab as Peter opened his door to talk to Mila, who was curious to know why they had stopped.

Chapter 16

"Everything OK? Have you finished talking, or can I sit in the back and join in while we're parked?"

"No, I'd rather you didn't," Peter replied. "Sam and I have to talk about things which I know he wouldn't want a lady to hear."

Sam didn't have to say a word; he had the same thought running through his head and Peter knew that. Peter kissed Mila tenderly on her lips and then both men watched as she walked back to her car to wait.

Sam noticed the gaze of concern on Peter's face as he looked at her. It was as though he knew she should be protected, shielded from knowing too much about Sam's dealings with the Barber for her own sanity.

"To hide in plain sight, Sam," Peter muttered, and then quietly posed a question: "Where would you hide where no one would think to look?" His eyes had not diverted from his wife as she sat obediently in their car. Peter continued, "Two days prior to you being arrested, a prominent human rights activist was abducted . . . and later found butchered. She'd been researching corruption in the higher echelons of the Indonesian police and was about to submit her findings to an investigating judge. Her abductors were two of your cellmates, who then delivered her to the Barber."

"Ah, so the police caught them, and that's why they were in the cage with me, right?" Sam asked.

"No, they didn't get caught, Sam." Peter's vague reply created a stilled moment while Sam tried to work out the conundrum that was woven within Peter's words: *how could they be detained by the police and put behind bars, yet not be caught.*

"You can't be serious?" Sam replied, his voice almost dismissive in tone as he realised the answer to the riddle. "God, you've got to have balls to agree to do that!" he exclaimed, and then heard Peter let out a nasal laugh, finding Sam's repost somewhat abstractly humorous, remembering he had said he'd bitten into one of the men's scrotum.

"Where no one would think to look," Peter answered. "The one place your friends could keep you safe while the uncorrupted sought you out beyond their citadel."

"Great," Sam sighed, "it just gets better and better. Now you tell me he's a hitman as well as a psychopath!"

"The Barber's not what you would call an out-and-out assassin, Sam, more of an extractor. His forte is to painfully extract information from some unfortunate soul for the benefit of his clients, in this case, Kazemi. Then he kills them, but not before he feeds his fetish for disembowelling them first. You may not think it, but you were lucky Sam, in more ways than one."

Sam stayed silent, thinking luck didn't come into it. He recognised that with the ensuing hubbub of him being rushed to hospital, it was a sadistic ruse for the Barber to slip out the cell, and back into obscurity.

The flash of the car's headlamps alerted Mila that they were on their way again, but questions still remained to be posed and answered.

Chapter 17

The Sisters

Both men *did* spend a moment or two in silent contemplation, their thoughts firmly on their own agendas. For Peter Faber and his wife, it was perseverance; Sam's was payback. He now knew the name of the man whose calling card was carved into his flesh, but he needed Peter Faber to bring the Barber into the present. Then he hoped he could put his physical ghoul to rest, one way or another.

Ah-ha, Sam mused, in recognition of a shrewd man. He had forgotten that Peter was, after all, a journalist, and a good one. He was now aware that his new German friend hadn't actually asked any questions, but what he had done was cleverly fill in the blanks while Sam talked of his brief but painful acquaintance with the Barber and Kazemi. Like a pathway, he had brought Sam's past into the present and there was no more reaching back.

But it was now Peter's turn to answer questions. "Talking of quotes and the like, have you ever heard the saying 'I'll show you mine, if you show me yours?'" Sam asked, observing Peter frown in response to the idiom. "I take it that's a no then," he continued. "It means: it's now your turn to explain why my past is of interest to *you*."

"Huh, you English, you love your play on words. It's like a passion with you, isn't it?" said Peter, responding to the obscure demand.

"Passion!" Sam retorted. "Passion doesn't come into it. Wait until I recite Shakespeare. No, better still, you should listen to Penny or her two aunts. Once they get the Bard rolling off their tongues, they'll get you in fits of laughter . . . or have you crouching in a corner with fear! Now that's passion!"

Only the sound of the car's tyres trundling over the tarmac filled the silence while Sam waited for him to respond, and when he did, he would find that the quote, 'absolute power corrupts absolutely' more significant than he could ever imagine.

"He – Kazemi – is a means to an end for Mila and me," Peter replied. "Do you remember hearing in the news about the two young French women, sisters, who had been released from jail in Indonesia?"

"Vaguely. It was a while back, wasn't it?" Sam responded. The word Indonesia had over the years become a trigger to his sub-conscious, hoping to read about or recognise the men who he now knew as Kazemi and the Barber. "Wasn't their father some high-ranking diplomat or something?" Sam asked.

"You could say that. He's the French ambassador to the United Nations in New York. The sisters, along with another woman, were all working for a Swiss-based charity in Jakarta. They were accused of being in possession of cocaine and, according to the police, they had caught the man who supplied them – who later identified the women, of course," said Peter scornfully. He then let out a groan akin to frustration, aware that the tale he would now relay to Sam was a tactic carefully orchestrated to achieve a specific end, instigated in part by a man who needed no introduction: Kazemi. "You see, my friend, the story of the drugs was to snare them, for the women to become pawns in a plot of political subterfuge . . ." Sam noted the poignancy in his voice and a gaze that confirmed that this was no everyday story of three unfortunate aid workers. "The French Government had agreed to build five fishery protection vessels for the Indonesian Navy. Only they weren't. They were heavily armed patrol craft which contravened an arms embargo put in place due to the Indonesian Government's poor record on human rights."

"I bet that pissed them off," said Sam, nonchalantly.

"Oh yes, it pissed then off, all right," Peter continued, "so much so that they detained the three women on the trumped-up drugs charge, knowing in advance who the sisters' father was. The pre-trial was a total farce. It was all done for the benefit of the world's media, particularly the French."

"I assume the French Government did some sort of deal with regards to the ships so that the sisters could be released? But I don't remember anything about the other French woman. I take it she was released as well?" Sam asked.

"No, and she wasn't French, either. Elsa was German and . . . Mila's elder sister," Peter replied.

"Oh," Sam whispered under his breath, in recognition of Peter Faber's unexpected admission. He took his eyes off the road for a moment, showing Peter a pointed glance. "So, *that's* what it's all about. There was I thinking you were investigating cretins like Kazemi on a purely professional basis, but you're not, are you? It's personal . . . well, welcome to the club, chum." Sam reached down for his bottled water and offered it to him. "Go on, take a swig, and then you should tell me why your sister-in-law is still in jail." The sureness of tone in Sam's voice brought a guarded frown to Peter's troubled face. But he was prepared to answer the questions of the one person he felt he could trust enough to confide in, the one man who would understand.

"Elsa's dead, Sam, she hanged herself in her cell."

A gasp of anguish spilled from Sam lips, a spontaneous and genuine outburst of shock. "Oh shit, God . . . I'm so sorry!" he exclaimed, resisting the temptation to elaborate further by saying he knew what he must have been feeling as *his* sister Ruth had taken her own life. The telling of those memories, he thought, seemed inappropriate, even insensitive, just at this moment.

"You're right, the French did deliver the ships," Peter continued. "They found a compromise – something to do with the guns. Unfortunately, although the Indonesian Navy got their vessels, that wasn't the end of it. The police couldn't be seen to lose face especially Kazemi who was now deputy commissioner. His ego wouldn't allow a trial not to take place, so although the charges were dropped for the sisters, they still planned to go ahead with the full trial of Elsa."

While they spoke, a light rain had started to fall, creating moments of wet and dry on the windscreen. Peter paused to listen to the distracting squeaking sound coming from the car's wipers, but it was a breathing space that wasn't to last as he continued with his wretched tale. "If she had been found guilty – which I'm sure Kazemi would have made certain of – Elsa may have got the death penalty . . . or life imprisonment at best.

"She was what you would call fragile, and when she was told the other two had gone home without her and what was going to happen to her, Elsa couldn't come to terms with it. It broke her, Sam."

The pant of impotent anger on Peter's breath seemed to freeze time. Sam remained silent. There was nothing he could add. Remorse was a blunt word, but the empathy that flowed through his veins was an emotion that had become glue that bonded him to the Fabers. As he reached out his hand to grip Peter's arm, he could hear the cracking of plastic as he squeezed and crushed the empty bottle of water held in his grasp.

"Sorry, I wish that was that bastard's neck," was the response from the German. He knew Sam was now desperate to know how he could use all the intelligence obtained about Kazemi and the Barber, and *if* it would involve him further.

"So, what plans do you have now, now that you've made me aware you know all about my past?" Sam asked.

"Ah well, they've changed since Mila and I first decided to go after Kazemi in retribution for Elsa's death. We planned to expose him for the corrupt policeman he is, but then we began to ask questions to ourselves, like why did Kazemi help the Navy obtain their ships? And when we identified one of the men in the photograph as your brother . . . why was a high-ranking police officer casually having a meal with a wanted drug dealer? It was easy to think that maybe he was involved with narcotics more than just having them planted on innocent women, but it turned out to be even more involved than that."

As Peter laid out the last pieces of the puzzle to Sam, he could see that they were now entering Portsmouth and soon would be near to the docks where they would part company. "I told you that your brother moved around a great deal to avoid capture . . . well, that's not quite correct, Sam," he continued. "I think he's got a bolthole in the Philippines and he's protected by a man called Tagaan - who happens to be Kazemi's brother-in-law. Tagaan supplies Muslim rebel groups on the island of Mindanao with weapons, and I wonder how and where he gets them from, don't you?" Peter then went quiet, leaving the subject open for Sam's own reading of the covert question.

"I know of someone who runs a yacht charter business over there," Sam replied.

"A friend of yours?" Peter enquired.

"No, not anymore." Sam then pondered whether he should elaborate as to who the ex-friend was. "He's the guy who ran off back to the ship before I got arrested by Kazemi. We haven't spoken since then, but his mum still sends me Christmas cards with the odd letter attached. Henning – that's his name by the way – tells her that drug-smuggling and people-trafficking is rife over there. It's a far cry from Norway where he's from . . ." Sam then added a caveat to what he'd said, words of caution: "If you're going after my brother to bring down Kazemi, you don't need me to tell you to keep Mila out of it. Sidney doesn't damage people with his hands, with him it's cerebral and, like the Barber, he has no regard as to who he hurts, and that includes women."

Their journey together had come to an end and while they waited for Mila to arrive, Sam lowered his car door window to savour the salty essence that wafted in on the sea breeze, but there was one last question on his mind that hadn't been answered: "You haven't said anything more about the whereabouts of the man you think is the Barber, why is that?"

Peter Faber ignored the enquiry and climbed out of the car to welcome his wife as she parked nearby. But he turned to see Sam's eyes fixed on him. He returned a blank expression - indicating to Sam he had little to add.

"I wish, my friend, I could tell you . . . and I hope we are now friends, yes?" Peter asked.

Sam replied with a nod and a handshake, thinking of the man he was reminded of every time he removed his shirt.

"The Barber is like a ghost," Peter then said. "He appears and disappears as he has done for over thirty years. Three days after that photograph was taken, a trade union leader was abducted and when they found him in a drainage gully; his body had all the hallmarks of the man you seek. But that's all I know, I'm sorry."

"Don't be. He'll face his day of reckoning. God willing, I'll be there when he does," Sam replied coldly. Mila then distracted the men as she waved at them. "Now, do you mind if I say goodbye to your wife?" he asked.

"Certainly, please do. I know she wants you to," Peter replied.

Sam walked over to her, to savour her hypnotic blue eyes – not expecting to gaze upon them again in the future. *There is no reason to*, he thought, never considering their paths could cross again.

After a brief conversation between the three of them, Sam left to continue on his journey. He left Peter pondering the information he had gleaned from Sam - and the unsuspecting Cissy.

Chapter 17

"So, did you get a name?" Peter asked his wife, who looked very pleased with herself.

"Yes, I did: Harry Topp. The old lady said he's a retired detective chief inspector and an old friend of hers."

"That's good. He may be of use to us. I take it you got his phone number?"

Mila nodded to confirm, and then placed her lips tenderly on Peter's cheek. "Do you think she'll say anything about today to Miss McCain?" Peter wondered.

"No," Mila replied. "She thinks we wanted to speak to Sam about Miss McCain's ex-boyfriend, Toby, who she hates. No, she won't say anything."

Chapter 18

Christmas Come Early

February

"Good morning, Maggie, and how are your two rascals today?" Duncan asked.

Duncan was a vet with a wealth of knowledge regarding the care of a wide range of animals, be it a gerbil with an eye infection, or an orphaned baby elephant whose mother had been slaughtered by poachers for her tusks on the plains of the Serengeti. Now settled in a small town in the Yorkshire Dales with his family, Duncan shared his veterinary practice with a young woman whose father called her Mayhem Maggie for her zest for life and intolerance of fools, but above all, those who mindlessly intended to do harm to innocent animals.

"The buggers," Maggie heatedly exclaimed, giving the two seven-week-old Highland puppies a stern glare. "These little monsters have only gone and chewed the heels off a pair of my Jimmy Choos, and they cost me a bloody fortune. The buggers!" she repeated.

"Well, I think it's time you started to think about finding homes for them soon, don't you? You've done your bit," said Duncan.

He observed Maggie gently lifting the puppies out of the wicker-shopping basket that she had carried them around in, and had done ever since she took on the role as surrogate mother when they were less than a week old.

"I know, and yes, you're right of course, but I'm keeping the boy. He can come around the farms with me, but the girly has got to go," she replied, giving her two charges a smothering hug. "Here, hold her for me will you while I take a picture of her. I know just the person who will give her a good home," she said, her dreamy smile masking the tear-jerking past of the two loveable, but mischievous, shoe-chewing puppies.

"Hi, Trudy!" chirped Penny, openly pleased to see her again.

"Ready for round two, are you?" Trudy joked.

Trudy was once again Belinda Carson's PA after being away to organise Penny and Sam's forthcoming wedding. Their unrestrained hug was so different from six months before when Penny had last appeared on Belinda's chat show. It was then that her defences had jangled at the sight of Trudy fixing her practiced alluring gaze on her future husband, but now the three of them had become close pals and, as Sam put his hands on her shapely waist and petted her on both cheeks, only smiles ensued.

"Come on, Penny" said Trudy taking her friends arm. "Same old, same old: sign in and then to make-up."

"Ah, here you are darling!" boomed Belinda, tracking Sam down to the last place he would expect her to look . . . but then maybe not? She prided herself on being a resourceful and wily woman who always kept one eye on the ratings and, should she finally persuade Sam to appear on her show with Penny, well, that would be the cherry on the cake. She tilted her head for a desirable peck - which was more of a gesturing pout from Sam: stage make-up never was a delectable delight to the taste-buds.

"Now, Sam!" Belinda boomed again. "Considering what is planned, I rather hoped that you would reconsider and join Penny and me on the show. It'll make a wonderful moment for when, you know who arrives . . ."

Her plea was a mix of appealing charm and intimidating self-interest, that was then followed by a broad grin from Sam, acknowledging where she had cornered him.

"Well, this is novel for me," he replied, drying his hands on a paper towel. "I've never been accosted in a gent's toilet before - not by a woman that is," he sighed, in exasperation at her fortitude. "Sorry, hun, but the answer is still no. The look of curiosity on the faces of those who witnessed them leaving the washroom only fed their instinct to tease and enjoy the funny side of what she'd done. "Your place next time, sweetheart?" Sam said jokingly, blowing her a kiss.

"Fifteen minutes, Miss Carson," came the call from the informative Trudy, who had appeared from the hospitality lounge with a mug of lemon tea for her boss.

Sam then reached for Belinda's hand and gave it a light squeeze. "I'll leave you both to it," he told them, intending to be with Penny for a chat and coffee while they waited for her turn to appear on the show and sit on the sofa that now replaced the uncomfortable chair she had to endure the last time.

"Not so fast, Sam," Trudy hastily requested. "I need to talk to you privately while Penny's still in make-up."

"The gent's is free," Belinda quipped. She turned to walk off in the direction of the set, a flag-like hand waving in the air.

Then a humorous spiky repost followed, echoing in the confined space of the corridor: "Ha, I hope you have better luck with him than I did, Trudy darling. He said no to me!"

Trudy wasted no time in leading Sam to a more appropriate place to be alone; somewhere even the desperate wouldn't consider entering without prior permission. The small informative sign on the office door with the inscription: Beware the Bitch Bites, had Belinda written all over it. The two cream leather executive chairs that faced each other across an imposing desk remained redundant as Trudy stood close to Sam, so near he could feel the heat of her breath as she spoke, saying, "I spent the evening with Mila last night. She sends her love by the way."

"Oh, did you now, and how are they both?" Sam enquired. Then in that single moment he became conscious that Trudy's repartee for banter and quick wit had been put aside for a more solemn tone of voice. Even her gaze, as his pointed frown searched her eyes for ungifted answers, told of a tension, even a glimmer of fear as he noted how her pupils had become dilated with untold fretful thoughts.

"I realise you must be wondering how I know Mila and Peter," she said, "and if I helped them find out about your past in any way." She glanced down at her wristwatch, ever mindful of how time flies – and this was one occasion when the pressure was on her not to waste it with idle chitchat. "Very quickly, Sam," she continued. "I know the Fabers very well. We've been close friends for years, in fact. They're nice people, Sam, and they know, as I hope you do, that I wouldn't betray friendships – yours or theirs."

The impulse to hug and comfort her as he would any friend who seemed uneasy was checked by the manner in which she spoke: she was asking for his attention, not his sympathy.

"Yes, I know that," he replied, endeavouring to reassure her, and then added, "You're like me, sweetheart. We bear too many scars to talk of each other's pasts cheaply."

His words of understanding brought a glaze to her eyes, that made her instinctively turn away from him for a moment; loss of composure was the last thing she wanted to happen. Again, she checked the time. "Penny should be out from make-up soon." She now paused to stare directly into Sam's eyes, wanting to feel his emotions as a friend. "You remember the car accident Penny had last year, and that the police never caught the person who caused her to smash into the central reservation?"

"How could I ever forget that . . ." he replied firmly. "It was one of the darkest days of my life. I was at the airport waiting for her to pick me up, and all the time she was in hospital, broken-boned."

Then the bombshell was dropped.

"It most likely wasn't an accident, Sam. Someone may have intended to kill her . . . or you. It was your car she was driving, after all, wasn't it?"

The unimaginable, unthinkable idea that anyone would contrive to do harm to Penny - his Penny - was beyond comprehension. He gasped as if the oxygen in the room had been sucked out in the instant his mind had taken to absorb Trudy's statement. For a few moments, she became just a spectator as Sam tussled with his emotions, and for control of his state of mind. His eyes strained, as did his jaw muscles – speechless movements that needed no sound to express his reactions. But she knew that like anyone who had been given such emotive information, he would demand answers to the barrage of questions; questions that waited for him to catch his breath and ask.

"Don't say a word, Sam, please, just listen to what else I have to tell you . . . please?" she pleaded.

"OK, I won't. But you'd better come up with a good explanation as to why you've just . . . scared the shit o-out of me," he blustered.

Then he observed her crouch down by the side of Belinda's desk to reveal a small drinks chiller that was built into it. "Help me up, will you?" she asked, reaching for his hand - that now felt like hard, unbending iron.

He silently watched as she put the bottle of Perrier water to her perfectly made-up lips, and how she savoured its refreshing zest. "Here Sam," she said. "I know in times like this you would prefer a dash of single malt with it . . . sorry . . . maybe later, huh?"

No sooner had he started to quench his thirst, than Trudy started to explain: "You've heard the name, Harry Topp, haven't you?" she asked.

Chapter 18

"Yes. He's a retired policeman, an old friend of Cissy's. You've met her – she's Penny's next door neighbour. Why?"

"Peter and Mila hired him to do some digging around for them. According to her, he was eager to put his skills as a detective back into use – especially if he got good money for doing it."

Once again, she glanced at her watch. *Bollocks*, she thought, combing her black bobbed hair with jittery fingers, aware Belinda's first guest would soon be introduced to her audience. Now the clock was really ticking for Trudy to say what she had to, and finish in time for them both to see the shows last guest appear: Penny.

Trudy's tone now became metronomic in presentation. If Sam wanted to know the facts, then he'd better keep up.

"The Fabers," she continued, "pointed the old blood hound in the direction of Birmingham to see if any of your brother's past acquaintances were still around. They knew it was twenty-odd years ago, but thought it was worth a shot. For a while he drew a blank, and then he called in a few favours from someone he knew who was still serving in the police force, someone whom he had helped up the promotional ladder when he was his boss."

Sam had no trouble keeping up with her – in fact he hung off every word she spoke – but he could tell by the way they had eye contact with each other that she didn't want to sound cold and uncaring; to Trudy, presentation was everything.

"Harry Topp," Trudy continued, "was passed a name by a serving policeman: Terry Button. He'd been released from prison in January last year, after serving six years for the attempted murder of his ex-wife. Apparently, he prided himself on being an out-and-out thug. Old Topp found out that soon after Button was let out, he flew to Acapulco, Mexico, supposedly for a holiday. Topp believed it was most likely to meet the person who paid for his ticket to fly out there."

"Here, babe, take a swig," Sam ordered, seeing her pause long enough to ensure she had a drink. "Sorry the water's not warm, as you prefer, but like you said – maybe later."

"Thanks, but don't distract me, Sam, please." This statement was followed by a strained smile to soften her somewhat terse rely. "Shit, now where was I?" she huffed. "Yes . . . Topp. He regularly kept the Fabers up to date with his progress. He'd tracked down a prostitute in Birmingham who Button visited from time to time, and according to the tart – well, after some financial incentive that is – she told him that a week or so after Button returned from Mexico, he was in her flat and boasted that he'd been down south playing dodgem cars on the motorway to teach someone a lesson, to silence them. That was the day after Penny had her accident, and I don't know if the police told you or not, but they found a car on fire in a lay-by just off the motorway. It had been stolen the night before in Birmingham."

Trudy then decided to let Sam have a say; his change of expression left her in no doubt that he intended to speak whether she wanted him to or not.

"Please tell me the Fabers have gone to the police with that information!" Sam questioned.

"Mila wanted to talk to *you* first, and then couldn't because the situation changed." Trudy's reply was instant; for her that was all the time she was willing to give him to talk. "You see, Sam . . . Harry Topp is dead: murdered."

"What do you mean murdered? Murdered by whom? When . . . and where?"

Trudy glanced nervously towards the office door, concerned that Sam's stern interrogative tone of voice would not be confined within the thin flat-pack-styled partition walls; her reply was undertone in comparison. "That's why I had to talk to you urgently," she responded. "You see, the police interviewed Mila a few days ago. Peter is out of the country at the moment, so she had to deal with them on her own . . . poor cow."

Trudy then sighed, which only added to her desperate sense of urgency. "Mila thought there was something very wrong from the start with the way the cops were treating Topp's death," she continued. "She couldn't understand how they found out the connection between Topp and them. He wouldn't have freely divulged who he was working for – client confidentiality and all that crap – but she was told that Topp was attacked six days ago, getting into his car at a service station just north of Birmingham, and died on the way to the hospital. But according to Mila, their version is spurious at best. She was sure the police weren't telling the whole truth, because Topp had said that he didn't drive anymore because of an eye condition, so he used taxis and trains instead."

Sam moved to rest himself against the corner of the desk as he grasped what he was hearing and it filtered through to every sinew of his body. The notion that the British police were whiter than white would be a belief based on pure naivety, but the possibility that they were covering up the true facts of the man's death introduced a dimension that would hang like a shadow of doubt over them.

Was it Topp's old police colleague who betrayed him to the thug, Button, and if so, why? Sam wondered. And then another overriding thought struck him like an ice-cold spike driven down his spine: *By poking around into Sidney's past, had old Topp inadvertently awakened Button's deadly interest in Penny and him? Who the hell is this man?* he mused, *he obviously knows me, but how?*

For a moment, the distraction of his own intense thoughts muted the sound of Trudy's voice, and the sensation of her hand gently soothing the side of his face.

"We'd better get a move on, Sam, if you want to see Penny before Belinda springs her surprise. But there's a couple of other things you ought to know . . . important things." Trudy frowned thoughtfully at Sam. It was out of friendship for Mila and him that she had agreed, somewhat reluctantly, to be the bearer of the bad news. She was conscious that with Sam heeding every word she uttered, any deviation of the facts that Mila had conveyed to her could lead Sam up a blind alley of thoughts; a misdirection that could understate the possibility that he may become the victim of circumstance because of factors that were out of his control. "Like I said, Sam, there were two detectives. The senior. She's called DCI Tamworth," she eventually said.

"Tamworth, ha! – that's an appropriate name for a police officer, isn't it"! Sam laughed.

"Why? What's so funny about her name?" Trudy asked, mystified as to his sudden burst of humour.

"Tamworth is a breed of pig! I thought – you being a country girl – you would have known that."

"Shit! You're right! It is, isn't it? Now that's done it – we'll have to call her Miss Piggy from now on, won't we?" She grinned like a naughty schoolgirl, allowing herself a moment of light relief.

"Did I hear you say *she*? So, the DCI's a woman . . . What was she like with Mila?" he asked.

"Apparently OK, very professional and business-like. But it was the pushy detective constable who was with her . . . Mila thought he seemed to be out of step with his boss, like he had his own agenda. You see, instead of just asking questions about Topp, he wanted to know what she knew about your brother Sidney. Mila said that she could see Tamworth – aka Miss Piggy – was clearly unimpressed with her colleague, as if he knew more about what was going on than she did."

Trudy paused and opened the office door to check the corridor was clear and then closed it again, her voice now quieter as she continued in an almost secretive tone, saying, "Yesterday morning Mila had another visit from Miss Piggy, but this time on her own, and 'off the record' so to speak . . . and she didn't beat about the bush either. She said that she had found out that her young colleague, DC Davis, had been approached by a very high-ranking police officer – who will remain nameless – to retrieve some files about your brother for him. That person then passed Button's name on to his old friend and ex colleague, Topp.

"According to Miss Piggy, Davis thought he'd do a bit of snooping around for himself to earn some brownie points towards his promotion. He found out about Topp, and then approached Button in the belief he could use him to gain intelligence about the main drug dealers in the area. But Davis hadn't done his homework on Button, and found out, to his cost, what a thug he could be. He ended up telling Button everything he knew about Topp and the Fabers."

"Christ, that's all we need, a rogue cop! Who's next on Buttons hit list I wonder? The Faber's? Me?" Sam's severe words were tempered with the knowledge that you don't shoot the messenger; you take her hand and pull her to you for a reassuring hug. "OK, answers time, hun," he calmly said, knowing without Trudy needing to glance at her watch for the umpteenth time that they only had minutes left to make some sense of the calamitous situation. "What possessed DCI Tamworth to own up to Mila about DC Davis? She risked her career to do that. I'm not saying Mila or Peter would . . . but what if the media got hold of it? It would be feeding time of the police."

"That's because Miss Piggy needed to take a calculated risk and not have the spectre of the Fabers causing future problems for her. Like us, she wants to see Button locked away for the murder of Harry Topp. He was one of theirs after all."

"So, what about Button? Does she know his whereabouts?"

"No, Sam. Unfortunately, before they could arrest him, he flew to Amsterdam and then disappeared; but he'll be nabbed if he ever comes back."

Hearing Trudy say the thug had left the country filled Sam with twin emotions. On one hand, he was relieved that Penny was unlikely to come in contact with him again; but on the other he experienced a sense of annoyance that it would be more difficult to find out why Button had wanted to kill Penny or him in the first place.

"Come on, let's get out of here," Sam told her.

He felt they'd talked enough. Anymore and they'd just be going around in circles . . . or so he thought.

"I'm not finished yet, Sam," Trudy replied abruptly. An uneasy frown had appeared across her brow, and she knew that what she was about to repeat had angered her friend Mila when she was informed by DCI Tamworth of the same information – and Trudy understood why. As for Sam's reaction . . . she was in the dark, still unaware of the connection that was a bond between him and the Fabers.

"Sam, it's like this. When Tamworth realised that her rooky detective was up to no good, she felt that she had no other option but to confront the senior officer who passed Button's name on to Topp. It was then decided, by the said person, to pass on some recently received intelligence to the Fabers via Tamworth, to placate them and, he hoped, direct their attention away from Birmingham – and, of course, him."

As Trudy talked, she wiped a tear away that had formed out of caring sympathy for the Fabers, and she somehow sensed that that tear was also for Sam. Her voice then became stuttered. Even for someone like Trudy, whose past life in the gutter had seemingly strengthened her, the utterance of a man's name still withered her defences. "Kazemi . . . Kazemi is in London, Sam . . . he's here for another three days."

Sam stayed strangely silent. Only the look of devilment that appeared told of what was seemingly going through his mind. Then he cracked a brittle smile. It may have only been February, but to Sam Christmas had arrived early. *Now it starts . . . all things come to those who wait.* That thought was then followed by a tender lingering kiss on Trudy's cheek; he tasted the saltiness of tears on his lips.

But for her, that was now a pleasing distraction to what had unfolded. "You'd better go, Sam," she said. "I'll follow in a minute or so."

She watched as he walked to the door, and then stopped to turn and look back at her. "Just out of curiosity," he said, "there are a couple of things I'd like to know. What happened to the traitorous DC Davis?" he asked.

"Oh him . . . I think he's back 'directing traffic', as the saying goes." Trudy at least expected a cautious smile from Sam, but instead he was deadpan, his sense of humour replaced by preparation. "And the other, Sam? You said you had two questions?" she then said.

"Yes, I did. You said Peter Faber was out of the country . . . I just wondered if it was in connection with Kazemi, that's all?"

"No, Sam. He's gone skiing with their five-year-old son Kurt in Austria. Mila was planning to go with them, but she's a bit under the weather at the moment, so she stayed behind." Even after she gave her reply, her mouth was still poised to speak. She had words in limbo, and was wondering if it was necessary for him to hear them. "I'm the boy's godmother. His parents seem to think I'll be a good influence on him!" The delivery of her words had an ironic tone. Her close friends knew of her now distant involvement with drugs . . . yet she found it humbling to be considered as a good influence for a child.

"I like the Fabers," Sam replied, showing Trudy a genuine smile of pleasure. "Despite their profession, they're sensible people. And having you as the boy's guru only confirms it."

He then left to be with Penny; but Trudy realised that what they had talked about was only the beginning . . . One person was already dead, and she doubted it would stop there.

Chapter 19

The Mexican Wave

"Ah, back from the broom cupboard, are we?" Penny quipped teasingly. She glanced across her shoulder as she felt Sam's strong arms embrace her waist from behind. Her relaxed banter only told of the pleasure of seeing her man again, not insecure curiosity as to why he wasn't waiting for her in the hospitality lounge when she walked in from make-up. "Belinda said you'd disappeared with Trudy."

"Oh shit! Found out, am I? It wasn't a broom cupboard, it was Belinda's office, sweetheart. Some desk she's got!" he jokingly replied, aware that Penny would have realised all too well that Trudy, as chief organiser for their wedding, would use any opportunity to discuss how her plans were proceeding, and he felt strangely calm considering what they had really talked about . . .

With Topp dead, Sam silently mourned his passing, and felt sympathy for Cissy – who had lost a lifelong friend. But his overriding focus was now fixed on Kazemi and how he could exploit the next three days before he left the country.

It wasn't long before it was Penny's cue to be Belinda's last guest, and this time Sam didn't stay in the lounge to watch the show on television. Instead he took up the offer of one of the show's directors to have a bird's eye view and observe from the studio floor; an interview that he wouldn't want to miss for the world.

The predictable prompted clapping by the studio audience was the cue as Penny, once again, sauntered onto the set to be greeted by Belinda Carson with a cautious 'don't crease my blouse' hug. Since her last appearance on her friend's show six months earlier, the set had been unexpectedly redesigned. Gone were the fake marble pillars; they had been replaced by a cosy lounge with rugs and two country-style sofas, complete with huggable scatter cushions.

"Hey, this is great! It reminds me of my lovely new home in Devon," declared Penny.

She was then directed by her host to ensconce herself on the vacant sofa opposite the one from where she would stage-manage Penny's seemingly off-the-cuff interview. In between them was a stripped pine coffee table – the final piece of furniture to set a scene. Belinda wanted the set to be something different, something novel from which to interview her close friend – unlike Penny's previous appearance on the show when they had both soothed their feet in a foot spa, reminiscing about the past. Now the cottagey scene was set to transport Penny into the future: at home in her beloved cottage on the edge of Dartmoor.

"Well, it's lovely to see you again, darling," said Belinda, her joyous tone sounding as if they hadn't seen each other for quite a while; but in fact, hardly a week went by without them bumping into each other; that was of no consequence now, however, as the chat show diva started to channel her inquisitive audience's interest down a path that she had craftily laid.

They both sat on the edge of their sofas straight-backed, knees together, with their right foot tucked behind the left. Their mirrored ladylike demeanour was akin to two peacocks not wanting to appear slovenly in front of the cameras; cameras they knew would zoom in on any inappropriate posture or unexpected emotion; and, unknown to Penny, Belinda had every intention of putting her guest's self-control to the test.

Belinda continued, saying, "In some ways, I suppose it's hello *and* goodbye, isn't it?"

Her question initiated the desired response, as Penny spoke

with mixed emotions about how she would soon be leaving the play she was staring in in preparation for her wedding in Devon – a wedding that Belinda proudly had an invitation to. Now Belinda's tenuous 'thin line' that she'd dare not cross came back into play, and she knew that she would be the instigator of emotional anguish and tears – tears she hoped would move her audience. But the consequence of her actions would depend on her timing and ability to hold it together . . . and hold *herself* together. One question troubled her: *Will Penny still think of me as a friend by the end of the show?* she wondered.

Belinda outwardly showed interest in what her guest was saying, interjecting from time to time to keep the conversation flowing. Then she broached a question that caused her audience to hush in anticipation, and prompted a gaze of puzzled curiosity from Penny: "Now Penny, there is one thing you haven't said anything about, isn't there, darling?" Belinda paused, and she timed it to perfection; long enough to stir the juices of thought, but short enough for Penny not to openly query her host's statement. "I believe you're expecting . . ." Again, she briefly paused, purposely to let her question hang in air, before she continued, " . . . an addition to your future family."

Penny gasped, a look of perplexity on her face as the premature reaction from the audience was heard: a misguided response of cheering and clapping. Again, Belinda's timing was impeccable, calming her now elated onlookers with subduing hands and words. She then rose from her sofa to sit next to her guest, who on the inside felt bewildered, yet outwardly showed a strained, patient calm; but it was a calm that was soon replaced by a bellow of relief as Belinda passed off her misdirection as a seemingly poorly timed choice of words.

"Christ, Bel!" said Penny with urgency in her voice. "For a moment there I thought you knew more about what was going on in my womb than my gynaecologist!" She hoped her jokey retort would kill off any notion that she was pregnant . . . but it was subsequently followed by moans of disappointment from the studio audience.

"What I really meant was . . ." Belinda replied, swiftly moving on from her deceiving theatrical ruse. She tenderly took hold of Penny's hands, placing them in hers, aware that emotions would be stirred as she again engaged her audience, leading them once more like a pied piper on a touching journey. "This wonderful, dear friend of mine and I were recently in make-up together getting ready to record a celebrity quiz show . . . weren't we, darling?" Belinda continued.

Penny instantly developed a deep frown across her brow, now astutely aware of where the conversation was leading. Her host continued, reciting the moment when Penny received a text message and a picture from Maggie. She had been told about five abandoned days-old puppies who her sister Estelle had found squeezed into a large biscuit tin on a harsh winter's day, dumped next to a builders' rubbish skip, and how she drove through the night to rush them to her sister to save their lives, only for two to survive. The oohs and ahs rising from the audience directed Penny's now tearful eyes to a large screen . . . and a picture of an adorable puppy with a charcoal-black coat, with streaky highlights of tan and white, appeared, long lashes framing two wanting dark brown eyes.

"She's beautiful, isn't she? I can hardly wait to take little mite back to Devon with me and give her a happy life," Penny said. But behind her dreamy smile, she knew Belinda Carson too well to believe that that was it, that that was the full extent of her devious rouse.

"So, when are you . . ." Belinda asked, again her timing was exact, "expecting to meet your 'little mite', as you call her?"

Penny was cautious in her reply, slipping her friend a pondering smile. "Hopefully next week," she said. "And her name is Bourbon. Her brother is called Hob-Nob because of the biscuit tin they were found in."

Like a Mexican wave, Penny's words raised row after row of laughter intermingled with resonating tones of more pre-practised oohs and ahs.

"Really?" Belinda replied; but her tone didn't quite sound as casual as it should have . . . it was more of a questioning, *are you sure*? She glanced over Penny's shoulder; it was the giveaway sign that made her guest instinctively twist to look behind her. The audience did the rest, confirming that she *wasn't* the last guest on the Belinda Carson Show after all. Both of them rose to their feet to greet the surprise company. Belinda was thinking of how her show's ratings would go through the roof; Penny stood in disbelief, thrilled to unexpectedly see Maggie and Estelle – sooner than she had thought – with their two charges held in their arms: Bourbon and Hob-Nob.

"It seems you have an extra mouth to feed, Sam?" Trudy said, as she slipped her arm through his.

"Yes, it looks that way, doesn't it," he replied, watching his two much-loved daughters with fatherly pride as they seamlessly engaged in conversation, unfazed by the proximity of the television cameras or elated studio audience. *I wonder who they learnt that from*, he marvelled. His thoughts then drifted back to Kazemi, who like a storm cloud loomed on his horizon, and he knew a decision had to be made: should he take shelter and wait for it to pass, or confront it and face it down . . . face Kazemi down? "I need you to do something for me," Sam asked quietly, his every word then spoken with cold, calculated purpose. "I want you to arrange for Kazemi to receive two theatre tickets for Penny's play . . . say the day after tomorrow, and with a 'carrot' that he'll be invited to meet her in her dressing room afterwards. With your contacts, it shouldn't be difficult to find out what hotel he's staying at. You can leave the rest to me."

All the time he spoke, and while he waited for her reply, Trudy noticed that he never deviated his gaze once from Penny and his daughters; an empty focus that was devoid of emotion.

Chapter 19

He felt her arm tense against his as she replied, and soon realised her reason: "Yes, I'll arrange it," she said quietly, "but take a good look at those three women, Sam. They love you in spade-fulls." She paused, wanting to have eye contact with him. What she needed to express now required his full attention. "Be careful what you wish for, Sam. Kazemi isn't the type of man you toy with . . . you know that, don't you? I'd hate to see them standing over your grave because of him, or . . . or you standing over theirs."

Chapter 20

Cause and Effect

"Hello, baby," said an excited Penny, going in and closing her dressing room door behind her at the end of another evening's performance. She crouched down, her arms out stretched, and with a smile that beamed at the, *I'm excited to see you too!* Bourbon. The puppy had, after her television debut two days' earlier, become a bit of a celebrity in her own right with cards and gifts for her from well-wishers arriving at the theatre daily. "No Sam? I thought he'd be here by now. He usually is," she added.

Mavis her dresser peered over the clothes rack to reply. "He *was* here, dear, but left saying he'd not be long. Popped out to have a chat with someone or other, I think."

Sam was in fact standing patiently to one side in the theatre's foyer, his eyes searching out the face of a man who was among the play's audience as they made their way out of the auditorium, slipping on their coats and hats in preparation against the winter chill; they were faces of people who once again confirmed why tickets to experience this rollercoaster of a play were so sought after. He knew that a man like Kazemi, who enjoyed the trappings of office, power and wealth, wouldn't turn down the opportunity to be at the theatre; especially with the enticing pleasure of being introduced to the leading lady afterwards.

Within moments Sam caught his first fleeting sight of his prey - who then seemed to disappear, shielded by unsuspecting fellow playgoers. Sam took in a deep, deep breath, taking his time to prepare himself – and if that meant keeping Kazemi waiting, then so be it. He wanted to relish that moment, an opportunity to have sway over him, an opportunity he suspected very few had had. *And live to savour it*, he thought. He would be the instigator of disappointment and entrapment, a living presence from Kazemi's past that would have him searching back into every crevice of his sordid mind to unearth a memory of the man who would become his nemesis.

On the wall opposite to where Kazemi stood hung a framed theatre poster of Penny; her contemptuous gaze appeared to be directed at him, mimicking Sam's own thoughts. He daren't think what her reaction would be should she be aware that he was about to embark on a compelling, unstoppable desire to open Pandora's box, to once more stand face to face with the man, the instigator of all the torturous pain he endured at the hands of the Barber.

His natural instinct – when he hatched his plan to entice Kazemi to the theatre – was to physically hurt him, an ability that came easily to Sam. Two punches . . . that's all he would need to land. He would lead by feigning with his left to line up his victim's head to the oncoming flash of a right and left to the face; but with smouldering memories of what that man had put him through, would it end there? Or would he feel the thrill of inflicting the ultimate payback? That notion of doing Kazemi bodily harm was balanced with cold calculative reasoning, and an opportunity that would be squandered for the sake of a moment of selfish indulgence. If it wasn't for the Fabers, Sam knew that he could be standing next to Kazemi and wouldn't have a clue it was him, or what a monster of a man he continued to be. Because of them he could exploit Kazemi's perceived self-importance and arrogance to his advantage - an advantage that he needed in order for the corrupt police chief to react exactly as Sam anticipated he would. It was a judgement Sam hoped that would protect those he loved.

Sam didn't approach Kazemi until the foyer was almost cleared of people. Only the theatre staff – who stood by the two sets of double entrance doors ready to shut out the din of the pavement traffic – were present. It was the first time he had seen Kazemi in the flesh for over thirty years; they were years that were a living testament that no matter how hard you tried, your face will always show your true self. Kazemi's jet-black, grey-less head of hair failed to disguise the ravages of an indulgent lifestyle. He had pillow-like bags that hung from under mean, emotionless eyes, washy, light brown eyes that were set in an almost jaundiced backdrop, semi-eclipsed by lash-less, ragged eyelids. His thin-lipped mouth turned down at the corners, unable to defy the gravity of sagging jowls. It was the face of an altogether despicable man.

Kazemi had been asked to wait in the foyer to be met – *so he thought* – by someone who would escort him to Penny's dressing room; but he wasn't alone. With him was a young woman, and her long flowing red hair and catwalk-like figure wasn't lost on Sam - or anyone else who scrutinised her. Her designer clothes and flawlessly made-up face shouted high maintenance; expensive maintenance that only a sheik or an oligarch or, in her case, Kazemi could afford to fund. Even her jewellery – slipped over her bright red-nailed fingers – could be classed as hand luggage on its own by most airlines, and confirmed her services didn't come cheaply.

Sam's first words weren't to Kazemi but to the whore. He reached for her hand, his eyes not deviating from hers. "Please accept my apologies. I don't make a habit of keeping a beautiful lady waiting," he said.

By greeting her first Sam knew he had created a cause and effect situation. He was aware that Kazemi would feel he was being overlooked, second in line of importance – *the cause* – and well aware that etiquette dictated that Sam should have presented himself to the gentleman first, who then would have introduced the lady to *him*. But Sam wanted to put Kazemi off balance from the onset – *the effect* – and his deliberate and controlled manner ran like a deep vein, pulsing with disdain; but it was a calm disdain that made him realise that he was actually enjoying himself.

Gently releasing her hand, he nonchalantly turned to face Kazemi, wanting again to show a lack of respect towards him. His face was deadpan as he spoke, a distinct contrast to Kazemi's cutting glare at the stranger . . . a man he thought he didn't know. "I'm afraid you will be unable to have the pleasure of meeting Miss McCain," he said. Sam's words flew like poisonous arrows into Kazemi, verbally inflicting another wound to his already deflated self-importance.

"Why? I was very much looking forward to meeting her." Kazemi's curt, yet disappointed, reply only added another tick in Sam's box.

"As was I. I do hope she's not ailing," added the well-spoken and still un-introduced lady of the night.

"No, she's in fine fettle, thank you." Sam's polite reply included a smile for her. But only for her. For Kazemi more of the same was to come: degradation. "There never was going to be a meeting. You see, I brought you here on false pretences," he added.

"What do you mean, false pretences? Who are you, and what do you want?" boomed Kazemi. His eyes now fixed uneasily on Sam, confused and unsure as to whether he should make for the exit or stand his ground. He fiddled for a moment with the top button of his black woollen suit; but his stubby fingers failed to pull the fabric across his bloated torso.

"What, only three questions? Well, I shall answer two of them," Sam replied, his self-assured tone undermining the urgency in which the questions were asked. "Firstly, your second question: who am I? You already know that, it's just that you haven't remembered me yet. And what do I want? Well, the answer to that question is . . ." Sam reached into his jacket's inside breast pocket.

Suddenly Kazemi took a step backwards. His eyes became

wide like dinner plates as his mind conjured up the possibility that this man of mystery may pull out a knife or even a gun.

"Ha! No need to pee yourself just yet. I want you to have this." Sam moved his hand slowly, giving his actions a sense of drama, and then handed the now perspiring Indonesian an envelope. "Here, take it. Its contents should jolt your memory as to who I am . . . and at the same time, tell you what I want."

Kazemi nervously grasped the envelope, his tense fingers bending it out of shape. He slipped it into his suit pocket.

"I-I won't f-forget this," Kazemi blustered, "or y-you, whoever you are. I don't take kindly to be treated with . . . with . . . disrespect."

"Oh, I'm counting on it," Sam replied, turning his attention back to Kazemi's female companion; he had noted that when her date moved away, thinking something violent may happen, he hadn't made any effort to protect her. *Very unchivalrous of you*, Sam thought. He once more took hold of her hand. "May I ask you your name?" he enquired.

"It's Anya," she answered, with a soft, alluring smile – and a look that said that whatever the aggravated man who gripped her arm thought of him, her impression of Sam was the complete opposite.

"Well, Anya, it's been a pleasure to meet you," Sam told her, and then fixed his eyes back on her client while extending an arm in the direction of two theatre staff who waited to close the doors for the night. "Have a safe flight home, Mr Kazemi."

Sam's words were direct and final. He watched Kazemi and Anya disappear amongst the throngs of people passing the theatre's doors, knowing he had set the clock ticking and that it was only a matter of time before Kazemi would respond; and hopefully, if Sam had read the man correctly, he would react in the manner he envisaged. He knew it was a gamble, and he wasn't sure if anyone would be brave enough to give him odds. *Would I give myself favourable odds*? he wondered. Only time would tell.

Chapter 21

The Man with No Name

"Oh dear, what's happened here? The police seem to have closed off your road, Miss McCain," said Andrew, Penny's driver. (One perk that was written into her contract when she agreed to play Katherine, was that a car should always be available to take her home at the end of an evening performance.) "Good evening, officer," said Andrew politely as he lowered his window. "Would it be possible to drive through?" he asked, "I have a lady who lives here."

"May I enquire what house number you live at madam?" asked the officer, crouching down and seeing Penny leaning forward between the two front seats. Even through the dim light of the street lamps, he could see she was showing concern about what was happening.

"I live at number 22. What is it, officer, what's happened?" she asked, peering anxiously through the windscreen at three police cars and an ambulance that between them fired off a constant stream of flashes of blue light.

"Ah, right, number 22. And your name, please?"

"Penny McCain, officer," she hastily replied.

Then she heard him relay her name swiftly to a colleague through the radio that was attached to his black anti-stab vest. "OK, will do," he answered, replying to a soundless voice from his concealed earpiece. "I'm afraid there's been an incident, madam, near to your house."

"Oh my god, what sort of incident?" she asked, gasping with concern.

Unwilling to give more details, the officer simply pointed to the right. "If you could drive to the female police officer over there, that's as far as you can go, sir. She'll escort Miss McCain to her front door."

Sam was back in Devon and, as always, was expecting a phone call from Penny once she arrived back home, although not before she had settled herself on the settee with a glass of her favourite wine and, no doubt, with Bourbon snuggled on her lap. But the call he received wasn't the normal bubbly Penny; it was from a woman who sounded distraught, barely able to compose herself to speak.

"Cissy's been attacked in the street on her way home from playing bingo! She's dead, Sam, *dead!* The poor darling, she was really frail. I'm so upset!" Penny cried.

On hearing the terrible news, Sam had no intention of waiting the three days he had planned before travelling back up to London. Within half an hour of putting the phone down he was already on his way to be with her. The few facts that he knew, relayed by a distraught Penny, were that Cissy had been set upon by a man only yards from her front door . . . and her neighbour's door . . . Penny's door. That detail wasn't lost on him. Kazemi was still fresh in his thoughts as he headed up the motorway, anxious to reduce the time Penny had to spend mourning the death of her friend without being comforted in his arms. The likelihood that Kazemi was somehow behind the attack on Cissy was soon dismissed, though. He knew the truck Kazemi had with him didn't require bumping off a frail old lady; no, he wouldn't do that to send a message that it could be Penny next. He had no doubt that he was going to hear from Kazemi sometime in the future, he was banking on it, but it wouldn't be in that way. Besides, Sam reasoned, Cissy's attacker had all the hallmarks of a thug, and the only thug that came to mind was Button, who may have known about Cissy by beating it out of Harry Topp; but Button was supposedly out of the country, and if he did come back he would be arrested in connection with Topp's murder. The more he thought about her, the more it appeared Cissy was simply mugged. No conspiracy, no smoking gun. Or so he thought . . . it wasn't until two weeks later when Sam and Penny were back at his cottage in Devon that things began to make sense, and in a way neither of them could ever imagine.

"I don't remember you ever leaving the driveway gate open, Sam," Penny casually commented as they walked back to the cottage after their stroll with Bourbon. She peered through the fading afternoon light at the unfamiliar vehicle that was parked outside their cottage.

"Company," Sam replied, and then observed a pair of black cotton trousers and a woman's shoes swing out from the front passenger seat.

"Mr Farmer?" enquired the woman, taking hold of his helping hand as her feet reached for terra firma from the black Mercedes RV. "Bloody tank. I need a step ladder to get in and out of the thing . . ." she hissed, turning her attention to Penny and showing her a polite smile. "Firstly, may I apologise to you both for calling at this unusual hour," she said, handing Sam her police warrant card. "DCI Tamworth, West Midlands Police, and my colleague DC Pitt.

So, you're Miss Piggy . . . I wasn't expecting a visit from you, Sam mused. His mind rushed through possible reasons, notions of thoughts compressed into the time it took him to draw a deep breath . . . and consider why the police had found it necessary to pay him a visit and, chiefly, why Tamworth?

He felt Penny nudge closer to him, slipping her hand into his. His fingers gripped hers firmly as they observed Detective Constable Pitt approach them, followed by another man, a man who appeared un-introduced from the other side of the vehicle.

"Go and put the kettle on, sweetheart," he said giving her a tender kiss; her lips were normally moist and supple, but they were now dry and taut.

"We had hoped to talk to you in London, sir, but just missed you," explained the junior detective.

"Sorry about that. We came back down here last night," Sam replied. "We had to go to a funeral yesterday in London . . . Penny's next door neighbour."

Sam showed his uninvited guests into the lounge, which prompted the predictable observations and comments about the quaintness of the room from detective Tamworth. Like most mammals, she was instinctively drawn towards the warmth of the open log fire, and stood next to Bourbon, who had already staked out her place on the rug.

The woman, who was in her late forties and had light brown hair left to go grey naturally, sought out the fire's comforting warmth, her petite frame silhouetted by the blaze of the flickering light. Despite her diminutive size and genteel femininity, Sam knew he would be foolish to underestimate her position of authority. You don't get to be a detective chief inspector by looking cute and demure. She had those letters in front of her name by merit, and rose through the ranks of her profession by being diligent and impersonal. *Such a compelling contradiction compared to Kazemi in regards to merit*, he thought. One question that instantly came to mind was how much did she know about him and his involvement with the Fabers? Was she aware that the information she passed to them about the Indonesian was then relayed to him? There was only one way to find out. He stood next to her as DC Pitt sat himself at the solid oak dining table at the far end of the room and placed a laptop computer in front of him.

"I hope this chap is an improvement on your last DC. I hear that one couldn't work out who the good guys were," he said, giving her a fleeting glance.

She turned to face him, her eyes looking inquisitively into his.

He then noticed that the left side of her mouth had turned up at the corner, causing a dimple to appear on her cheek.

"If you're referring to the eunuch, Mr Farmer," she said quietly, "the one lesson he failed to learn was that no matter what information you possess, if it's not relevant to your enquires, such as now, you keep it to yourself." She paused for a moment, distracted by Penny placing a tray of mugs on the dining table. "Sometimes, Mr Farmer, you have to be aware that maybe not everyone knows all the facts, and I've no doubt it's done to shield them. In those cases, it's wise to keep it that way, don't you agree?"

Sam slipped her a surreptitious look that confirmed the predicament she may have put him in. Without him saying a word, she knew that Penny may have been unaware of the dealings he had had with the Fabers, and their raking through Sam and his brother's pasts. And she would keep it that way . . . for the time being at least.

"I take it you all drink tea?" Penny asked, turning to the as yet un-introduced man, seeing him tip his head with a tense smile in response.

"Shall we all sit down?" suggested DC Pitt.

The sound of his drawling Brummie accent made the words he spoke sound longer, and they cut into the air of apprehension that filled the room's normally tranquil setting.

Sam and Penny sat opposite the two detectives; the silent man, the man with no name, walked about the room, pausing to gaze at the pictures on the wall of Dartmoor and of Sam's two daughters with Penny. His eyes showed weariness, and he squinted at the pictures, instinctively studying everything he gazed upon. He was tall and muscular, with rugged features and a close-shaven head that showed signs of a less-than-genteel life with its unfollicled scars; their whiteness was prominent against his sun-tanned scalp.

"May I?" he asked with a deep and rather gruff North American accent. His light blue eyes were flecked with shards of green, and carried the look of a man who was genuinely interested in her treasured theatre award.

"Oh, he speaks . . ." Sam muttered, and then felt Penny nudge him with her elbow in response to his flippant remark.

"Feel free," she replied, curious as to why this aloof man with the rugged appearance was showing such interest in an accolade given in recognition of her theatrical prowess.

"My wife and I saw your play six months ago," he told her, running his fingers around the rim of the crystal disc which was displayed upon the oak shelf where Sam had proudly placed it. "She couldn't stop talking about you . . . Jeez, she got me to promise to take her a second time."

"So, have you?" Penny asked.

"No. Circumstances changed," he replied. It was an answer spoken with an air of sadness, as if personal memories of his recent past had mingled with his motives for being there.

"OK, when we're all ready, I'd like to get started," said Pitt, his impatient tone bringing to an end the momentary rapport between Penny and the American. "Remember this?" Pitt asked, spinning the computer around 180 degrees.

"Ha . . ." Sam responded with a nonchalant, half-hearted breath. "So, who am I looking at? The one on his knees picking up what remains of his teeth? Or the other man I've got pinned across the front of their car?" he asked, his eyes now revealing tension at the sight of the two men on the screen. They were men he had briefly met at a time when his back was against the wall, and just about everyone in front of him was baying for this blood.

"Sweetheart," Penny said, her voice not hiding her disapproval at the picture.

He turned to her and replied in an unrepentant tone, "They

threatened me and my family, demanding recompense for Sidney running off with their boss's money, so I gave it to them … my way!"

Penny then slipped her hand into his, not for self-comfort, but realising what must have gone through his mind when the two strangers had tried to terrorise him, especially if it had involved his late wife, Annie, and his beloved daughters. Her gaze returned to the screen and then to Sam, studying him while she thought. "I prefer you now to how you looked then," she told him with a loving peck on the cheek.

"So, what's this all about? Have they, after all these years, decided to sue me for damages?" he asked.

The picture on the screen then changed to that of a young boy sitting on a swing in a park. A man who, for Sam, required no introduction was pushing him.

"Sidney . . ." Sam murmured. With his elbows on the table, he leant his face against his clenched fists, distorting his cheeks as if he was taking a punch.

Penny stayed silent, as did the three other people in the room. Sam could feel her breath like a warm breeze as the two of them peered at the face of a man who was not only a stranger to her, but also in one sense to himself also; but he stirred nothing in Sam anymore, be it anger or betrayal, Penny had seen to that. She had teased those emotions out of his soul.

"OK, I give in. What's this about?" he asked, directing a frown across the table at DCI Tamworth, who responded with a twitch to Pitt – a message clearly.

"Right . . . I'll move on then . . ." was the hesitant reply from the young DC, who Sam sensed had been read the riot act by his new boss about getting above himself. It may have seemed that he was leading the way, but Sam could tell that the arms-folded, sitting back in her chair DCI had him on a tight leash - which was probably tied to his genitals. "You've recognised the man as your brother Sidney, but the boy on the swing you wouldn't know about. He's your nephew, Mr Farmer, and his name is Auner. He's five years old and has been taken . . . kidnapped by one of the men you fought with."

"Oh no! When did this happen?" Penny asked. Her voice was full of concern for the child's welfare.

Sam studied the picture of the smiling boy. He had an Asian appearance, and his broad dark eyes and jet-black hair – that looked like it had been cut around a pudding bowl – added an air of endearing innocence to the free-spirited-looking child. The tropical surroundings of the T-shirted youngster, and the knowledge that Sidney had a bolthole, indicated to Sam where the picture may have been taken; but it wasn't for him to say, so he decided to ask instead to see what response he got.

"So where was the picture taken? It's obvious it wasn't around this neck of the woods, was it? Sam asked.

"It wasn't, sir, no. It was taken in Alongapo City in the Philippines," answered Pitt. "Then they moved to live in Manila. That's when he was abducted. Dusty-looking place, isn't it?" Pitt said, describing the playground and surroundings that were parched and unkempt.

"I've heard of Alongapo," Sam replied, briefly glancing over his right shoulder to look up at the man whose presence was beginning to bug him. "There used to be a massive base for the US Navy nearby at Subic Bay," Sam continued. "Before the Filipino Government threw the Yanks out, that is." Again, he turned in his seat to look across at the American, clearly irritated by his apparent arrogance in not introducing himself; he was aware, however, that that was how he had treated Kazemi when they'd met in the theatre lobby. "Just, who are you?" he now asked the mystery man forcefully. He seemed to shadow the proceedings, as if he was there purely as an observer. And if that was the case, Sam wanted to know why.

DCI Tamworth thought it wise to intercede. The last thing she wanted was for the American's aloof attitude to be a distraction for Sam, aware he would require every ounce of concentration and fortitude he possessed to understand and carry out what was going to be asked of him next.

"I must apologise on behalf of our American cousin for adding a touch of the Hitchcock to the proceedings," DCI Tamworth said. "This gentleman is Mr Spatz, and he's here in an advisory capacity."

"Oh yes, and what advisory capacity is that?" Sam asked sternly, eyeballing the American.

"If you don't mind, we'll come to that later," replied Tamworth, endeavouring to take control of the situation that had all the ingredients of becoming fractious. She put her hand on her colleague's shoulder, lightly, as if to say, I'll take from here - and she did. Her role as a seeker of truth was now set aside to become the bearer of information, knowledge she would have to convey skilfully to Sam for the singular purpose of saving a child's life . . . his nephew's life. "Right, let's paint some background to what's happened, shall we?" Tamworth suggested.

She used her right forefinger to direct Sam's attention back to the laptop. Her first aim was to bring a man – a particular ghost from Sam's distant past – into a line-up of individuals that included his own brother. She would introduce them like characters in a play, with one similarity between them: they were all criminals.

"One of the two men in the photograph . . . and if you're wondering about the picture, by the way, you were under surveillance just in case your wayward brother turned up," said Tamworth, who paused for a fleeting moment to draw breath. "The man on his knees, the one you said was picking up what remained of his teeth, is a rather unsavoury character by the name of Terry Button. He is one of the men who has your nephew."

The utterance of that name had barely left her lips when Sam responded with a judder, an uncontrollable reflex as the question he had once asked himself – *who was he, and why did he want to kill Penny or me?* – was answered. The glare of his eyes betrayed his anger at hearing the name of someone he had not only met in the time it took to lay two ferocious punches to Button's face some twenty-plus years before, but the same man who had boasted that he'd caused Penny to crash his car, almost killing her. And now he had the boy?

Penny's voice was then heard, bridging the silence that had been created by Sam's reaction, and her softly spoken tone implied that she wished to soothe him and draw him back from the brink of reliving the time when his life and family were in turmoil; but Sam's anger was very much in the present, not the past.

"Sam, calm yourself sweetheart, please. There's no need for all the hurt anymore. You were OK when you saw his picture, so why all this? It's only a name, and it was a long time ago. Time to move on . . ." She rubbed his white-knuckled fist as it lay on the edge of the table like an inanimate object, hard and unyielding.

Sam turned away from DCI Tamworth to show Penny a poignant smile, revealing that for both of them, Button wasn't just a name from his past, but someone who had just gate-crashed their future life together, like a shadow of hate. New questions then arose in his mind: *Why did Button abduct his brother's son? And why now after all these years?*

The only consoling element was that the beautiful, caring eyes shining at him were innocent of the truth, and still oblivious to the fact that Button had once tried to kill her.

"So, if it was this man Button who's snatched Sidney's boy, who's he working for?" Sam demanded. Again, he glanced over at Mr Spatz; he was still observing, still silent. "Button is just a thug. He's like a mindless clockwork toy you wind up and set on its way, not someone capable of organising a kidnap."

"Yes, you're right about him," replied Tamworth, mindful that Sam knew a great deal more about Button than she needed to say. He noted the reappearance of the dimple on her cheek, reflecting the need for caution and to choose her words wisely. "He's just what you said, Mr Farmer, a blunt instrument, as is his accomplice. Another clockwork toy as you would say." Her words were then followed by a wry smile that made her dimple become even more pronounced.

The smile faded as Penny's voice broke into their exchange. She was becoming increasingly anxious to know the answers to her own burning questions. "Would someone please tell me what this has to do with Sam? This is happening on the other side of the world, for Christ's sake. There's nothing he can do about it . . . is there?"

A series of penetrating glances shot between the two detectives and the American, glances that stirred the American to finally take a seat at the table. He ensconced himself in a captain's chair; but not next to Sam and Penny or the detectives . . . he sat at the head of the table and adopted a look as if to say *this is where I take over*.

Chapter 22

Achilles Heel

Spatz filled the room with the persona and arrogance of a man absorbed in his own self-importance . . . a man whom Sam thought acted as though he had watched far too many B movies as a boy. Few words had yet passed the lips of the American, and only a dull, throaty grunt was heard as he fixed a look on Sam, a pointed intimidating stare seemingly done to set out his parameters of authority. His left hand slipped across his broad, shirted chest, and disappeared in a motion as if he were reaching for a gun that was concealed in a shoulder holster beneath his brown corduroy jacket.

Ah, you're a southpaw, Sam noted; for him an observation of habit as it was the term used for a left-handed boxer. With his chin resting on laced fingers, Sam observed Spatz produce what, at first glance, looked like a credit card from his breast pocket. He then placed it down on the table . . . and with two fingers slid it across as if it was a tarot card foreseeing Sam's future.

"Can we stop this nonsense? It's all very melodramatic, isn't it," Penny spouted. Her commanding tone of voice set the bar higher with regards to theatrical presence – higher than Spatz could ever hope to attain. With her brief master class put to one side, she peered curiously at Sam's hand, which was now holding the piece of plastic pinched between his forefinger and thumb. With the dexterity of a magician, he flipped it over to read the details with somewhat subdued interest.

"So, you're Mr Spatz, Mr Special Agent Spatz, of the US Drug

Enforcement Agency. Apart from what Penny has just stated, that all this is rather theatrical, why do I get the feeling that this ID card of yours has my brother Sidney written all over it?"

Sam's unambiguous question was followed with a pondering stare at the now confessed DEA man, an enquiring glare as to why his lounge was full of law enforcement officers, and especially one who, so far, had only managed to reveal that his wife loved the theatre.

Spatz's comeback was to run his hands slowly over his head in a fashion reminiscent of a time when he had hair. Another pointless action, Sam thought, that seemed to be part of his repertoire to add unnecessary drama to the proceedings. When he finally broke his silence, Sam didn't know whether to laugh or castigate him in response. It was an absurd demand that on the face of it was inconceivable; but his brother Sidney knew there was a chink in Sam's strong and loyal persona that was his Achilles heel, a perceived weakness that Sidney would ruthlessly exploit.

"Your brother wants *you* to get his son back for him."

"Really," Sam replied. "And what makes him or you think I would consider doing such a thing? I don't know how much you know about what Sidney did to our family, but it culminated in the suicide of our sister . . . my twin sister, by the way. For that alone I could never forgive him."

"He's not asking for your forgiveness, Mr Farmer, just your help to get his kid back."

"Oh yes, and how is he going to do that?" Penny interjected. Her hand now firmly grasped Sam's forearm as if to indicate that *he* wasn't going anywhere soon. "What is he expected to do? Put on a Rambo costume or something and jump out of a plane at thirty thousand feet with all guns blazing. How can his brother ask him for help after what he did? He's a sodding thief and drug dealer for Christ's sake–"

But her scornful tirade was prematurely halted by the looks on the faces of the three uninvited visitors; they looked like hunters priming themselves for the kill. Now her feminine instincts screamed like a banshee, feeding her intuition and telling her that there was something more at stake than just the safe return of the boy. Her searing glare picked out detective Tamworth, whom she sensed was someone, unlike the American, who could give a straight answer to a straight question. "This isn't . . . only about the boy, is it? Because if it were, Mr Spatz wouldn't be here . . . would he?" she said slowly.

Tamworth let her eyes momentarily sway from Penny to give Spatz the same look she'd given Pitt a few minutes before, that of *I'll take it from here.*

"You're a very astute woman, Miss McCain. And yes, you're right, there is another reason why Mr Spatz is here," she then turned her attention to Sam. "You see, Mr Farmer, your brother has offered to pass certain information on to the Americans in return for entry into the USA, and new identities for him and his family."

"So . . . so, what's that got to do with me? Just let Mr Spatz here and his buddies get the boy back. I've no skills in that sort of thing. I'm just 'your average Joe', as the saying goes," Sam replied.

"We can't be seen to be directly aiding criminals, Mr Farmer, even if a kid's life is at risk," Spatz answered as he muscled in, his interjection teasing the limelight once more from his English counterparts. "Button and his accomplice have demanded nine million dollars, US of course, for the safe release of your nephew."

"Nine million? That's an odd amount. Why not round it off to ten?" Sam asked.

Spatz didn't respond to that, but said, "Either way, your brother says he can't raise that amount of money. He's desperate. So, the DEA have offered to assist in exchange for cooperation to apprehend certain individuals who are of great interest to us, particularly those who deal in drug trafficking from the Asian Pacific into the US, with the Philippians as the hub."

"I thought you just stated that you don't aid criminals? What you've just said sounds a lot like you're doing a deal with one."

"There are deals . . . and deals, Mr Farmer. Our involvement is purely to assist and expedite matters as quickly as possible."

"That still doesn't answer my question as to why Sidney wants to involve me. As Miss McCain eloquently put it, I'm no Rambo."

"On the contrary, from what I've heard you're a resourceful man who can take care of himself. That's why your brother needs you. He wants someone who he can rely on and trust; someone who will make sure his kid is safe," replied Spatz.

"Huh, he should choke on the word 'trust'. He hasn't got the right to speak it, and now he asks for my help, the bastard."

Sam's grievous words tore into Spatz's face; but Spatz showed no great response to what was said, as if he already had an antidote to these words that were spoken with such venom. Instead he replied, "Your brother said I shouldn't be surprised by your lack of enthusiasm, Mr Farmer. But he said you'd agree to go, anyway."

"Oh, he did, did he? And what makes him so cock-sure I'll do his bidding?" Sam questioned.

"Apparently, it's to do with what your father drummed into you as a boy, something about protecting those in need and family . . . and he did say one other thing: he said to remind you . . . *don't forget the man in the woods.*"

Those emotive words emotionally winded Sam like a left uppercut to his stomach. His mouth felt dry and stale with inner pain at being underhandedly reminded of a man who shouldn't have been used as a moral lever for him to say yes.

Penny instinctively reached with both hands to clasp his face, to focus his eyes on hers, and only hers; it was an act of love from a woman who had herself been fortunate to be guarded by him at a time when her own life was in turmoil. She wondered, as did the others, why such spurious words caused Sam to react in that manner. They were like a trigger that had reincarnated thoughts of a man who'd cast a long shadow over his family, but a man who was most definitely his Achilles heel.

Sam soon regained his composure, and with the gentlest of touches held Penny's hands to his lips to lovingly kiss them. But he had the look of a person still suffering the wounds of his brother's painful despatch. The last thing she expected to see now, however, and the last thing she *wanted* was to see, was the soft kindly smile that followed, an accepting smile that told her Sidney was prizing him away from her.

"No, Sam! You can't consider going! Please no! Tell me I'm wrong . . . *please*?" she pleaded, and her eyes now filling with tears. "Your brother doesn't deserve you helping him! You know that better than anyone, so why?" Penny rose from her chair and walked towards the fireplace, turning her back on those whom she painfully realised were there for the sole purpose of taking Sam away from her, and away from their tranquil life together. She'd had a sweet taste of the future, and that had now turned bitter by Sidney's selfish pull on Sam's moral heartstrings.

"Sweetheart, please . . ." came the calm, placating words as Sam joined her, his hand rested gently on her shoulder, easing her around to face him. "If I were to do what they ask . . ."

"To do what Sidney asked, you mean!" Penny retorted.

"I don't care a toss about Sidney, you should know that," he replied calmly. "But, like you, I'm naturally concerned about the child, he's only five for Christ's sake. Button is a heartless thug. Imagine how lonely and scared the boy must be." He gently picked up Bourbon, who was lying peacefully by the log fire, and placed her in Penny's arms. "If it wasn't for Estelle and Maggie, this puppy wouldn't be alive, and you wouldn't have had the chance to give her the happy life she has now. The boy is just a puppy. What else can I say?"

His poignant analogy caused Penny to go quiet for a moment. She knew Sam could never turn his back on those who needed his help.

"I'm scared for you, Sam. I'm scared for us. I know you're no fool, sweetheart, but I just don't trust Spatz, let alone your brother," she then said, her voice sombre.

Unlike the American, who even with a deep, guttural accent that endeavoured to command and cajole could never match her verbal punch, Penny's voice carried to every corner of the room, and those who listened were left in no doubt that what they asked had put her and Sam's life together on hold.

He leant forward to kiss her face, still moist from tears for him, only to be intercepted by Bourbon who was eager to show her own affection. Penny smiled and let out an almost strangled laugh. "You see, Sam, even Bourbon wants to let you know how much we love you."

Her heart-piercing statement gave way to a thoughtful silence that neither of them found the desire to break. Even Spatz and company seemed distant, quietly allowing two people to come to terms with the reality that the tectonic plates their future together was based on had shifted, causing Sidney's past to erupt around them.

"Go and have that soak in the bath you promised yourself, sweetheart," he suggested, and then succeeded in teasing a kiss from her lips while Bourbon was distracted.

With Bourbon still cosseted in her arms, Penny politely excused herself to the two detectives. As for Spatz, his sincere interest in her profession was in stark contrast to his arrogant persona, and that perplexed her. She sensed that underneath his rugged appearance, he was a troubled man with more on his mind than that which had been discussed around the table. Did she detect a hint of guilt behind his eyes as she smiled at him before turning to go upstairs?

Sam returned to the table and the trio continued their conversation. The details of the situation became more horrendous as DC Pitt once more reincarnated the face of the thug on the laptop screen. His features not only showed the rigours of the years since Sam first laid eyes on him, but also the consequence of being on the receiving end of a freight train of punches that had shattered more than just his ego.

"Not a pretty sight is he, Mr Farmer?" Pitt proclaimed.

He waited with interest for Sam's reaction at seeing, this time, the face of the man who'd encountered Sam's fists close up. Now the result of that brief encounter was starkly visible. Sam looked across at Spatz and wondered what *he* would have done had he been put in the same situation. Both men were of a similar build, with Spatz slightly taller, and his scarred, knuckled hands were evidence that was confirmed by the American's empathetic stare.

"According to Button's medical records," Pitt continued, "you shattered his left cheekbone right up to his eye socket. Metal plates were required to repair it, and the injuries you caused resulted in residual nerve and muscle damage, that's why his left eye droops."

Sam was then shown another picture, this time of his mouth, which even for Sam was gruesome in the extreme.

"No . . . you can't be serious?" Sam blustered, with a look of disbelief etched across his face. "My God, his teeth, what has he done to himself? That's gross. Surely there must be laws about having those fitted?"

He leant back in his chair, taking in the sight of a man who, in his own mind, thought that Button was definitely out of his and it made him realise that it was almost certainly *him* the thug wanted to kill and not Penny after all!

"Ahem . . ." came the small cough from DCI Tamworth, who

until that point had stayed relatively silent while Pitt displayed the visual blow by blow account of Sam's violent actions. Her facial expressions were hard to read, and Sam wondered if she thought that he was as much of a thug as Button, whose grotesque grin glared at him from Pitt's computer screen.

"They're dentures, Mr Farmer," said Tamworth. "And no, there's no law to say he can't wear them; teeth are teeth, whether they have a porcelain finish or are made completely of metal – and in his case I believe, titanium."

Then the voice of DC Pitt was heard, and his timely interjection reminded Sam of Penny's two aunts who had the coordinated ability of jumping in and out of each other's conversations without seemingly being disrespectful to the other – an action the young DC was learning fast. The manner in which he delivered his words had become punchy and factual. "When you hit him the second time, Mr Farmer," said Pitt, "you broke his lower jaw so badly that he had to have all his teeth removed, hence the dentures." Pitt paused for a moment to let out a subdued sigh. "Considering the fact that Button now aspires to emulate the appearance of Jaws from the James Bond movies, I can't imagine, should the two of you meet again, that he might have forgiven you for what you did to him–"

Before he could continue, Sam raised his hand and said, "Second punch, you said? Actually, that was my first punch. My father always taught me to make the first punch the bone-breaker, and then floor him with the second. He worked in the docks, you see. He knew a thing or two about taking care of himself, did my dad."

Sam made sure there was no hint of regret in his words. He felt no shame in what he had done to Button, and was even comfortable with the fact that if he found himself in the same situation again, and possibly soon, he wouldn't hesitate to fire his fists at the thug, or anyone else who was foolish enough to threaten his family, again.

Then Spatz spoke, saying, "With all things considered, Mr Farmer, you seem to be very calm about all this."

Once more Tamworth grasped the mantle with the intension to quietly subdue the DEA man's inquisitive powers of detection, aware that Sam knew more about Button's recent activities than were being divulged; she wanted to keep it that way. Penny had made it openly clear that Sam was no fool, and that she didn't completely trust Spatz – a fact which wasn't lost on Tamworth – and like Penny, she was conscious that the American and his department had their own agenda which wasn't wholly conducive with what was being asked of Sam.

"This isn't the Wild West, Mr Spatz," she said. Sam couldn't help but let out a quiet laugh at Tamworth's droll retort. "In your country, you have your own ways of dealing with adversity. Over here, as Mr Farmer is duly doing, we take it in our stride and don't rush in like Rambo with all guns blazing," she concluded.

They then discussed Sam's journey to the Philippines, and the arrangements to be made once he arrived. They were about to leave when Sam recalled the one missing piece of information, and he wondered why it hadn't been given to him.

"By the way," he said casually, "you never told me who the other man with Button was . . . his 'accomplice' you said?" He turned to Tamworth for the answer.

She shot him a look as if to say *I hoped you weren't going to ask me that*, but then said, "He's Moses Jones, Mr Farmer."

That name resonated through his body like a tidal wave of fear, remembering, like any parent would, that when his daughters were just young girls, Moses Jones had become infamous for abducting young children, never to be seen alive again.

"If that's the Moses Jones I think you mean, I thought he was locked up for life? How the hell did he get out and get hooked up with Button?"

Sam's blunt and angry questions were greeted with

embarrassment by Tamworth, who knew it was for her to answer. "Three years ago, Moses Jones was transferred back to Jamaica in a prisoner repatriation scheme to be near his family," Tamworth said, and then paused, mindful of the significance of what she was about to tell him.

"And . . .?" Sam impatiently asked.

"And six months later he escaped. He made his way to, where he hid . . . until recently."

"Huh!!" Sam huffed. "Let me guess . . . the same place Button was hiding?"

"Yes, that's right. Acapulco, in fact. Button was in the same prison as Jones, and when he was released early last year he flew out there to meet up with his old cellmate. The rest is obvious."

"*Obvious*. Is that what you call it? Every policeman on the island must be after him, let alone the boy!" Sam replied.

"No. They're not. Kids go missing all the time over there, Mr Farmer," said Spatz. "The cops have enough on their hands trying to keep a lid on the drug and people trafficking gangs. You see, they've been led to believe it's a domestic issue, not a kidnapping as such."

Sam took in what the American had said, and then read between his verbal lines. On the face of it, the less interference, the better chance of getting the boy back alive; but Sam had an inkling it was mostly to do with the fact that Sidney was dangling a big fat carrot under the DEA's noses . . . that of the heads on a silver platter of the criminals on their most-wanted list, minus one of course: Sidney's.

He walked with the two men back to their car, and shook DC Pitt's hand in a farewell gesture. He then shook Spatz's hand and found he was more than a match when it came to firmness of grip. He then waited for Tamworth in the porch – she had asked to use the bathroom – as he had another question he wanted to ask, but this one was personal.

"May I ask your first name?" Sam enquired, as he helped Tamworth put on her mint-green cotton overcoat when she returned.

"Mr Farmer, please," she replied, sounding like he had just made an improper suggestion; but her shadowy smile, illuminated by the porch light said otherwise . . . it was a teasing, feminine trait of a smile that required no words of explanation.

She knew something else about him.

"Apparently, the last lady you asked that same question to thought you were gorgeous by the way, a real gentleman, in fact. And yes, you pissed off your friend Mr Kazemi no end."

One moment he was indulging in a polite and cordial farewell to a lady who he had first become aware of a few weeks before; the next, and not for the first time that evening, he now found himself surprised by what he heard, and the realisation that DCI Tamworth knew all about his meeting with the corrupt Kazemi; it utterly derailed his train of thought.

"Don't worry, Mr Farmer," Tamworth said, noting him staring at her, "as I said earlier, if information you possess isn't relevant to your enquiries, you keep it to yourself. Your meeting with Mr Kazemi isn't my concern, Button is." She then paused for a moment and smiled. "It's Jane, by the way," she added, and reached out her hand for Sam to shake.

"Well, Jane," he replied with an air of relief in his tone, "have a safe journey back, and please keep in touch."

"There is one other thing . . ." Tamworth said as they walked towards the car. "I hear you're an avid fan of Shakespeare. Have you read *Julius Caesar?*"

"Yes, a while ago," Sam replied, and noticed a subtle flick of her head towards the American passenger sitting behind her as she climbed into the car.

"*Et tu, Brute,*" she whispered. "Goodbye, Mr Farmer."

Sam slowly closed his front door, annoyed with himself that he had missed the clue when Trudy had informed him that Kazemi was in London. She'd used the word 'intelligence', and that alone should have alerted him to the fact that Kazemi wasn't only of interest to him, but also to those who do their work in the shadows. Sam became aware that although DCI Jane Tamworth indicated that she wasn't interested in his involvement with Kazemi, that wasn't to say others weren't.

Penny lay back in the hot soapy water and handed Sam her empty wine glass. He had said very little since he'd sat on the edge of the bath and, like her, he wondered how long it would be before he was able to enjoy these quiet moments together again.

"Who was the man in the woods, Sam, that Spatz mentioned?" she asked. With all the questions that consumed her thoughts, that was one she hoped he could answer. She looked deep into his eyes.

Sam immediately betrayed a sense of sadness. "He was more than just a man . . . he was a man amongst men. If I were to tell you now it would seem like an excuse as to why I must go. I'll tell you all about him when I return, and I will return, I promise."

He then helped her from the bath and carried her to their bedroom to take her body and soul on a journey of passion before he had to leave to journey without her.

Chapter 23

The Photograph

"Hello, Farmer."

"Archie, now this *is* a surprise. Ah . . . and Trudy! Hello, sweetheart," said Sam curiously; these were two people he least expected to turn up at his cottage, especially considering he had only spoke to them in London the day before, about why and when he would be leaving the country. He then realised they obviously didn't want Penny to know, and had been prepared to travel two hundred miles to make sure she didn't. "Come on in, you're making my doorstep look untidy," he quipped.

"So, this is Penny's bolthole . . . cosy!" said Archie, slipping his gabardine overcoat off his shoulders and laying it over the back of a chair.

"Sit yourselves down while I'll get some drinks," Sam said.

"I'd rather stand, if it's all the same to you," Archie replied.

"I'll get mine, Sam. You see to Arch," Trudy insisted, and headed towards the kitchen for a glass of warm water – her version of Darjeeling or an espresso.

"Whisky?" Sam asked, aware that he too enjoyed a fine single malt – and considering it was a Christmas present from Archie in the first place, he wouldn't gift anything to anyone if he thought it was inferior to his own exacting palate.

Still surprised to have his friends standing in his lounge, he looked intriguingly at Archie, not only because he was there, but also because he wasn't the Archie he was used to seeing. Missing was one of his flamboyantly coloured suits, complete with waistcoat and cravat. They had been replaced with dower and understated charcoal pinstriped attire, white shirt, and a silk royal-blue tie. It was still a Savile Row suit nevertheless, but well below par for the man who exuded style with aplomb that few could afford to match. Even his chirpy, slightly feminine tone of voice had gone, replaced by more masculine and monotone straight-to-the-point speech.

"OK, Arch, why are you here?" Sam asked over the faint sound of crystal on crystal as the two men chinked their glasses.

Archie failed to acknowledge his question. Instead he turned to gaze around the lounge that previously he had only seen in photographs.

"Since I've known you, Farmer, you've caused me to question my own trust in people . . . or rather the lack of it," he said, and his gaze fell upon the pictures of Sam's daughters, hung to please and cause one to reminisce. "I know as well as you do, Farmer, what drives you . . . its trust and loyalty, isn't it?"

"We should all strive to trust and be loyal, Arch."

"But for you it's your nemesis, isn't it?" Archie pointedly replied.

"You reckon so, do you, Arch? Nemesis means I have an adversary. To me trust and loyalty is a commitment."

Archie then turned to face Sam, the aroma of the single malt making his nostrils flair as he stared unflinchingly at his friend.

"I know all there is to know about you, Farmer. When I read that letter you sent me, you showed that you were willing to risk everything you had to help finance Penny and enable her to become Katherine in Aaron's play. I had to know about the man who *trusted* me with his money, and not run off with it as his own brother had done." He then reached into his breast pocket to retrieve an accessory, an Archie trademark he had made his own: a canary-yellow silk handkerchief which he used to wipe the palms of his hands, thus absorbing the signs of tension seeping from his pores. "I know all about how you were attacked in the police cell by that maniac," he then said.

Sam almost became a spectator then as Archie passed his glass to Trudy and, with pampered, manicured hands, started to unbutton Sam's light blue linen shirt, wanting to expose his tortured and scarred torso. Sam didn't stop him or object. It was as though he knew it was important for Archie to see them.

"Did you ever wonder about the true identity of the man who did this to you?" asked Archie as he continued to undo Sam's shirt, button by button, slowly and caringly, as if he was undressing a lover.

"All I know about him is that he goes by the name of the Barber." Sam then paused with a shudder as Archie's fingertips began to explore the tracks of scars that littered a once unblemished and muscular torso, one that was now covered with ridges of flesh like fault lines, flesh pulled out of shape having been stitched together by a doctor whose ability was impaired by the influence of barbiturates.

Archie let out a muted cry, akin to that of a startled animal as his eyes then fixed on a sight that was beyond his comprehension. "Oh my god, Farmer, your nipples!" he exclaimed.

"Yes, as you can see, Arch, the Barber cut them off," Sam confirmed, and he turned to look at Trudy, whose hand had clasped her mouth to silence any desire to whimper. Tears trickled down her cheeks.

Sam moved across to her, passing Archie back his glass of whisky, knowing he was in need of it. He restrained himself from the natural compulsion to wrap his arms around Trudy's shoulders and comfort her, thinking the last thing she would want was to be brought closer to the abominable memento of the Barber; but he had forgotten she was the multi-faceted Trudy, who, like him, carried physical scars from her own violent past.

She took his hands, and with look of a friend who understood his hesitation, she placed them around her waist while she rebuttoned his shirt.

"The man who did this to you, Sam, is a Brazilian called Rodrigo Domendez," she said. The name from Trudy's lips, her voice now chillingly cold and concise, was of a man who for Sam was one part of a jigsaw from his past that piece by piece was coming together. "His name makes him sound almost aristocratic, doesn't it?" Trudy suggested. "But his upbringing couldn't be more of a contrast. Brought up in the squalor of the Favelas in Rio de Janeiro, he learnt to steal, mug and eventually murder his way out of that place. The reason why he got that nickname, the Barber, was because in the early days he would shave his victims with his cutthroat razor, before he slaughtered them with it. He's in his late sixties now, but he's still out there as a killer for hire . . ." The tone in which she ended her sentence seemed more of a pause than an indication that that was it, that that was all there was to know about the Barber.

Sam peered curiously at Trudy; something about her frown told him that she and Archie were holding something back.

"And . . .?" Sam asked. "There's always an and . . . So, which one of you is going to tell me what it is?"

Archie passed him his recharged glass, and with a straight-backed stance, his chin up, he looked Sam straight in the eyes in order to reveal the dire situation his friend was getting himself into. (Unbeknown to both Archie and Trudy, what Archie was about to say was, in fact, just what Sam wanted to hear.)

"The Barber, Domendez, flew into Manila two days ago, even before you agreed to go out there," said Archie, who briefly paused for a sip of his whisky. Trudy noted the wry expression on Sam's face; it was not what she was expecting. Then Archie continued saying, "They're all there waiting for you, Farmer, and it doesn't take a genius to know they want you dead. Button for what you did to him and the Barber because you were the one that got away. But not only that . . . Kazemi has hired his services once more, this time because you humiliated him at the theatre."

"How the blazes do you know all this, Archie? I know you have your contacts, but this is detailed information and no doubt classified."

"Archie didn't get hold of it, Sam, I did," said Trudy.

"So where did you get it from?" he asked.

"I'll tell you in minute, Sam. I'm not ready to yet," she replied.

"OK, as you wish, but what of Sidney and the boy? Where are they in all this?" Sam asked.

"I don't know, Sam. You know your brother better than anyone. And as for the boy, he's caught in the middle by the sound of it," Archie replied, voicing his own interpretation of the facts.

"Hang on a moment, Arch," Trudy questioned. Her searching gaze fixed firmly back on Sam. "You did humiliate him at the theatre, didn't you? You planned it? Tell me!" Trudy demanded, recalling his less than grave reaction when informed that the Barber was in Manila. "You spooked Kazemi at the theatre knowing damn well that he'd most likely get the one person who, pun not intended, also wanted your guts. You did, didn't you?"

"Yes, I did," Sam, answered with a shrug of his shoulders. "You see I had no choice. Your friends the Fabers, they showed me an incriminating photograph taken of Kazemi in a restaurant, and with him the Barber who, as we all know, is a perverted assassin, and Sidney, my brother, the drug dealer. I soon realised that it would only be a matter of time before the Fabers would use that picture as part of their condemning evidence to destroy Kazemi in revenge for the death of Mila's sister, Elsa." Sam lingered to savour a sizable mouthful of his single malt before he carried on with his reasoning. "That night at the theatre I handed Kazemi an envelope, and inside was a copy of the photograph with my name written on the back, nothing more. I wasn't going to make it that easy for him to remember who I was. I needed to force his hand and, on my terms, to come after me, not the Fabers, or those I love and care for, like you or Penny and my daughters. Only me. Because he would, you know. He'd get someone as nasty as Button or the Barber to pick you off one by one, and all because of the one person who links all of you to that picture . . . *me*."

Sam remembered his conversation with Trudy at the television studio a few weeks before when she'd first informed him that Button was on the rampage, and that Kazemi was in town. What he didn't know was that the fact that she told him weighed heavy on her mind.

Both men observed her move to sit herself on the settee. She now had an out-of-context dreamy smile, and eyes that were momentarily lost in memories of happier times at the cottage when she would sit by the log fire with Penny and Sam, laughing and relaxed as they talked through their wedding plans. She would be sipping a glass of warm water, while her two dear friends saw off a bottle of wine. Now, reluctantly, she had to inform him of an incident, an action by a heartless thug, that would not only reinforce the reason why he had to put his life in harm's way and extract a young child from the clutches of Button and Moses Jones, but the realisation that those close to him *were already* in harm's way.

"Oh God, what a bloody mess," she muttered, ending her brief reverie, and wishing she didn't have to reveal the information that was not hers to keep.

"I'll get you another drink," Sam told her hoping the water would refresh her.

She thanked him and when he returned with the glass, began to speak. "Our friend Miss Piggy . . . it was her who gave me all that information, Sam. She contacted me late last night. She told all about the Barber's true identity and his whereabouts." Trudy fell silent, reluctant to continue.

"I'll tell him the rest, sweetie," Archie offered, his tone gentle and sympathetic, recognising the pressure Trudy was under. His yellow handkerchief was once more brought back into use as he also knew the gravity of what required telling.

"No, Archie. Thank you anyway, but it's for me to tell him," Trudy replied.

She then gestured for Sam to sit next to her, if anything for her own self-comfort, aware she wouldn't have to ask him if a reassuring hug was required.

"Miss Piggy, DCI Tamworth that is, also informed me that Button unexpectedly came back into the country, and was arrested and questioned in connection with the death of Harry Topp. But he was later released on police bail as there was insufficient evidence to charge him." She stopped to take a sip of her water, staring trance-like. "Within two weeks of the police releasing him, and with no passport - which was taken from him when he was arrested - he managed to sneak out of the country again, to eventually reappear in the Philippines. According to Tamworth - and she didn't know this when she called here with the American - it's highly probable that it was Button who killed Cissy while he was out on bail. A partial fingerprint which matched his was found on her walking stick . . . it had been used to beat her over the head." She had no desire to continue. She bit her bottom lip, but there were no tears. She knew Archie would spare no expense in making sure Penny and Sam's daughters would be looked after while he was away. She feared only for Sam.

"You're right, you know," Sam admitted, and on cue he reached out to her with his intuitive hug.

"Right about what?" she asked, savouring the moment of consolation from her friend.

"It is a bloody mess," he answered. "But that's why I'm going . . . to put it right once and for all."

"I hope for yours and Penny's sake you can. She wouldn't look good in black, Sam," said Trudy mournfully.

Then she reluctantly freed herself from Sam's arms to stand

once more next to Archie, who by nature was a wily and resourceful individual. As Sam once said of him: 'If you take him at face value, you're a fool'. He made sure he used his wealth and flamboyant lifestyle to his advantage - a lifestyle that was like a magnet to those who were worth knowing and useful to him - but Archie's prowess always came to the fore to help his friend.

"You're going to need this," Archie said, and reached into his inside suit pocket to retrieve a small, sealed bag. "I'm assured by this lovely woman here that it will fit into your phone."

"Thank you, Arch. What's on it?" Sam enquired, resting the innocuous but tiny memory card in the palm of his hand.

For the first time since he'd walked through the door, Sam observed a glimpse of the usual, mischievous crafty Archie that seemed to have been left behind in London like one of his more garish suits.

"Ah yes, well. I know this sweet little man at the American Embassy," Archie chirped, and the alluring roll of his eyes spoke far more than either Sam or Trudy wished to know. "On that card is all you need to know about that Spatz fellow and, according to my dear man, as well as being a shifty piece of work, he also has personal problems. I hope it helps."

"I've also put some information on it for you, Sam," said Trudy, but without the same look of enthusiasm as Archie. She seemed stressed now as a vivid memory of someone from her past was resurrected. She reached for Archie's hand, and held it like a child would her father's, a supporting hand from a man who knew all too well how her words would pain her. "Sam . . . do you remember when we first met, how I told you that Archie sent me to Ireland to straighten my life out?" she asked in a small voice.

"Yes, like it was yesterday," Sam replied quietly, which mirrored her sense of pain.

"Archie sent me for rehab to a commune in County Kildare

which was run by a priest, Father Patrick O'Toole-Quinn, ex-IRA, and he hates the English . . . well, not all of them," she added with a small smile. "He's six foot three of pure God-driven red-headed stubbornness. He'll break you metaphorically speaking, and then put you back together again as a better person.

"This wonderful man, Sam," said Trudy, indicting Archie, "saved my body from the gutter where he found me. But that mad Irishman saved my soul . . . and I love them both. The reason why I'm telling you all this is that he has a new flock of lost sheep now. They're in the Philippines, Manila, in fact. He runs an orphanage there for street children. If you find yourself in need of help or sanctuary, he's your man; but be cautious . . . he may be a man of the cloth, but he'll exact a high cost for his assistance, one that you may not be willing to pay."

"I'll keep him in mind, thank you, but I can't think of anything I've got that he'll want," Sam answered. He felt both humility and endeavour. Humility brought on by the willingness of a friend, a very dear friend to open her own Pandora's box to unselfishly help him; and endeavour to do as Trudy had done: to prevail in the face of adversity.

"Why don't you take one of my chaps with you, Farmer?" Archie suggested. "My minders are all capable of looking after themselves, you know that. Take James, he'll watch your back for you. He's ex–"

"Come on, Arch, put your coat on," came the motherly interruption from Trudy. "We'd better get back before people start missing us."

"Thanks for the offer, Archie," Sam replied, "but I already have someone on their way out there, someone who'll watch out for me."

Archie looked intrigued, wondering who that someone was; and then it dawned on him . . . there was only one man who Sam would trust with his life, someone who was capable of breaking bones with his bare hands. Archie said nothing, but just looked at Sam wide-eyed, salivating at the thought of the formidable bone-breaker.

As if it was a requisite for females leaving the cottage, Trudy had disappeared to use the bathroom, so Sam led Archie back to his car . . . and noticed with astonishment the type of vehicle he had arrived in.

"Christ, Archie!" Sam blustered in astonishment. "You came all this way in a London taxi! It's going to cost you a fortune!"

"Worth every penny, sweetie, if it helps me save the life of a dear friend," he replied.

Sam usually said his goodbyes with a handshake, but this time he thought Archie deserved better, something personal. He held him in his arms and kissed his cheek – just a peck, he didn't want to give his friend the wrong impression! – as he knew Archie would like that.

"I'll see you again in nine days, Archie," Sam informed him, cracking a smile at the reappearance of that yellow handkerchief. "I promised Penny I'd be back in time to watch her last performance of Katherine, and we'll all meet up and party like mad," he added, smiling at Archie, who was clearly moved by Sam's farewell hug and kiss.

Archie shuffled himself onto the back seat of the car as Sam left to find Trudy. She'd waited for him under his front porch to say her own goodbye – and Sam knew that wouldn't be easy for either of them. Although Sam loved Penny to distraction, and she had become the lungs that put breath into his body, Trudy was that rare breed of friend who, like him, had had her share of physical suffering, and it had formed a bond that was unique to them.

Sam stroked his fingers across her cheek and placed his strong hand on her shoulder as he kissed her lips, a kiss that said goodbye.

Chapter 23

"I'd like to believe you weren't thinking of Penny when you did that," Trudy said, with tears now trickling down her face.

"I wasn't. That was for you. Had I been thinking of Penny, we'd still be kissing," he replied, with a caring smile.

"She's a lucky woman, Sam."

Holding her hand, he walked Trudy to the car and waved them off. As he swung the five-bar gate across his driveway, Trudy's words, 'She's a lucky woman', played on his mind. *I'm the lucky one,* Sam thought. *'It's my love for her that's going to give me the strength to stay alive, and come home . . .*

Chapter 24

The Commitment

Oh God, what are they doing here? thought Penny, unexpectedly hearing two familiar voices call out as they opened the front door to her London home.

"Hello maid!" said Maggie cheerfully, popping her head around the lounge door.

Penny returned a strained smile from where she lay on the settee.

"Right, you ready then? We haven't got long if we're going to catch the ferry," said Estelle, as if nothing was amiss.

"I told you both last night when I phoned that I won't be going to France this time. I'm just not up to it," Penny said. She sounded very tired, almost breathless.

But even though they noted her forlorn and tired *leave me alone* voice, it didn't have any sway with them; their minds were made up. Like her they too were concerned about their father and the reason he'd had to go to the Philippines; but for them that was no excuse to postpone their trip to see Madame Renard and carry out the fitting of Penny's wedding gown.

"Yeah, yeah. Blah, blah," Estelle nonchalantly replied, reaching for Penny's hand to pull her up from the settee. "Don't waste your breath on us. Like father, like daughters. Now come on, get your arse into gear. We're going to France, and for Christ's sake girl, put some make-up on, you look scarier than Maggie!"

Chapter 24

Penny gazed up at the sisters, realising in that very moment that Sam in some ways hadn't left her at all. He was right here in the form of his two lovely and determined daughters; a lot more determined than she could have possibly imagined!

"What are you looking at maid?" Maggie asked, watching Penny craning her neck as she gazed up at the sky from the deck of the ferry.

"That plane up there, it made me wonder what country your dad's flying over at the moment."

"Well, if he's on schedule he'll be landing for his stopover in Hong Kong before too long, so I suppose it could be China," replied Maggie, conscious that she had just blatantly lied. Like Penny she fixed her eyes on the vapour trail from a faint spec high up in the sky, aware that her father had planned to make a detour to visit someone before he flew out, someone who, as yet, Penny was unaware of, and due to that delay Maggie knew that that could be his plane they were looking at.

"Hadn't we better think about going below and getting our bags? You know what the rush is like when the ferry docks," said Estelle.

They agreed, and she opened the heavily varnished mahogany door that led them from the observation deck to the bowels of the ship.

As always, the dependable Monsieur Paul was waiting in the car park ready to drive them back to the chateau – better known as 'the farmhouse' – but not before an enthusiastic embrace and kiss for the three women. Up until that point Maggie and Estelle seemed carefree, almost indifferent, as to how Penny was feeling who, as much as she tried, couldn't mask her low spirits on missing her beloved Sam. Once in the car, however, the sister's moods changed, becoming pensive, as they knew it was time for Penny to be taken to a place that would lead her to the answers . . . answers to puzzling questions that had eluded her. Who were the airman and the sailor about whom Sophie had got short shrift when she spoke of them? And who was the man in the woods? When Sam had been reminded of him, he became the catalyst that made him decide to risk his own life for that of a young boy on the other side of the world.

Maggie twisted around in the front seat and reached behind to take hold of Estelle's hand, bringing a smile to Penny's face as she witnessed the genuine sisterly gesture.

"We're not going straight to the farmhouse, Pen," said Maggie, whose voice had now become soft in tone. "Sis and I are taking you to meet someone, someone very special. It's not too far out of our way."

"OK, sweetheart, that's fine by me," Penny replied, curious to know where she was being taken and who that person was. At the same time, she became aware that from the manner in which Maggie had ended her sentence with the gentlest of smiles, little more would be said regarding where they were heading.

It took just under three quarters of an hour to reach their destination, Bayeux, a town that Penny had visited once before. On that occasion, she had been taken to see the famous Bayeux tapestry, the seventy-metre-long work of art that depicts the Norman conquest of England in 1066. Her history lesson this time would be set in the twentieth century and Penny, now realising where she was, also knew the precise date: 6th of June 1944 – the allied invasion of Normandy.

As she stood by the car and looked around, she felt a deep sense of humility. She gazed at row after row of immaculately kept white headstones, all precisely positioned as if they were on parade to those who came to visit. Each one was, in its own right, a monument to the brave soul who was buried there and who had been denied the luxury of dying in old age. Their headstones stood in narrow beds of an endless infusion of flowering colour, with pencil-sharp borders defined by a carpet of lush, manicured lawns that lay above the dead like a protecting blanket of green.

"Come on, maid, let's go for a little wander, shall we?" said

Maggie, who with Estelle had linked arms with Penny. They left Monsieur Paul to wait for them in the car.

Penny had said very little since they had arrived at the war graves cemetery, and had only offered polite acknowledgements and comments on the beautiful dry spring day that it was. Other than that, she thought it crass to ask anything like *why are we here?* or *who have we come to see?* She knew the sisters well enough to realise that it must be important to them for her to be there and, despite their sometimes-childish games, like their father, she also trusted them.

"There must be thousands buried here, it looks vast," Penny commented. She paused and freed herself from the sister's arms to stop and gaze at a tall limestone cross set upon a four-stepped octagonal base that stood like a beacon to the fallen.

"It's called the cross of sacrifice. Powerful, isn't it?" said Estelle, who could see Penny was moved by her surroundings. "There are nearly four and a half thousand graves here, and there are even a few hundred German solders buried here too; but as they say, in death all men are as equal, aren't they?"

Estelle's profound words produced a forlorn and solitary "Yes" from Penny's lips.

"Come on, Pen, we haven't got far to go . . . he's just over here," came the encouraging voice of Maggie, her outstretched hand once more reaching for her friend.

"Penny?" said Estelle.

"Yes," she replied, her eyes now fixed on Estelle, whose questioning tone had gained her attention.

"Do you remember when you first came to the farmhouse and Sophie asked you whether you were told the story of the airman and the sailor, and then wished she hadn't?"

"Yes, very much so, and I remember the disapproving look Madame Renard gave her as well. Why?" Penny asked.

"Well, Pen, Mags and I . . . we . . ." Estelle paused as the sisters then stopped to stand in front of the particular grave of a man whose story they knew would take Penny on a journey from the beaches of Normandy to the present time, a journey that would not only answer puzzles, but would make her understand what it meant for Sam and his daughters to carry the name Farmer. "We'd like to introduce you to the sailor, Sammy Farmer. He's Grandad's brother."

At first Penny said nothing, muted by a strange sense of excitement that filled her thoughts. It was an emotion she most definitely wasn't expecting to feel considering she was standing in front of a war grave. It was obvious that there was a particular grave the sisters wanted to show her, but never imagined it would be Sam's uncle. Neither he nor his daughters had ever spoken about Sammy. *Why not? Was it because he was dead and they didn't think he was worth mentioning?* she pondered, but straight away she dismissed that thought. *How could anyone think that of a man who gave his life for his country?* She read the inscription on the headstone with a voice so quiet that it was almost a murmur: "*S. A. Farmer. 86594. Leading seaman. Royal Navy. 7th June 1944.*"

Penny had noticed that Estelle had brought with her a red carrier bag; Monsieur Paul had handed to her as they left the car, but she hadn't mentioned it at the time.

"Here, Pen, we have one each," said Estelle, and produced three single flowers from the bag. "They're beautiful, aren't they? They're Normandy poppies, so different from the bright red Flanders poppy you normally associate with remembering the war dead. These have lovely pink petals . . . look."

A fond laugh was heard coming from Maggie; she was thinking back to when she was a child. "Do you remember, Estelle, when we young we used to call them panda poppies, coz of the single black dot on each petal? There's a certain area on Renard land where they grow in abundance. Madame Renard picked these for us," she said.

For the first time since they had arrived at the cemetery Maggie, who rarely let sentiment get the better of her, now had a thoughtful frown as she talked of where the poppies grew.

The three women stood quietly for a moment, each with a poppy clasped in their hands, united in respect for a man who never made it home to his mortal family. Maggie and Estelle placed a tender kiss on their flowers, and then crouched down to lay them alongside two other poppies that had been recently placed there; both of the sisters knew who by, but made no reference to them.

Penny laid hers, and then slowly ran her fingertips across the cold limestone. "Tell me about him. That's why you've brought me here, isn't it?" she asked.

With a gentle nod of her head, Maggie then pointed to a granite stone bench that was some twenty feet behind them; it had room for the three of them to sit. "You start to tell the story, sis," said Maggie, knowing Estelle had the gift of drawing a mental picture that, for the sisters, was imperative for Penny to not only know of the past, but also what the immediate future held for the three of them.

Penny gazed down at her hands to find once more that the sisters held them in theirs, an act of support for each other as Estelle opened a portal for her to travel in her mind, back to the 7th of June 1944.

"Oh gawd, it's hard to know where to start really. I've not had to talk about him to a stranger before. Shit, I didn't mean it in that way, Pen. I'm sorry, it's just you're the first person outside the family who we feel needs to know; but you are family, isn't she Mags?" There was no hiding the desperate look on Estelle's face as she tried to correct herself. The last thing she had intended was to make Penny feel she was an outsider – but Penny knew that.

"Don't worry, sweetheart," Penny replied, her smile intended to ease Estelle's awkwardness. "We all fluff our lines from time to time, believe me, I'm a past master at it. When your father asked me to marry him, I was just busting to say yes, but what came out was 'I can't'. So, no, don't worry about it. Just carry on. Please."

"Yes, she's right, you know. Now come on, sis," said Maggie.

"OK, OK, don't rush me!" Estelle pleaded. She closed her eyes for a brief moment to refocus her thoughts on leading seaman Sammy Farmer and his journey to immortality. "Well, it all started for him about three months before D-Day," Estelle said, her rhythm and composure returning to her. "Sammy's ship was in for repairs at Scappa Flow, in Scotland, after being damaged in air raids on Arctic convoy duty to Russia." She then leant forward to peer across at Maggie. "Mags, we didn't mention that Sammy was a medic, did we?"

"No, don't think so," Mags replied.

"Right, OK then," said Estelle slowly. But before saying anything further, she stood up and walked over to a cigarette packet that lay crumpled on the grass a few feet away from where they were seated. "Sorry, it was bugging me. Some people who visit here have no respect." Estelle's expression of irritation as she dropped the rubbish into her carrier bag quickly dissipated, though, replaced by a more equable pose – essential if she was to calmly continue with the story of Sammy. "While he was in Scotland, a signal arrived asking for medics for special duties. So, he put his name down, and you don't need me to tell you where that led him . . .

"On the morning of the invasion, the British landed on the beach that they code named Sward. The same beach near to where our ferry docked, in fact. Sammy came ashore in the second wave; he was part of a naval shore party. He and other medics were tasked with setting up a first aid station for all the wounded." Estelle then paused to allow herself time to consider what she would say next. Her eyes flittered between Penny and her sister, but now sought out her great uncle's headstone, a wanting connection between her and a man whose final hours of life were about to be described. Now she spoke in earnest, setting a tone for what was to come.

"Sometime during that day," she continued, "he treated a wounded commando who had made it to the first aid station. He said a glider that he'd been towed across the channel in, during the early hours of that morning, had crash landed in a field near to some woods to the southwest of Sward beach, and that two of the men on board were so badly injured they had to leave them behind. Apparently, the glider clipped a tree as it tried to land and broke apart. Uncle Sammy found out that a reconnaissance unit was heading into that area and volunteered to go with them so if they came across the plane, he could help the two casualties – if they were still alive that is. It was late afternoon by the time they found it."

Once more she paused for a brief moment, and then Maggie's sisterly intuition kicked in, sensing that it was now time for her to pick up the mantle and complete the tale. As a vet, she often had to deal with life and death situations, and even those of animals could be emotionally stressful; but Maggie had learnt to be stoic and detached, a trait that would prove to be her strength, even after Penny knew the full story.

"I'll tell the rest, sis," she told Estelle. Then her attention focused on Penny, who had barely said a word. "You all right there, maid? Ere, I don't know about you, but this stone ain't 'alf chilling my arse. Never mind though, we'll have some of Madame Renard's *Obstler* when we get to the farmhouse, that'll wake up your circulation."

Only a faint "I'm fine thank you, sweetheart" was heard in reply; Maggie was right, Penny thought the granite seat was cold, but the least she could do was endure it for the sake of their Uncle Sammy.

"Right, now, where were we? Yes . . . the glider," said Maggie. "You have to remember, Pen, that there was a war going on, with Germans all around who were either retreating or putting up a fight and, with the American and British planes flying over their heads trying to bomb the crap out of the enemy, the soldiers that Sammy were with took it slow. Apparently, they saw some Germans near the crash site but skirted around them. Their job was to reconnoitre, not pick a fight. Anyway, when they got to what was left of the glider, they found the two men. One of them, a commando, had died of his wounds, but the other guy was alive – just. He was the pilot and was still jammed in the mangled cockpit. They managed to get him free and take the edge off his pain with morphine, but he couldn't be moved far because of his severe injuries."

As Maggie talked, Penny imagined the scene in her mind as if she were reading a script for the first time. There was Sammy desperately trying to save the life of the pilot, while the soldiers, weary of their exposed surroundings and the proximity of the enemy, tried to decide what to do next.

"The officer in charge," Maggie then said, "said it was too dangerous to stay and may draw attention to the site, so decided it was best to leave the pilot there and withdraw. Either they or another unit would go back the next day for him. By then he reckoned the area would be clear of Germans."

Maggie then rose to her feet with an air of defiance in her posture and pointed a finger like an arrow towards the grave of Sammy. Her voice was passionate in its delivery, unrestrained in its bluntness, Maggie-style: "Do you know what that brave bugger over there said in reply to the officer's decision?" Her unyielding stare fixed on Penny, who became conscious of the eerie motion of her upper body: she was gently rocking forward and back as the emotion of the scene played out in her head.

"'Bollocks, bollocks!'" Maggie repeated, "'You lot can piss off if you want, but I'm staying here. I'm a matelot, and I don't have to take orders from squaddies!' And he stayed behind – with a heavy machine gun he'd found in the glider as company, that is."

"Help did come," Maggie continued with a huff, "but it wasn't from the British. Things didn't quite go to plan on that first day of the invasion. They tried and failed to take their main objective, Caen, but they feared a counter attack by an SS Panzer Division that was defending the town. It was French Resistance that got to the crash site late in the morning the following day. At first, they didn't find Sammy, but what they did find was the pilot who he had kept safe and alive, and four dead German soldiers near to the wreckage of the glider. It turned out that two young sisters were hiding in the woods because of the allied bombing and shelling, and it was they who found Sammy."

"Oh my god, it can't be . . ." Penny muttered as her mind filled with past stories of how two young sisters would run errands for the local French Resistance. With eyes wide with fear, she'd dared to imagine what other scenes Maggie would continue to describe to her.

"Just after dawn the two girls heard gunfire coming from the meadow. It lasted on and off for about half an hour or so, they think. Then sometime later, after the shooting had stopped, they watched three German soldiers drag a man into the woods and tie him to a tree – not far from where the girls were hiding – and beat him with their rifle butts. They did that for several minutes, before one of them shot him in the head and then they left, leaving Sammy there still tied to the tree." Maggie then sat down again, but before she talked further about Sammy, she asked a question that in itself would raise new questions and answers, and would make Penny think that, in matters of life and death, some things are preordained: "You know who the sisters are, don't you?" Maggie asked.

"Yes, I think I do," came Penny's reply.

"Weird, don't you think? Those two young girls who witnessed dad's uncle get murdered by those bastards, would in years to come be mine and Estelle's grand-mère and Madame Renard," said Maggie.

Penny's reply came only after a moment of reminiscing,

thinking back to how she first met their father seemingly by accident on the steps outside the National Gallery in London, and how she became convinced that Maggie and Estelle's late mother, Annie, from somewhere in the heavens had laid out the road ahead for Sam to find his future happiness with her.

"There are things that happen to people, good things, due to the sacrifice of others that can never be explained, but you can only be thankful for," Penny said.

"That is so, so true, Pen," said Estelle. "Something good did come out of Uncle Sammy's sacrifice," she continued. "Years later, dad and grandad were sitting here, just like we are now on this same seat. They'd come over to commemorate D-Day. As they sat here quietly, two men showed up and stood by Sammy's grave. The older man then dropped to his knees and started to weep. Of course, seeing him in such distress they went to him to find out why . . . The old man turned out to be the pilot whose life Sammy had saved. He was with his son, Oak . . . later to be Aunty Ruth's husband and our darling uncle. You couldn't make it up if you tried, could you?" Estelle asked.

Penny nodded her head in sombre acknowledgment that something special had been born out of the tragedy of Sammy's death, and realised that a single word would forever be associated with his sacrifice: commitment; the word that she knew had been drummed into Sam by his father to become his moral compass. This was why he reacted as he did when Special Agent Spatz uttered the words *the man in the woods*. It was an underhand trigger from his brother Sidney to remind Sam of what commitment meant: to be unselfish to those who need your help.

"Thank you," said Penny, hugging the sisters closer to her. "I now know why you brought me here, and why your father felt he had to go to save his nephew. Thank you, it helps." Then Penny stared poignantly at the grave, seeing the two other poppies that were already placed there. "He's been here? Your father? He put those flowers there, didn't he?" she asked.

"Yes," answered Estelle. "Dad and Madame Renard came here before he flew to the Philippines."

Maggie then coaxed Estelle with her eyes, who then reached into her carrier bag to retrieve a small jewellery box.

"Oh my god . . . is that what I think it is?"

"Yes," replied Estelle, placing a medal that was struck from bronze gently into Penny's palm; she held it like a precious jewel. "Grandad Farmer," Estelle continued, "said many times that his brother would be shocked to think he had received the Victoria Cross for valour. Apparently, he was a modest man who would never see himself as a hero. Maybe that's why we don't make a song and dance about the fact, because Sammy wouldn't want that."

The three of them then remained silent for a few moments, the desire to speak muted by the serenity of their surroundings and their own inner thoughts.

Maggie reached out her hand to hold the treasured family heirloom for herself. She caressed the medal with the tips of her fingers, feeling every indentation, which charged the words as she spoke and reinforced her stubborn will: "This medal is a legacy that our family, to this day, endeavours to uphold. That of never turning your back on those who need your help."

Suddenly it was as if an echo jolted Penny's memory, a *deja vu* moment on hearing the exact words that were spoken by their father only a few days before. Penny now peered deep into Maggie's dark brown eyes in the forlorn hope that her intuition was wrong this time, and that she had misread the passionate tone in which Maggie delivered those words; but her body told her that what she feared was in fact right, and a wave of emotion ripped through her from head to toe.

"You're going, aren't you?" asked Penny, her voice now taut with a rush of anxieties. "You're going to follow your dad . . . Why? Why on God's earth . . .?"

"Because I'm a Farmer, that's why, doing nothing isn't in our DNA. You should know us well enough by now, and understand that we don't sit on our arses and twiddle our thumbs. I'm flying out tonight. MP is driving me to Paris later. And if you're wondering if dad knows – he doesn't, and I want to keep it that way… well, for the time being."

Penny was under no illusion that Maggie was adamant and that her decision was final; but although she was anxious that one of Sam's beautiful daughters was also heading into a situation fraught with untold risks, Penny was impressed with Maggie's analytical approach to what she intended to do, however. No rash, female, hysterical, off-the-cuff reasoning. No, Penny could see that she had thought it though. She was after all like Estelle had described them earlier: like father, like daughter.

Penny turned her attention to Estelle, who had kept noticeable quiet while Maggie explained her plans. "Please tell me that you have no intention of going with her?" she said. "It's going to be hard enough now with Maggie and your dad out there. I'll be beside myself if you both go."

Penny's desperate tone of voice brought a caring smile to Estelle's face; it confirmed the decision that both of the sisters had made for her sake. "No, I'm not going with Mags," she replied, sounding somewhat disappointed, though. "I won't deny that I want to, but it was decided that one of us should stay here and support our future mum, whom we care about very much."

Penny responded to what Estelle had said in the same manner as she normally did when the sisters made her feel as if she were already their mother – she hugged them with all the love she could muster, tears springing to her eyes.

"Any message for Dad when I see him?" asked Maggie, using her own hanky to dab away the tears from around Penny's eyes.

"Yes, there is. Tell him that I'm running short of jam, will you."

Chapter 24

"Ha! I'll tell him!" Maggie replied, fully aware what the obscure message meant.

Chapter 25

The Tourist

Day One

With his fifteen-hour flight from Paris now behind him, and Manila time telling Sam that it was 10.52 in the morning, an eight-hour leap was what his body clock was experiencing just now. Sam wearily observed the two airport customs and immigration officers diligently examine his documents and the contents of his travel bag, item by item. One of the officers asked him questions from behind a white dust mask that obscured his face, and his blue latex-gloved hands gave an air of sterile interrogation.

"I see you have a British passport, but you flew out from Paris not England. Why was that?" The muffled question came from a rather portly middle-aged officer who sat the other side of a long aluminium table where Sam's bag had been placed.

"I have relatives in France and I called in en route to the airport," Sam replied, intent on answering his questions with as little detail as he deemed necessary.

"And what's your reason for coming to the Philippines?" he asked. His approach was as laid back as his posture, and only his fat buttocks squashed into the chair made the difference between remaining in that position or sliding onto the floor like an overweight jellied eel.

"I've got a brother who lives here in Manila."

"Do you intend to stay long? Mr Farmer, is it?" enquired the still precariously slouched inquisitor, whose stubby fingers flicked through the stamped pages of his passport.

"No, and yes, it is. I'm only here for seven days maximum," Sam answered, placing his hand across his mouth to stifle a yawn.

"Are you traveling on your own or with others?" the younger officer then asked as he rifled through the side pockets of his black canvas bag.

"Alone," he replied, glancing at the other travellers who, like him, were waiting in turn to have the contents of their luggage examined. One similarity that became blatantly obvious to him was that those who weren't waved through to continue on their journey were mostly men. Middle-aged European men like him, traveling alone and light. He concealed a wry smile as he retrieved his documents and bag, aware that in the eyes of the two customs men, he was seen as just another sex tourist come to savour the flesh pots of downtown Manila.

"Welcome to the Philippines, Sam," he muttered quietly to himself, observing the chaos of the taxi pickup point that was more like a free-for-all with ill-tempered and frustrated cab drivers foul mouthing each other as they engaged in car horn combat and crude hand signals to win a fare. He stood for a moment deciding which company he'd prefer to fall victim to. *Yellow cab, white cab?* he thought. He'd read on the Internet about the pricing scams between cab companies that would have him out of pocket by several hundred Philippine pesos, if he weren't so wary of them.

As an ex merchant seaman who had sailed to similar countries in the past, it was nothing new for him to experience scenes just like those being played out right in front of his eyes. They were day-to-day scenarios exacerbated by the pull of poverty that spawned a need of survival of the fittest – a mentality he intended to draw upon and use to his advantage whenever the opportunity arose. Sam was under no illusion that if he was going to succeed and get the boy away from the clutches of Button, and be on the lookout for the Barber, he had to be wily and alert to those around him – and that included Spatz, who was supposedly there to help him. Penny and her two aunts had enlightened him regarding the art of acting, and how actors were predominately governed by set scenes and scenarios. The character would respond to these influences and perform within the constraints of the script, and this vital skill would be used to his advantage. Sam would, for the purpose of misdirection, play the part of the compliant brother who had travelled halfway across the world to be directed by Spatz and Sidney, with one or two rebellious moments thrown in, just to keep it real; but behind the scenes, Sam had devised his own script, one that only he knew about and one that gave him the freedom to act independently.

"Take your bag, sir?" offered a taxi driver who had darted out from the driver's seat to open the passenger door for Sam.

"No thanks, it stays with me," Sam answered, giving his surroundings one last look before ensconcing himself on the rear seat of the yellow taxi.

"Where to, mister?" enquired the voice that came from a reflected face in the rear-view mirror. A young man with clean-shaven appearance and dark enquiring brown eyes looked at Sam with an aura of streetwise youth.

You'll do Sam decided. He moved to the edge of the seat, his right hand resting against the front passenger headrest to talk to the driver, whose name was clear to read from a permit attached to his dashboard. Above that was the fare meter that already showed fifty-six pesos even before they'd set off.

"Paco, is it?" Sam asked. Then, almost instantly, he felt his body thrown with a jolt back into the seat by the force of the car as it drove off like a bullet from a gun. *Well that didn't work as planned, did it?* Sam thought, with his hand now soothing his neck for signs of whiplash.

"Hey, Paco, slow down a bit would you please? I need you to

do something for me and there's twenty-five dollars in it for you, if you're interested?" Sam asked loudly, trying to make himself heard above the din of the revving engine as they avoided the competing hazards of all the other taxis negotiating their way in or out of the airport terminal.

Paco glanced in the mirror to see Sam staring right back at him. "So, what's the deal, mister?" he asked, his reply sounding more indifferent than curious, as if being approached in that way was an everyday occurrence.

"Easy really. Twenty-five dollars on top of my fare if you keep an eye open to see if we're being followed," explained Sam.

"Hey, you're not in trouble, are you? I don't want any trouble. I could lose my license!" came the hurried response from Paco in his version of an American accent.

"No, nothing like that, I assure you," Sam replied, and having learnt his lesson, now remained firmly in his seat to talk. "You see, I was told to wait in Arrivals to be met by certain US Government people, but I decided not to. That's why I'm sitting in your cab instead. Oh, by the way, it's the Manila Hotel."

"You're a cop, mister?" asked Paco.

"No, I'm here purely to help find someone, that's all," Sam replied.

"What, like a tracker, man hunter sort of thing?" Paco enquired, and Sam noticed by the way he was repeatedly flitting his gaze from mirror to mirror that he had taken him up on his offer.

"More of an honest broker, Paco," answered Sam, peering out at Manila Bay coming into view as they drove along the highway towards the city that lay under a thick cloud like a veil. Even on an overcast day like this it was hot, in the high eighties and humid (suffocatingly humid), and so far removed from the approaching Devon spring he'd left behind.

"Got-cher!" cried Paco with gusto, as if he had just hooked a fish. "You're right, mister, we've got company. They're hanging back behind a truck. A black SUV with US plates. Do you want me to lose them?"

"No, there's no point. They're probably the same people who I should have met up with at the airport," Sam replied, certain that they had probably found him by tracking his mobile phone. It was a hunch that stemmed from Spatz's insistence that he kept the phone on him at all times. In normal circumstances that wouldn't have been a strange thing to ask: his two daughters had often tried to contact him, only to find out that his phone was either turned off or left at work; but this was Special Agent Spatz of the DEA, a man that Sam realised, due to the sheer nature of his profession, would want to keep tabs on him.

Once that thought had entered his mind, it only took Sam two minutes on the Internet to find out what means were available to agencies like the DEA, and tracking people via their mobile phones was at the top of the list. Sam smiled to himself knowing that Spatz must be thinking that he'd got him on a leash, and couldn't roam far without being traced. *Ha! That's what you think, buster,* he mused. "If you want to know, Paco, they're DEA," he said.

"Thought so, them and the CIA are like flees on a dog's back on the islands. They behave like they still run the place," Paco replied.

His less than enthusiastic regard for the American law enforcement agents was exactly what Sam had hoped to hear. Paco was someone who would be cautious to not break the law and put his taxi license at risk, but wouldn't be disinclined to give Spatz and his colleagues the proverbial run around, enabling Sam to continue unrestrained with his own plans.

"How would you like to earn some extra dollars on top of what I already owe you?" Sam asked, now thinking ahead to what he would do next, or rather, what Paco would do next. As for himself, he knew exactly what he was going to do once he arrived at his hotel: sleep; but not before a visit from Spatz, and he knew that after the cat and mouse antics at the airport, it would be sooner rather than later.

"What have you got in mind, mister? Is it to do with those guys behind us?" said the now slightly cautious Paco.

"Yes and no," Sam answered.

His reply sounded detached and distant as he became distracted by the madness he was entering, a chaos called Manila City with twenty million inhabitants – more than twice as many as the land space was really capable of accommodating. All around him, street after street was a contradiction of urban planning, with modern high-rise buildings that bullied their way up into the skyline sharing precious space with rickety, corrugated roofed structures made from nothing more than leftovers from building sites. An unsynchronized racket of vehicle horns added to the bedlam of sight and sound, invading Sam's jet-lagged senses.

"Ha! Would you believe it?" he muttered, hearing the unmistakable crow of a cockerel calling out from some rare piece of real estate that hadn't been built on . . . yet. "Sorry," Sam continued. "As I was going to say . . . once we get to my hotel I'd like you to wait. The black car behind us will probably also stop. Then, when it drives off, I'd like you to follow it. I'm guessing it'll go to a private address somewhere in the city. Once you know where it is, remember it, and then you can go... Then at eleven tonight I want you to pick me up by the hotel's kitchen loading bay and drive me to Alongapo – well, Subic Bay to be precise. Can I rely on you to do that?"

Nothing was heard from Paco immediately, which Sam felt was a good sign. To him, that meant he was thinking it through carefully, street-wise carefully, and of course there was the matter of the money.

"That's going to cost you a great deal more than another twenty-five dollars, mister."

"Yes, I'm aware of that. How much do you get to take home a day taxiing, Paco? Fifteen . . . twenty dollars?"

"Mostly around eighteen. On a good day, twenty-five," Paco replied.

"Really? Wow, that's not a lot, is it? So, if I rounded up your twenty-five to a hundred – that's including seeing where that SUV goes – and two hundred for taking me to Subic Bay and back, does that sound agreeable?"

Sam's eyes flitted between Paco's mirror and a wad of one hundred dollar bills he had retrieved from the buttoned pocket of his white shirt.

"If I agree to do what you want, I'll have to get a hire car. This taxi goes back at the end of my shift for another driver to use."

"OK, no problem," Sam replied calmly. "So, that's one, two, three hundred, plus the hire car . . . so let's make that a round five hundred, shall we?"

"Subic is a long drive. It'll take at least two-and-a-half to three hours. How long do you expect to be there?" asked Paco.

"Oh, not long. I'm going to meet a couple of people and may bring one of them back with us, but I'm not sure yet. And I mustn't be late back at my hotel for breakfast or our friends behind us may realise that I wasn't tucked up in my bed all night."

"For someone who's just arrived, you sure sound like you're in a hurry, mister."

"That's because a young boy's life is at stake, Paco, and when it comes to our American chums, I want to stay, as the saying goes, 'ahead of the curve'."

With only the thickness of the car's glass separating him from the realities of abject poverty, Sam knew money was a slayer of caution and a maker of hope, a realisation that he thought would sway Paco to do what he asked of him. He knew relying on a complete stranger to help was at the least fool hardy, but he didn't have the luxury of time, and if he was to stay ahead of the curve, he knew he had to take risks – Paco was one of those. One thing he couldn't buy was Paco's trust in him, however; loyalty yes, at a cost to his wallet, but trust no, that had to be earned. In Sam's book, not trusting in someone caused hesitation and doubt, and he needed Paco not to doubt him. The only way he could gain one and eliminate the other was to be honest, upfront and truthful . . . well, almost.

Sam continued, "There is one other thing, Paco. When I said I'm not in any trouble, that wasn't quite true. You see, there are two, possibly three men, who want to kill me, and if they succeed, the story of the boy doesn't have a happy ending either."

Sam wasn't totally sure what Paco's reaction would be to his statement; but he knew if his previous responses were anything to go by, he would take his time, and he did. Then came a series of questions.

"Has the boy been kidnapped? That's big business here. And what have the DEA and those guys who you say want to kill you got to do with it?" asked Paco, whose face in the mirror betrayed a modicum of concern; but Sam wasn't sure if it was genuine interest for the child's wellbeing, or annoyance at finding out that his passenger was possibly a dead man walking.

"The boy's my nephew, Paco. His mother is a Filipino, but his father, my brother, is a wanted drugs dealer, and yes, the child's been kidnapped. As for the DEA, it's complicated. And the men who want to kill me, well, one of them has the boy."

"So why do those guys want you dead? Are you a gangster like them?" Paco's questions were pointedly direct; his words spoken in a manner that said to Sam *don't bullshit me.*

Sam knew his reply would have to be just as straight, even if it required reluctantly exploiting the consequences of his past as a means to an end.

"The man who has the child wants to kill me because over

twenty years ago I knocked all of his teeth out when he threatened my family. He came looking for my brother, who by then had long disappeared." Now Sam made sure Paco was looking at him in the mirror as he spoke so he could see what he did next. "The other man is a psychopathic assassin who did this to me when I was in the wrong place at the wrong time. He wants to finish off his handiwork."

Paco almost brought the taxi to a halt as his eyes bulged at the sight of Sam's physical nightmare. "Oh Mary mother of Jesus! He did *that* to you? And he wants to kill you? You mean you're going to kill him, yes?" Paco's tone had become fretful, even to the point of enthusiasm about what Sam should do to.

In reply Sam leant slightly forward in his seat and raised an eyebrow with an air of confidence. He shot Paco a wink. Then Sam knew, as Paco's reflection showed an agreeable nod of his head, it was game on: Paco was on board for the duration.

"Room 698 for Mr Farmer," said Louisa, a quietly spoken, almost whispering receptionist who handed Sam's room key to Marco, an equally softly spoken porter.

He reached out his hand to carry Sam's travel bag for him. "This way, sir," said the obliging Marco, his free hand indicating the direction to the lifts, and then seemingly from nowhere, he found a one-dollar bill trust into it.

"That's all right, I'll show Mr Farmer to his room," came the deep-toned voice of Special Agent Spatz who, with an intimidating glare, coaxed Sam's bag and room key from Marco's hands. "That was very dumb, Mr Farmer, to make your own way here," said Spatz; it sounded to Sam as if he was being chastised. Other than the brief rebuke, Spatz's attention was then taken up with watching the floor numbers for the lift slowly decrease as they waited. Then he said, "You've gotta understand, you're in *my* world now, Mr Farmer, and in it some folks see visitors like you as fair game. You're lucky the taxi driver brought you here. Some people leave the airport never to be seen again." Spatz paused then turned to look at Sam with cheerless eyes that endeavoured to show displeasure at the Englishman's antics; but they couldn't hide the truth: behind the façade, like a veneer that covered over imperfections, Spatz's world, as he called it, was in reality falling apart.

"Well, thank you for your concern," Sam replied, "but I did make it clear that I'd organise my own travel arrangements – and that included taxis."

He knew that even with his mild retort, an impasse had been reached between the two men. The timely ping! that rang out as the lift doors opened made Sam aware that both of them had had their say and he didn't want to overplay the situation. He now needed the DEA man to think he had won the argument, and that Sam would be agreeable with every instruction he would be given from then on. Spatz then made sure Sam entered first, and dissuaded two female guests from sharing the lift with an abrupt "Take the next one."

Any desire for either man to make small talk while they trundled upwards to the sixth floor was quashed by the next well-chosen words from Spatz that were made to sound like suggestions rather than their true intention: demands. "If I may, Mr Farmer," he snapped, "I'd advise that you stay in the hotel until arrangements are finalised for the ransom to be delivered. And to pass the time, this hotel has an excellent restaurant, swimming pool and gym." Spatz cracked what he perceived to be a gentle smile, but the stiff manner in which he spoke only confirmed the obvious to Sam: that Spatz and the DEA wanted him kept out of the way for the time being or, as the American indicated, to be kept safe and out of harm's way.

"So, when will I be required to do what I've travelled all this way for?" Sam asked.

Spatz's reply was curiously lacklustre, as if he didn't have a definitive answer – which troubled Sam. It had been, as far as he was aware, over ten days since the boy was kidnapped; ten days he had had to endure his captors, Button and Moses Jones. "Not sure yet," he said. "We're still waiting for the ransom to arrive from stateside."

"Surely it's not that difficult to get your hands on the money?" Sam asked.

Spatz fixed his eyes on the neon light on the lift's control panel, and then pressed the emergency stop button that brought them to a premature halt between floors – a rather dramatic way to obtain some privacy, Sam thought, but this was Spatz, who he already realised seemed to thrive on the theatrical.

"Not money, Mr Farmer, diamonds . . . nine million dollars-worth."

"Wow. Forgive me if I'm wrong, but back in my cottage I'm sure you said they wanted nine million in cash, so why the change?" Sam's question was directed to himself as much as to Spatz. It was a 'thinking out loud' moment to consider if there was any reason why Button and Moses Jones had decided to change from dollars to an altogether different form of currency. Dollars were certainly bulkier than diamonds to conceal, and traceable, but there was one other possibility that he thought was just as feasible: maybe the kidnappers, or even the DEA, had a desire to slow the pace . . . but for what reason? All Sam was sure of was that whatever the other parties' timetable was, he would stick to his own plan, no matter what.

"It's not unheard of in situations like this for plans and demands to change, Mr Farmer, and we don't want to provoke them into doing something dumb like hurt the kid, do we? We all have to be patient," said Spatz, who, with a prod of his finger, set them on their way again to the sixth floor. "Stay in the hotel," he continued, and with a flick of his wrist tossed Sam his room key. "I'll phone you later to see how you've settled in."

"If it's all the same to you, could you make it tomorrow? It may be morning here, but back home it's my bedtime," said Sam with a yawn. "And not before nine. Considering that they've got a pool here, I'll probably go for an early morning swim before breakfast, and won't have my phone with me."

As Sam watched the lift doors close – with relief that Spatz was out of his hair for the time being – he glanced at his wristwatch. It was still set to UK time and he wondered how Penny and his daughters were coping, unaware that he was not the only one who felt the pull of commitment to *the man in the woods . . .*

Chapter 26

Gift of Good Fortune

Sam was sure he must have been dreaming as the sound of the buzz-buzz, buzz-buzz relentlessly invaded his mind; but he wasn't, and the tone eventually awakened him into a drowsy, hazy state.

"Yes, what is it?" he snapped, with barely enough energy to lift the bedside phone's receiver, sandwiching it between the pillow and his head.

"Hi, good afternoon, Mr Farmer, this is Louisa at reception. There is a lady here at the desk – a Mrs Farmer – she says you're expecting her. Would you like me to get the porter to show her to your room?"

"Sorry . . . did I hear you say *Mrs Farmer*?"

"Yes, sir, that's correct," replied Louisa, who then waited patiently for Sam's answer. He reached for the watch that was on his bedside cabinet and through strained eyes could see it was 3.17pm.

"No, be so kind as to ask her to wait in the lounge," Sam said, knowing his blissful sleep was now permanently interrupted. "And give her my apologies. I'll be down in ten minutes."

Sam made it in nine. He had a quick shower (a cold one at that, and for all the wrong reasons), then a wet shave. Whoever the woman was, Mrs Farmer or not, the least he could do was to present himself in a befitting manner to meet his guest, even if she did invite herself.

Chapter 26

The hotel's lounge area was more of a sprawling link between two cocktail bars and the restaurant, and Sam thought it most likely that she would ensconce herself on one of the plush seats as near to the lifts as possible; the only problem was, *did she know what he looked like*? If the lady who called herself Mrs Farmer was indeed his sister-in-law, as he suspected, at least he had the advantage of knowing she was a Filipino. The downside was, which one? But there was one particular female who caught his eye. She was stood next to a glass-clad pillar, and its integral coloured lighting gave her an iridescent glow; but it was her acknowledging wave that alerted him she may be the lady he was looking for. Either way, there were several undeniable facts about her: she was very pretty and petite, with long, naturally flowing black hair that was parted to one side and kept in place with a tortoiseshell clasp, and despite her slightly anxious smile, she had the air of a happy disposition. *No wonder*, Sam thought, *the immigration officers at the airport came to their own conclusions as to why I'm here.* What lonely man, whose years of youth and vigour had abandoned him, wouldn't cross to the other side of the world to hold a beautiful, young woman in his arms if she was anything near as delightful as the one who stood in front of him now?

Like most Filipino women, he noticed that she wasn't as tall as European ladies, and even in her three-inch heels, she still only stood at five feet two, possibly. (The style of shoes she wore intrigued Sam, suggesting that it was more than just a fashion accessory.)

He reached out his hand to her, careful not to crush the slender fingers on her delicate hand with his manly grip; her hand seemed to disappear into his palm.

"Mrs Farmer, I presume?" Sam asked, his face showing the remnants of an interrupted sleep. "Please," he continued, guiding her in the direction of two-leather buttoned high back chairs, "would you like a drink?" He raised his hand to get the waiter's attention. The high wings of the chairs provided privacy as they eyed each other across a table – a leather pouffe with a slab of blue tinted glass placed upon it.

"Yes, please. Thank you," she answered. Her accent was, he thought, so different to Penny's, which was warm with hints of her Scottish roots that wrapped around you like a comforting friend; this young woman had a high-pitched, almost girlish, and Americanised voice.

"So, Mrs Farmer . . . I can't keep calling you that, can I?"

"It's Ma . . . Freya," she replied, and then in an instant averted her gaze from Sam, hoping that he didn't make anything out of her Freudian slip. So far Sam was open to the possibility that she was indeed Sidney's wife; but there were other factors that dissuaded him that he couldn't ignore.

"Well, Freya, allow me to ask you a question . . ." Sam waited for a moment to gauge her response to being put under pressure with such a direct demand. She had already put herself on the back foot as soon as she opened her mouth, and he wanted to keep her there until the truth of whom she really was came out. "Do you know what the word fastidious means?"

Sam then paused while the waiter brought their drinks to the table. For her, mineral water, and for Sam, a double shot of single malt whisky – although he was wishing it was a night cap rather than a pick me up.

"No, you don't, do you?" Sam said quietly, seeing the subdued shake of her head. "Fastidious, amongst other things, means fussy or finicky. Let's take your engagement and wedding rings, for example." Sam gestured for her to place her hand on his. "You will notice that your engagement ring is a paler gold than that of your wedding band, which, by the way, doesn't fit does it? Also, you haven't stopped fiddling with it . . . and that's because it was made for someone with less dainty fingers than yours."

As he began to dismantle her ruse, and with her hand nervously resting in his, he realised that a little friendly reassurance that he meant her no harm wouldn't go amiss. So, he gently released her hand and became more measured in his tone, from one of intimidating inquisitor to that of a storyteller who, sleuth-like, would as calmly as possible describe how her ploy had so quickly fallen apart.

"Now, let's bring Sidney into the equation, shall we? He's finicky, and if you know him like I do, you'll be aware that he's also a pain in the arse . . . anyhow, Sidney would never bring himself to purchase two rings of different carets of gold, in this case, by the looks of them, nine and eighteen. Neither would I, for that matter. So, my guess is that the engagement ring could be yours, but the wedding band belongs to someone else, possibly your mother?" Sam wasted no time in waiting for a reply; whoever she was, he wanted her to be aware that he may well be jetlagged, but he certainly wasn't going to sleepwalk into being fooled. "Now, let's discuss your name. You flunked your lines. It happens, believe me, it happens. And as this is a predominately Catholic country, my guess is that your immediate answer – 'Ma' – is either Mary or Maria, and as I've read somewhere that most girls are christened Maria, I'll go on Maria, and hazard another guess that Freya *is in fact the boy's mother*, which makes you possibly his elder sister or aunty?"

Sam leant back into his chair and sipped at his single malt. It was now for her to say if his assumptions were correct, and if so she had some explaining to do. He watched as she slowly raised her right hand and swept it across her forehead to remove a non-existent, hair away from her face.

"Yes, Mr Farmer, my real name is Maria, and Freya is my sister, Auner's mother," she answered. A look of dejection was etched across her face at having fallen at the first hurdle; but Sam needed to understand why she wanted him to think that she was the boy's mother.

"Please call me Sam. Whether you're the boy's aunty or mother, it makes us family."

He watched her lean back slightly then, cocking her head to one side, contemplating the significance of what he had said . . . and all the time not taking her eyes off him. "I told Freya I thought it was a dumb idea pretending to be her," she said. "She seemed to think because I work on a cruise ship as a singer and dancer then I must be able to act, but it didn't take you long to work out that I can't, did it Sam?"

"Ah, I thought you possibly had something to do with dancing," he said.

"How did you think that?" Maria questioned, again surprised at his powers of deduction.

"Cuban heels," he responded.

"What about Cuban heels?" Maria asked.

"You're wearing them." Again, her curiosity was aroused as Sam explained, "Estelle, my youngest daughter, when she was a teenager and having dancing lessons, made me buy her a pair of shoes that were very similar in design to yours." He laughed as he reminisced. "'Got to be *Cuban* heels, Dad! They have to have *Cuban* heels!' she'd begged."

"Is she a dancer now?" Maria asked.

"No, she went on to become an art restorer; but she still likes to cut a rug now and again. And you? I take it that you've left your cruise ship to support your sister and Sidney while we try and get the boy back?"

She shot a look at him. "Freya was right . . . you don't know, do you?" she said. Pausing only long enough to draw breath, she continued, "Three months ago, Sidney walked out on her, taking Auner with him. And yes, I'm taking a vacation to be with her." She looked down and chewed her bottom lip, obviously deeply concerned about the boy; but there was more on her mind, and Sam waited until she continued, "Freya is dying, Sam. Once Sidney knew she was very sick he left, leaving her all alone. She has cancer of the colon, and the only thing that is keeping her alive is her willpower and belief that she'll see Auner again soon – and it'll have to be soon, Sam!" Her tone was now desperate in its delivery. "She's got days left in her, that's all."

When Sam responded, it wasn't only with words. He rose to his feet and stood next to Maria, his outstretched hand guiding her to her feet. Maria felt his arms close around her and was cocooned in his embrace; she barely knew him, but was thankful for his comfort.

He began to speak with a tone that was as gentle as his hug, and he looked at Maria as he spoke, her head barely reaching his shoulders. "My wife Annie sadly died two years ago, and my daughters, in no uncertain terms, would always say that hollow words are no substitute for a cuddle." He felt the squeeze of her hands on his back acknowledging his caring words. "Come on, sit down," he said. "I've been kept in the dark about Freya's illness and Sidney walking out on her, and now I need to work out why."

"Freya is being kept in the dark too, Sam. That's why she asked me to be her. She hoped that you'd tell me what's really happening about getting Auner back. Sidney told Freya that it's because of you that Auner was taken. Something to do with your past."

Sam gasped at her statement, consciously winded that anyone would think or imply that he was to blame for the boy's abduction. "What the hell are you talking about?" Sam's retort was direct but quiet, aware that Maria was simply repeating what Freya believed to be true. "Auner was taken because *Sidney's past* has caught up with *him*, not my past," Sam continued. "Yes, I don't deny that I briefly met one of the men who has Auner - a nasty piece of work by the name of Button - but I put him in hospital soon afterwards. I can only surmise that Sidney is lying to portray himself as as much of a victim as Freya and the boy are. Believe me, he's good at manipulating people. It cost the life of our sister for me to find that out!"

Maria stared searchingly at Sam, letting her instincts guild her, wondering whether to believe him or not. "Sidney said that this man from your past, who has taken Auner, is demanding a million dollars for his release, and that you're here to pay the ransom," she said.

"Really? Is that so?" Sam replied, puzzled as to why Sidney told Freya it was only one million dollars, and making it sound as if *he* was paying it. He was equally mystified that Special Agent Spatz had told him that Button and his co-halt, Jones, had demanded nine million in cash, and then changed it to diamonds. Then the fog of Sidney's subterfuge began to lift enough for him to put daylight between the truth and his brother's lies. "Oh, Sam Farmer, you idiot!" he blurted.

"What? What is it? What are you thinking?" Maria asked, confused by his outburst.

"I was thinking I'm an idiot, that's what," Sam answered annoyed with himself for being duped by someone who he should have known couldn't be trusted. "Since I mentioned that Sidney is fastidious, a thought has been rattling around my thick scull about that word, because it has another meaning, you see?" He paused to give himself thinking time, and be sure that he was right. *Sidney is working a blinder on Spatz and the DEA . . . they're being conned by him,* he thought. He then sighed as another thought, another scenario, dug its heels in: *Spatz . . . could he be in cahoots with Sidney? If that's true, you know why, don't you Sam?* With those thoughts ringing alarm bells in his mind, and now aware it was more than a simple pay off to Auner's captors, he needed information that only one person could supply. "It's a shame your sister is so ill. I'd have dearly liked to talk to her."

Maria then looked into Sam's eyes, deeply, as if she was searching into his soul for a decision she had to make. "Wait here, will you. I have to make a private phone call," she said, leaving him to ponder.

When Maria returned, it was with a heavy frown of intent, and her voice was direct and impatient. "OK, Sam. Freya will talk to you but only if she's up to it. I've told her that she should trust you. She can trust you, can't she?"

Sam could see Maria was a little doubtful, naturally. *She* was clearly questioning her decision to trust a man she had known for less than an hour, a man that according to his brother was the reason why her nephew was kidnapped.

Sam responded by taking hold of Maria's hands and holding them in his, and with eyes that did not flinch he endeavoured to reassure her that she had done the right thing. "I promise on the lives of my two much-loved daughters that Freya and you can trust me . . ." he said quietly, "and you *must* trust me if we are to get Auner back alive."

Sam followed Maria into the taxi, confident that after realising what Sidney and possibly Spatz were up to, the notion that he was being watched didn't seem credible any longer. *Why?* he thought, *why would they?* Spatz had told him to stay inside the hotel for his own safety, and as far as the DEA man was aware, he had gone to bed to sleep off his jetlag. But his tiredness paled into insignificance as he listened with sadness to Maria speaking about her sister and how her life had been torn apart by disease, not to mention the treachery of her husband, his brother, who had once again double-crossed his family for his own ends.

With the sticky humid afternoon beginning to darken into an equally humid night, the taxi pulled up outside an apartment block in a suburb of Manila where urban decay and deprivation were like fingers that reached out to tear at the morality of his soul.

"Freya lives here?" Sam asked, cautiously slipping a twenty-dollar bill out from his wallet for the taxi fare.

"She does now, Sam," Maria replied with a resigned sigh. "Up until three months ago, they all lived in a plush apartment on the outskirts of a city called Alongapo. When Sidney abandoned Freya, he left her with no money. I'm paying the rent on this place. It's the best I can do."

Again Sam thought that sympathetic words would be pointless. What was required was action, and he felt that Freya herself held the answer as to how he could return the boy back to her before the ever-approaching cloak of death sadly descended.

Maria slipped her latchkey into the lock of the ground-floor flat; the sound of the oil-starved hinges as the door creaked open was almost lost in the din of a resident on the floor above shouting along the landing at children playing on the bare concrete steps. Sam looked up. The steps were littered with empty beer cans and discarded syringes.

They entered straight into the main living area, a room that despite being no larger than ten feet by twelve feet, functioned not only as the lounge, but also doubled as the kitchen. There was a shabby vinyl two-seater settee in the room, and a small table and two chairs. The only privacy from peering neighbours was a white sheet draped down from a curtain rail across the dirty window.

"I take it you sleep there?" Sam asked, looking across at an ex US Army camp bed along the wall by the window, an opened suitcase next to it serving as Maria's wardrobe.

"Yes . . . but it's OK . . . you get used to it after a while," Maria replied, her attempt to put a brave face on her temporary lot not wasted on Sam. He looked with disdain at what his brother's contemptible actions had resulted in. "Give me a moment, I'll see if Freya is OK to see you," said Maria quietly; but her hand had barely moved the handle on the bedroom door when they heard Freya's voice calling out for Sam.

Sam entered with vivid memories of how he'd cared for Annie who, like Freya, had refused to stay in hospital to die. She wanted to be surrounded by photographs of Auner as they gave her the strength to stave off the inevitable for another day. The scene before him was even worse than the mental picture of what he'd expected to see. The grim stagnant air, a cocktail of vomit, urine, faeces and stale perspiration, filled his nostrils and stung his eyes;

but he was able to respectfully restrain himself from placing his hands over his mouth and nose as they adjusted to the sensory assault.

Across the room lay Freya, the light from the shade-less bulb that hung from the ceiling unsympathetically exposing her wretched situation, stripping bare any final morsel of dignity. With a hand that she barely had the strength to lift, she beckoned him to sit on the edge of the bed next to her, and despite the fact that the cancer had spread to her liver, her jaundiced eyes revealed to him her hope that at last there was the one person she must trust – Sam Farmer – if she was to see her son again.

For someone who was near to the end of her life, Sam found Freya remarkably lucid, and although her voice was strained, she spoke with perseverance and clarity, all too aware that the sands of time were against her.

They say that every picture tells a story, and Sam was keen to listen to Freya who, though her photographs, described the life she and Auner once enjoyed, memories of events and places that were now her only link with her stolen son. Sam's attention was drawn to one particular photograph, that of a place she described as their 'hideaway'. *An appropriate name considering the present circumstances . . . but it couldn't be that obvious . . . or could it?* Sam thought.

She gestured to Maria to show him another item, a framed newspaper cutting. It wasn't hung on the wall like the others, but Sam's sharp eyes had spotted it partially concealed by a carrier bag, one of many that now represented the full extent of Freya's worldly belongings.

With it held in his hands, the sisters observed Sam with curiosity, unaware of its significance. A slow smile spread across his face as once again he took the long reach back to the edge of the vivid memory, when he and his sister Ruth were dubbed 'awesome' by their peers. The cutting was from the distant past when they were in their late teens, and it documented a decision they had both made, which to them seemed like the right choice.

"Sidney never spoke about you or your sister," said Freya, with a voice that suddenly sounded more laboured. "I found this in a drawer when I was tidying up at . . . home, and I asked Sidney about it, but he snatched it out of my hand and threw it to the ground, smashing the glass, as you can see. He then slapped me across my face shouting 'Like you, they're two stupid people who didn't know the true meaning of unrivalled!'" For someone so frail, and who deserved all the love and compassion in the world, not this terrible hurt and pain and disease, Freya gave Sam a pitiful gaze that, with ochre eyes, revealed a genuine and deep sadness. "Why does Sidney hate us?" she asked in almost a whisper.

"I don't know. Believe me, I've asked myself that same question for over twenty years," he replied.

Sam felt as if he had a chasm to cross to find the answer to that. One thing he did know was that Sidney wasn't the type of person to absorb himself in nostalgia; to him yesterday was history, only tomorrow mattered. *So*, he thought, *could the answer be staring at me from the two young faces peering out from the newspaper cutting? Why did Sidney find the need to frame it, yesterday's news, history?* He knew if he could find the answer to that, then he may be able to find out why Sidney turned from a loving brother into a man who would use anyone – family or friends even the DEA – to fulfil his single-minded desire to do whatever he pleased, no matter what the consequence to others, even his own son.

In the short time that Sam had spent looking searchingly at the scrap of newspaper, Freya had drifted back into a drug-induced sleep. Sam's heart ached. She was slipping ever farther away from her chance to see Auner one more time. Her wish to see the boy safe and well depended on him and how he used the time that was left before she died.

Chapter 26

"At times like this, shouldn't a priest be calling in on her to give her spiritual solace?" he asked.

Maria's reply was glum and despondent, almost echoing her sister's own thoughts: "She had a priest in Alongapo who would visit, but with Auner being taken, and the cancer, and your brother's abandonment making her live like this, she feels somehow that God has deserted her."

Maria watched as Sam placed a tender kiss on Freya's forehead. The idea that anyone, be it his brother or God, had deserted her, angered him.

"No one should end their life thinking that," he muttered.

He was aware that the taxi Maria had arranged to take him back to his hotel would be waiting; but having to leave made him feel as though he was turning his back on a woman who had come to view servitude as a vocation, and that being married to his brother, a position in life that had caused her to end her days in squalor, was her lot. As he went to leave, he gave Maria a parting kiss on her cheek, a gentle peck. Her response was a questioning look, a copycat stare like the one she had given him at the hotel when she questioned whether she could trust him.

"Wait, Sam," she ordered, "I have something for you." She retrieved an object about the size of a credit card from a small inner pocket of her suitcase, her makeshift wardrobe. "It's my portable hard drive. I keep all my music and dance routines on it," she said. With the seemingly innocuous piece of plastic grasped in her hand she held it up close to Sam's face in a gesture of boldness, and with words that laid bare the myth that Sidney was somehow superior to those who he saw as subordinates. "Your brother is scum, Sam. He thinks I don't know what he is. Look around you. You think Freya and me don't belong here, don't you? Well you're wrong, we do. These are our people. We were brought up in a dump much the same as this, where drug dealers like Sidney prey upon anyone, even using children to sell their shit."

In the desperately short time that had elapsed since he had met Maria, she had shown caution towards Sam, and much concern for her sister, but her indignant words, scornfully delivered, now revealed her to be a woman with a repressed anger, whose awareness of her surroundings made her a dangerous adversary should anyone cross her – and Sidney undoubtedly had.

"There's a file named EH112 which belongs to Sidney, and I'm trusting you to put it to good use."

"How did you get this?" he asked, and then almost instantly wished that he hadn't as her face portrayed an expression of utter desperation; instantly he was aware that she had had to demean herself to obtain it.

"Tell me, Sam, do you think one of your daughters would fuck a man she hated purely to obtain what she wanted?" She paused long enough for that thought to impact on him. "Sidney always wanted me, and he became quite forgetful about shutting his computer down, especially when I was on my knees in front of him . . . and he snores like the pig he is," she replied.

Sam knew that Sidney had reincarnated his Achilles heel – *Sammy* – to lure him to the Philippines; but it took a woman to exploit a man's time-old weakness to gain access to his brother's own Achilles heel: the kryptonite that could destroy him. And it was now that Sam must wisely use this gift of good fortune.

Chapter 27

The Tourist

Day Two

If Sam wanted to re-enter the hotel without being noticed (even if the reason was no longer an issue), he didn't count on the seemingly ever-present receptionist Louisa. From nowhere she popped up in front of him with a rather curious grin across her face, and with information that would once more deny him any chance of a quick nap before his rendezvous with Paco.

"Hi, Mr Farmer. It's lucky I saw you. I was just going off duty. I've been calling your room to tell you there's another lady to see you," she said with a concerned tone in her voice. "She's been waiting for over two hours, and looked pretty tired and upset that you weren't here, so I've put her in the lounge to wait for you like I did the other lady. Is that OK?" she asked.

Had it not been for the fact that it was his intention to enter the country unannounced, and he'd only booked his hotel during his stopover in Hong Kong, he would have made some witty quip about mystery women taking it in turns to see him; now it was beginning to seem like an open secret that he was in Manila.

"Yes, that's fine, thank you," he replied, slightly puzzled. "I'll go and find her. Did she give you her name by the way?"

"No, sir, she didn't, but she sounded as though you know each other."

Sam acknowledged Louisa's helpfulness with a smile and whispered, "Thank you."

"Sod this for a game of soldiers," he then muttered, making his way into the previously tranquil setting of the sprawling lounge, where earlier that day he'd met with Maria. Now it was a hive of frenetic activity with guests spilling out like a rising tide from the lifts, cocktail bars and the restaurant, along with the ebb and flow of attentive waiters, diligently keeping their visitors amply watered. For Sam, the thought of a needle in a haystack came to mind, and he felt too tired to trudge around the seemingly endless body of people, so he stood by the pillar of glass where his last mystery woman had waited, and hoped the iridescent glow would catch the eye of whoever she was and alert her to his presence.

Then something distracted him . . . the colour blue. It was a blue that was imbedded in his memory, but this time it was the gorgeous, distinctive deep blue of eyes that belonged to a woman who made him shudder at the realisation that she was there. But those eyes were not as he remembered them. The woman had changed from when he'd last seen her only a few months before. The palette of anxiety had replaced her natural, healthy glow that had once defied the need for make-up to enhance its beauty. Her bleak gaze, with dark rings around her eyes, told of days without sleep. Sam opened his arms to her, the desire to ask why she was there secondary to showing her that she had found her friend. With his hand slowly caressing her back, he felt her suddenly weeping in his arms, her stuttered breath straining to find the energy to talk.

"Sam . . . S-Sam . . . I-I don't know where t-to begin."

"Don't say anything more, we'll go to my room," he said softly. He needed to find out why Mila Faber was in his arms thousands of miles away from where he expected her to be, but first he had to get her away from the crowds. "Is this all you have with you?" he asked, taking her leather and blue canvas holdall.

With the traffic of people leaving or entering the lifts, and in the corridor, Mila hung on to Sam's arm intent on not being separated from him. Only when she reached the security of his room did she release her hold, to stand like a forlorn and lost soul drained of any ability for positive thought.

"Right, my girl, let's get you freshened up, shall we," Sam ordered; his quietly spoken but firm tone was a well-practiced approach, honed by having two daughters from whom he would have expected a robust debate had he shown any leniency in his voice. Mila knew that his fatherly direction was what she needed at that present time. "While you're having a shower," he continued, "I'll order us something to eat and make us a couple of stiff drinks from the mini bar . . . and then you can tell me what's happened."

Sipping at a vodka and Coke and wrapped in a hotel bath robe, Mila sat on the bed as she described in vivid detail why and how over the previous two days she had flown from London to Jakarta, Indonesia, where her husband Peter had been arrested by the state police, and then flown on to Manila in a desperate quest to find Sam.

"Don't be mad with Trudy, Sam, for telling me where you were staying. She said you'd only text the hotel details to her in case of an emergency. I was desperate, and I'm sorry."

"Don't be, and considering the circumstances, I would have done the same," he replied; but the fact that she was now there concerned him. The prospect of Mila staying wasn't an option, and going on what she'd just told him, he thought it was a fair assumption that she may have unwittingly become the bait to draw him into a trap that was planned in Jakarta, and most likely by his adversary Kazemi. "I'm booking you on the next flight home to London. It's too dangerous for you to stay here," he then declared. His no ifs and no buts demand hid from Mila the possibility of what he had to do, and if it went pear-shaped and he didn't die, he may also have to leave the country in a hurry.

Mila didn't argue; instead she lay down and closed her eyes, her exhaustion now too overwhelming.

He looked out across at Manila Bay from his balcony, a visual distraction to stave off his own tiredness. All that concerned him was that Mila caught the 8.40am flight for Hong Kong. Then on to London and far away from the world Sam had entered, a world where the likes of Button, Moses Jones and the Barber resided. Setting the alarm on his phone for 4.00am he placed it by the bed; Mila was fast asleep, the combination of jet lag and the traumas of the last two days etched into her face. He left his room shortly before 11.00pm, hoping that the next time he met Mila those beautiful blue eyes of hers would have regained their sparkle.

"Hi," said Paco, as Sam slumped into the seat next to him.

The car seat provided instant respite as the relentless desire to close his weary eyes overwhelmed him, and sleep was a welcome pause from the realities of why he was going to meet two men in the early hours of the morning. One of them he trusted beyond doubt; the other was someone he once thought he could trust - a shipmate from thirty-two years before who'd run away, leaving Sam alone to face the horrors of what Kazemi and the Barber had in store for him. The nudge-nudge of Paco's hand on Sam's shoulder brought to an end to that slumber; although it had been nearly two hours, it felt like two minutes to Sam. He couldn't stifle the yawn that followed.

"We're getting into Subic Bay . . . where do you want to go?" Paco asked.

"To South Marina," Sam replied. He coughed to clear his throat, and then continued with precise instructions: "When you arrive at the barrier, give the name Farmer, and it'll open for you. You'll need to go to the South Quay. You'll see a two-masted schooner tied up there. The skipper will be waiting for us."

The schooner came into full view as Paco parked the car as directed. The masts stood out, poles naked of their sails and backlit by the full moon radiating its glow over the marina. The rigging from the yachts chimed in the breeze, accompanying the sound of waves lapping against the schooner's hull. On the quayside waited a tall, well-built man, his pale blue canvas pumps, navy linen trousers and black T shirt blending into a bland grey against the shadow of the vessel's hull.

"You want me to wait here?" asked Paco, peering over the back of his seat.

Sam opened the door and prepared to meet a man who was another part of the jigsaw from his painful past. "No, I need you to come with me," he answered turning to be greeted by a man he hadn't seen for over thirty years.

"Hi, Farmer . . . it's been too long . . ." said the man quietly; the deep remnants of his Norwegian roots would normally bellow out like a sea horn in the fog, but not tonight.

"Hello, Henning," Sam replied, staring at him through the near-darkness. This was a man whom he had once despised. "Yes, you're right," he continued, "it's been far too long." Paco walked around the car to stand next to his temporary employer. "This is Paco, my new buddy," he added.

"Can we trust him?" asked Henning, giving Paco a worried stare.

"As much as I can trust you . . . And *he* hasn't let me down so far . . ." Sam pointedly replied, his venomous memories of the past getting the better of him.

The terse remark wasn't lost on Henning, now under no illusion that Sam still simmered with hurt remembering how his so-called friend had abandoned him the last time they had been together, and that that would take some healing. "You'd better come on board. Your brother-in-law, Oak, is waiting for you in my day cabin," he replied.

Once on the deck and with only the light of the moon, Henning guided his visitors towards the stern; for Sam, being on such a classic yacht was a welcoming distraction from the reason he was there. Then Henning led them down eight mahogany steps into a passageway with cabins and the galley leading off from it.

"Hi there, fella," came the unmistakable welcome from Oak; even in the relatively confined space of the cabin he still managed to give a suppressed version of his infamous bone-crushing hug.

"First things first. Where's the heads? I'm busting for a piss," Sam asked, his less than genteel manner swayed by a sense of urgency over politeness.

"Third on the left," Henning replied, gesturing with his head towards the door they had entered through. Shuffling himself into the cramped toilet compartment an aroma aroused his senses: the heady essence of a woman's perfume hung in the air.

Returning to the cabin, Sam sat with Paco on a green leather bench that was crafted around the curvature of the hull. He smiled at Henning, who was holding a bottle of Jack Daniels in his hand. "Whoever the lady was you've had on board, Henning, she sure has expensive taste in perfume. With three women in my life, I should know better than most!" he remarked unwittingly. (He didn't notice the surreptitious eye movements between Henning and Oak, who hoped that he wouldn't recognise that the fragrance belonged to his daughter Maggie, who'd only left to return to her hotel near to the marina less than an hour before.)

Sam was interested in learning more about his probationary friend's yacht charter business. The only contact he had had over the years was that each Christmas he had received a card and a short letter from Henning's mother in Norway. She knew what had happened to Sam but never gave up hope that one day he would forgive her son for not standing by his friend, as friends should, a circumstance that Sam hoped could be rectified as, once more, he needed to rely on Henning.

With every minute wasting away with idle chitchat, Sam casually knocked back what remained of his whisky, and exhaled as he prepared to breathe life into his plan regarding how they could rescue the young boy. This was a plan that entailed trusting three men; but he knew that only one of them, Oak, was beyond reproach.

Paco would be willing to dip his toe into trouble at a price . . . but up to his neck in it? That was something else. As for Henning, Sam felt he wanted to atone for deserting his friend . . . but again, to what extent? He now had a thriving charter business. If, like all those years before, it came to a matter of self-preservation, would history repeat itself? Then there was Oak, a man whose life had been torn apart by the suicide of his wife Ruth, Sam's twin sister. A life destroyed by the treachery of her own brother Sidney, who Sam was beginning to realise was embarking on a scam of self-interest and financial gain, possibly at the cost of the life of his own son Auner. He also knew and relied on the fact that Oak was prepared to kill to save the life of the child, and at the top of his list was Sidney; it was a blinding desire that Sam saw as a danger that had to be contained if any of them were to survive.

As for Sam, well all he wanted was to close two painful chapters in his life forever, ready to start a new one with Penny. But to do that, first he had to keep a promise to Freya before she died . . . and time was running out for her.

"OK, let's get down to business, shall we?" Sam said. With the information that Freya had given him - that was as much visual as spoken - he was reasonably sure he had worked out where his nephew was being held. But that was still pure hypothesis made on the basis of limited evidence. What Sam required was for someone to take a look . . . and he knew just the man . . . but first he had to get there. "Henning," Sam continued, requiring from the burly Norwegian his local knowledge, "there's a bay south of here, isn't there, called Sweetwater, and a river that runs down from the surrounding hills onto the beach?"

"Yeah, there is, and the river you mentioned is the Binanga. It flows through a plantation before it reaches the bay. Let me get the chart and I'll show you."

"Do you think that's where the kid is?" asked Paco; his enquiring tone had a tinge of surprise that Sam picked up on.

"Yes, why? Do you know it?" Sam replied.

"Sure do. My uncle was a US marine and stationed in Subic Bay when the Americans had their base here."

While they waited for Henning to return from the chart room, Paco spoke of the times when as a child he would spend his holidays at a bungalow near to the beach. It was similar in description to the one in the photograph that Freya had shown him. Paco continued, "When the base closed they weren't used so much. Most of them have gone now, either swallowed up by the plantation or demolished by developers who moved in and built beach resorts in the bay."

"I know for a fact that there's one still there," said Sam.

"Like I said, that may be so, and it would be at the north end of the bay by the plantation," Paco replied.

Yes, Paco's right, Sam," said Henning, with a navigation chart rolled tube-like in his hand. "Clear away there," he ordered, laying the chart across the cabin's table with his broad hands, flattening the curl of the corners with whisky glasses. "Any of the bungalows that are still standing would be on the edge of the plantation. That area to the north is supposedly national parkland now and can't be built on for commercial use. Recently one burnt down, and kids were blamed; but the truth is that over recent years, developers have muscled in wanting to expand the resorts along the whole length of the bay. If the one you're looking for is still there, it won't be for long."

"Well, we'd better find it, hadn't we, before it goes up in smoke," said Oak, glancing briefly at Sam. He then refocused on the chart. "I take it that there's a road?"

"Yeah," Paco eagerly replied. "It leads to the south of the bay and the resorts, but after about a mile there's an old single track road, that branches off to the north and through the plantation. It ends on the north side of the river. To get to any of the bungalows and the beach is a short walk across a timber foot bridge."

"Can you drop me off there on your way back?" Oak asked.

"I'll take you to where it branches off. It's about two miles from there," Paco cautiously replied; like Sam he thought that driving down a rarely used road in the early hours with the possibility of coming face to face with kidnappers was a bit more than dipping his toe . . .

"That's OK, fella, that's good enough for me. I'll make my way from there," said Oak.

"Is there anything else you need to know?" said Henning.

"Yep, sure is," Oak replied, giving Henning a long stare. "Where can I get a rifle from, no questions asked?"

He pouted his bottom lip and shook his head from side to side: a wordless "No."

"Any particular rifle you have in mind, mister?" asked Paco.

Oak replied without hesitation: "Yep, a .308 calibre Remington 700 with a Bushnell scope and a silencer. Can you get me one?"

"Got a pen and paper? I'll give you the address of my uncle, the marine. He's retired now and runs a gun shop in Alongapo City. He'll have everything you want." Paco turned to look at Sam, curious to know what his weapon of choice would be. "So, what do you want, gun or rifle?"

"Neither," Sam replied, showing Paco two clenched fists side by side in the stance of a prize fighter.

"Huh? They ain't gonna stop a slug," said Paco, half-laughing.

"Ah, but the trick is to fire these off before he pulls the trigger."

"You have to get close to him to do that. What makes you think he'll let you?"

"Would you believe me if I said vanity?" Sam's reply may have seemed naïve to Paco, but he knew Button's thirst to get even with him wouldn't be quenched by using a gun. If the thug reacted true to form, and working on that premise, then vanity would rue his day. For Sam that scenario was a bridge that would wait to be crossed. His immediate focus was to confirm that the bungalow was in fact where Auner was being held and to formulate a plan for them to get the young lad out alive.

Using his fingers as a pair of dividers, Sam measured the rough distance from where the schooner was birthed to Sweetwater Bay, a journey by motorboat he calculated at less than an hour, weather permitting.

"So, this bay, Sweetwater . . ." enquired Sam, directing his question at Henning, who was in the process of topping up three of the chart's corner weights with Tennessee Whiskey. It's aroma of sweet maple and charred oak conjured up the scene of a gambler playing his hand at the tables on an old Mississippi paddle steamer as it wound its way from Memphis to New Orleans. That, for Sam, fitted the setting he found himself in precisely. It was a gamble, a presumption based on the probability that he held an ace: he knew Sidney's flaw, or as gamblers call it, his 'tell'. "How long would it take you, do you reckon, to motor around from there to Manila bay, say, to the marina below my hotel?" Sam asked, only to pause while he savoured the refined taste of the unmistakable malt. "That's based on the assumption," he continued, "that you can get in and out of Sweetwater Bay in the dark without arousing any interest and not using navigation lights?"

With his hand moving across the chart in various directions like a glass on a Ouija board, Henning frowned as he pondered Sam's question. When it came, his reply was considered and well thought through: "Hmm. I've got a thirty-six-foot sports fishing boat, and she'll do thirty-five knots if you want to get from A to B in a hurry . . . that's as long as you don't look at the fuel gauge," he quipped, but his frown still remained fixed. "This coastline is awash with smugglers, drugs, people. You name it, it comes and goes out of Subic, so the authorities log all movements of craft in and out of the harbour." Stopping to put his glass to his lips, Henning gave a sweeping glance at the three men around the table, and with a deliberate jerk of his head sank his drink in one unflinching gulp. With a face that was windswept and ruddy in complexion, his eyes were now fired up with a glare akin to a pirate devising a devious plan. "I could inform the harbour master that I'm taking a party of tourists on a night fishing trip to a popular spot I know, and then on to Manila. There's a shipwreck, the *Osaka Maru*, she's a Japanese freighter that sunk after she hit a mine in 1944. She's nineteen nautical miles southwest from here, and she's near enough on the same heading as Manila. It'll be easy to make a detour into Sweetwater Bay en route. From there, and depending on the sea state, at twenty knots, it'll be a four to five-hour run to your hotel's marina."

"There you go, fella," said Oak, with an agreeable smile. "You said yourself this guy is going to be handy. It sounds to me that all we have to concern ourselves with now is, when?"

"Tonight," Sam replied, with a look of urgency. "It has to be tonight . . . My guess is that Mr DEA man, Spatz, should have received the ransom sometime today and will want to hand it over to Sidney as soon as possible and complete the deal. We must get the boy out before that happens."

"How much is the ransom?" asked Paco.

"Nine million dollars-worth . . . of diamonds."

"Wow, nine million in diamonds!" gasped Paco, his eyes now wide, pondering the thought of what he could do with just one or two of them. "I take it that those guys who have the kid and want to kill you have demanded that you deliver them, yeah?"

'Yes, my friend, they have," Sam answered, knowing that Paco and Henning only knew about the boy being kidnapped by two men, and that one of them, Button, also intended to kill him. The thing that Sam neglected to mention was that the other man, Moses Jones, wouldn't let the child go free even after they had the diamonds. Moses Jones was already a convicted child killer, and Sam knew leopards never change their spots.

Henning loomed over Sam, the bottle of whisky poised to refill their glasses; but his question wasn't whether his guest wanted a top up - he was getting that like it or not - it was to do with the welfare of the child. "Are you sure the kid is still alive? It's not unheard of on these islands for people to be killed long before the ransom is paid, and all relatives get for their money is a corpse," he said.

Sam swung his gaze from Henning to look at Paco, who had a bottle of ice-cold lemon soda warming in his hand. The bleak look etched across his face showed that he agreed with Henning's opinion that Auner may already be dead.

"Oh we're sure, fella," Oak boomed, addressing Henning's question forcefully with the intention of putting an end to that idea. Oak knew Sam too well to not realise that if he, for a moment, thought Auner was dead, they wouldn't be sitting in a ninety-two-year-old schooner in the early hours of the morning planning on how to rescue him.

"So how are you going to get this DEA guy to delay you handing over the diamonds?" Henning asked, his stare giving Sam nowhere to hide.

"Don't know yet, but I'm sure if I need to, I'll think of something," Sam replied with a sly wink of the eye.

By the time, Sam returned to his hotel room, with a laptop computer and a mobile phone that he had borrowed from Henning, it was approaching 7.00am. Mila had gone to catch her flight back to London but had left a note, and Sam knew even before he read it, that it would be a plea for him to help get her husband released from the clutches of Kazemi.

"One problem at a time, Sam, one problem at a time," he muttered, slumping down across his bed; it was calling at him like a mermaid, enticing him into a deep, deep sleep; but it was sleep that he knew once again had to wait. *Right, let's go for a swim before Spatzy turns up,* he thought.

"Thank you," Sam replied with a small smile to the waitress, as the wonderful aroma of the fresh coffee she had just poured gently wafted around by the light morning breeze coming off the bay. The chaos of the city he had witnessed the day before now seemed like a world away as he sat on the veranda by the swimming pool in relative seclusion, with only four of the twenty or so other tables being occupied by guests having their breakfast. He purposely sat near to the low glass screen that bordered the pool and outside eating area. It's view of the harbour, and particularly the hotel's small marina almost directly below him, was of particular interest; but his observation was interrupted by the recognisable monotone voice of a man who had approached from behind him: "Good morning, Mr Farmer. I trust you have caught up on your lost sleep?" The American's hand briefly rested on Sam's right shoulder as he walked past to then stand opposite him blocking out the view that Sam so wanted to concentrate on.

Spatz stood there, stiff and imposing, the tight-fitting pale green cotton shirt that he wore over his muscular torso an intimidating statement that showed that, despite being in his fifties, he was still in good physical shape. With a wry smile, Sam wondered if Spatz once had had aspirations of being a showman before becoming a law enforcement officer, noting that at his cottage when they first met, and even in the hotel's lift taking him to his room, Spatz couldn't resist to signature his appearance with a subconscious caricature of James Cagney.

"Yes, I did, thank you. I slept like a proverbial log. Please . . . pull out a chair and join me for breakfast. Mmm, it's very good," said Sam munching away at a piece of buttered toast.

"No thanks, just coffee," Spatz replied, pulling out a chair. He then spun it around to straddle it, and rested his arms crisscross over the backrest.

The Long Reach Back

God, you have to be so bloody different, don't you? Sam thought in bemusement at another of the DEA man's actions.

"So, what's the latest on the items that you're waiting for? Do we have a go, no go? Isn't that what they say?" Sam's slightly flippant question was asked with the intention of not sounding fazed regarding whether the gems had arrived or not. For him, if there was any expectation, it was waiting for his own, go, no go phone call from Oak, who he hoped by now, had found the bungalow and confirmed Auner was inside, alive. Then he would have to lie through his teeth to distract Spatz and his brother from his own plan; or as Penny would call it, acting!

When it came to performing, Sam knew Spatz would want to continue to take centre stage; and he wasn't wrong, as the DEA man replied in a reluctant manner, wanting to make Sam feel he should be grateful for being kept in the loop.

"They're arriving by courier tonight from our office in Chicago," he said. "Then tomorrow we'll get the remainder of the information we want from your brother."

Good, it's on, we go for the boy tonight, Sam thought, relieved. The more he thought about it, the more he was convinced that he was being set up. Once Spatz handed the diamonds over to his brother in exchange for the information he promised, Sidney would have no intention of giving them to him to free the boy, even though he was his own son. If he was going to save Auner, then he had to do it before Sidney got his hands on the so-called ransom, or the child would surely die at the hands of Moses Jones, no ifs or buts about it. "The remainder of the information?" Sam questioned, eager to know more. "So, what has he given you so far, that is worth knowing?" Sam wondered just how much of a carrot Sidney had dangled in front of the DEA. Enough to stump up nine million dollars-worth of diamonds for?

"Can't tell you that," answered Spatz, reaching forward for his cup of coffee, the handle a redundant fixture. He paused with the rim shadowing his lips, and with a heavy frown set upon his face, he then spoke in a cold intimidating tone: "If I did, then I'd have to kill you."

Sam had not expected anything less than for the man to use a touch of the dramatics in his answer, and like most people at some time or other, he had also used those words, but purely in jest. He had the feeling that Spatz wasn't joking, however. He pondered whether this was because Mr Special Agent was just doing his job, and had fired a warning shot across his bows in order to protect the DEA's investment in Sidney. Or was he? Sam returned a spear-like smile in response to Spatz's words, but again he wondered: *was Spatz in fact protecting his own personal involvement with his brother?* Sam knew he had to probe further to find out. *Just whose side are you on?* he thought.

"All things considered, I think it odd that my brother is prepared to hand over any information to you before he gets his son back. Sidney's a snake. I'm surprised you trust him. Don't you think it odd?" Sam then said.

"No," Spatz replied defiantly. "Your brother's arse is in a sling Mr Farmer, and he knows that. To get our help he had come up with some of the goods first, and the rest before we hand over the stones to him. Our business with him ends once he hands over the data and we confirm it's kosher."

"How long is that likely to take? Hours? Days?" Sam asked.

"An hour. Then that's it for us – we're done. It's then up to you and your brother to deliver the ransom and get his kid back."

While the waitress refilled their coffee cups, Sam had a moment to consider what Spatz was telling him; he realised he wasn't in the loop after all, but on the outside looking in.

"Forgive me if I'm wrong," Sam swiftly interjected before his breakfast guest could continue further, "but you said that part of the deal is Sidney and his family get to live in the States with new identities once we get the boy. So, who is going to watch my back while I hand over the ransom to Button and Jones? I thought you lot were?"

"Sure, it's all arranged. They'll be part of our relocation program," replied Spatz. "That ain't to say that the DEA are gonna get involved in getting the kid back . . . that's your job."

"Oh, I see. This is your way of squaring the circle, is it?" Sam hissed. "Like you once said, you don't aid and abet with drug dealers. So how do you explain away the nine million in diamonds? Expenses?"

"Investment, Mr Farmer, investment. Worth every dime if it helps the DEA to close down drug routes into the US."

Surprised by Spatz's candour, Sam wondered just how forthright he would be when it came to answering a question a little closer to the bone. "So, what's in store for you when you've bagged the baddies, wife and retirement?" he asked.

Sam could instantly tell that a nerve in what Spatz considered was his impregnable skin had been touched. He leant slightly back as if his seating position had become uncomfortable, but it was his jaw muscles that gave him away. Their involuntary tensing pulled at his jowls to show a more defined and intimidating jawline. "Why do you ask?" he retorted, his tone seizing on the fact that Sam had dared broach the subject in the first place.

"Well, just curious really. Everyone has a use-by date, especially in your line of work." Using the information Archie had supplied him, Sam couldn't resist probing Spatz's thick skin a little further, and this time with a verbal stick. "I reckon you must have pissed someone off big time to be handed this job."

"Huh, is that so?" came the curt response. It implied that Spatz intended to bring to an end any further discussion on his future employment plans, and his breakfast meeting with Sam. He stood up, returning his chair to its original position, and reached out his hand to Sam; the strength of the grip made Sam feel that he was being tested, by the American bearing down on him.

Chapter 27

"So, when do I get to see Sidney? Sometime today, I take it? Not that I'm looking forward to it," Sam asked.

"That's up to you two, Mr Farmer. He knows you are here, why not give him a call? I'll text you his cell phone number but, like I said, arranging the exchange is not our concern." Now Spatz couldn't resist one more change of persona, this time from a DEA man who liked to overplay his self-importance, to a cop with eyes at the back of his head. "One word of advice." Again, Spatz paused, unable to resist the urge to carry the scene. "Sleepwalking can be darn dangerous . . . just make sure if you do it again you don't screw up the DEA's deal with your brother."

Sam should have felt concerned that Spatz somehow knew of his nocturnal activity, but he didn't. Instead he smiled, as the knowledge was laced with a sense of relief. A nagging question had just been answered: Sidney didn't have Spatz in his pocket. But that raised another problem: if what he thought was true, and his brother had planned to rip off the DEA for nine million dollars, then when was the best time to inform Spatz that Sidney was conning him? He couldn't say anything yet. It was too soon. Button or Jones would, without doubt, kill Auner, and, like Sidney, would disappear. He had to stick to his plan . . .

He thought back to when Penny had taught him how to conquer his shyness of playing his guitar in front of people, and her words were now ringing in his ears: *'Timing and concentration, Sam. Timing and concentration.'*

Chapter 28

Distant Glow

Undeterred by the fact that Spatz was aware of his 'sleepwalking', Sam still left the hotel via the kitchens. He knew that within twelve hours he would either be on a flight out of the country . . . or dead. The latter was not an outcome he envisaged, or one that swayed his determination that the ghosts from his harrowing past, alive and incarnate, who had destroyed, scarred, manipulated or murdered, must once and for all be silenced. This had to end now. Today.

"No need to come on board this time, Paco, I won't be long," Sam said.

"Sure thing, Mr Farmer," he replied as the masts of the schooner once more came into view.

A more menacing dark backdrop had replaced the milky light of the moon from the night before and Sam strained his eyes into the darkness to see.

"What's happened to the weather, Henning, it's not going to be a problem, is it?" Sam asked, gazing in the direction of the pontoons at crafts of various types and sizes. They were dancing at their moorings, yawing and pitching, pulling at their tethers, a monotonous clanking and whistling like unruly sirens from the deep now replaced the gentle clatter of the rigging of the previous night.

"It's a squall, blows in from the east. Give it a few hours and it'll be as calm as a millpond out there," Henning roared, and with a swagger that was in sync with the roll of the deck, he and Sam made their way below. "Oak is in the galley getting himself something to eat. I suggest you do the same, Sam. It's going to be a long night."

"Here, fella, I've saved you some," said Oak, pointing at a plate of sandwiches. "Don't know what the meat is . . . apparently, they eat dog in these parts. If it is, then it's a mongrel," he laughed; but Sam knew that as a hunter in the beloved forests of his native Ontario, Oak was a master at survival. He had to be to endure, sometimes for weeks on end, tracking and checking deer for the regional government, and if that meant eating squirrels, raccoon or even dog, then he would. Whatever the contents were between the two hearty slices of white bread, Sam sat down on a bench seat opposite his brother-in-law but declined the offer. He did have a hollow feeling in the pit on his stomach, but it wasn't pangs of hunger – it was nerves churning at his gut in anticipation for what lay ahead.

"Well, if you ain't gonna eat, I bet you'll not turn your nose up at this," Henning exclaimed, his words followed up by a thud as a bottle of dark Jamaican rum landed on the galley table in front of him. Three shot glasses that were balanced on the tips of Henning's fingers like thimbles appeared to then summersault into the upright position. The three glasses were filled to their brims, so much so that only steady hands could put them away without a drop being wasted. Henning lifted his first then halted in mid-flight as he glanced at his two companions. "Skal!" he toasted, and with an almost mechanical movement of his elbow and wrist disposed of its contents in one effortless gulp. Within moments the echoing sound of the three now empty glasses rang out as their upturned rims were plonked downwards onto the table top. The deep intake of satisfying breaths from the three men soothed their senses, causing a distracting veil from the task that had brought them together.

But there was no doubt it was a task that Oak had now to lay out for Sam. He produced a piece of paper from the breast pocket of his hunting vest, and spoke with the tone of a hunter who had stalked his prey to their lair: "Your buddy Paco was right about the outlay of the bungalow," he said, ending his sentence with a dismissive huff, "if that's what he's calls it. It ain't no log cabin, that's for sure, more of a shack with a rusty corrugated roof."

Sam's eyes were inadvertently drawn to his manicured fingernails as he raised his replenished rum glass, and noticed that they were trimmed right back to the skin - necessary attention to detail, as the sound of fingernails against gunmetal could carry even amidst the nocturnal noises calling out from the canopy of the plantation. With the aroma of distilled molasses from the rum flaring his nostrils, Oak poured over the floor plan of the shack that he had roughly sketched, with Sam picturing in his mind every minute detail, from the terrain to the colour of the drapes that hung across the French windows.

"Once our friend Paco drops us off," Oak continued, "it's a brisk forty-minute walk along the track to the bridge. From there it's another two minutes to the shack. We'll come up from the rear. There's no back door just two windows; one is the bathroom, the other is the bedroom. The kid's in there, asleep on the floor."

"How do you know that? How can you be sure it's the kid?" Henning asked.

Oak only gave Henning a fleeting glance, and instead he rounded his stare on Sam. With a heavy frown, he said, "Sam knows how I track an animal, don't you, fella? One of my methods is an old Indian way. I follow their perfume - by that I mean their piss. Deer, bear, moose, they've all gotta piss, and it's all different; even a man's piss is different to that of a woman's, and a child's – theirs is sweeter. The shack . . . bungalow . . . whatever you want to call it, is built on top of low stilts. I managed to crawl underneath. Its bare floorboards are covered in some sort of hessian matting. Unless they've got a woman holed up there who's soaked in her own piss, then it's the kid."

Oak's words brought a moment of silence as each man

confronted his own sense of despair at the thought of what the five-year-old boy must be enduring after so many days of being held captive by two of the nastiest men on God's earth.

"OK, so you found the boy . . . but what of the two men who have him? Did you see them?" asked Henning, who split his questions between Oak to Sam. "That's what you said, Sam, wasn't it? Two men?"

"Only one of them," Oak replied. "A black guy. And he seemed to be keeping watch, drinking beer - and by the caseload by the looks of all the empty cans that I came across. I think the other fella was asleep on a settee in the middle of the lounge. I could hear heavy snoring. As much as I could make out, there's a small kitchen area down the far end on the left, then the bathroom and the bedroom on the right."

"The man outside . . . that'll be Moses Jones," Sam answered. "He'd most likely have a gun and would know how to use it; whereas Button, even if he does have one, he'll not use it on me – I know him. 'Putting a slug into me', as Paco would call it, isn't what he'd have in mind."

"Well, I wish I shared your confidence, Sam. Over here men with guns use them!" Henning's brash retort wasn't lost on Sam, who was aware he was openly showing what he and Oak were trying to conceal: nerves.

"So, what's the front of the place like?" Sam asked, pointing his finger to an area on Oak's drawing marked with a shaded box.

"French windows that open out over the bay. There's a six-foot wooden veranda - that's where your Jones fella was sitting. It runs the full width of the shack, about twenty feet or so, and in front of that are grassy sand dunes that slope down to the beach. Laying down in the dunes, I reckon from sixty, sixty-five feet away, I'll have a clear shot at anything that moves. Further away, then I'll have to take the shot standing up."

"Why don't you get closer, say up to the veranda, then you

can rush them can't you?" Henning asked, his voice now clearly showing signs of anxiety.

"No!" Oak boomed. "Sam has to somehow get the drapes open so that I can see my targets inside. If I get too close, I'll become one."

"Sorry, have I missed something here? It sounds to me that Sam's going in on his own and you're staying put outside?" asked Henning.

"Yep," Sam answered, "that's exactly how it's going to be."

"What? You just gonna knock on the door and invite yourself in?"

Now Sam saw the same look of fear in Henning's eyes as he did all those years before when he ran off leaving his friend to be arrested. The possibility that the Norwegian was going to bottle out again was a risk he had no option but to take.

"Look here, fella," Oak then said, aware like Sam that Henning was a key element on saving the boy and needed to be reminded of that, and fast, "this guy ain't stupid enough to walk in through those doors if we weren't there to cover his back. You gotta trust me and Sam. We know what we've gotta do and we need you be there on your boat waiting for us. You will be, won't ya?" came the pointed ask from Oak, taking hold of Henning's right forearm as if to say, *we must stick together. No running away this time.*

"Yeah, yeah, sure I'll be there. It's just I didn't imagine Sam being so dumb and handing himself to them on a hook like a piece of bait."

"Got it in one," replied Sam, showing Henning a smirk of a smile. "That's exactly what I want them to think. Like you said, who would be stupid enough to turn up without backup? Besides, I'm banking on another man turning up before any harm comes to me, and by then I may have levelled the playing field a bit."

Through the spilled light from the headlamps, Paco stood in front of the hired car smiling nervously at the two men he had come to like in the last twenty-four hours, and especially Sam, with whom he felt he now had a mutual trust.

"OK, young man, you know what to do. I'll see you again as arranged," Sam said. Gone was Sam's usual firm business-like handshake; instead he clasped Paco's hand caringly, as a father would say farewell to a son.

"Come on, fella, we'd better be on our way," whispered Oak, and with a rifle now slung across his back, was eager to slip into the surrounding habitat. For him, repeating the same walk he had made the night before - along a rarely used track in the blackness of night - only served to hone his senses. He set the pace for Sam to follow close behind, and in silence, the need to talk replaced by the need to arrive at their destination unannounced. Oak got them to the footbridge within a minute of the time he said it would take to get there. They savoured the breeze that blew in from the direction of the bay. It cooled their sweat-soaked bodies after the claustrophobic canopy of the plantation. After a handshake that said 'good luck', both men now knew they were on their own, and each with a synchronized timetable that would only start once another piece of Sam's jigsaw from his past had arrived.

Sam watched as Oak, his rifle now clasped firmly in his right hand, quietly walked across the footbridge and then disappeared like an apparition into the night. With a glance at his wristwatch, Sam knew it was now time for him to make his move, starting with two phone calls. The first one was to Sidney. Convinced that his brother was double-crossing him, he put his suspicion to the test. If Sidney did what he told him to do, then Sam knew he was right! (His version of walking up to the bungalow and knocking on the door.) The dozy 'hello' was the cue that Sam needed.

"Sidney, it's Sam. Don't bother saying anything, just keep quiet and listen. Tell those two goons in the bungalow that I'm outside and have come for the boy. Have you got that?"

"What about–" blurted Sidney, only to be cut off mid-stream

by his brother who was in no mood for conversation, not just yet.

He hoped his next call would be his ticket home. The call went straight to voicemail, and again he wasted no time on chitchat: "Spatz, it's Sam Farmer. It's now 1.20am. Be at the safe house where you have Sidney at ten this morning and bring the diamonds." Sam then broke the phone into two pieces and threw it into the river, aware that like his own, the one that Henning gave him could also be tracked.

By the time, he had walked cautiously from the footbridge to stand in front the wooden steps that lead onto the veranda from the dunes, Moses Jones was waiting for him. Sam now knew, Sidney had failed the test. Moses Jones stood next to the open French widows with the drapes that Oak had described partially pulled across. The shaft of light escaping from between them cast an eerie shadow behind Sam like the gnomon on a sundial. He stood there and waited without saying a word; there wasn't much he could say at that moment. They already knew why he was there, and with Jones pointing his semi-automatic pistol straight at his face, it seemed a sensible decision. Jones then shuffled sideways, stopping in front of the drapes, and beckoned Sam with two flicks of his gun to walk towards him. No sooner had Sam stepped across the veranda, he was forced to stop. With the muzzle of Jones' Glock 19 now pressing hard into his cheekbone, the need to be compliant was, at that moment, his only option. Jones stepped slowly backwards into the lounge still with the weapon threatening to blow Sam's teeth out through his ear.

As the first words left the Jamaican's lips, fractious and demanding, Sam felt that a plague of vermin had attacked his senses: Jones' breath stank. The forty-eight-year-old had a distinctly unhealthy appearance. His dreadlocks were dyed an unflattering burgundy-red and smelt as bad as his breath. What a wretched person he truly was. Now Sam had to breathe the foul air in the room that reeked just like he did, and of beer and cigarette smoke.

"Who else is out there? Don't bullshit me mon, or I'll drop yer where yer stand."

"No one. If there was, you'd be dead by now," Sam replied, following that lie with an unflinching and intimidating stare back at Jones. Despite the fact that there was a pistol agitating the air around his face, he felt calmer than he thought he would be. So far what he hoped would happen, had happened: he had made it to the lounge and was still alive.

"If he dies, so does the kid," came the reply; but it wasn't from Jones, his mouth had remained closed, for now letting the Glock do his talking.

Sam leant slowly to his right to gaze behind his gun-toting intimidator to put a face to the distinctive accent that could only be one man: Button.

"Bring him over here and keep his hands behind his back," Button ordered.

Now Sam could clearly see for himself the Button *he* had turned him into. He still bore unsightly scar tissue above and below his right eye, wounds that also continued across his cheek and under his chin. His flesh was torn apart by ferocious punches that were, for Button, like battle honours that he thought enhanced his hard-man persona. But those disfigurements were eclipsed by his *piece de resistance*: titanium teeth, a grisly demonstration of insanity bordering on the psychotic.

But that was nothing compared to the awful sight that now greeted Sam. He shuddered in revulsion at a scene that was as pitiful as it were degrading, a sight that burnt away any notion that kindness had been extended towards the five-year-old child, his nephew. When Oak informed him that Auner was probably soaked in his own urine, he didn't imagine for a moment that he would be also be naked and soiled in excrement. Button stood with the entrance to the bedroom at his back. He held Auner to his hip, his left hand grasped across the boy's mouth and nose. Only his eyes were visible, eyes that should have been full of childish mischief and sparkle were now barely alive, dulled and dilated by drugs. In Button's right hand he held a military-style lock knife, with only his thumb preventing the blade from cutting the boy's throat – an action that Sam knew Button was clearly capable of.

Sam's whole body now raged with adrenalin-fed anger at seeing the condition of the child. He felt the desire to break free from Jones' firm hold and lash out at Button with even nastier venom than years before; but there was an obstacle: Auner. With Button's thumb the only barrier that was keeping the boy alive, Sam realised he had to restrain himself from such a knee-jerk reaction and instead use a ploy that would have him, for the sake of a child's life, try to manipulate the evil mind of Moses Jones. He had to play Moses Jones's desire for Auner off against Button's. A desire he hoped would, for the time being, free the child from the clutches of Button long enough for him to have the time and opportunity to erupt the cauldron of malice that was now simmering within his whole being.

With his arms held behind him, and forced up and against his spine, Sam focused his gaze on Button's face, a face that glared back at him in a frenzied scowl.

"Your pal here behind me," said Sam, struggling to speak as coolly and suggestively as he could. "I'm sure he won't take kindly to you slitting the kid's throat . . ."

Sam left his words hanging in the air for Moses Jones to think about, and to gasp for breath through the pain as his captor increased the pressure of his torturous hold.

"Oh, don't you worry, mon, that kid's mine," said Jones, sniggering into his ear with a bravado that fired his accomplice's glee with the knowledge that Sam was there to die . . . maybe not by *his* hands . . . but that didn't inhibit Button from his burning desire to inflict pain on Sam that would not only be physical – payback for smashing his face – but a terrorising emotional pain that would goad him.

Despite Sam's racing pulse pre-empting what was to come, the only heartache he experienced was for Auner, who he watched being manhandled by Button back into the loneliness of the darkened bedroom. Within moments of the door being slammed shut, Button laid his first punch, a swinging haymaker to Sam's face, landing on the brow of his left eye with such impact that it made his head wrench to the right. Two more blows quickly followed, this time a left and a right to his stomach. In great pain, Sam felt the air driven from his lungs. Button continued with one more and then another two in quick unyielding succession. This time they crashed into his ribs with a body-twisting force that almost brought him to his knees.

"Go easy there, bro, he's ready to drop," said Jones, his voice now sounding a warning to the man opposite him, who was shuffling and side-stepping like a boxer in front of a defenceless opponent, lashing out blows at will. "Remember what the mon said," Jones continued, "this guy is for him, and he's not to be harmed."

"Oh fuck him!" spouted Button dismissively. With eyes ablaze with hatred he spat into Sam's face.

Then Button, as if he were a coin, flipped to show his other side, a new face, a calmer pose than that of seconds before. Now he inflicted on Sam a verbal reminder of why he was called 'the thug', a description he wore with pride, a self-made position of evil he acted out on innocent people's lives. "How's that bitch of an actress of yours, these days?" he asked. They were nettled words that were intended to sting Sam to his very core. "Got over her next-door neighbour getting done in has she? You should have seen the old girl go down. I swear when her head hit the road it bounced like a ball." With a satisfying smirk now glowing from his vicious face, Button took a step teasingly closer to Sam, intent on feeding off the painful gasps coming from his captive's mouth, and goading him yet further. "Getting back to that bitch of yours," Button continued, "I heard that you know that it was me who got her to crash your car. Ace, it was. It was meant to be you. No matter though . . . if at first, as they say . . ."

Button paused, and then glanced over Sam's shoulder giving his accomplice a satisfied nod as if to confirm what both men had planned. "Me and Moses here, we've been talking about her and those daughters of yours, and we reckon we can turn that bitch into a basket case. When I leave here, I'll go back and do her aunties like I done the old lady . . . oh yes, and her dog. Then I'm going to call on those pretty girls of yours. I've got friends who'll turn them into crack heads in no time. They'll be fucking anyone for their next fix, I promise ya. That'll fuck her mind up good and proper, she'll spend the rest of her days bouncing off padded walls, you mark my words. Shame you won't live to see it."

Button's boast only confirmed what Sam had feared: that all those he loved would themselves become victims to the depraved that gathered on this island. Sam closed his mind to Button's bluster, and put into play a plan that now meant putting his faith in two men: one who was not yet present, an adversary whose evilness even surpassed those of Moses Jones and Button. The other was Oak, reliable and true to their friendship, a man who Sam knew was out there, like the hunter he was, listening, watching, waiting for the right moment to close the trap on their prey with Sam inside as the bait.

Now, with his fists clenched to his chest, Button was posturing in a slow trance-like weaving motion, salivating at the imagery of what he'd described. But he was distracted by Sam's uncompromising rejoinder: "Ha! Are you aware that the police back home call you Metal Mickey because of your stupid teeth – which, by the way, I'm going to knock so far down your throat that they'll need a metal detector to find them."

Sam showed Button a nonchalant grin, and then prepared himself for the reply, which wasn't long in coming: "Like fuck you are!" he spouted. The words were accompanied by a stinging thump to Sam's face, again landing on his brow and this time breaking the skin above his left eye. With the punches now beginning to hurt more than he let on, Sam knew it was time to take Button out of the equation. With the memory of Cissy, Penny's nosey but kind neighbour prominent in his thoughts, let alone the terror he had inflicted on Auner, Sam felt no qualms for what he was about to do. Taking another blow to his face, Sam slumped forwards, his arms straining at the hands of Jones.

Thinking Sam was concussed, Jones relaxed his hold on Sam's muscular frame to let him drop to his knees. Good fortune for Sam; bad news for Button. Even with arms that now felt like lead, he eyed his target, and with a rolled fist he quickly slipped Jones' hold to strike out a punch like a whip into Button's groin.

"*Anaiah*! Fuck you, you ass-hole!" screeched Button, but those were the last legible words that anyone was to hear from him again. Now grasping his crotch instead of pounding Sam's face, he stooped in pain to unwittingly align his jaw for Sam's second blow, a blow that neither swung nor looped. Sam unleashed his fist so straight and powerfully that Button's face crumpled under its force, an impact that undid all the hours of surgery that had been necessary to put his face back together the last time their paths had crossed.

As he rose to his feet, Sam wasn't sure if it was the crack to the back of his head from the butt of Jones' pistol, or the pepper spray that was squirted into his eyes that brought him once more to his knees. Either way he was down and blinded, coughing and gasping for breath with the sensation that his face was on fire. Body spasms then kicked in, forcing him into an uncontrollable desire to lie in the foetal position. After that everything was a blur. He knew he had been dragged along the floor to another room, and that his hands had been trussed up in front of him.

Sprawled on the floor and with his watery eyes still smarting as if pins were being driven into them, Sam blindly explored his cell. He stretched out his legs and shuffled around until his feet came into contact with what he hoped would be a wall. With a little more shuffling, and using his bound hands to clumsily survey the surface, it didn't take him long to realise that he was in the bathroom. He felt the cold smoothness of porcelain and reached out to identify the toilet pan. Raising himself to his feet with the aid of his elbows on its seat, he ventured to his right, hopeful that he would come in contact with the basin and was able to bathe his eyes. He could sense there was a light of some sort coming from somewhere, as its brightness seeped through his reddened eyelids. Suddenly, and about to fall sideways, he crouched down aware he had bumped into the side of the bath. Leaning tentatively to the left he slid his hands along and around the rim until at last he found a tap. Slowly he managed to crack it open, pausing as a greaseless squeak pricked his ears. As he awkwardly managed to collect water with bound hands, it was his sense of taste and smell that returned to him first from the obnoxious chemicals in the pepper spray. Sam then became aware of a sweet taste on his lips, and a tainted smell, strong and odorous like rotten eggs or worst still . . . flesh? With his mind racing, he hurriedly cleansed his eyes. He then opened them, painfully, and what he saw caused his heart to pound hard in anger and heavy with despair. A sorrowful moan escaped his lips at the sight of a corpse that had been his friend Mila, her naked, mutilated body bathed in her own congealed blood.

"Hell is empty and all the devils are here," he muttered, almost instinctively quoting Shakespeare at the gruesome and wretched act that had taken place.

Sam dropped to his knees and looked into Mila's eyes, those beautiful, mesmerizing dark blue eyes that were now redundant opaque orbs staring out from death. Sam was oblivious to the door opening and Moses Jones calling to him to come. Only the prod of the pistol to the side of his face stirred him from his grieving stupor. He turned his head lethargically to look up at Jones, and with an absent gaze then turned away and gently, with his bound hands, closed Mila's eyes from the world she had so brutally left.

Being prodded back into the lounge, his thoughts reeling with remorse, he didn't register at first that another man had arrived. He was looking down at Button lying on the settee in a semi-conscious state. Only the faint sound of gurgling coming from what remained of his face indicated any sign of life.

"Ah, Señor Farmer, at last we meet again. Please," said the man calmly, his left hand pointing to a dining chair that had been positioned in the middle of the room.

"No thanks. If it's all the same, I'll stand," Sam replied, struggling to concentrate on the present after what he had seen in the bathroom.

"As you wish, señor, but we can't have you running away," said the man, stepping closer. The spicy fragrance of his aftershave failed to distract Sam from the stench of death that filled his nostrils. "Please, señor, I need your belt . . . or can I call you Samuel?" he asked.

"No, no one calls me that anymore. Farmer will do," replied Sam as the man slipped the black leather belt from around his waist and passed it to Jones' out-stretched hand, the pistol in the other still pointing at Sam's head.

"Your brother does señor, but no matter, Farmer it is," said the man with a courteous nod. He continued, "Please forgive me. I haven't introduced myself. I neglected to do so the first time we met. My name is Rodrigo Domendez, or you may know me as the Barber."

Sam made no effort to reply straight away. He had waited thirty-two years for this moment, and now time stood still, remembering how all that time ago, Domendez had not only disfigured his body but also scarred his life.

"Yes, I know who you are, and I know you've been expecting me," said Sam coldly. The yearning to do to Domendez what he had done to Button was almost irrepressible, but with Moses Jones now tying his feet together with his own belt and the gun now pointed at his genitals, it meant that regardless of the desperate pain tearing at his gut, he would have wait for Oak to make his move – a move that Sam had planned would only happen once another piece of his past had arrived, and that piece was now standing in front of him.

"Please allow me to untie your hands, Señor Farmer," said Domendez in a polite, gentlemanly tone as he picked away with dark-skinned fingers and manicured nails at the taut cable biting into Sam's wrists.

Sam studied Domendez and thought how his attire looked so deceivingly out of place with the surroundings. The cream cotton suit and tieless white shirt, right down to his handmade brogues were more appropriate for cocktail lounges than a place where death presided.

Sam knew that the illusion could never deceive or cloak the fact, however, that the grey-haired man with an age-wrinkled face was nothing more than a perverted monster. With Jones once more firmly holding his hands behind him, he could only observe as Domendez unbuttoned Sam's shirt, his eyes flaring with anticipation at once more gazing at the torso that he had disfigured, a torso that also had his initials scarred into it. Sam could then feel the sensation of Domendez's quickening breath on his skin, like a salivating animal wanting to gorge himself on his captured prey.

"Ah, Señor Farmer, how I have prayed for this day. For me you are my unfinished canvas!" His jubilant words were followed by a pondering smile. He paused to slowly run his fingertips across his face, and Sam remembered that Domendez was known to shave his male victims prior to slaughtering them, a perverse act that would be carried out with a savage item that in the hands of the Barber would be wielded as if it were a surgeon's scalpel. Domendez slipped his hand into his inside jacket pocket to produce a hard leather case that opened like a clamshell; but instead of a priceless pearl inside, there was only an object of death. His eyes became dreamy and nostalgic as he removed a cutthroat razor from its cushioned velvet-lined bed, and he opened the blade out fully to hold as if it were an extension of his hand. "It's unique, Señor Farmer, you see," he said, brandishing the four-inch blade against Sam's face. "I'm informed it's made from Damascus steel. Metals forged together to give its unique fingerprint design. Beautiful, don't you think? It has been in my family for over four generations."

"Well I hope for my sake it's sharp. I can't think of anything worse than being shaved with a blunt razor," Sam replied.

"Ah, for you, señor, I have something different in mind. But yes, it is very sharp. I'll show you . . ." Domendez answered. He walked over to where Button was lying, still moaning, still hanging onto life but not for much longer. Standing behind the settee, and with a swift slice from left to right, Button's throat was cut from carotid to carotid, his arteries spewing blood skywards like impromptu fountains.

"Fuck me, mon, what a way to go!" said Jones in shocked exhilaration. "So, what are you going to do to this mon, cut him up like you did that German bitch?"

"You didn't have to do that to her!" Sam cried out in anger, hoping that at any moment time would finally run out for Domendez and Moses Jones.

"It is my profession, señor. We took her as she left your hotel. Señora Faber had information about a certain client of mine, and I had to find out what it was. It's business; it's what I do."

"Really. Well I'm going to make sure you're going to burn in hell for her," Sam snarled.

Domendez shrugged dismissively, confident that he would finally fulfil his desire to finish where he'd left off all those years before, an arrogant belief that made Domendez drop his guard and elaborate further as to another reason why he was in the Philippines, and why it was also business.

"Give me his right arm!" ordered Domendez to Jones with a look of evil intent.

Now Sam knew it was back to business as usual for the Barber.

With his feet bound together and one arm held firmly behind him, Sam realised he had to slow the pace his fate was heading as Domendez was yet again engaged in having his fun, this time with Sam's forearm.

"Do you want to know what my daughters call you?" Sam then asked, watching the Barber brush the flat of the blade along his forearm, effortlessly removing the hairs. "Le lâche," he said, and waited for an answer, but none came. "It's French for coward, so what have you got to say about that?" His intention was to mock, giving himself fighting time before his one-man cavalry arrived . . . he hoped. "You're no better than the playground bullies I use to have to contend with when I was a lad. Would you agree?"

"Shush please, Señor Farmer, no talking, or I will be forced to cut out your tongue like I had to do to your friend Señora Faber. She would not stop screaming. Very, as you would say, 'distracting'," said Domendez, placing the razor against Sam's forearm and looking deep into his eyes with a smug, self-satisfied grin. He knew that what he would say next would have every muscle in Sam's body tense to near bursting point. "Tell me, do you think that Señor Faber was aware his wife was pregnant?"

He was right, Sam could hardly contain himself as he was once again confronted with the horrors the Barber was capable of.

"Please God, give me the strength to rip this man apart," he muttered, his breath ragged.

Then, with a dismissive snort, Domendez, after waiting three decades, turned the blade at a right angle to Sam's arm and sliced into his flesh once again. As he bit down on his bottom lip to suppress the urge to scream, and with Moses Jones peering in bloodthirsty silence over his left shoulder, Sam heard a faint tinkling sound, as if the fake crystal lampshade had rattled in the non-existent breeze, then, another sudden and brief noise, like the crack of a whip, *thwack,* as the bullet impacted and entered Jones' scull. The impact jolted him forward, and as he collapsed his body struck Sam's left shoulder to inexorably make his last unassisted journey to the wooden floor.

With his feet still tied together, Sam faltered to his right, the momentum making him act like a felled tree as he began to topple and then he instinctively reached out with his now freed hands, pawing at Domendez's torso whose reactions were in a state of flux due to the sudden demise of his accomplice. Sam managed to grip tightly to the lapels of his jacket, enabling him to use the force of gravity and his body mass to draw Domendez into him as if he was a beautiful woman, his woman, who he wasn't going to let get away. The time it took Moses Jones to begin his death fall, to Sam ending up sprawled on top of the now crumpled Domendez, was less than eight heart-stopping seconds, eight seconds that gave him the chance to fight for his life on his terms.

Sam rolled off Domendez who he thought, by the sound of his coughing, had only been winded by the fall, but he was wrong.

"Ah . . . this is not good, señor," uttered the Brazilian breathlessly.

The irregular panting from his partially opened mouth at first suggested that nothing more serious was happening, but blood began seeping from between his lips. It was then that Sam saw the gaping laceration across Domendez's abdomen, the blade of his razor embedded within it. He realised that the killer, after trying to resist his hold on him, had fallen on his own blade. Sam frantically untied the belt restraining his feet and surveyed the carnage around him.

He quickly glanced down to where Moses Jones had come to

rest, suddenly aware that he had been coated in the indescribable human cocktail normally held within the confines of the now dead man's head. And then at the Brazilian, who was weakening by the second, his eyes rolling in his head.

With his senses now reacting to the slightest sound and movement, he diverted his eyes to the French windows as they smashed open, to see a burly sixty-year-old Canadian with an intimidating high-powered rifle in his grasp.

"Hi there, fella!" boomed Oak jovially, not making any effort to speak quietly, as normally he would do when stealthily tracking deer in his native Ontario. There was the sound of the broken glass under Oak's boots as he stepped further into the room, and he smiled, pleased to see his brother-in-law was still alive; bleeding, yes, but still very much alive.

"That was one helluva shot you made through the gap in the drapes! Scared the shit out of me!" Sam told Oak; but Oak slowly shook his head, reluctant to acknowledge Sam's accolade.

"Yes, it was a helluva shot, wasn't it fella?" he replied, glancing back into the black canvas where once there were French windows. "But I didn't take that shot," Oak added, "he did."

They watched as another man walked in from the darkness with an even more intimidating high-powered rifle, its night vision sight being Sam's salvation.

"What the hell are you doing here?" Sam blustered, wondering why James, a former captain in the Royal Artillery, was standing in front of him - and dressed like a Ninja. Then he muttered, *"Sam, you stupid idiot!"* as he answered his own question. His close and dearest friend Archie, James' employer, only had the finest of everything, the best that money could buy: the best suits, the best meals at the best restaurants, and obviously, he also employed only the best minders, the best of the best, ex special forces SAS best.

"He's with me, Dad," came the reply from a female now

appearing from the shadows, the ill-fitting trousers and rolled back sleeves of her black camouflage shirt looking more like a fashion statement than simply garments which were too large for her. "Bugger me! What a mess!" Maggie then said, skirting around the pools of blood seeping from Button's throat and what remained of Jones' head.

"Yes, well, high-calibre rounds tend to do that, I'm afraid. But I needed a round that could go through glass and still hit my target," James explained.

Sam sucked in air as if he had been punched in the gut, a reaction to what he had heard, aware that if Jones had moved in the split second prior to James squeezing the trigger, Maggie could be staring down at him! He watched as she walked towards him, and he struggled to hide his anger at seeing her enter into a situation *he* didn't want to be in, let alone his beloved and beautiful daughter.

"Have you got any frigging idea what danger you're in?" he cried, his eyes wide and searing into her.

"Get over yourself, Dad, I'm a vet, remember? Seeing animals like them two dead doesn't worry me." She felt his arms wrap around her, wanting to hold her safe in his embrace; despite her cavalier attitude she, like her father, knew they were still anything but safe. "Is that him, the bastard who cut you up?" she then asked, moving to crouch down at the side of Domendez, who had managed to prop himself up against a wall. "Ooooh, that don't look good, got your spleen . . ." she said gleefully. "Now don't go away will you, coz you and me are going to have a little chat." Maggie then rose to her feet and walked towards the rear of the bungalow. "Where's the boy, Dad? In here?" she asked with her hand poised to open the door to the bathroom.

"No!" yelled Sam. "Not that one! I'm begging you, don't open that door, please." He was distraught at the thought of Maggie seeing Mila and the barbarity Domendez was truly capable of.

Puzzled by her father's outburst, Maggie hid her thoughts

behind a small smile. "OK, Dad, whatever you say," she replied, disappearing into the bedroom instead; she was followed by Oak.

Ignoring his own wounds, Sam peered down at Domendez with a sense of irony at how, in an instance, events had conspired against him. "Well, Rodrigo, by the looks of you, you've given a twist to an old adage. Shall we rephrase it a little: do onto yourself as you have done to others. There are more of course, such as 'live by the sword, die by the sword' etc., etc." Sam paused for a brief moment, staring reflectively at the bleeding man. When he did continue, his casual, almost cavalier, regard towards the man who lay dying in front him almost seemed inappropriate. What with the boned crater that was once the head of Moses Jones, and then Button, the gaping wound across this throat like a rouged and pouting mouth, it was like the scene from a bad movie; but conversely, foremost in his thoughts was Mila, her once brilliant blue eyes that had the ability to set any man's pulse racing, now pierced his mind in death, soulless, a vision that would haunt him forever.

"Remember what I told you?" Sam then said. "You're going to burn in hell. Well, prepare yourself, you . . ." But suddenly distracted by movement from the corner of his eye, Sam watched as Oak appeared with Auner cradled in his arms, wrapped in a dusty curtain and oblivious that his family had come to rescue him.

"I'm taking this wee fella to the boat, Sam. James knows what needs to be done," he said, and with his rifle once more slung across his back, Oak started to make his way towards the front of the bungalow.

"Hold on there, Oak!" Sam ordered, resting his blood-stained hand heavily on Maggie's shoulder. "You're going with him Mags. You're getting out of here as well. I need you to look after Auner."

"No, Dad. It's you who's getting out of here. You're all cut up, look at you."

"Na, it's nothing, sweetheart," Sam replied, giving his arm a cursory glance.

"That's not nothing, Dad, besides, it's not that that I'm too concerned with, it's this!" Maggie replied, pulling to one side her father's blood-soaked shirt. "That bastard's got your tummy again!" she said with concern, viewing the four-inch slash with a medical eye. "It's a good job I brought a sewing kit with me. But I can't stitch you up here, I'll do it on the boat, if it's not too rough that is."

"Here, put this around him," said James, tossing Maggie a battle dressing from a pouch he wore around his waist.

"She's right, fella," said Oak. "Let them finish off here. You've done your part."

"Go, Dad, please. Like Uncle Oak's said, you've done your bit," Maggie repeated.

"Oh alright, you win," replied Sam reluctantly, knowing he didn't call her stubborn for nothing.

"You gonna say your goodbyes to him, Dad?" she then asked, only briefly diverting her scornful eyes from Domendez, who she hadn't finished with yet!

"No, I've got nothing more to say to him. He knows he's going to die, that's good enough for me." For a moment, Sam wondered why he didn't feel any sense of remorse for what he had just said, but it was only for a moment. "And no more Rambo-ing!" Sam cried as he walked away from his daughter, leaving Domendez in her charge.

James had emerged from the carnage in the bathroom, but his training had kicked in and he restrained any emotions. "Here, Sam, I thought you may want these to give to her husband," he said, placing Mila's blood-smeared wedding ring and a gold chain and locket into his palm. "I'll treat her decent, Sam, and make sure there's nothing left of her, you have my word on that."

Sam clenched his fist tightly around the items, and with an ache that reached deep into his memory, he tried desperately to remember her as she was, for his own sake. "Thank you," he replied quietly, and then left, turning his back on another part of the jig-sawed past that had only two more pieces left to fit.

Maggie knelt down again next to Domendez and pulled the razor from his wound, knowing all too well it was possibly acting as a plug to any severed vein or artery. She poked at his blood-soaked jacket with the tip of the razor, and in a voice that did not hide her revulsion towards him, said, "Because of your fucking cruelty to my darling daddy, he is reminded of what you did to him every day." She turned briefly to gaze across at James, who was pouring gasoline over Moses Jones and Button. "Now, where were we?" she asked, her chillingly cold stare telling him that his fate wouldn't only be by bleeding to death from his stomach wound. "Oh yes, did you hear me say that I'm a vet? Have a guess what my specialty is? . . . No? Give in?" she asked, waving his razor in front of his face. "*Castration . . . I'm gonna cut your balls off!*"

Sam stopped and turned, hearing the high-pitched wretched sound coming from the direction of the bungalow, and then nothing, only the endless nocturnal chatter from the animals of the plantation that broke into the still of the night.

Sailing out of the bay, and with the salty sea air cleansing his lungs of the stink of blood and body parts, he watched the distance glow of the bungalow as it burnt to the ground. *God bless you, Mila. I only wish that I could have saved you. I'm truly sorry.*

Chapter 29

The Showdown

Day Three

Watching the sun rise over the horizon three hours earlier was already a distant memory for Henning. Now his attention was on navigating his boat through the inward bound channel of Manila Bay.

"If Maggie's finished sewing him up, you'd better get Sam up here . . . not long now," said the boat's skipper, sending James back down below to the forward cabin space where his passengers had been resting.

"The hotel's marina is coming into view to starboard, Sam. Should be alongside in about fifteen minutes," said Henning, who with his left hand was masterfully altering the boat's course. He blindly moved the wheel to port or starboard as he kept a watchful eye not only on commercial shipping, but the smaller craft like his all wanting to navigate the same expanse of water. In his other hand, he held a mug of black coffee laced with more than just a small tot of rum.

"It's 8.43. You've make good time considering it wasn't such a baby's arse out at sea as you said it would be," replied Sam. He looked out over the harbour, now with hardly a ripple on the water.

"Yes, it was a bit lumpy out there, more than I thought. How's the kid doing now?" Henning enquired.

"He's OK. Still a bit out of it due to the drugs he was given – strong sedatives Maggie reckons. They'll take a while to work out of his system, the bastards," he seethed.

With the city of Manila sky-scraping through the early morning heat haze and pollution, Sam now had to concentrate his thoughts on what lay ahead for him in the next three hours. Up until then his overriding concern was to get Auner safely back to his dying mother. Now he planned to confront Sidney in a meeting at which he intended to unravel his brother's double-crossing subterfuge, an artifice that Sam now realised had its roots laid a lifetime before, when he and his twin sister Ruth were just teenagers, and when the world was their oyster.

"Here, Sam," said Henning, gesturing to him to take the helm, "take over will you. Me and James can tie up. If you fuck up those stitches of yours, Maggie will keel-haul us."

"Sure thing, skipper," replied Sam, smiling at Henning's serious wit. Looking out over the bow as he brought the fishing boat slowly alongside the pontoon, Sam caught sight of a familiar face smiling with a welcoming wave.

"Hi there, Paco," said Henning, feeling the trust of the two powerful engines as Sam put them gently into astern to bring the fishing boat to a stop. "Here, make yourself useful, take this stern line and feed it through that ring, then come on board."

"Who's that, Dad?" asked Maggie appearing from the cabin through an arched door to the left of the boat's helm.

"That young man, sweetheart, is my friend Paco."

"Mmm . . . 'ansom ain't 'e. Uncle Oak told me about him. Is he married?"

God, you're such a flirt, Sam chuckled to himself. "Where's the lad, asleep?" he asked her.

"I've left him in the cabin with Uncle Oak. I don't want anyone seeing him. All he's wearing is a girly T-shirt from my bag that Henning brought on board for me."

"Yes, know the feeling," he muttered – he was still wearing his ripped and blood-stained shirt. "In a minute, we'll go down to the cabin and I'll explain what I need you to do next," Sam added, but knew there was something else that he needed her to do after that, something she had to do on his behalf. "Once you've done a little errand for me, you need to go with Auner to an orphanage."

"No way! I'm not taking him to an orphanage, Dad, he's family!" Maggie replied, her angry voice setting her father straight on what she obviously perceived to be an inconceivable idea.

"Sweetheart," Sam responded, placing his hands on her shoulders to stare into her fearful eyes. "I need you to do this for Auner, but not in the way you think . . . please hear me out."

"Sorry, Dad, I've got it wrong, haven't I?"

"It was a natural response. Like you said, he is a Farmer after all; but I haven't risked my life, or yours, to stick him in an orphanage, you should know that, but he needs to go there. Paco will drive you. It's in one of the poorest parts of the city so be careful. There's a priest by the name of Father Patrick O'Toole - Quinn."

"Gawd, that's a name and a half," she responded.

"Yes, well, as I was saying, Father Patrick will be there and he'll be expecting you. There will be food and a bath waiting for you both and some clean clothes for Auner. Take your bag with you. You won't be coming back to the boat . . ." Then Sam paused as sadness filled his thoughts. He knew Maggie would do what he asked of her and do it with kindness and understanding, but this was something he wanted to do himself, he'd made a promise. "Then . . ." Sam continued with a voice that was choked with emotion, "you're to go with Father Patrick and take Auner to his mother. I want you to stay there until it's all over, then text me please. We'll meet back at the orphanage."

"What about Auner? Who's is going to look after him when his mother's gone?"

"Not sure yet, sweetheart. By rights it should be Sidney, you'll have to speak to Maria, his aunty, about that," Sam replied.

Paco had to sit on one of the steps leading down to the cabin, with Henning's motley crew squeezed in on two small benches.

With what remained of the rum being shared out into mugs, Sam looked around the cabin beholden to those who had come to his aid and risked their lives to help rescue Auner. The boy sat quietly on Maggie's lap, her arms lovingly wrapped around him.

"Right, sweetheart, you first," Sam started with a small chuckle, thinking about what she had to do for him. "Go to the hotel's reception desk and ask for Louisa. Tell her who you are. She'll probably laugh."

"Why, Dad?" she said.

"Because you're another woman, that's why. It's a long story . . . but she's OK, you can trust her. I left my room key at the desk. When Louisa hands it over to you, go to my room. Pick me up some clothes and my razor and then open the room's safe. The code, oddly enough, is your date of birth. Inside you'll find a money belt, four flash drives and a larger portable hard drive. Bring them to me, but you're to keep hold of the hard drive and return it to Maria when you meet her. Tell her I said thank you. Oh, yes, I forgot . . . my phone . . . it's in the safe as well."

"Wearing a tie in this heat, Sam? It's a bit over the top, isn't it?" asked Henning. Both men were listening with amusement to Oak grumbling as he tried to take a shower in the cramped toilet compartment that doubled as a bathroom.

"Maggie thought I should wear it. She thinks that, despite the cuts and bruises on my face, it sends out a calm business-like statement – and considering what I've got to do, I tend to agree with her. "Hmm . . ." Sam then muttered, with Maggie's orders still ringing in his ears: *Don't go getting into any more fights. Those stitches will come apart like a zipper . . .* Easier said than done, considering he would shortly be confronting a man who wanted him dead.

Henning then had another question for Sam: "Oak said that, as a result of what your brother did, his wife – your sister – committed suicide. Is that right? And that he intends to kill him?"

"Yes . . . yes, he does," Sam replied.

"Are you going to let him?"

"Don't know yet . . . that depends on Sidney."

Sam then walked out onto the deck to find James at the stern, coolly puffing away on a Havana cigar that he had commandeered from Henning. He was talking to two bikini-clad yachtswomen; he had just helped them tie up their sailing boat to the pontoon.

"Are you all ready, then?" he asked, giving James a farewell handshake.

"Sure am."

"Well, good luck, Auner's counting on you."

"He who dares, Sam . . . he who dares," replied James, casually quoting the motto of the SAS.

"Where's he off to, Sam, he wouldn't tell me?" asked Henning with a farewell wave.

"That's his military training. He's gone on an errand for me, that's all. You won't see him again," he replied.

"You ready there, fella?" said Oak, being offered a cigar.

"You want one too, Sam?" asked Henning.

"No, thanks, not until the fat lady sings, as they say," Sam replied, knowing it was also time for Oak and him to leave.

The two men paused at the driveway leading to the address where Paco had tailed Spatz, two days before. They found themselves barred from going any further by a man and a woman. Both had a hand behind their backs and both, Sam knew, would more than likely have the safeties off the pistols they were concealing.

"Hi there, can I help you guys?" asked the woman with a courteous American accent. She showed the two men the outstretched palm of her free hand in a gesture that said *any further and I'll show you my other one!*

"Remind you of anyone?" Oak asked, his words coming from lips that barely moved.

"Nah . . . Mags doesn't need a gun to scare the crap out of me, you know that," Sam jested.

"Good morning. Lovely day, isn't it?" came his polite Englishman's greeting, directed at the dark-haired woman. "I'm Sam Farmer, and this gentleman with me is Oak. I believe your Mr Spatz is expecting us."

"Oak who?" was asked abruptly by the other member of the duo.

"Just Oak, that's all you need to know about me, so you just open them two gates and let us go up to the villa, that's a good fella."

Sam cut Oak a cautious smile as they walked up the drive, aware that his brother-in-law was showing untimely traits of the hunter in him, sensing that his prey, his human prey, was soon only the thickness of a door away.

"I know you aren't going to like this, but I need you to stay here," said Sam, watching as Oak took a mighty intake of breath, charging his pent-up wrath. "Yes, I know you want to bounce Sidney around the walls every which way, and I'm not going to stop you. But if you, like me, want answers as to why he turned on his family, then you have to let me go in on my own, otherwise the pain we both feel for Ruth's death will continue to fester in our souls. You have to ask yourself, would *she* want that?"

Oak just stood there motionless, silent, with his eyes boring into Sam; they were hardened eyes that, as he spoke, became softer as memories of his late wife temporally extinguished the fire of hate for Sam's brother.

"You find out whatever you want, fella, but once yer done, I'm coming in and I'm glad you won't stop me. I sure as hell don't want to open up them stitches of yours," he said. His tone of voice didn't have to be loud or terse for Sam to understand that the hunter intended to have his kill. They shook hands like titans; two men who now found themselves with opposing agendas on how to deal with a man who was once family.

No sooner as he entered the villa, Sam again found himself being prodded by the barrel of a gun.

"Hands on your head," he heard, and was then frisked by a man whose black trousers and matching T-shirt seemed to be the order of the day. Then a nod was exchanged from his frisker to another man, who at first stood at ease in front of a pair of double doors, his hands clasped behind him; but then he turned in almost military stiffness to open one of them for Sam, who was now prompted into a spacious lounge. The room, apart from a luxurious Murano glass chandelier that hung from the high vaulted ceiling, was sparsely furnished. Only a coffee table and a deep white leather sofa gave the room any sense of being used. Finding that he was the only person in the room, Sam walked towards the open French doors to see two men standing on the patio looking out over the bay of Manila in the distance. One he knew: Spatz; the other he once thought he did.

"Hello, Samuel," said Sidney, offering his hand to Sam, who made no effort to reciprocate the welcoming gesture. Instead he slipped his hands behind his back, defiant that their meeting would be anything but affable.

Showing little regard for Sam's actions, Sidney walked nonchalantly into the lounge, pouring a large glass of locally distilled coconut brandy from a tray on the coffee table. He then ensconced himself on the sofa.

"Help yourself, why don't you? It's all courtesy of our friend here, Mr Spatz," he said.

Sam remained silent; he hadn't as yet been asked a question worth answering he decided. Instead he looked deadpan at his sixty-three-year-old brother, whose unhealthy gaunt features, Sam thought, were a deserved reflection of the wasted and twisted man he had become.

"So, where's my kid? You got him back. I want him," Sidney demanded, his tone now showing no sign of cordiality towards his younger brother.

"All in good time," Sam replied, and then turned to talk to Spatz, who had reminded him several times that, as far as the DEA where concerned, they were only interested in the information Sidney was going to hand over to them. "Has this brother of mine kept to his final part of the deal yet?" he asked.

"No . . . he's been waiting for you to turn up with the kid. I must say, it took some balls to go for the boy before the arrangements were made for the ransom drop," said Spatz. Then his tone changed to being less complementary: "You forgot though what I told you. I warned you, Farmer . . . don't fuck with me, this is DEA business, now, so, where is he?" Spatz demanded.

"He's safe. One of my daughters is looking after him."

"Your daughter?" replied Spatz, perplexed.

"Uh-huh. Maggie," Sam answered, enjoying seeing Spatz baffled.

"She popped up out of the blue . . . well, that's not quite how it was . . . more popped up out of the darkness to come and help her old dad," Sam answered, but not to the DEA man. His reply was directed at his brother from whom he expected at least a reaction of surprise that Maggie was in Manila and Auner was with *her*, not him.

Maybe you don't want to overplay the bluster, he thought, reminding himself that everything around him was just a farce, a con. Gazing at the open French windows at the stunning view, Sam knew that timing and concentration – Penny's watch words – would be the ploy that would have him take command and able to dictate, intent on subduing his brother while he unearthed the painful and indisputable truth, past and present.

"OK, down to business," Sam then stated, clasping his hands together as if he was organising who was going to do the washing up. "Sidney," said Sam sternly, "hand over that info to our friend here, and while it's being checked through, you and me are going to have little natter about old times."

"No . . . I'm not prepared to hand over anything until you return my kid to me," Sidney answered.

"Really, is that so?" Sam calmly replied; but for his brother that was as nice as he was prepared to be. "It hasn't got anything to do with the fact that once Mr Spatz has what he wants, he'll have you on the next flight to the States and obscurity. But is our American friend here aware that you've heartlessly abandoned your wife because she's dying, and according to Filipino law, if you take a child out of the country without permission of both parents, and you don't have hers, it's classed as a felony. And, if the DEA knowingly assist you, I believe the legal term is 'an accessory after the fact'? You will only become sole legal guardian once your wife Freya has died, and that couldn't come soon enough for you, could it? That's why you reduced her to living in abject poverty, hoping that if the cancer didn't kill her quick enough, her rat-infested environment would. You shit of a man. Now give Mr Spatz that sodding information," Sam seethed, staring fiercely at his obstinate-faced brother who, despite Sam's angry retort, still remained comfortably leaning back into the deep cushioned sofa.

It was Spatz who now realised the ballgame had changed, unaware until then of the circumstances regarding Sidney's wife.

"If that's the case, the kid stays. If you wanna see the diamonds, then do as your brother advises, and you'd betta do it pronto."

With Spatz's demanding voice echoing around the room, Sidney begrudgingly reached for his phone to send the information that he had stored on it.

"There, now you have it, so let's get our deal concluded. I want out of here – and with my kid," said an impatient Sidney.

"It'll be a while," replied the DEA man, now distracted with transferring the file to be authenticated, a procedure that allowed Sam time to confront his nemesis. He was now aware that a certain event from the distant past was the catalyst that had unlocked a vain of gross immorality, and made a seemingly loyal brother turn on his own family in a way that would cut like a scythe; but why? The answer to that question had eluded him until now.

"Ah, Mr Spatz, if I may, now you've finished with your phone," said Sam, his tone revealing his desire to ask the American a question, "you're a theatre buff, so you must have heard of the saying 'All the world's a stage, and all the men and women merely players'? So–"

"Huh. Shakespeare. I might have known you'd bring him up. I've heard that . . . that . . . woman you're marrying is an actress," said Sidney, rudely cutting in.

Sam leisurely turned his head to respond to his brother's outburst and fixed him with a glare while he continued with what he intended to say.

"I apologise for my brother butting in. Obviously, he must feel that that question hasn't any bearing to any of this . . . but you're wrong, Sidney," said Sam and, as planned, redirected his question to his brother: "You see, it *was* a stage, wasn't it? A stage where two innocent young people, a lifetime ago, made a joint decision to shun the limelight. A decision that seems to have affected *you* more than it did us."

The sneer across Sidney's face showed Sam that he knew exactly what he was referring to. From his pocket, he then produced a folded piece of old newsprint that Freya had found, which Sidney had kept as a twisted reminder of when, as Sam realised, Sidney had become the Jekyll and Hyde of the family. Reading the caption and part of the paragraph for the benefit of Spatz, he then needed to know from Sidney why and what had driven him to become the monster he had turned into.

"'*Brother and sister sailing phenomenon turn their backs on Olympic gold*'," he read. "'*Twins, Samuel and Ruth Farmer, declined the chance to be part of the British Olympic sailing team, sighting career commitments . . .*'" With a clenched fist, he tossed the crumpled cutting onto the white marbled floor, now intent on prompting his brother into an explanation. "What possessed you to think that Ruth wanting to concentrate on becoming a midwife and me joining the Merchant Navy was so wrong?"

"Because . . . in my eyes, Samuel, both of you showed a lack of ruthless instinct. And your mundane, narrow thinking proved to me how superior I am compared to you both." Sidney now relaxed in his own narcissistic world, where his inflated sense of superiority and self-importance showed its ugly head. "I fooled you. I fooled you both. Over the years when you thought I was struggling and you were lending me money, I was, in fact, making more in one day that you would in a month. Then when you came to me with that investment deal, I saw my opportunity to finally show you what fools you and that sister of yours really were."

"Ruth was also your sister, or had you forgotten?" Sam hissed.

"No, I never had siblings after what you both did, rejecting an opportunity to make something of yourselves," Sidney replied, shaking his head. "After that I always considered myself as an only child, with two imposters who called me their brother." Sidney laughed in Sam's face, a nonchalant conceited laugh. "The truth hurts, doesn't it, Samuel?" said Sidney coldly.

Had there been a morsel left of benevolence towards Sidney,

Sam would have felt it drain from his body on hearing his brother's twisted rant. A brother he once loved. But now, sure in the knowledge that he and his sister Ruth weren't fooled, it was something more devious and wicked.

"You're wrong, Sidney, you didn't fool us . . . you betrayed us, and you betrayed our whole family. If Dad were still alive he'd call you a 'wrong 'un'. The only time you fooled me was when Button first paid me a visit twenty-odd years ago, after you ran off with all our money. He made me think that your drugs boss had sent him and, amongst other things, told me to keep my mouth shut or else he'd harm my girls, and *you* know what I did to him! Well, I did it to him again last night, but not before he told me that it was you who sent him . . . *you* were his boss, *you*." He paused to clear his throat with a small cough. The dryness of the air-conditioned room was bad enough, but having to conceal from view on the outside what he was experiencing on the inside – raw, emotional hurt – was an endeavour that made his throat dry and taut.

"Any chance of some water? It's a bit early in the day for me to start drinking brandy," he asked Spatz.

"Sure thing," he replied.

As he waited for his water, Sam wasted no time in asking why his brother wanted him dead. "Tell me, Sidney, why, after twenty-odd years, did you get Button to try and kill me?" he said.

"Yes, I heard that he almost did that woman of yours by mistake . . ." Sidney paused, allowing his brandy to work its way down his gullet, still with his arrogant expression firmly fixed on Sam. "The reason why . . .? Loose ends, dear boy, loose ends," Sidney continued. "Button contacted me soon after he was released from prison. He said that he had seen your picture in a magazine with those daughters of yours and that actress. I couldn't have you drawing attention to yourself, now could I?"

"Drawing attention towards you, you mean, worried that people would start to poke their noses into my past and find you festering in some corner of it," said Sam, reaching out his hand for a welcome bottle of ice-cold water. "Thanks, Mr Spatz. Maybe when this is all over you'll allow me to call you by your first name."

"Spatz. Spatz will do just fine."

What no dramatics? Sam pondered. "Well, now you're back, I was just asking Sidney – considering he got you to persuade me to come over here and help get his son back from Button – why he hired the same thug to kill me two years ago? Odd, don't you think?"

Not expecting a denial or rebuff from Sidney, Sam left Spatz to cogitate about what he had just said, while he calmly unscrewed the blue top off the bottled water.

Now it was time to move around. *Change of props*, Sam thought. He walked across the room to stand at the back of the sofa, and produced a photograph from his wallet. "Here, Sidney, take a look. If this isn't drawing attention to yourself, I don't know what is." Sam could see from the corner of his eye, Spatz lean slightly forward, his chin leading the way in curiosity.

"So . . . what about it?" Sidney shrugged. "It means nothing. I'm in a restaurant having a meal with some people I know," he replied, tearing the picture into small pieces and tossing them into the air like confetti.

"It may mean nothing to you, but it sure pissed off your Indonesian police chum Kazemi when I gave him a copy. Of course, you know that, don't you?" Sam retorted.

"Woah there! Are you talking about the deputy commissioner of police, Sohaed Kazemi?" now asked a rather inquisitive Spatz.

"Ah, now I've got your juices flowing, haven't I? Yes, I am. I've met him a couple of times. The last one was a few weeks ago, when he was in London, and I passed him a photograph of him in company with Sidney and another lowlife who you may also know – Rodrigo Domendez, aka the Barber."

"Jesus, you know what that guy is, don't you? The FBI has been on his tail for years!" replied the stunned DEA man.

"What he *was* . . ." Sam answered coolly. "There's no *is* anymore. They're all dead: Moses Jones, Button and the Barber. Dead and burned." Putting his hands on the back of the sofa, Sam peered gleefully at Sidney and now spoke in an *I know something you don't* tone. "You didn't know the Barber was here in Manila though, did you, Sidney? Kazemi didn't tell you that, did he? Now, don't you wonder why that was . . .?" Sam asked, not really bothered if there would be a reply, or what expression would appear on his brother's face. Sam now moved back to stand by the French windows, with Spatz to his left and Sidney still seated on his right, aware that the longer he and Sidney continued to joust, the sooner the deal for the diamonds would be done. But unbeknown to Sidney, that's exactly what Sam wanted to happen . . . well, almost. So, he continued to ruffle his brother's proverbial feathers by enlightening Spatz in a spot of theatrical skull-duggery.

"Do you know, Spatz, it took a beautiful young woman to remind me – in fact, it was Sidney's sister-in-law to be precise – that this self-proclaimed superior being, who is so cocksure he can out-clever anyone, is in fact as readable as a book? Well, by those like me who know him, that is. For starters, when it comes to being superstitious and having foibles, he's no different from any of us. For instance, take the nine million dollars in diamonds. First, ask yourself: why did Button and Jones only demand nine? Why not ten? Is it because Sidney was born on the ninth day of the ninth month, and his lucky number is . . . nine?"

"You're talking utter rubbish again, Samuel. I'm not even going to waste my breath in responding further to that stupid assumption." Snidely, Sam's brother reverted back into his smug comfort zone, content to let the minutes tick away. "Actually, Samuel, I should thank you. You see, with the kidnappers dead, I get to *keep the ransom*. Once again I win out on you."

With his brother's contemptuous smirk beaming at him with perceived satisfaction, an unfazed Sam returned an equally jocular smile; then looked away to once more engage with Spatz, continuing where he left off.

"As I was saying," he said, "Sidney is readable. You see, clever clogs here, when it comes to such things as remembering people's names and passwords, has a crap memory." Now he looked at Sidney, and as he hoped the smirk had gone. "So how does he remember them without doing what most of us do – write them down? Well, simple really.

"But first, back to Domendez, aka the Barber. I had the misfortune to meet him thirty-two years ago . . . or was it thirty-three? Well, anyway, I found myself in a police cell courtesy of Sohaed Kazemi, and keeping me company was Domendez, who hours before had carried out a contract killing for the said Mr Police Chief. While the rest of the cops were out looking for him, he was hiding in plain sight under their noses . . . and that's what Sidney does with his computer passwords. He hides them in plain sight to trigger his memory, *don't you, bro*?" Sam asked, casting his last three words firmly in the direction of his brother, who seemed more interested in Spatz's reaction that showing his own.

As he opened his mouth to continue, Spatz called "Stop!" cutting Sam off abruptly. He reached for his phone and read a message with an undecipherable face.

Had that been me, Sam thought, *I would have apologised for interrupting, but not Spatz.*

"OK, continue," was then heard as he slipped the phone back into his pocket.

"Hmmph," Sam grunted, thinking that just at the moment when he was about to expose his brother's Achilles heel and shatter his mask of ultra-confidence, Spatz had momentarily stolen the scene. "Like I said," he then continued, "Sidney had devised a way to prompt his memory – and his choice was as cynical as it was simple." He paused to walk over to where he had dropped the crumpled piece of newsprint that he had read earlier. He handed it to Spatz with an unsmiling face, embittered by another of his brother's contemptuous actions. "That young woman with me in the picture is Ruth, our sister. We're shown sailing over the finishing line of a race we'd just won." Sam then stared pointedly into Spatz's eyes, willing him to voice the answer that was in plain sight. "Tell me, what can you see in that picture that isn't organic? Something that to you probably means nothing, but to Sidney it is the key . . . or to make it even clearer: passwords to open restricted files on his computer."

"I don't know what the hell you're talking about? He's bluffing you!" Sidney blustered, directing his indignant tone at Spatz, and with energy fed by fury, shot to his feet to confront Sam head on.

"Oh stop wailing, Sidney. Go and sit your sorry arse back down," Sam ordered, now clenching an intimidating fist at his brother. "I'm sure Mr Spatz would like to know exactly what is really going on."

"You can bet fifty years to life I do," Spatz barked, folding his arms like a head teacher waiting for an explanation from two naughty boys. "If either of you are trying to play me or the DEA, I'll have you on a flight so fast, you'll be pissing yourself here and shitting bricks in a penitentiary stateside by sundown."

"That sounds fair enough, can't argue with that," Sam replied coolly. "But I can't vouch for him," he added, noticing Sidney's ultra-confident façade had paled, his eyes rounding on him. "Right, now that I've got your attention," said Sam, "I'll try to be as brief as I can." He was aware that for Spatz to know all the facts he would have to, and he hoped for last time, exhibit himself. "You don't get to share a cell with a man like the Barber and go away with a short back and sides," he then said.

Even before Sam had fully unbuttoned his shirt, Spatz had seen enough, gesturing with a push of hands for him to stop.

"Now, where did I get to . . .?" he continued. "Oh yes, the

newspaper cutting; but I'll come back to that in a moment. It was a photograph that started the ball rolling for me, so to speak. The same photograph that I handed Sidney a few moments ago. You see, at the end of last year I was shown that same picture by a journalist, Peter Faber, who was with his beautiful, but sadly late, wife Mila. Together they were on an unrelenting mission to destroy Kazemi in revenge . . . because he perpetrated the death of Mila's sister Elsa. The photograph shows the three men I hate the most: Sidney, Kazemi and Domendez, all sitting enjoying a meal together. Then it became a question of who gets to them first, the Fabers or me?

"Yes, like them, I wanted to settle old scores; but now I was aware that Sidney tried to have me killed by Button and would probably try again. I also had to protect my family, as he wouldn't just stop with me. So, I rattled Kazemi's cage, calculating he would inevitably contact my brother . . . and then I waited to see what the wind blew in . . . And it was you, Mr DEA man, along with a very able policewoman, DCI Tamworth who, unlike you, was already aware that Button was tidying up, as Sidney put it, 'loose ends'. Button had already killed a retired policeman who'd been nosing around in dusty corners in Sidney's past; but Button's murderous spree didn't stop there. A prostitute and a lovely, harmless old lady were next to be slain by him . . . Am I right or am I right, so far?" Sam asked, posing the question in the direction of Sidney, who was still leaning comfortably back into the sofa, but now with his hands clasped behind his head with an air of haughtiness, as if his version of the truth was contrary to what Sam was describing. "Huh, I wouldn't get that comfortable if I were you, Sidney, I'm just getting started," said Sam sharply, hell-bent on chiselling away at what he perceived to be a poisoned mind lost in his own detached world.

"So, as I was saying. Button . . ." Sam continued. "Well, seeing that he had already cocked it up once to kill me, Sidney devised his own plan to deal with me, partly because he now had Kazemi demanding that I be dealt with for humiliating him in public. So, he came up with the idea that involved heartlessly using his own five-year-old son, Auner, as bait to lure me here. That's where you came in Mr Spatz. Sidney knew it would take more than a phone call for me to help him, so that's why he thought of involving the DEA . . . if you turned up on my doorstep, then maybe I could be persuaded. He also needed you to remind me of my own Achilles heel – our uncle Sammy, and how he never turned his back on someone who needed his help. He knew I couldn't turn my back on a helpless child, now could I? I'd have to be as sick as him to do that, and Auner is family."

Sam watched as Spatz turned his head towards Sidney, and for the first time the American was relatively speechless, only a muttered "Continue" was heard.

"So, to get the DEA on board and, I may add, make some serious money at the same time, he enticed you with presumably sought after intelligence pertaining to the shipments of narcotics through the South Sea Box which, correct me if I'm wrong, is the area between the Philippines, Vietnam, Singapore and Malaysia – information supposedly of dealers including what, to whom, when and by what means. All for the not-to-be-sniffed-at price of nine million dollars. And, in case you had forgotten, Sidney's lucky number."

Stopping for water, Sam couldn't believe that Sidney wasn't countering his every word. *Strange*, he thought, and he continued. "Now ask yourself why the demand for cash changed to diamonds? It was to slow the pace down while I made my way over here. After all, you wouldn't have priceless gems rattling around in a filing cabinet, would you? Sidney knew it would take a few days for you to get your hands on them. And, of course, you offered him a new identity, which I doubt he would have taken you up on. Once he got his hands on the diamonds, he would have disappeared into the ether, but probably back to Acapulco where he has another bolthole."

"Poppycock, Samuel, that's pure speculation. You're guessing.

I've handed over all the information I possessed. Even if you do know the passwords to access my files, you still require my bio's code, as without that you can't access my computer, and I guarantee you don't know that; no one does, except me."

"Well, that's sort of true," Sam replied, nodding his head in agreement. "I'll give you that. But there are other methods to get at the files. One is to take your hard drive out and fit it into another computer – or were you dumb enough to think your sister-in-law really wanted to have sex with you? – then you would need to be sufficiently careless to leave your computer open. So, while you were snoring your head off, Maria was downloading every file she could . . . Ha! Now that's what I call being shafted!" Sam smirked; but Sidney didn't. "Ah . . . I thought that would take the wind from your sails," Sam then said, expecting a further verbal response – but none came. Only eyes wide and fixed confirmed that the inflated sense of his own invulnerability had been struck a blow.

Now Sam turned his attention back to Spatz and the scrap of newsprint. "Got it yet?" he asked.

"Think so. Is it the pennant numbers on the sail?" Spatz replied.

"Give the man a coconut! That's exactly it. EH112 . . . like I said, in plain sight. There was a file named 'Just the two of us', which to Maria meant nothing, but was in fact the name Ruth and I had given our sailing boat, and the pennant number on the sail decrypted the files. They contained names and bank account details of dealers, corrupt police officers and politicians in over thirty countries worldwide going back years . . ."

Sam again paused to quietly observe the American, aware that his interest was well and truly aroused. "What's that phrase you Yanks use – a 'plugged nickel'? Well, the file that Sidney has handed over to you, compared to the ones he hasn't, isn't worth a dime, and certainly not nine million dollars. I know because I've seen it," he said soundly. "It's all right, I suppose. You'll be able to close down a few routes into the States, and it names a dozen or so dealers there and here in the Philippines you've been after. To Sidney they've become expendable, but it's nothing like what I can give you."

"You?" asked Spatz.

"Oh yes . . . how about a certain US congressman's brother, who is laundering drug money through the family's car parts company? That's only a teaser, by the way. The only good thing I'll say about my brother is when it comes keeping records and diaries, he's fastidious – and I mean fastidious with a big 'F'. Aren't you, Sidney? And don't look so pathetic. You were never going to get away with it anyway. Kazemi had no intention of relying on you to kill me, that's why he sent the Barber here to tidy up the mess – and that included *you*. Seeing first-hand what his methods were for extracting information, you would have quickly told him about these files, then died a gruesome death . . . so much for friendships, eh?"

Sam had been expecting that at any moment Sidney would again intercede, aiming to cut him down in an attempt to rubbish the stark daylight of truth, the truth that his plot had failed, and that his friend Kazemi had now turned on him. Instead, he remained impassive, aloof like a person in his own egocentric bubble with the world outside contrary to his own perceived superiority. Sidney had in fact closed his mind to reasoning, and now Sam felt he had carte blanche to speak at will. Nothing that Sidney could say could disrupt his intensions.

Spatz, however, was showing increased interest. With the tease of a motherload of intelligence improving the DEA man's expectations, Sam knew he now had the upper hand.

Then the inevitable intervened, untimely but predetermined. "Oh, excuse me for a moment?" Sam asked politely, reacting to the text ring tone on his phone, a sound that made his heart pound in apprehension, but then sink like a stone, heavy and numb, as he read of Freya's passing, a soul freed from pain. He walked out onto the patio to be alone with his thoughts of a woman who'd wanted nothing more than to be a loyal wife and a loving mother, thoughts that made him angry that that hadn't been the case.

"Mr Spatz," said Sam as he re-entered the lounge, now speaking with an even, more commanding voice. "There's a man waiting patiently outside. Can you tell him to come in?"

"Sure, what's his name?" Spatz replied.

"Oak," Sam answered, turning in the direction of his brother, knowing that Sidney may have detached himself from the present but he could no longer hide from consequences of his past.

Entering the room, Oak knew he was now at the end of his quest, but not to seek and ask why. He had left that to Sam. Oak regarded Sidney as one who had turned rogue, like an animal that casts itself out from the herd to roam unchecked and uncaring in the jungle of life. Sidney, as far as he was concerned, should be destroyed for the sake of the herd. He took a few steps, then paused, still some eight feet from his intended prey; but it was only an instinctive pause to take stock of his surroundings before, like the hunter he was, he would go for the kill.

Sidney now realised that Sam had added a dimension that even he knew was at odds of him leaving alive, let alone with the diamonds. He tentatively rose to his feet, glancing first at Oak and then at Spatz with a look that, until then, was not an expression he expected to show; that of fear.

"He's come here to kill you, Sidney, and I told him I won't stand in his way," said Sam bluntly, though positioning himself like a buffer in touching distance of both men.

Spatz remained by the closed door, and diligently and calmly assumed 'the position' as he moved his right hand behind his back, prepared in an instant to produce his pistol if the need arose.

With the slaying of Mila raw in his memory, and now the passing of Freya, a deep pain consumed Sam knowing that another young boy had lost his mother. It hurt more, however, that it was Freya's own husband, his brother, who had conspired to quicken her demise for the sake of greed, and a selfish single-minded desire to have everything for himself. Now Sam wanted Sidney to experience the true pain of loss in the way only he could understand. To be denied what he thought was rightfully his, then turn it into a mirage that would always be in his mind's eye, a vision that would never diminish with time. To achieve that, there was an obstacle, a man whose sheer presence scared Sidney to his core. Despite all his rhetoric, Sam knew that Oak, although a hunter, wasn't really a murderer. Yes, he was prepared to take a life if that's what it took to save Auner's; but to kill for no other reason than revenge for the death of his wife? That, in Sam's eyes, was letting Sidney off too lightly.

"Sidney, sit down," Sam ordered, pointing again at the sofa. "Oak won't be so rude as to kill you while I'm talking, will you?" he asked, with a face that was now bleak, void of any endeavour other than to finish the job. "I want to read you a message I received from Maggie just now and . . ." He paused, conscious that he could feel raw emotion tearing at his heart. "And Sidney, if you show the slightest sign of pleasure in what I'm about to tell you, I promise you I'll kill you myself."

"I'll hold his arms for you, fella," Oak offered with a tone resonating from deep inside his diaphragm, booming in the direction of Sidney.

But it was an offer that Sam barely noted as he pressed ahead with his message: "'*Daddy . . . just to let you know that Freya has passed away, with Auner in her arms and Father Patrick by her bedside.*'" Sam stopped talking as he just stared at the screen, silently once again reading the remainder of the message to himself. No one in the room made a sound, and certainty not Sidney. He didn't even dare to blink in case his brother misread him. "Mr Spatz," said Sam, breaking into the stilled atmosphere with a voice that was now business-like, direct and unwavering.

"I take it the text you received a while ago was verification of the files Sidney passed to you, all be it reluctantly?"

"Sure was," he replied.

"So, considering that Sidney has, according to him, kept to his part of the deal, would you be averse to doing one with me instead?" he asked.

"No, no, he wouldn't!" Sidney retorted, sensing that his brother was about to pull the rug from under his feet.

"That depends, Mr Farmer, on what else is on those other files you have and what you want in exchange," Spatz replied.

"Two things: firstly, I want a private jet – you do have them available at short notice, don't you? Thinking about it, you must have one fuelled and ready to go as you planned to fly Sidney out of the country, am I right?"

"Yes, Mr Farmer we do," Spatz answered. He relaxed the hold on his gun and stood astride with his thumbs resting on top of his belt. With eyes turned down at the corners he waited, curious to hear the rest of Sam's deal.

"Good. So, here it is. I want you to fly my daughter Maggie back to England. But she won't be alone. She'll have Auner with her. But you don't have to worry about being an accessory after the fact. You see, Sidney is going to give his consent."

"I won't!" Sidney bawled. "He's my kid and he's coming with me!"

"You. Shut up and listen to the man, Sidney," Oak boomed, his hostile intervention breaking his silence, a contemptuous leer on his face.

Secure that Oak was content, at least at that juncture, to do nothing more than bide his time, Sam continued. "In Maggie's message, she said that Freya pleaded with her to take care of her son and to bring him up as if he was her own boy. So, in the presence of Maria, Freya's sister and the priest, Maggie swore on the Bible that she would."

"Freya can't do that! She's dead! Priest, or no priest, that now makes me his sole legal guardian. Auner's my kid and like I said, he's coming with me!" shouted Sidney.

Now Sam decided it was time for a brandy, leaving Oak with a clear path to his brother.

"Look at it this way, Sidney," said Sam, taking a sniff of the curious-looking liquor, "either Auner leaves the country with Maggie, or Oak kills you – and he'll snap your neck long before Spatz manages to stop him. Then, when Maria becomes his legal guardian, she'll want Maggie to have the boy anyway," said Sam happily. "Besides, it's not really up to you, it's up to Mr Spatz here, isn't it?" he asked, glancing away from his brother to catch the DEA man's eye.

"And what is the other thing you want, you said there were two?" said Spatz.

"Well, the next one is what we can do for each other. I'll give you this," said Sam, producing one of his four flash drives. "It's one of two that you can have. This one contains information about illegal arms shipments organised by none other than Mr Kazemi. The Malaysian Navy ships them to the Philippines, to a man you may well know. His name is Tagaan, and he's Kazemi's brother-in-law. He then supplies them to the rebel separatists on the island of Mindanao."

Fuelled by the bitterness towards his brother, Sam's demands came across as uncompromising, and Sidney shouted, "Liar, liar!"

Sam continued with undaunted vigour. "In return for the said information, I have a journalist friend of mine, Peter Faber, who's in a spot of bother. Kazemi has him locked up and I want him freed, ASAP–"

Again, Sam was interrupted as Sidney shouted, "We had a deal, Spatz, we had a deal! Don't believe him, he's lying!"

"We'll leave that to Mr Spatz to decide, shall we?" Sam countered. "If he'll settle for your piffling information, that's fine, I'll hand over what I have to Oak. He'll pass it onto the Canadian authorities. I'm sure they'll be pleased as punch to have up-to-date intel on yours and Kazemi's narcotic's network in North America, instead of the Yanks." Again, he directed a question at Spatz: "So, what's it to be? Do we have a deal or not?"

Spatz stared at Sam, unflinching, and then, without giving a reason, left the room.

"Ha, I think you just pissed him off, fella," said Oak with a grunt.

"No, I know him," Sam replied. "He likes a touch of the theatricals, you'll see."

Waiting for Spatz to re-enter the room, Sidney reverted back into his ego-bubble, looking at Sam as if he were transparent. As for Oak, he hardly took his eyes off his quarry. Only when Spatz returned, and with the same two agents they had met at the entrance gate, did he get distracted. Oak found himself gazing at a very pretty face, but a stolid one, as the female operative positioned herself in front of him with both her hands behind her back, her muscular T-shirted body leaving little to the Canadian's pondering imagination.

"I see what you mean," said Oak, his wilderness-beaten face peering over her left shoulder at Sam, who stood quietly confident that the penultimate piece of his jigsaw was about to fit into place.

"Ha-ha," Sam chuckled, reminded of when he first met Spatz at his cottage, and like then, he now drew attention to himself by simply staying silent. He chose to dictate his will by sheer presence. With Sidney also being watched over, Spatz gestured using only his eyes that Sam walk out onto the patio with him, and hopefully confirm that Freya would have her dying wish granted.

"OK, we have deal, but I'll have to log a new flight plan with DEA headquarters in Virginia. How long before you'll be ready to get to the airport?" Spatz asked.

His question and outreached hand was all that Sam wanted, and the two men shook, this time with the desire not to out-firm each other.

"Two hours, but I won't be leaving with them. Sadly, I've got a funeral to attend."

"I see, so when do you plan to keep *your* end of the deal?" Spatz asked.

"When you collect my daughter to take her to the airport and hand over the diamonds to me, I'll give you another one of those flash drives. You can check it out while they're in the air. I'll not have Auner waiting around on the tarmac while you go through it all, there's too much of it." Then Sam asked for something else, something extra: "Oh, and I almost forgot . . . I'd like a diamond, to take with me now, just one will do, please."

Re-entering the lounge, Sam noted with relief that although he was still steely-eyed, Oak had erred on the side of caution and remained at bay.

"On your feet, Sidney, and don't say a sodding word," Sam ordered, and his directness caused his brother's minder to react by reaching for his holster.

"That's OK, let him be," said Spatz, and again followed with wordless motions for his colleague to stand down.

Sam reached for Sidney's hands that, compared to his own, were small and soft, and with eyes flaring with satisfaction said, "You're screwed, Sidney; or to use your words: 'I've won over on you'." He then gripped his brother's hands tightly, crushingly tight, his eyes drilling into his. He felt him flinch with discomfort.

"Can you feel that, that pain as your bones and sinew compress? That's your sister's neck as she hanged herself. She may have put the rope over her own head, but *you,* Sidney, tied the knot!"

Letting go of his brother's hands and taking a step back, Sam observed Sidney show little response to his brother's actions other than a wringing of his hands and a conceited smirk.

"Seeing you die at the hands of Oak would, in my mind, be a waste of his energies. I want you to live and experience the true meaning of loss, to have what you considered yours taken from you. I've stolen your deal with Mr Spatz, taken your diamonds and, more importantly, your son."

"You can't do this to me!" Sidney raged, with words that literally spat into Sam's face. "You're making a big mistake. If you think I won't get my kid back, then you're more stupid than I took you for."

Relentlessly Sidney continued to condemn and belittle in a ranting stupor of wrath, which, for Sam, was almost as embarrassing as it was pitiful. Then with a sudden and exerted push with both hands, Sam made Sidney reel backwards to land clumsily on the sofa.

"Oak, come over here," said Sam, seeing the big Canadian, unopposed, sidestep his female obstacle to stand next to his brother-in-law. "Do you trust me?" Sam asked.

"With my life, fella, you know that."

"Well," Sam said, his eyes focused and wide, reddened with hostility as he looked down at his brother. "On the life of my daughters, I swear to you that if this piece of shit or anyone associated with him comes near our family, I'll drop him down a hole so deep that to rescue him they'd have to dig a tunnel on the opposite side of the world to get to him."

Chapter 30

A lesson in Morality

Day Three

Whether it was the lush Devon countryside that Sam longed to return to or, for Oak, the lakes and forests of his native home, the lands of Shangri-La seemed unfitting desires when all around them the sights and stench of poverty clawed at their senses; but they were images countered by the endeavours of one man, a holy man, who unashamedly broke rules for the sake of the children in his care.

"Are you sure your buddy Spatz has dropped us off at the right place, fella?" asked Oak, his eyes surveying a face peering at them from behind a barred window. The building appeared on the outside to be a derelict three-storey block whose weather-washed walls disguised a sanctuary within.

"Apparently in its previous life it was a police training centre – an appropriate place if you want to keep children safe, don't you think?" Sam replied.

Both men looked on as the sound of security bolts being slid aside gave way to the creek of the steel-clad entrance door opening into a word of hope.

"Yes, may I be of assistance?" enquired a softly spoken lady who, despite being rather elderly and short in stature, used her rotund waistline to amply fortify the partially opened door.

"Ah, good morning, yes you can. My name is Sam Farm–"

"Oh, Mr Farmer, welcome. Come in, please," the lady replied, and the door was flung wide open. "Father Patrick is expecting you. He's in the infirmary with your lovely daughter. Please follow me and I'll take you to them," she said, leading the two men along a corridor towards a single door at the end.

"Quiet for an orphanage, ain't it?" Oak commented, noting the absence of the sound of children being children.

"Oh, if it's noise you want," answered the lady, and in a manner that made Oak feel that he was about to be chastised, "you'll have to wait for when the children are outside playing in the courtyard. They're about to have their lunch. We teach them to be silent and orderly. Here we are," she ended, her spiky retort replaced with a polite smile as she knocked on the door, opened it, and then walked away.

"Hello, sweetheart, what are you doing and where is Auner?" Sam asked, frowning at the somewhat surprising sight that greeted him.

"Oh! Hi, Dad! What's it look like I'm doing? And Auner's fine. He's about to have lunch with the other children," said Maggie, giving her uncle Oak a little wave as he stood next to her father, equally mystified to find his niece laying on a hospital bed with a tube protruding from her right arm.

"Well, I can see you're giving blood, but why? Who's in need of it?" Sam asked.

"Those who are able to give us what we want in exchange for the blood, that's who," came the direct reply from behind an old hospital bed screen, which partitioned off a small area in one corner of the room. Its tubular painted frame was chipped and stained with rust and, like the room itself, had seen better days. Even before a face was put to the voice, a mystery it certainly wasn't. The unmistakable northern Irish accent and profound conviction in his words told Sam that he was in the company of one Father Patrick O'Toole Quinn. A man of whom Trudy had said, if you ask for his help he may want something in return that you may be 'unwilling to give'.

He was a man who dared to be defied, with an imposing stature and an aura that, despite wearing a dog collar, he was happy to exploit for the parentless souls in his care. The priest was everything that Trudy had described, with a full head of curly red hair and a bushy beard that virtually concealed his mouth; it was streaked with grey, giving him an almost biblical image.

"You see, Mr Farmer, here we use blood as a currency – untainted blood to be more precise, that in this God-forsaken city is a rarity. We have an agreement with a small research laboratory; they take it in exchange for drugs that we desperately require." The priest paused, removing a pair of surgical gloves, and then shook the hands of his two visitors. He took particular interest in one of them – Oak – his eyes scanning the big Canadian. "What blood group would you be?" he unashamedly asked, turning briefly to Maggie with raised eyebrows at the prospect of another donor ready to hot bed once she had recovered.

"It's O positive, and the name's Oak," he replied, still gripping the resourceful clergyman's hand.

"Mr Farmer . . . I have a question that needs an answer, so I have," said the priest, releasing his hand from Oak's grip so that he could check the blood bag that, for him, was slowly filling with manna from heaven. "Did our mutual friend, the prodigal daughter, ever tell you the main reason why she only drinks water now?"

Sam hesitated to reply to what he knew was a surreptitious question, aware that as a man of the cloth, Father Patrick could never admit that it was he who had guided their close friend Trudy through the tortures of cold turkey as she fought to kick her dependence on heroin, an addiction that resulted in her having to take antiretroviral drugs. The memory of her words rang in his ears: *I drink water. The only drugs that pass my lips now, are the ones that keep me alive.*

"I think you already know the answer to that," Sam pointedly replied.

"Yes, I do indeed, but what *you're* not aware of is that we have twenty-seven children just like her, and all of them depend on what we do in this room. These children, Mr Farmer, are not only orphans, they're outcasts, consequences of their parents' immorality." Father Patrick's sermon-like tone left no room for debate or further justification. For him it was this or the children died. Sam stood there feeling the fervour of his words humble him. He was in the presence of a priest who ignored the ethical boundaries of his mother church and interpreted the will of his god in favour of his charges.

Sam looked across at the bag that was filling up with his daughter's blood, an unselfish gift that for her would be replenished in time – time that Sam now knew was the one thing that wasn't on the children's side.

"So, when do you want us to roll our sleeves up?" Sam asked.

"No, not you Dad, you can't," replied Maggie.

"Unfortunately, your daughter is right," said the priest. "Maggie informed me that you've lost enough blood already; but if I had my way, I would bleed the English until not a drop was left . . . with exceptions of course," he countered, with a glance at Maggie.

"That's put you in your place, fella," Oak laughed, and then rolled back the sleeves of his shirt to expose both forearms. "Here, I'll pay for Sam's; you can take one out of each arm." Again, he laughed.

"Sorry Mags, I was watching Oak give blood. Poor man, he's looking a little on the pale side now," he laughed. "Still no Auner, where is he?" Sam added, finding Maggie on her own in what Father Patrick called his office; but with its small window and security bars, it had the air of a prison cell.

"No. I left him playing quietly with the other children for a while longer. He's OK. One of the sisters is keeping an eye on him, but you can see he doesn't want to be far from me, which is nice . . . but the little mite misses his mummy. Almost ready though, Dad. I've been transferring the few items Auner owns into my own bag, the poor sod," she said, looking sadly at Auner's sparse belongings. "After all he's been through it comes down to two bloody carrier bags . . . two. I tell yer, Dad, had I been there when you let that shit go, I would have marked him for life. That so-called 'uncle' of mine has got away scot-free, and it's wrong," Maggie hissed. "What if he comes for Auner? What then, eh?"

"He won't, sweetheart, he knows what I will do to him, brother or no brother."

"Well, I'd like to see him try, coz I'd fight to the death for Auner – I promised Freya that. There you are, Dad, all done," she said with a final tug of the zip on her travel bag.

"Good, so let's go through what I need you to do once you land," said her father, and he saw that her grim expression from moments before was now child-like excitement at the thought of her journey home.

"How cool is this going to be? Having our own private jet to take us home? Do you think they'll let Auner go up to the front and see the pilot?" she asked.

"Can't see why not, after all, you two will be the only passengers on board. But let's get on shall we, Spatz will be here soon to take you to the airport," he replied. He was mindful that getting Auner back to England was the comparatively easy part. Being allowed into the country without immigration documents wouldn't be. "OK," he continued, "remember the four flash drives you brought to me from my hotel room?" He showed her one that he had pinched between his finger and thumb. "When you land in London, and if it all goes to plan, you'll be met by Detective Chief Inspector Jane Tamworth. Hopefully she'll be waiting for you as soon as you get off the plane. You're to give her this, no one else, only her – is that understood?"

"Yeah, yeah, Dad, loud and clear. Only her. So, what's on it?" she asked, taking it from her father.

Sam knew she would ask him that, and it had to be the truth he told her, as she could smell a lie a mile off, even if it were for her own safety. "It's the remaining files detailing Sidney's present-day involvement in the import and distribution of heroin and cocaine into the UK, not only on Tamworth's patch, but many others. It also includes illicit payments to serving and retired police officers going back nearly twenty years."

"Wow, no shit. But you said remaining files? So, I take it she's got some files already, the same as you've given to that DEA guy?"

"Yes. Well, she will have about six hours before your flight lands. You see, I've sent James on ahead of you with the first part, to get the ball rolling. He'll be there to make sure you and Auner get home safely. With what he's capable of, no one is going to mess with him, are they?"

"Bloody hell, Dad, it sounds like real spy stuff, don't it? But what are you getting out of it?" Maggie asked.

"Nothing," Sam answered. His daughter looked perplexed. "Hopefully Auner is going to be the beneficiary, sweetheart. If all goes to plan, he'll get a British passport and with a Miss Margret Louise Farmer listed as his mother and sole guardian."

"Oh my god, that's great news!" she cried. "Then no one can take him away from me, or us, his family! Thank you, Dad." She kissed him and flung her arms his neck, crying unashamed tears of relief.

"Don't thank me. Thank your – hopefully hiding under a rock – Uncle Sidney. The police will be falling over each other to get their . . ." Sam stopped, distracted by the sound of a familiar American accent talking with an equally recognisable Canadian.

"Sounds like your ticket home has arrived," he said. "I'll introduce you."

Maggie didn't stay long. Mr Spatz and she could talk on the way to the airport. For Maggie, Auner was her sole priority, and she needed to prepare him for his new life with her and Hob-Nob, the dog. But Sam still had plenty of talking to do, and some of it would leave his acquaintance, Mr Spatz, lost for words.

"Oak," said Sam, "do me a favour, mate. Mr Spatz and I have few things to sort out in private. Could you go and find Father Patrick and bring him back with you in about ten to fifteen minutes?"

"Yeah, sure, fella. No probs," replied Oak, not giving it a second thought. For him it was job done, and his hunting skills were no longer required.

As for Sam, Oak knew the end game was still a work in progress. Over the last thirty-six hours he had witnessed with awe as his brother-in-law had, at a relentless pace, put together and executed a plan that culminated in the successful rescue of their nephew, and the demise of Button, Moses Jones and the Barber. To do that he'd not only had to put his own life on the line, but also outwit and out-manoeuvre his heartless brother.

Then, with a battered body that was weary with fatigue, still have the mental stamina to find answers to questions that had eluded him for over twenty years, whilst at the same time skilfully steal the deal from under his brother's nose. He then had to cast him into the wilderness, and Oak was satisfied that would be a place where those who thought Sidney had betrayed them would be searching with their own brand of retribution.

Now though, after all his manoeuvring, for Sam the end game had turned into a game of patience as he waited for the final piece of his past to fall into place.

Closing the door, Sam couldn't fail to notice the large brown leather attaché case that was handcuffed to the DEA man's right wrist by a short hardened steel chain, the contents of which were gained by the sheer fact that he didn't want his brother to profit from the torture he had put his son Auner through, or the senseless and barbaric murder of his friend Mila Faber.

"Hmm," Sam quietly mused, thinking how the past three days now seemed like one long surreal dream, an unimaginable dream that now bizarrely continued as he stood in front of the United States drug enforcement officer. The man was about to hand over nine million dollars-worth of diamonds, diamonds that for Sam had long since lost their lustre.

Spatz rested the case on Father Patrick's desk – that was nothing more than a rehashed dressing table, and its pink melamine top was littered with ignored correspondence from the Vatican, the Papal seal embossed into the 'no expense spared' high quality paper. The priest appeared to have his own personal watermark: rings where numerous cups of coffee had been placed, no doubt laced with the peaty essence from the bottle of Irish whisky that stood appropriately by an empty cup.

"Here they are, want to count them?" said Spatz; but his remark received only a silent shake of the head from Sam, who seemed more interested in what the DEA man had to tell him rather than what he had to give him.

"So, is Peter Faber free, and what of Kazemi?" Sam asked, feeling that *his* two questions deserved more of an answer than Spatz's. He hoped the answer wouldn't make the uncomplicated complicated, that it would be simple.

"No, not as yet," he replied, noticing Sam's frown. "This is because your buddy is a German citizen, and diplomatically the US State Department doesn't want to be openly involved in his release. So, the Germans are handling it and, of course, will take the credit," Spatz said. He turned away, placing his unchained hand flat on the makeshift desk to check whether it would take his weight, but clearly decided the diamonds alone were putting it close to collapse.

"So, when is Peter likely to be freed?" Sam asked impatiently.

"Should be within the next two or three days," came the casual reply. Pausing, he turned around and did what Sam wanted him to do – look him in the eye. "You should know better than most, Mr Farmer, that getting out of Indonesia isn't that straight-forward. Dealing with the appropriate authorities is like dealing with a rattlesnake in a henhouse. The cops have already charged your guy with subversive activity against the state, and despite giving them the intel about the arms shipments going to Tagaan and the rebels, they won't let him go just like that. You know what they're like, Mr Farmer. To them it will be seen as losing face. I've heard, but it's not been confirmed, that they will hand him over to the German Consulate in a bogus prisoner swap; so, like I said, two or three days."

If Spatz had hoped that Sam might have relaxed his stare on him once he knew Peter Faber could be released, he was wrong, and instantly sensed the next words that were about to roll off Sam's tongue. "As for Kazemi," said Spatz quickly, pre-empting Sam's question, "you used a well-known saying earlier: 'plugged nickel'. Well, I have one you Brit's use: 'done a runner'. Sorry, bud, your guy slipped away."

The Englishman's expression changed from one of expectation to a look of utter dejection in the time it took him to utter, "The bastard."

"According to our embassy in KL – Kuala Lumpur – your man Kazemi was obviously tipped off. It seems someone high up gave him time to high-tail out of town while the others on your list were bush-wacked. My guess is that with his contacts, he'll be somewhere like the Regina Hotel in Singapore by now, giving those who couldn't catch him the finger while drinking the best there is of this stuff," said Spatz, pointing at the bottle of Bushmills on the desk. (At that moment, Sam would dearly have loved to take a large mouthful of that whisky, aware it was among the best money could buy.) With Kazemi escaping the wrath from his own country that he duly deserved, Sam knew that no amount of questions would change the fact that the last piece of his past still eluded him: a man he would never forget as long as he had scars covering his body.

With a huff, Sam looked poignantly at Spatz and said, "C'est la vie." But he had been denied closure of his quest for retribution on the last of three men that had each in their own way shaped his life, mentally and physically, and the words sounded hollow.

Sam patted the pockets of his trousers to retrieve the one remaining flash drive, showing it to Spatz. He seemed almost resigned now at this turn of events. "Well, that's it then, time to 'bring the curtain down', as the saying goes."

Spatz reached out with his free hand to take the item from him, an innocuous piece of two-tone plastic that, like the three that preceded it, held within its memory card the capacity to disrupt a future that, for many, had looked very profitable. But now? Well, now it would be bleak.

"And while we're on the subject of lowering the curtain," Sam continued, "have you checked any emails recently from your wife Cindy?"

For Sam, it was like watching in slow motion as Spatz tried to pigeonhole the curve ball that had just been thrown in his direction, out of the blue and out of context with all that had just taken place. Then, like all delayed reactions, Spatz's response shifted into top gear, demanding answers with a bluster showing that Sam had unsettled him.

"How the goddamn do you know about her? And what the hell do you mean by curtain?"

"Well you see, Truman – you don't mind if I call you by your first name, do you? I know very little about your wife, that's to say compared to Thelma," said Sam, hoping his revelation was taken with the sensitivity and understanding in which it was meant.

Spatz stared stunned and wide-eyed at Sam's face; but Sam showed no malice or judgment towards him. He observed the DEA man glance at the closed door, as if to convince himself that they were alone. Then, and without saying a word, he retrieved a small key from the breast pocket of his shirt and released himself from the restraints of the leather case.

Now with both hands free, Spatz twisted his wrists, and his knuckles cracked as he flexed his fingers. He then spoke with a tone that was uncompromisingly stark: "Don't for one moment think, Samuel – you don't mind me calling you that, *do* you? – that because you're still breathing, I may not be considering breaking every bone in your body – *comprendez?*"

But Spatz's unambiguous retort only produced an accepting nod from Sam, a nod that was also laced with a soft agreeable smile, as were his words: "Do you know I had the same thought myself, about you and me going toe to toe, last man standing and all that shit, just to find out which one of us would come out on top?"

"Yeah, and what did you decide?" asked Spatz.

"Pointless in this instance. It would be like beating myself up, and I'll tell you why. You see, I remember when we were first introduced at my cottage, and apart from you pissing me off for being so bloody arrogant and aloof, I saw in your expression when you held Penny's theatre award in your hands, something that reminded me of me as I once was."

Sam turned and looked away from his threatening slayer to cast an eye on the bottle of desirable malt, then the coffee cup, tide-marked and with a deep brown sludge-like sediment lying in the bottom. *That'll do, Irish coffee. Besides, whisky is a good sterilizer*, he decided. Pouring enough of the amber liquid into the cup to lose his driving license, he savoured the hearty swig, and then passed what remained to the disgruntled Spatz, and watched him swiftly put it away in a fashion purists would say was wasteful.

"I have a good friend who passed me some information about you; but please don't ask me how it came to be in his possession," Sam continued, fully aware that none of what he was about to say was any of his business. "I'm aware that one of your co-workers

– that's what you call your so-called work colleagues, isn't it? – and you were involved in some sort of undercover surveillance in Miami, codenamed 'Thelma'. The rest of the facts I must admit I know little of, other than you hit this co-worker of yours so hard that he's still in a coma. The reason why – and I can only guess – was probably due to the rage you must have felt when you hit him, and that it had something to do with your family. I think this because when I hit Button again last night and put him down for good, I was thinking of those I love and keeping them safe from him. But what I do know for sure is that, because of your actions, you're not able to keep the promise you made to your wife, are you? At my cottage, you told us you'd promised to take her to see Penny's play again before she leaves. I realise now that that's what I saw etched across your face. You reminded me of when I was desperate to keep a promise to my dying wife Annie." Sam awaited a response, gaining in confidence that Spatz wasn't about to take up his idea of last man standing.

Reaching for the whisky bottle, Spatz then gazed thoughtfully at Sam and spoke in a manner that was void of his usual practiced melodramatics. "The guy's called Chuck Booth. We worked together on and off for over twenty years. I considered him as someone I could trust with my life, and those of my family." He paused taking another sizable amount of whisky before handing Sam what remained. "Chuck and I were in a bar. We'd been on a stake-out together in Miami – Thelma, like you said. To cut to the chase, he advised me that I should put in for a transfer, because if not the lives of my family were at risk. I realised instantly that he'd sold the department out . . . and our friendship . . . and that we were getting too close to his acquaintances. So, I hit him, and got transferred, like he advised, and to this shithole. At least I know my family are safe." Spatz waited for a short moment while Sam finished off the whisky, then he wanted his own question answered. "So, you contacted my wife . . . why?" he asked.

"I didn't." Sam paused while Spatz pondered. "A PA friend of mine contacted her to say she's managed to get the two tickets you wanted for Penny's final performance. I guess you wife's email is to arrange your flight to London . . . but you'd better get a move on, chum, you've got five days."

"You've done this for me . . . why?" Spatz asked, puzzled, and with a faltering voice.

"I don't like betrayal, no matter how it's dished up," Sam replied. "Being stabbed in the back by my brother, or not being able to keep a promise – it's all the same to me. You're an honest man, Spatz; but at first I didn't know that. You see, when you left my cottage, DCI Tamworth glanced at you and said quietly 'Et tu, Brute', and at first I thought she was indicating that I should be wary of you . . . but she wasn't. You probably know that that sentence comes from Shakespeare's *Julius Caesar*, when his close friend Brutus stabs him in the back? It wasn't until I knew more about you that I realised that, like me, you'd possibly been betrayed by someone you trusted."

"Jesus, you Brits, you love your conundrums, and I see now what you meant by the curtain coming down . . . reference to Miss McCain's last performance . . . clever," Spatz said, but hadn't finished. He was curious about something Sam had mentioned. "Tell me, if you don't mind me asking . . . did you keep the promise you made to your wife?"

"Yes, but sadly I had to wait until after she had died . . . but that same day I met Penny. Now, that is a puzzle!" replied Sam, his face a perplexed frown. "Oh yes, and by the way, I do mind being called Samuel. My friends call me Sam."

Spatz responded with a handshake that was firm and equal to the Englishman's; a handshake that was abruptly interrupted by the distinctive sound of knuckles tapping against the door.

"Tell me," Spatz asked, "what did you do with that diamond?"

"Nothing yet. It's for my taxi driver friend, he's earned it," Sam quickly replied.

Oak led the way into the room, followed by the priest – who

took an instant interest in Spatz, dispensed with the niceties of being introduced, and went straight for the blood group.

Maggie came in holding Auner in her arms, his waif-like body clinging to her, not wanting to let go. As much as she wanted her father to fly home with them, she knew he was staying two more days for Freya's funeral and to catch up on old times with Henning; Oak was in no hurry to go home either.

With one hand resting on the leather case, Sam realised that, whether it was due to the fine Irish whisky he had just consumed, or the fact that sleep deprivation was once more clawing at his mind, he had almost forgotten that there was still the matter of the diamonds.

"Father Patrick," said Sam, putting on a sheepish voice as he glanced across at Spatz, who, like Oak and Maggie, was unaware of what he intended to do with the gems. "My friend here and I have a confession to make. I'm afraid we've drunk all your whisky, but I hope this will recompense you for it," he said, handing the case and its contents to the one person they knew deserved them, a man who would now be able to give his flock of diseased and destitute children life-saving care without the need to worry about where the next vein was coming from.

"That's better than any kidney, ain't it, Father Patrick?" said Maggie.

"What has a kidney got to do with it?" Sam asked.

"Oh hell, Dad, did you not know?" Maggie smiled with the look of mischief about her. "Father Patrick here, he gets bonus points if he comes up with a kidney," she laughed; but she wasn't joking.

Chapter 31

The Land of his Birth

Seven days. Seven long days he had been away. It took astronauts only six to travel to the moon and back. Sam at times had felt as if he had been on the moon, and on the dark side, where home was blanked out by the evil people; but from the time Penny had collected him at the airport she'd hardly let him out of her sight – not that he minded. All he had done for the first couple of days was sleep, in between being spoon-fed her love. And it was love and adoration for her that spilled out with gusto by an entire theatre audience, including Spatz and his wife Cindy, as they watched a tearful Penny take her final bow portraying Katherine. Now her energies should have been solely focused on becoming the future Mrs Farmer, but there was something she had to tell Sam, and she knew it was time.

"You bugger, that's the third time you've dropped the soap in as many minutes," laughed Penny.

The sound of her playful saucy giggle as she lay in the bath while he soaped her body was, for Sam, his heaven compared to the hell he had just been through. And then there was the hell that for Peter Faber had now just begun. There was never going to be an easy way for him to tell his friend that his wife, Mila, was dead. He felt for the sake of Mila's memory and the sanity of her husband it was best not to elaborate on how she met her fate. The sight of Peter with darkened eyes clutching his wife's wedding band and locket confirmed to him that that visual torture would remain solely his burden to bear.   Even with the knowledge that

Kazemi still eluded them both, Sam hoped that, like him, Peter would find a way to move on for the sake of his young, now motherless son. For Sam moving on was now splashing him with water in between kisses and caresses as he sat on the edge of the bath. Penny's memories of when she anxiously waited for Sam to return were cast aside. Now for her and the love of her life it was the future that filled her thoughts... as parents!

"Sam, sweetheart . . ." she said, smiling. "You're going to be a daddy again . . . I'm pregnant." her words hung in the air and like her glowing smile combined to produce a moment that neither of them would forget in a hurry, a comical moment instigated by the sound of the front door slamming shut, followed by the sudden appearance of Estelle.

"Christ, it's like Piccadilly Circus in this house, where did you spring from? You're early," Sam boomed, clambering to his feet and intending to give his daughter a welcoming kiss.

"No way, Dad, you go and get changed first, you're dripping wet. You're meant to take your clothes off when you have a bath," she grinned, noticing Penny as she coyly gave her a little wave and beaming from ear to ear.

"Are Maggie and Auner with you?" asked Penny stepping out of the bath, aware that there was only one reason why Estelle needed to rush up the stairs as soon as she arrived.

"Yes, yes . . . but you or Dad need to give her a hand, she's in a bit of bother," Estelle hurriedly replied.

"Mags, what on earth has happened to you? Wait, let me help," cried Penny as she hastily made her way down the stairs to the hallway while quickly tying the waistband of her bath robe into a bow.

"Ah, thanks, maid," said an appreciative Maggie, her smile not hiding the discomfort she was experiencing: her right arm was in a sling. Penny helped her slip off the lightweight Parka jacket she was wearing.

Standing quietly and shielded behind Maggie was Auner, still trying to come to terms with his new life and extended family.

"You must be the gorgeous Auner I've heard so much about," said Penny softly. Her comforting smile was the opposite of his shy gaze as his fingers reached for the security of Maggie's hand.

"Do you think we should tell Aunty Penny what your silly new mum has done?" said Maggie, and with Auner's hand grasping hers walked through the lounge into the kitchen.

"Christ, it was so embarrassing, wasn't it Auner?" she said sheepishly, looking at the young boy who Penny lifted up onto a stool at the breakfast bar. "We had just parked up at a farmyard and I said to Auner to be careful as the courtyard could be slippery . . . and no sooner had I said that, I fell arse over tit. Dislocated my right shoulder and cracked a bone in my elbow."

Words of sympathy followed, as did a collection of amused huffs from her father. Sam stood by the archway to the kitchen, buttoning up the cuffs of a dry shirt, still quietly distracted with the realisation that Penny was going to have his child.

"Well, a mug of tea is called for, and I expect you would like some juice, wouldn't you, sweetheart?" asked Penny, shooting Auner a gentle smile.

"Ah, good. Let's put the kettle on, I'm gagging," Estelle declared, rubbing in some of Penny's hand cream from the bathroom. "We're sorry for not letting you know that we were arriving early, but being a Friday we thought we'd catch an earlier train and beat the rush, and sorry again if we disturbed you."

"I wouldn't fret, sis," Maggie replied, rolling her eyes. "You know what they two are like when our backs are turned. They can't get enough of each other," she joked.

Sam let out a small laugh. He was so pleased to have his family around him, even more now as he walked over to the mother-to-be and put his arms around her waist. Her radiant smile, he knew, contradicted her once strong belief that motherhood wasn't for her. Penny whispered in his ear and he replied with a kiss to her lips and a wink of his eye. The peering faces of his two daughters were filled with curiosity.

"Take my advice, young Auner," said Sam. "Enjoy every minute of love you can get from these women, it's priceless."

"I still think you should stay behind and rest that arm of yours," Sam advised, giving Maggie a farewell peck on her cheek. The three most important women in his life were once again about to board a ferry to France.

"You know I can't, Dad. Fanny's foal is due the day after tomorrow. And with Papa Goss away, I have to be there for her. Besides, Madame Renard and everyone at the farmhouse are so looking forward to meeting Auner."

"Don't worry, sweetheart, Estelle and I will look after her," said Penny, blowing him a kiss as they disappeared through the double doors that lead to the ferry.

That's all well and good, but they should be looking after you, he thought.

He stayed to watch the ferry leave, the lights on board becoming ever fainter as the ship sailed further into the blackness of the night, and with what he now called his baby stowaway on board.

"My god, look at all the visitors there are, and it's not even 10.00am yet," Penny commented.

"Yvette asked me to drive you around to the rear entrance. She will be there to meet you," said Monsieur Paul.

"Yeah," replied Estelle, and like Penny peered out of the car window as they approached the chateau. "Sophie said they're pretty busy, mostly due to the craft school and the lace museum, of course; but ever since one of Madame Renard's cousins blurted out in pubic that your wedding gown was being made here, loads of people, mostly media, have been nosing around hoping to get a glimpse of it."

"Yes, I know, but it's safe though," Penny replied. "When Yvette phoned last week, she said my dress is now kept locked away in her mother's rooms, which is reassuring. I can't wait to try it on now that it's finished."

"Well, I know what Auner and I are going to do later. We're off to the stables to check up on Fanny."

"No, you're not," came the stern reply from Penny. With Auner sitting quietly between them she leant slightly forward and looked severely at the impatient Maggie. "You're going to bed, sweetheart. You said yourself you couldn't get comfortable on the ferry last night and that you hardly slept a wink. The stables can wait, and don't worry about Auner, he'll be spoilt for choice for people happy to look after him," said Penny, giving a little tug to the peak of the boy's blue canvas baseball cap.

"I'll be all right, maid, don't fuss. Honest, I'll be OK," said Maggie, who as much as she tried couldn't conceal the malaise that was wearing her down.

"Penny's right, sis," said Estelle from the front seat. "I'll phone the stables and if there's any news, I'll wake you, but there won't be. We all know Fanny's in the best of hands."

"Yeah, really?" Maggie replied. "Bernard doesn't give a damn about Fanny, you know that. He hated Sabine because Papa Goss favoured her over her brother. He always wanted to run the stables, and now he does."

"Tell you what, sis, I'll ask the stables to contact us if anything happens, yeah? Anyhow, there's a vet on call at a moment's notice, isn't there? So, stop gassing girl. Like Penny said, you're going to bed."

"Yvette, have you seen Penny? I've been looking everywhere for her." asked Estelle, finding her in the grand hall as the last of the day's visitor's left the chateau.

"Yes, she's with ma mère, trying on her wedding gown," Yvette answered.

"Ah, silly me, I forgot she'd be there. I'll pop up and see her, and I can't wait to see the dress!"

"No, you can't, you'll have to wait until the wedding, Estelle," Yvette insisted. "Ma mère has given strict instructions that she will be the only person to see Mademoiselle Penny wearing the gown before then."

"Oh . . . OK then," Estelle replied, feeling slightly stumped at what to do next. "It's just that MP is taking Sophie and me into Bayeux tonight. We're all going to the festival to watch the candle-lit procession of the statue of Our Lady of the Rosary being carried through the town. I wanted to ask Penny if she fancied coming along, that's all."

"Yes, I know you are, but I don't think she will," Yvette replied. "Paul asked her earlier and I believe I heard her say that she'll stay and keep Maggie and Auner company." Yvette let out a small chuckle as Auner came to mind. It wasn't long before smiles and timid chatter had replaced his shyness. It was Monsieur Johnny, the chateau's cook, whose broken English had soon found a universal language the young boy could respond to: baking cakes!

Penny stood in front of the full-length gilded mirror and gasped. It was a vision that began in her mind's eye that had brought her to this moment, a moment where all she could do was mutter, "Oh, how it fits like a glove." Trembling with tears of delight that now glazed her focus, she reached, in need of Madame Renard's hand. As matriarch of the Renard clan, she exuded a mystique, a quality that was honed over a lifetime. Now Penny would soon realise that she not only had the ability to detect what was not on show, but also predict the unexpected!

Placing Penny's hand to her made-up lips, she stared deep into eyes that soon flared with a truthful smile.

"Have you told Sam you're pregnant?" she asked, and with a voice that was as gentle as her question.

Penny's eyes then fixed on her. *Oh my god . . . you know?* she mused, wondering just how the Devil she had found out.

Madam Renard smiled one of her enigmatic smiles.

"Yes," she then said, remembering Madame Renard's question. "I told him yesterday, and he was so happy, but we've agreed not to tell Maggie or Estelle yet. We're having a family get together with my aunts and Archie when we get back. Sam and I plan to tell them then. We know they'll be over the moon with the news, as we are." She paused as she recalled the moment she told Sam and laughed. "Ha! The poor darling! He was sitting on the edge of the bath and leant over to kiss me. Then I heard the front door slam shut as the girls and Auner arrived. I suddenly moved and he slipped into the water. Not a very auspicious way to respond to the news that he's going to be a daddy again, but it made me laugh,' she giggled. Then Penny asked, "How did you know, you haven't felt my tummy? Not that I'm showing yet . . ."

The reply that followed made Penny feel slightly saddened that her secret was realised by logic rather than Madame Renard's supposedly unique gift of deduction. A gift that Maggie and Estelle had said she possessed.

"When we had lunch, I noticed that you preferred to drink water this time, to your usual wine you like so much." Madame Renard paused giving an eye browed shrug. "I'm informed by Sophie that these days, mothers-to-be pay more attention to what they consume. It was never like that in my day . . . I'm very happy for you both, for all of us." The wise ageless lady sensed Penny's disappointment that she hadn't put her gift to the test. "Slip out of the gown." Penny did as asked, and then stood silently as Madame Renard laid her hands on her tummy to utter a word that Penny was defiantly not expecting to hear. "Deux."

"Oh my god . . . two?"

"Oui. Pourquoi pas? Why not? You are a twin. Sam is a twin."

Penny's reaction was to hug her tummy, the elation of possibly carrying two of Sam's babies had just doubled.

That evening, soon after supper, Penny decided to go to bed early. It had been a day beyond compare and now she lay in the dark, drifting off to sleep with visions of her wedding gown and, if Madame Renard was correct, her twins. But those dreams were about to be abruptly interrupted by a desperate sounding Maggie.

"Penny, wake up . . . please!"

"Oh . . . what is it? What's wrong?" she replied, teasing open her eyes against the glare of her bedside lamp and peering at her watch which showed 10.42pm.

"It's Fanny, she's in trouble. I've got to go and see what's wrong with her. Can you come with me, please? I'd like you to come!"

Pulling herself up to sit on the edge of the bed, Penny ran her fingers through her dishevelled hair and stretched.

"Sure . . . sure I will, sweetheart. Did the person who contacted you say what has happened to her?"

"No, not a lot. It was one of the staff, and she said Fanny's become agitated and is kicking out. Someone's coming to pick us up."

"What about Bernard and the vet, surely one of them are there?" Penny asked, slipping on her cream Aran jumper and red denim jeans.

"No, neither of them are," was Maggie's furious and blunt reply. "It sounds as if Bernard has gone into Bayeux with two of the stable maids to see the bloody festival and, as for the vet, it's anyone's guess."

"Are Estelle, Sophie and MP back yet?" Penny asked.

"No, I tried to call them both but their phones go to voicemail. I left messages."

"So, who's looking after Auner?"

"He was sleeping with me, and luckily he didn't wake up. Yvette is sitting with him," said Maggie. She looked into the dressing table mirror at the same time as Penny. "I hope Fanny won't get even more frazzled seeing us without our make-up on," she quipped; but Penny knew that like father like daughter, in times of stress, humour was her release valve.

"Come on, Mags, I'm ready. Where's your coat? I'll help you put it on," said Penny, wondering just how Maggie was going to be of any use with her right arm in a sling and painful as hell to move.

Maggie hardly spoke on the way. Penny knew she was going through possible scenarios in her mind, preparing herself for the unknown; but what greeted her, she wasn't prepared for.

"My God! What is this, what is wrong with you people? Why isn't she in a larger foaling box? Look at her hay, it's filthy with shit. Clean it up now! And she needs more hay, lots of it . . . *rapide, rapide*!" Although seething with anger, Maggie made her feelings clear without overly raising her voice, and her tone and wide eyes were enough to put the fear of God into the two stable maids who were supposedly tasked to watch over the pregnant mare.

Penny stayed out of the way in the background, watching and listening as Maggie stood for a moment just inside the mare's box, observing her. "How long has she been rolling around like this?" she asked, directing her question at the older of the two stable hands, Colette, who Maggie had known since she arrived at the stables some years before.

"On and off for two hours or so. She would walk around a while and then back herself into a corner and drop down onto her forelegs. That's when I phoned Monsieur Goss," said Colette.

"We're talking about Bernard here, aren't we, not his father

Raymond?" Maggie impatiently asked. "Come on, girl, yes or no?"

"Yes, yes Bernard. I phoned him to say Fanny was showing signs of labour, and I noticed her teats were waxing. He told me not to worry and that he'd contact the vet himself."

"Two sodding hours ago, the poor darling, no wonder she's fretting," Maggie seethed and turned to Penny. "Pen, I'm going to need you to assist me. Right, you two," she said, briefly giving orders to the two staff, "we need to get Fanny onto her feet and you two are to keep her calm while I examine her. Where's the birthing kit?"

"I'll get it," replied Colette.

"Right, Pen, while they're sorting themselves out, I need you to help me scrub up. Help me off with my cardigan." For Maggie, there was no time to waste on polite requests: only the wellbeing of Fanny and her foal mattered now.

Penny did exactly what she was told, rolling up the sleeve of Maggie's blouse and washing her hand and forearm with warm soapy water from one of two buckets that had been placed in the box.

"At least they've had the forethought of taping up her tail," said Maggie, as Penny coated lubricating gel onto the fingers of her long-sleeved surgical glove. "Right, let's have a feel." Caringly Maggie started her internal examination. Nothing was said by anyone as they waited, and only the winces of discomfort could be heard from Maggie as she awkwardly tried to manoeuvre her injured arm out of the way. Then it was done, but the torturous look on her face confirmed something that she had feared, something that she knew she was in no physical condition to deal with. When she spoke, her words were glum and dejected: "It's dystocia: the foal's breeched, a complete arse about face . . . it wants to come out backwards."

"Oh shit," came the reply from Colette.

"Yes, 'oh shit'. She's in need of a caesarean and it can't be done here. The nearest veterinary clinic is an hour and a half away. The foal will be dead by then and possibly Fanny too."

"Have you had to deal with this condition before?" Penny asked.

"Yes, many times, mostly with cows. Sometimes you can go in and help it to come out backwards, but it doesn't always work out. If it doesn't you have to cut it up with a type of cheese wire and bring it out one piece at a time to save the mother."

"Oh my god, Maggie . . . you can't do that, you can't!"

"It may come to that. I wish MP was here, he'd know what to do," Maggie replied, then took a long sad look at Penny. "I can't help her, Pen, not with this arm, but *you* can, you can be my arms."

Penny stepped back in fright; she didn't have to ask Maggie to repeat herself, she knew exactly what was being asked of her.

"No way . . . I can't . . . I won't. How can you expect me to do that? I know sod all about what you're talking about. Why don't you get one of those two to do it?"

"I need them to keep Fanny calm, and she knows them."

With Penny now near to tears and visibly shaken, Maggie moved up close to her, and like Madame Renard hours earlier, placed her hand on her tummy. What Maggie said next, and unaware how near to the mark she was, brought home to Penny that it could be her in the future.

"One day, maid, you and Dad will hopefully have a little foal of your own. But what if, like the little bugger in there . . ." Maggie paused to glance at the mare. "What if yours got into trouble? You'd want someone to be there to help, wouldn't you? Well her foal needs *your* help."

"God, you can be a ruthless cow at times," Penny replied.

"Yes, when I have to be," replied Maggie.

Chapter 31

"I'm scared I'll hurt her, Mags."

"We've got nothing to lose, trust me. Together we can do this, I'm begging you, help her, please?"

Despite her apprehension, Penny removed her cream jumper and found herself scrubbing up – a surreal task as she did not know how she was going to do what she had to do.

"Right, maid, first things first," said Maggie, handing her a pair of nail clippers.

"No, not my nails, please! I've been nurturing these for the wedding."

"Sorry, Pen, you said yourself you don't want to hurt her. I'll buy you some stick-ons. Now, come on, time's running short. Once Fanny's waters break, her natural instinct will be to get the foal out quickly."

Listening to Maggie's disciplined demands reminded Penny of her profession, that of an actress in the theatre. There, a particular person would guide her: her director. Remembering that, Penny knew she would have to concentrate like never before and follow Maggie's instructions to the letter; but as for the idea that they could, 'do this together', Penny still wasn't convinced.

"You look the part if nothing else," said Maggie, with a fraught smile.

"I find it hard to believe that, standing here in only my bra and jeans and covered in iodine up to my armpits . . ." Penny somewhat nervously replied.

"Oh, I think it's the surgical gloves and blue hair net that does it, maid . . ."

"Well, if you think so . . . Just make sure no one takes a picture of me like this, that's all, please!"

"Don't worry, Pen, if I find someone with a phone in their hand, I'll personally insert it where the sun don't shine! Now, ready?"

Penny frowned and shook her head, in one last-ditch effort of protest.

"Right, Pen, I'm going to give you a crash course in what you're looking for using Fanny's leg as an example, OK? In a normal delivery, the head comes out first with its hind legs coming out last. But in this instance, the foal's backside is where the head should be. Now you're going to feel two lumps. A large one – its rump – is just here," said Maggie, with her hand on the mare's rear. "Got that?"

"Yes, the rump," Penny replied, with barely breath to talk.

"Now, the other lump will be a smaller one – that's the tail. That'll give you your bearings as to where you are. From the base of the tail make your way down the foal's buttock and along the leg, which you should find is in line with its belly. Make your way down the leg and then you'll come to this joint, the hock." Again, Maggie paused, now crouching down, her hand the centre of attention. "Then along the cannon bone to the hoof – the foot to you. Now, this is the tricky part. Cup the hoof in the palm of your hand then manipulate the leg backwards, keeping it in line with the foal's body as much as possible. Remember to keep the hoof in your palm and then gently pull it out towards you so that I can get a hold of it. Then you'll have to repeat it for the other leg." Maggie didn't bother to ask Penny if she had understood everything that she had said, as with the mare showing the final signs of labour, the on-the-job training was over. "OK, maid, I've prepped her for you . . . in you go."

"Aah, I don't believe I'm doing this," Penny groaned.

"Close your eyes, Pen, it'll help you visualise where you are without being distracted."

"Really? I wish it worked for my sense of smell!"

"You'll get used to it. Now, have you got to the neck of the womb yet?"

"Yes, I think so. I can feel a mound . . . God, she's squeezing my arm."

"That's normal, Pen," replied Maggie. "Now you'll have to feel through the amniotic sac. Don't worry, you won't break it, it's pretty pliable. Then do as I instructed you to do."

"Yes . . . OK . . . bugger, where am I?" Penny muttered. "Christ, my arm's not long enough."

"You've probably gone too far, keep trying," said Maggie, who was watching and assessing every movement that Penny made as she twisted her shoulder, raising herself up on her toes then crouching slightly, only to twist once more. Then encouraging but terse words broke through the sounds of pain and exertion as Penny grunted, "Got you, you sod," and very slowly she withdrew her arm . . . and the foal's small hoof appeared.

"Good girl, Pen, now let me take . . ."

"Shit, it's gone back in. Sorry, Mags, it slipped out of my grasp, sorry . . ."

"Don't be sorry, maid, that's good. It means the foal is still alive in there. Now change your gloves and go back and get it. Come on, chop, chop."

Again, Penny used every contortion she could possibly make, once more retrieving the allusive hoof. When she did, there was no letting go, not before Maggie had tied a tether to it, ready for its twin.

With constant mutterings to herself of, "Come on, you stupid cow, no . . . that way," Penny finally followed with "That's good, that's good. Right, you little hoof, you're coming with me," and at last she had her matching pair.

So engrossed had she become in the endeavour, defying her lack of belief that she could do this, Penny had lost all track of time; but Maggie knew that from the moment she cut the amniotic sac, when the foal's hooves were visible, that time would conspire against them and reduce the chance of the foal being born alive.

"Right, Pen, you've had your fun, now we've got to pull."

"You what? I can hardly feel my arms and legs, Mags. I'm knackered."

"I know you are," said Maggie, desperate not to waste time. She now gave her instructions as they pulled. "Fanny can't push the foal out without our help, now come on and grab its legs above the hock and pull gently. We have to pull out and down once its hips are out. If we're not careful, either its umbilical cord will break and the foal could start to choke or, if not, the cord will pinch against the neck of the womb cutting off the blood supply."

"Do you want a hand?" asked Colette, moving off to one side and hoping to see what progress there was."

"No," Maggie replied who, like Penny, was weakening. "You girls just keep her still."

"It's coming, Mags, it's coming!" cried Penny, and she dropped to her knees to pull.

Maggie though wasn't so sure. "Come on, Fan, help us out and have a contraction. Don't be so bloody lazy."

But as Maggie cussed, Penny groaned, "Oh for Christ's sake, that's all I need."

"It's only amniotic fluid, it won't do you any harm," Maggie answered.

"Harm? She's soaked me and that's all you can say?"

"Just the shoulders, maid, then it's out . . . come on . . . we're almost there, now keep pulling," Maggie instructed.

"I'm trying to, Mags, honest I am," Penny gasped.

Then in the melee of exhaustion, desperate smiles of relief appeared on their faces as the man Maggie had wished for was there, and without uttering a word, took over. Unable to do anything but watch, Maggie and Penny, heaving for breath, slumped on the hay as Monsieur Paul cradled the foal safely to the ground and skilfully removed the remnants of its chaotic entry into the world.

"Ah, I feel so dirty and horrid . . . and hopeless," Penny said, trying to wipe her arms clean with a handful of hay.

"Well, you shouldn't, Pen, look," replied Maggie with an excited gasp. Her face broke into a relieved smile as the new life just feet away from them was greeted by the mother.

"You don't understand, Mags," she replied in a voice that now sounded ashamed. "I've peed myself."

"You, silly mare, is that all?" Maggie laughed. "The first time I did this, I did more than just pee myself!"

As both women sat on the hay, their minds dizzy with a mixture of fatigue and euphoria, the gate to the horsebox suddenly swung open – to the drunken bluster of a man's voice. It was Monsieur Bernard who, swaying and staggering, demanded answers, first from Monsieur Paul then from Maggie – questions he would live to regret!

"Wh-what's goin' on? Wh-hat in God's name have you done? And why is *she* here? If you've harmed her, I'll . . . I'll call . . ."

"Call who?" Maggie barked and, with her hand on Penny's shoulder, she pushed herself to her feet, fired by rage at seeing the stable owner's son who she believed had wilfully neglected his late sister's horse. "Not your father, that's for sure. He'll go ape-shit when he finds out, and he will find out, coz I'm staying here with Fanny until he gets back."

"You'll do no such thing and you can get this bitch out of here!" With the words barely out of his mouth, Bernard lunged at Penny, grabbing the top of her bare arm. But by the time MP could respond to Penny's yelp of fright, Maggie had already sprung to her defence with a single left-handed punch to Bernard's face that rendered him unconscious on the stable floor.

"Ouch, ouch! That hurt! But it was so worth it!" Maggie groaned

"Mags, you silly sod! Now you've hurt your good hand," said Penny, clambering to her feet.

"Do you want me to phone for a doctor for Monsieur Bernard?" came the question from one of the two stable hands who had prudently stayed out of the way.

"No," replied MP, pausing briefly from attending to the newborn foal. "He's out cold with drink. When I've finished here, I'll carry him back to his room to sleep it off, then I'm taking these ladies home. The stable hands can tidy up and keep an eye on Fanny and her foal."

"No, Paul, *I'm* staying here with Fanny. That drunken arsehole, Bernard, won't dare come anywhere near them while I'm here," Maggie replied.

It was an answer that came as little surprise to MP. He'd known Maggie all her life and, over the years, had affectionately called her his little '*vache têtu*' – stubborn cow.

Wrapped in a horse blanket against the chill of a cloudless night, and with it approaching 2.40am, Penny was barely awake by the time MP had driven the short distance back to the chateau. With Yvette caring for Auner, Madame Renard and Sophie waited at the bottom of the steps, primed by a phone call from Maggie warning them what to expect.

"Carry her to my boudoir, Paul. Sophie, run my bath for mademoiselle, then go to the kitchen and get the food Monsieur Johnny has prepared, quickly now," ordered the matriarch. Her calm instructions masked her concern for the welfare of the dishevelled women who only she and Sam knew was pregnant.

"Ah, this is bliss, thank you. It's just what I need," said Penny, moaning with a mixture of pleasure and pain as she slipped beneath the water perfumed with rose oil. But it was a pleasure tinged with guilt at the thought of Maggie, equally as tired, but denying herself a hot bath in order to protect the mare and her new-born foal. It was a decision that would have implications that she could never imagine.

"Sam, sweetheart . . . is that you? What are you doing here?" asked a startled Penny. Her eyes had barely opened, and here he was, sitting on the bed holding her hand and smiling at her.

"Hello, angel, sorry if I alarmed you," he said quietly over her protestations of discomfort as she pulled herself up the bed.

"Christ, my poor body, Sam. It aches from head to toe. I presume by the sheer fact that you're here, you know what happened and what I did?"

"Yes, hun, more than you realise."

"Sam . . . what do you mean? What's happened? It's Maggie, isn't it? Tell me, please."

"Calm yourself, everything is under control. Here, drink this water and don't look so worried."

"It is Maggie, isn't it?" she asked again, anxiously awaiting Sam's reply as all sorts of imaginary scenarios filled her thoughts.

"Estelle phoned me late last night to inform me that she'd had three missed calls from Maggie. She was worried for you both and said that MP had gone to the stables to see what was going on. Then later she phoned me again to say that you had arrived back here and in quite a state."

"Oh did she? I didn't know that. I only saw her briefly when she was taking some clean clothes to the stables for Maggie," Penny replied.

"Yes, well, I became concerned for you both so I decided to catch an early flight to Paris and then hired a car. I arrived just in time to see you open your eyes."

"What time is it?" she asked.

"Just shy of 11.00am. You've been out for the count, you poor darling."

"To hell with me, you still haven't told me about Maggie. She hasn't gone and hit that awful man Bernard again, has she?"

"No, luckily for him. Apparently after Bernard woke up from his drunken stupor, he was told that Maggie was still there with Fanny. He phoned the police to get her arrested for assaulting him."

"Oh no, poor Maggie . . . so she's been taken away to the police station?" She couldn't believe her ears; she had gone to sleep only to wake up in a nightmare.

"Nah." Sam grinned at her, his eyes full of fatherly faith in his daughter. "You should know Maggie by now. When she says she's going to do something, not even the police can stop her. She refused to come out of the Fanny's box until Raymond returned."

"And has he?" asked Penny brusquely.

"Just. I spoke to him shortly before you woke up and he wants to see you at the stables this afternoon. Estelle is there and has taken Auner with her."

"Oh, Sam, does he? Poor man, he must be furious with Maggie and me. He goes away to have surgery on his feet, only to find all hell's broken loose while his back is turned."

"I wouldn't worry, sweetheart. You don't know Raymond like I do. It'll be fine, trust me.

"Really?" she responded. "I wish I could share your optimism."

"The place looks deserted. Where is everyone?" Penny asked, with her arm squeezed tightly around Sam's. They walked across the stable quadrangle, now eerily quiet, with only the sound of horses moving in their boxes or neighing for attention. There were none of the normal everyday activities she expected to see, not even stable hands mucking out or grooming their charges. There wasn't a soul in sight.

"Let's ask the horses, maybe one of them can tell us?" Sam said.

"Don't be flippant, Sam, you know I'm not enjoying this," she hissed.

As much as he tried, he couldn't persuade her not to worry. It was as though she had convinced herself that because Maggie was in trouble with the police, that it was partly her fault, and that Raymond Goss was angry with her.

"Sorry, sweetheart, let's try the new barn where Fanny is, shall we? Maybe we'll find someone there," said Sam.

"Back to the scene of the crime," Penny muttered.

It was only a short walk to the barn's entrance doors, and as Sam opened one slightly he paused and said, "Ladies first."

"Oh, you sod, Sam Farmer!" Penny gasped, clapping a hand across her mouth.

There in front of her were all the smiling faces of the people who worked at the stables, all of whom were holding a glass of champagne in the air – in honour of her! The elusive stable hands were there, too, as well as Estelle and Maggie with Auner; but there was one particular person who stood out: Papa Goss. On previous visits, she had only ever seen him sitting in a wheelchair; now he was standing with only the aid of a cane. He walked – more of a shuffle, really – the few steps towards her, and then took her hand in his. Seeing his boyish smile, made Penny instantly realise how foolish she'd been. She had let her imagination get the better of her, as she was soon to find out. First, though, the charismatic Frenchman couldn't resist laying a carpet of seductive words at Penny's feet. The words he spoke were pure theatre:

"My beautiful Mademoiselle Penny, being able to walk again is all for you!" He paused and, savouring the moment, kissed her hand. "I thought that when you came to your senses and married me instead, I'd be able to walk up the aisle with my new young bride on my arm."

Now relaxed and flattered by his teasing words, Penny let out a carefree chuckle and replied with an equally flirtatious response, "Don't give up hope just yet. You've still got two weeks to persuade me to change my mind," and returning his affection for her, she placed a tender peck on his lips.

"You see, Sam, my dear friend," said Raymond, with a poise that was uniquely his, "She's . . . wavering!"

Joining in with the spontaneous laughter to Raymond's suave repartee, Penny became aware that she was no longer the centre of attention. From the far end of the row of horseboxes, Fanny was lead out, followed by her foal – that looked every inch a thoroughbred. Penny had often heard Maggie say that horses were not only intelligent but also perceptive, and Fanny proved to be exactly that. Unprompted, the mare, with ears pricked and her head gesturing in a nodding motion, walked up to Penny.

"Don't be afraid, mademoiselle," Raymond said calmly, taking hold of her hand. "Listen to her. Fanny's making faint nickering sounds. She's thanking you for saving the life of her foal."

She may have thought that that was praise enough, but as for Raymond Goss, he personally felt a debt of gratitude to her and Maggie. Fanny was Sabine's horse, the young woman who gave her life saving the lives of the animals she loved so much. The continuation of the mare's bloodline was his way of creating a lasting legacy to his dearly missed daughter and the future of the stables. With memories of that fateful day, Papa Goss had thanked Maggie the only way he knew how, and in a way Sabine would've wanted.

Now it was Penny's turn. It was a commission that filled her with pride, and Estelle called out with a chorus of laughter. "Just in case you hadn't noticed . . . it's a boy!"

Penny's eyes fixed on the chestnut foal huddled close to his mother and knew, without doubt, that there could be only one name for him. "Normandy," declared Penny. "The land of his birth!"

As she sparingly sipped her champagne, Penny couldn't help but notice that throughout the foal's naming celebration, Maggie seemed subdued, as though her thoughts were elsewhere.

"You OK, sweetheart?" asked Penny, quietly taking Maggie to one side.

"To tell you the truth, Pen, I'm not sure . . . not sure at all."

"Do you want to talk about it?"

"Well, yes, I think I'm going to have to. Come with me will you, please?" said Maggie in a tone that sounded more of a command than a friendly request.

"Of course, I will, as long as it doesn't involve me having to stick my arm back inside a horse again," Penny quipped – a jest that fell on deaf ears.

Leaving Auner with Estelle, they walked arm in arm from the new barn across the quadrangle to stop at the base of Sabine's statue. Up until that point Maggie hadn't said a word and Penny sensed she had no intention to.

"I'm sure the smoke from the fire has affected Papa Goss's mind, you know," she finally said, her hand stroking the bronzed fingers of her now ageless friend. "Do you want to know what that lovely man has asked me?"

Penny didn't reply. It wasn't said as a question. She knew it was Maggie thinking out loud.

"He's asked me to run the stables with him and take over when he's gone," Maggie said. "He . . . he said that's what Sabine would have wanted . . . can you believe that?"

Whether this time it was meant as a question or not, Penny replied anyway, and she didn't mince her words. "Yes, I can, and he's right. You should. He knows how much these stables mean to you, and besides, he treats you and Estelle like his own daughters, and you miss Sabine as you would a sister."

"So, you think I should?" asked Maggie.

"Raymond's no fool. He knows you're more than capable of running the place with or without him. I saw that for myself last night when you tore into those two stable maids for not doing their job. What about Bernard though?"

"Oh, that bastard's gone, and I broke his nose when I hit him," said Maggie gleefully, not hiding her satisfaction of the fact. "When Gossy heard that Bernard had attacked you he was horrified, really angry and concerned for you; that and Bernard being negligent in the care of Fanny infuriated him. Gossy told the police that instead of arresting me for assault, he wanted Bernard escorted off the estate. He won't be coming back."

"Look at it as a fresh start for you and Auner, Maggie. With the farmhouse just down the road, you'll be near Madame Renard and everyone."

For the first time since they had been there, Maggie raised a smile, turning to survey what she would be letting herself in for.

"Papa Goss put the lad on a pony earlier and he took to it like a duck to water. I have a feeling Gossy and Auner are going to be great friends. They really like each other."

"What's there not to like about either of them?" Penny replied.

"Oh my god, Pen . . . you know what this means, don't you? I'll have *two* boys to contend with!"

Chapter 32

Something Borrowed

With her shorter-than-planned fingernails manicured and painted in a vibrant red, and her normally long flowing hair now done up into a stylish chignon decorated with small pearls, Penny slipped off her bathrobe and stood sideways in front of her full-length mirror, her hand flat against her still baby-bump-less tummy. Suzie, her long-time friend and make-up artist had just left, her job done. That left Madame Renard and the one person that every leading lady couldn't do without, her dresser, Mavis. This was the last time Mavis would assist in preparing Penny for what she called, 'the most important scene of her life'.

"Mavis, do you remember . . .?" she asked, dreamingly glancing at her dresser, who took her bathrobe and hung it on the hook of the closed bedroom door.

Penny continued to reminisce, reminding herself and Mavis of the times when, as a young girl, she would accompany her aunts to the theatre and sit quietly in their dressing rooms. She would observe that amidst the frenetic and sometimes fractious atmosphere, there would be this calm and unflappable lady, the consummate professional who could replace a broken zip in less time than it took a panic-stricken actress to scream, *"Oh shit, I'm on in two minutes."* Penny recalled how privileged she felt when, taking on the role of Katherine, she was told that Mavis would be her dresser; but at that time, she was unaware that the elderly lady (as a favour to her aunts) had come out of retirement to do so.

Once Penny and Sam had found out that her landlord intended

to increase her rent to an amount she could no longer afford, they insisted, as a debt of gratitude, that Mavis move to Devon to live out her days in the cottage Sam also owned next door to them.

Penny knew she had no family, and few friends to speak of, as most of them had moved away, but if there had been any apprehension about how she would adjust to the slow flow of village life compared to the metropolis where she was born, they were soon put aside. Mavis being Mavis, it didn't take her long to settle into her home and make new friends. She was often seen with Penny and Sam and their dog, Bourbon, out for an evening stroll or, at the crack of dawn, in the village bakery for a fresh crusty loaf and a friendly chat.

Penny had also kept the promise she'd made to her two aunts who had felt that, over the years, the 'posh' people had hijacked Shakespeare and that his plays were still meant for the masses, not just the privileged few. "Well, I'm going to do something to address that," she'd declared. "I'm going to put on a production of Katherine in the village 'for the masses' – a one-nighter for the locals." It had been a special performance, and the evening an outstanding success, and Penny knew she couldn't have done it without her trusted dresser by her side, who she often referred to as her third aunt.

"Now, young lady," Mavis continued, "are you going to stand there thinking about your wedding night or are you going to get married first?"

Madame Renard stood to one side silently observing. She knew it was for Mavis and Mavis alone now to dress Penny, something she had done countless times and something that had a routine. Kneeling on one knee, Mavis felt Penny's hands resting on her shoulders, and with a small smile tightened with nerves, and an awareness that this was no dress rehearsal, Penny stepped forward and into her gown to experience the thrilling sensation of her skin being enveloped by satin and lace. Then, with a wiggle and tug here and there, Mavis gentle zipped her up. Penny reached out for a steadying hand to slip on her wedding shoes that, like the gown, had been made especially for her. Mavis pawed over her with busying hands, making sure that everything was as it should be. Madame Renard glanced at the dresser, knowing that with over sixty-two years of experience in the theatre, Mavis knew exactly what she meant by the look. Taking a step back to admire the young woman she had known since she was a young girl, and with eyes now moist with tears, she knew it was time to do what Madame Renard wanted and leave her alone with Penny.

"I congratulate you, madam," said Mavis, her voice choked with emotion. "You have made a truly wonderful gown for the most beautiful of women. I'll pop next door to see if Maggie and Estelle need any help with their dresses, then I'll be waiting outside the church in case you need me," she said, always the dresser.

Madame Renard gestured for Penny to sit at the dressing table. Like Penny, she also wore satin and lace, a very elegant turquoise-blue flowing dress. In her hand, she held a matching clutch bag, and from it she removed a cigar-shaped tube that was made of mother of pearl. It contained an item that she hoped Penny would wear; but Madame Renard knew that her gesture of kindness was a veil that masked a more sinister purpose; an instinct that would not leave her.

Her pulse now rising with every moment that took her nearer to the church and Sam, Penny sat unquestioningly on the stool to look up at a lady whose silvery voice, clear and pleasant, disguised how she was feeling inside. "I know it is traditional in this country for a bride to wear something borrowed, so I thought you may like this, for good luck," she whispered, and placed a large pear-shaped pearl hairpin in her palm, the likes of which Penny had never seen before. It was attached to a four-inch gold pin and chain.

"Wonderful, isn't it?" remarked Madame Renard. "It once

belonged to Marie Antoinette, and it is said that she used it to kill a lover who spurned her."

"Oh my gosh, really?" replied Penny, taken aback and humbled that the dear lady would lend her such a priceless piece of French history. "Sam better be waiting for me then, or he'll get this where it hurts!"

"Oh, I don't think for a moment you'll have to worry about Sam . . ." said Madame Renard, and then paused as she carefully placed the pin into Penny's hair. It was what she said next that had Penny staring into the mirror, mystified by her somewhat ambiguous statement. "You never know . . . like its original owner, you may find another use for it . . ."

Penny said nothing in reply, just smiled, swiftly dismissing the menace in her tone, putting her observation down to her own over-imaginative mind and bride-to-be nerves.

The two women now looked silently into the mirror. Madame Renard pursed her lips and brushed her fingers, feather-light, across her eyebrows, knowing it was time for her to wait outside on the landing to allow Penny a precious few moments on her own.

Penny remained seated, remembering. It was two years to the day that she – as she described it – 'crashed' into Sam's life, an accident of good fortune that she was convinced was made in heaven by his late wife Annie. From her dressing table, she gently held the filigree silver and porcelain rose that Sam had given to her for good luck on her first night of Katherine, and she quietly recited his words: *"May the wind fill your sails",* and placing two fingers to the lips of her own reflection she murmured, "Goodbye, Miss McCain . . ."

Archie had been pacing around downstairs like an expectant father for almost half an hour, excited and honoured to be escorting his niece down the aisle to marry his dear friend Sam. When she appeared from her bedroom, pausing on the landing with Madame Renard assisting her with the gown, she could see he was stunned. He stood fixed to the spot, dazzled like a rabbit in a beam of light, mesmerised by the sheer beauty of her in her wedding gown as she, step by careful step, made her way down the stairs towards him.

"For Christ's sake, Archie! Blink, sweetheart," Penny beamed, placing her hand tenderly on the side of his face.

"I . . . I'm speechless," Archie blurted, still unable to blink.

"I know what you need," she replied, slipping her hand inside his grey pinstriped morning suit to retrieve a brandy-filled hipflask from his breast pocket, knowing all too well that he wouldn't go anywhere without it.

"Here, Arch, take a swig. I'd have one myself if it wasn't for the fact that I'm light-headed enough already!"

Savouring her advice was like a magic bullet for Archie, and his customary aplomb returned to him with gusto, and he now added a scene of drama to the schedule of getting Penny to the church – which was in fact a guise, a touch of harmless theatre. While Madame Renard was adjusting Penny's veil, he walked across the hall and stood by the front door ready to take her arm in his and walk into the afternoon sun and the waiting limousine.

"Just to make you aware, sweetie, there's been a slight hitch with your wedding car." His untroubled carefree tone resonated with Penny in a way that instantly made her think he was downplaying the possibility that things weren't going to plan.

"Oh yes, Arch, do tell," she said, and her veiled stare was enough for him to realise that he had her undivided attention.

"You see, sweetie, your chauffeur took a wrong turn and got stuck in a ditch; but don't worry, I've arranged alternative transport."

"Alternative, like a milk float you mean?" she cried.

"Now, there's a thought," Archie replied with a grin, endeavouring to show her how unfazed he was.

Penny though knew better, and peering into his eyes, as a seasoned actress, she soon recognised he had overplayed his acting a tad. Then in one breath she demanded, "Open the door, Archie! Let's have a look at this milk float of yours!"

With a little flick of his fingers for her to stand to one side, he pulled down on the door handle.

"No, wait!" came a hurried shout from Madame Renard, who scurried off into the kitchen.

"Oh Christ, in all the excitement I almost forgot," said Penny, watching her return with the bouquet. "Archie, you bloody rascal! I hate you," she cried, seeing for herself what sort of 'milk float' was actually waiting for her. "No, I don't, I love you, you know that! But you're still a little bugger," she laughed, as an almost magical sight greeted her: a beautiful red and gold Landau open carriage harnessed to two muscular chestnut stallions! Holding the carriage door open for Penny to join Maggie and Estelle was Auner, who was dressed like a miniature version of Archie, right down to his ivory waistcoat and colourful silk cravat.

Standing right next to him was the coachman, steadied with the aid of a cane, whose unmistakable boyish smile and out-stretched gloved hand drew her towards him.

"Your carriage awaits, mademoiselle," said Papa Goss, whose lingering kiss on the top of her perfumed hand was accompanied by a doleful frown. "Ah, alas, I only wish it was me that these wonderful horses were taking you to."

Penny wouldn't have expected anything less than these touching words from him, for here was a man who had walked through fire to try and save his daughter's life and would, within the blink of an eye, do it again for her because, along with Maggie and Estelle, and despite his playful banter of marriage, he looked upon the three of them as his surrogate daughters.

"Raymond, my darling," said Penny, her alluring reply no less teasing, food to feed his insatiable appetite for harmless repartee between friends. "Sam will soon be my husband, but they say Frenchmen make the best lovers!"

To the sound of her own spontaneous chuckle, Penny held Raymond's supporting hand to step up into the carriage, followed by Auner and Archie, and then they posed as the first in a long day of photographs was taken.

Once the car taking Madame Renard to the church had driven away, Papa Goss settled himself onto the box seat at the front of the carriage, accompanied by a stable lad. Holding the reins in his left hand, slipped between his thumb and fingers, his riding whip in the right, and to the command to walk on, the carriage moved off with a gentle jolt and made its way across the driveway and onto the country lane to be greeted by enthusiastic onlookers, clapping their hands and wishing her well. A journey that by the end of the day Penny would know the true meaning of Maggie's phrase, *'You don't fuck with a farmer!'*

Chapter 33

Stepping Stones

Forgoing the normal splash of water in his whisky, Sam stood by the bar with his best man Oak and landlord Dave knowing it was more 'hair of the dog' than 'one for the road'. He glanced at his Breitling Navitimer wristwatch, a wedding gift from Penny. He was killing time waiting for the nod from Trudy to take the two-minute walk from the pub to the church. This place was not only the end of a journey for a once lonely man who never imagined he would love again, let alone remarry, but for Trudy, a realisation of eight months of meticulous planning.

From the first day she arrived in the village on her Harley Davidson – that would have been more at home on Route 66 than the narrow, twisty Devon lanes – she had worked tirelessly to bring Penny's desire to be married in the small, quaint church to fruition. That would have been straightforward enough on its own, but first there had been the matter of getting planning consent to erect a large marquee in the same field where there was a derelict mineshaft which, due to the colony of rare bats that lived down there, couldn't be capped. Trudy enlisted a local builder to erect temporary hoarding around the area, and then hired a local artist to paint the panels depicting a working tin mine, complete with the pump house and its iconic chimney, so that the wedding guests would have an insight into the once bustling mining village.

There was also the production of Katherine she had organised. No mean feat when the temporary theatre was the marquee which afterwards had to be transformed into the venue of a no-expense-spared wedding reception, complete with a stage for an eighteen-piece orchestra. No wonder the villagers gave Trudy a nickname that summed up what she was there to do.

"Ay up, the ring master's here," Dave now said, giving Sam a nudge as they heard one of the bar's outer doors clatter open. Trudy then appeared, the metronomic sound of her stilettos echoing as she crossed the wooden floorboards of the temporarily closed bar. With a chink of a smile she stood silent for a few moments before the three men, who all seemed to peer at her approvingly.

"Scrubs up well, doesn't she?" said Dave who, more often than not, had seen her in a baggy jumper, jeans and wellington boots. Now she was dressed in a style befitting a sophisticated woman, in a pale pink trouser suit complete with matching Yves Saint Laurent handbag looped around her wrist.

"When you've all finished getting an eye full," she said, pausing to snatch a look at the time on her cell phone, "Estelle phoned. They're sitting in the carriage waiting for Penny, so I suggest you guys drink up."

"Jeeez, better get on, fella! I reckon with that bag of hers, she could do a heap of damage," said Oak, his jest followed by a peck on her cheek. If Oak was expecting a softening of Trudy's tone and demeanour, Sam and Dave knew better. She was after all, the ringmaster!

"Wait a moment," said Trudy, and she positioned herself so that she could inspect each of them in turn before they left the bar and into the public gaze.

She checked Oak and Dave, and then turned to Sam, who stood obediently while she hand-brushed his morning suit and rearranged his cravat. Breathing in her light, flowery perfume, he imagined the abundance of flowers that he knew would be adorning the church.

Then, quietly, Sam said, "I had a missed call from Peter Faber last night. I tried to get back to him but the phone was engaged. I take it, it was to say he wasn't coming to the wedding?" asked Sam.

"No, he isn't," Trudy replied. "Could you guys give us a minute?" she asked, turning to Dave and Oak.

They didn't ask for an explanation.

"Yeah, no probs," answered Dave. "It'll give me a chance to have a quick ciggy." And he and Oak wandered outside.

Seeing the look of dread appear on her face, Sam sensed it hadn't just been a case of touching a nerve when he'd mentioned Peter Faber, but more a case of putting her on the spot. Trudy was never one for dogging an issue: whether it was the appropriate time or not, she dealt with such things head on. What vexed her was, could Sam?

"Peter also phoned me last night. It was to say he was leaving," said Trudy.

"Oh I see, going back to Germany? I wondered if he would. With Mila gone there's nothing here for him and his son now, is there?" Sam replied.

"He was already there, Sam, at his sister's in Munich. He . . . he . . ." She faltered, clearly reluctant to continue.

To comfort her Sam placed his hand on her shoulder. "Sweetheart, what is it? What did Peter say to you? Tell me," he said.

"He phoned me to say goodbye, Sam. He's left his son with his sister and . . . and gone . . ." Again, she faltered.

"Gone where, Trudy?"

"Peter has . . . gone after Kazemi. He's gone to track him down for the death of Mila. He told me to tell you that when he finds him, he'll contact you."

"Oh shit," Sam muttered, realising that the lid to his Pandora's box had just been cracked open once more.

"I'm sorry, Sam. I had to tell you the truth, you know that."

Taking her hands in his, he brought them to his lips and kissed them. He looked straight into her truthful eyes that he knew could never lie to him. That's why he loved her, as if she was his sister.

"Come on, ring mistress, get me married. It's what Peter and Mila would want," said Sam, trying to steer a course away from the undertow of emotions that neither of them wanted to be dragged under by. Not now, not today.

To the beckoning peel of bells, Papa Goss brought Penny's carriage smoothly to a halt outside the two large oak gates at the entrance to the churchyard. Patient crowds of onlookers had gathered and been corralled by high-vis-jacketed security personnel behind metal barriers on the opposite side of the narrow village road. Many of them had their mobile phones raised in the air, replacing the emotional pleasure of the first-hand sight of the bride-to-be and wedding party with the need to record everything. Buoyed up that so many people had come to see her get married, Penny gave them a measured wave in response to their adulation, which to her was par for the course of being the actress she was. Maggie and Estelle also took being in the limelight in their stride; but for Auner, his day in the public gaze would be limited, shielded by his family.

"You stay in the carriage, sweetheart, with Papa Goss," said Maggie, enjoying being a novice mother. Her fingers lovingly brushed through his straight black hair. "He'll take you into the church. I'll see you in there," she said softly, finishing with a lipstick-kiss on the tip of his nose.

Archie was the first to step out onto a red carpet that was laid all the way across the churchyard and right up to the alter, and then followed Estelle and Maggie. Penny remained seated for a few moments, while Mavis and Madame Renard, who had been waiting by the gates, gave the two maids of honour a final preen. Now everyone was ready and Penny rose to her feet to a spontaneous backdrop of jumbled voices confirming what she already knew: that her wedding gown was a visual phenomenon of beauty. Clasping Archie's outstretched hand, she stepped down from the carriage, snatching a moment to collect her thoughts as she too was treated to the fussing hands of the two elderly ladies who, with good luck kisses, scuttled away to take their seats.

After a final wave to her street audience, Archie looped her arm in his.

"Are we ready, ladies?" he asked, glancing over his shoulder at Maggie and Estelle who, with their posies of flowers, looked every inch maids of honour.

"Sure are, Arch," said the sisters in excited unison, their voices almost singing to him.

"Stop a moment, would you," said Penny, pausing halfway along the path.

She stared poignantly to her left across a carpet of bluebells in full bloom. There Penny could see a solitary rose bush, surrounded by pillars of granite Celtic crosses and slabs of slate that had been honed into gravestones, monuments to departed souls. The rose bush was a living monument to Emily, Dave and Sue's eldest daughter, and the spot where her ashes were laid to rest. Like Sam, Penny's one regret was that, although the little girl was never far from their thoughts, their wedding would be the poorer without her presence. Penny knew Emily would have loved to have been a flower girl alongside her younger sister Clare who, with Martin their pageboy brother, waited under the vestibule out of the afternoon sun that virtually had the sky to itself. Its gabled slate roof and cold granite walls, with clusters of lichen, added a sense of ageless reverence to the 16th century house of God.

"You look very pretty," said Clare, whose observation of Penny as she approached was simple and matter of fact, unambiguous in a way that only a five-year-old child could be.

"Why, thank you. You look very pretty too," Penny replied, smiling at the little girl in her dress of mint chiffon and ivory lace.

"Look! We look the same," said the excited Clare, endeavouring to do a little pirouette in front of Estelle and Maggie who were wearing identical dresses to hers.

"Don't show off," sniped her brother as he was steered by his mother Sue into position behind the two sisters.

Overseeing the final moments of preparation was, as always, the indomitable Trudy, as the celestial sound of a harpist played serenely in the church as the guests were shown to their allotted pews by the ushers.

"Wow, Penny! You look truly wonderful," she said. "That's sure is a dress and a half. There's going to be more than a few jaws dropping when you go down the aisle. Sam for one," she proclaimed.

"That's the general idea," Penny replied calmly.

"Hi, hun," said Maggie, calling out to James, head of security for the big day.

He was dealing with an unauthorised photographer who had been caught trying to gate-crash the ceremony. There were, of course, a few select photographers present, *professionals* who were discreet, but this was the one time that Penny didn't want to be Penny McCain the actress, camera fodder, whose picture of her walking down the aisle would be on Facebook or Snapchat by the time she reached the altar. There was nothing, however, that she could do about the people outside, phones permanently raised in the air.

There were two other people that James was also made aware of. One was a respected filmmaker who knew Penny professionally. Trudy had invited him because, as a special gift from her, he would discreetly record the bride and groom's special day, producing a film in his own unique style. The other was a man who required no introduction. Just the utterance of his name was enough for James to realise that he posed a dangerous threat to the unsuspecting Sam and his family. And although their paths had never crossed, James would not hesitate to use his deadly skills and do whatever was necessary to protect his friends.

Trudy and Sue walked back inside to join a congregation that they knew were about to be treated to a spectacle of breath-taking elegance.

The interior of the church was exactly how Penny had wanted it to be. Its vaulted ceilings and white-washed walls were a picture of colour, not only from the abundance of spring flowers that cascaded from ornate stands and at the ends of the pews, but from the shafts of coloured light that shone through from the stained-glass windows. On any given Sunday, the vicar, Rick the Vic as he was affectionately known, would normally have a congregation of around twenty to twenty-five parishioners. Now, ninety-seven close friends and family filled the pews almost to capacity.

The harpist fell silent, heralding the commencement of the ceremony, as the Reverend Victor Matthews appeared from the vestry and made his way to the front of the church cloaked in his black and white vestments. And instinctively, pew after pew of wedding guests rose to their feet.

For Sam, even though it was the second time around for him, the emotions and pre-emptive nerves were nevertheless being felt as he waited for his bride to stand beside him at the altar. It didn't make it any easier with the knowledge that his friend Peter Faber had, after all, decided *not* to move on, but instead had continued his quest for vengeance against Kazemi.

A nudge on the arm by his best man, Oak, was all that Sam needed to relegate his anxieties to another time. Now, he watched as the little girl Clare sauntered down the aisle to the harpist's dreamy interpretation of Delibes Flower Duet. With a wicker basket of pink and yellow rose petals in the crook of her arm, she tossed them into the air, where they floated and fluttered before coming to rest on the deep red carpet. It was beautiful, and there was choreography between the flower girl and the harpist that took his breath away.

Penny paused for the briefest of moments as seamlessly the church organ accompanied the strings of the harp and began to play Wagner's Wedding March: her cue to make her entrance.

Twenty-nine measured steps and fifty-eight seconds. That's how long Penny knew it would take to walk down the aisle. Stepping stones, she called them. Each stride took her nearer to a man who, when he'd asked her to marry him, had unintentionally blurted, *I can't!* Now the only words she had fixed in her thoughts were, *I do* . . . but before that, her invited guests and soon-to-be husband would be treated to a scene of dazzling magnificence. Her radiant smile from behind the silk veil was reflected in the faces of those who could be heard gasping as they saw, finally, the wedding gown they had long anticipated. And if there was a single word that could describe Penny in her wedding gown, it would be . . . spectacular!

Penny wanted Sam to be reminded of how, in the beginning, he gauged their friendship with make-believe roses, roses that would eventually become a barometer of his growing love for her. '*I love you four roses-worth,*' he would tell her. This was blossoming love, and when one afternoon she arrived home to find that he had left two dozen in a vase for her, she knew it would be a moment she would never want to forget. Now her gown reflected that that flower, above all others, said *I love you*. From the hem of her train, eight vibrant red roses were embroidered onto the delicately woven Normandy lace that overlaid her ivory satin gown. Their silver-threaded stems glinted in the shards of light as the sun poured through the leaded windows. Eight roses then became four as they meandered around the curvature of her body to the bodice. Like the flower itself, Penny's gown encapsulated the essence of the rose that was an embodiment of her love for Sam.

The last bar of music coincided with Penny's final steps as Miss McCain, and that realisation made her pulse step up a gear. Archie, though, who had led her down the aisle, was unexpectedly controlling his emotions more than she was. He was uncharacteristically calm and composed for a man who was not only renowned for colourful suits and equally colourful champagne-flowing celebrity parties, but for his emotional side. But as Sam and Penny had discovered, behind the guise of a jester, they had come to know the real Archie. And although he would always wear his heart on his sleeve, he was anything but a clown. He was her rock, guiding and steadfast compared to the tide of emotions that were flooding through Penny's body. Archie paused with the bride's hand resting on his while Maggie moved forward to take Penny's bouquet of red and white roses from her. Then, without a word being spoken, Archie gently lifted Penny's veil over her head and, with a smile, kissed her cheek. It was Maggie's hand Archie now took to take their place in the pews.

"You took your time. Oak and I were thinking about going for a coffee!" said Sam, whispering to Penny.

"Well, I still have your stand-in waiting over there," she responded with equal jest and a flick of her head in the direction of Papa Goss.

Their banter abated, and was replaced by the zeal that had drawn them to stand together at the altar where Penny would finally get to say, and without hesitation, "I do."

The ink of the fountain pen being sealed with the roll of the blotter brought a long-awaited sense of completion for Penny. Signing her maiden name in the church register was a formality, but that name would, from then on, only continue to be used as her stage name. Penny was now Mrs Farmer, and as she waited for Maggie, Estelle and then Archie to sign the register as witnesses, all she wanted to do was share her kisses between her new husband and the gold and platinum wedding band he had, today, slipped on her finger.

"There you go, maid, I've done my bit," said Maggie, shuffling up to the newly-weds in her flowing dress and putting her arm around Penny's waist. "You're stuck with him now! Erm . . . as you're our new mum and all that . . . any chance of a raise in our pocket money?"

Chapter 34

Secrets and Truths

"Penny, Penny, dear!" called out June, waving her arm. She tried to catch her niece's eye before she once again lost sight of her as she continued to go from table to table, mingling with her wedding guests.

The only time in the last two and a half hours that Penny had stayed in one spot since she and Sam stood at the receiving line welcoming their guests at the reception was during the wedding breakfast. June was concerned that, even fuelled to the gills with adrenaline, her niece was pregnant and needed to rest.

"Ah," she said, exhaling a breath of relief as at last she caught up with the elusive Mrs Farmer. "Penny, dear, May and I are going back to the cottage for a rest before the party tonight. We think you should do the same. You have to think of your babies, dear, and a little nap would do you the world of good."

"OK," replied Penny in an instance, her compliance surprising her aunt. "It's all right, June, I was going to anyway. My number one husband . . ." She giggled. "He's already suggested I should, and I could do with being out of this beautiful dress for a couple of hours. I'm just waiting for Maggie. She's gone to find Auner. He won't be allowed to stay up late tonight unless he has a sleep first. You go on ahead," she said. "Apparently, James is dropping us back to the cottages in Archie's limousine, so we'll see you later," she said, un-aware that James had an ulterior motive for wanting to do so.

"Oh!" Penny gasped, standing in the doorway to her kitchen as she felt for the cord of her bathrobe to pull it closed.

"Sorry, Penny, we thought you were asleep. I apologise for startling you," admitted an equally surprised James.

"Looks like our little secret is out, hun," grinned Maggie sheepishly.

"From where I'm standing, yes, it sure looks that way, doesn't it?" said Penny, smiling, as she made her way to the fridge, intent on feeding her craving for pineapple chunks and cottage cheese. She was very curious to know why, finding James pinning Maggie against the kitchen worktop with his lips passionately on hers and with their hands laced in each other's, it should be a secret! "It's no big deal, though, finding you two canoodling," Penny added. "Why keep it a secret? Sam and I have thought for a long time that there is chemistry between the two of you."

"I'm going through a divorce, that's why," James admitted. "Karen, my ex, and I have been separated for over two years now. She left me for one of my army buddies and she's the sort of person who, if she found out about Maggie and the connection with you, she wouldn't hesitate to try and use it to her financial advantage. I'll be free of her in two months. We both agreed that she shouldn't find out about us, for your sake."

Removing a spoon from the cutlery draw for Penny, Maggie reiterated what James had said, but she was aware that she would touch a nerve at the mention of someone Penny would sooner not be reminded of.

"James and I didn't want history repeating itself, and by that we mean the problems you had with your ex, Toby . . . remember?"

"Hmm. Him. How could I forget the shit? You shouldn't worry, honestly, we . . ." Pausing in the midst of reassuring Maggie, Penny shot James a look of irritation that would within moments turn her wedding day on its head.

"James, be a love and answer that for me," she asked, concerned that the ring of the house phone might disturb Auner, asleep in the guest bedroom above the lounge. "I should have disconnected it when we came in. It's over there on the small table by the settee."

"It's your Aunty June," said James quietly, returning to the kitchen and handing Penny the phone.

"Hi, June, what's up?" she enquired, and at that very moment her mind went blank. She wondered why her aunt would deliberately disturb her having advised that she should be resting. "Oh my god! He's doing what? Oh no! Sorry, yes, OK. I'll shut up and listen." Despite her make-up, Penny's face visibly paled, her eyes wide with fear, and Maggie pulled out a chair for the fraught and buckling woman.

"What is it, Pen, what's happened?" Maggie pleaded, her anxiety rising.

Obeying her aunt's terse command to be quiet and listen, Penny felt the need to reach out to Maggie for her hand for solace. "Yes, yes, I understand. Tell May to stay calm, please. I love you both. Pardon? Yes, of course I know it, but you can't think like that, and you mustn't. Just tell him . . . June, are you still there? June, June."

Penny placed the phone onto the table, giving it a push, as though she wanted to distance herself from the conduit that would force her to choose between the wellbeing of her two much-loved aunts, or confronting head-on a menace who was once more intent on testing Sam's resolve that you never turn your back on those who need your help, no matter what the sacrifice.

"Well, what is it, what's wrong?" Maggie demanded.

Penny remained silent whilst she weighed up the options, thinking through what June had said, particularly her veiled reference to what her aunt thought she should do. And then she spoke. "Your Uncle Sidney has turned up. He's in the cottage next door and is holding a cut-throat razor to May's throat."

"Oh my god! She must be terrified! And you don't have to tell me why he's here . . . he wants Auner, doesn't he?"

"Yes, he wants *you* to take him," Penny answered calmly; she knew she had to be calm for the safety of her aunts. "According to June, we've got ten minutes before he'll start to hurt May."

"Well, that's it, I'm getting hold of Sam, he'll want to deal with this," James said, his forefinger already tapping the screen of his phone. "I'll get one of my team to find him. In the meantime, we have to pretend to play ball. I'd been reliably informed earlier that Sidney was in the area."

"Who by? Who told you?" asked Maggie, grabbing his forearm.

"I can't tell you that, sorry. I promised I wouldn't say who it was."

"Stop, stop!" Penny demanded, looking straight at James with intense eyes, eyes that questioned his self-proclaimed position of authority. "Yes, you can contact one of your guys, but tell him to get Oak here and don't dare let Sam know . . . is that understood? And as for you, James, you're staying put to keep an eye on Auner. Maggie and me, we're going to deal with that bastard next door!"

"That is insane! No, you can't!" James cried. "For Sidney to risk being here, it shows how desperate he is to get his kid back, and that makes him dangerous and unpredictable."

"He hasn't got a son anymore, James, Maggie has! And besides, there's no such word as can't, not in the Farmer vocabulary, and you should know that by now, you're in love with one, after all."

"I still say it's too risky. Have you got a plan?" he asked, trying desperately to keep the ball in his court. "I've been trained in hostage situations like this, and with a razor at May's throat he'll have to be pacified first before he can be overpowered."

"Yes, I've got a plan and, as I said, it doesn't require you or Sam, only Maggie and me, and then Oak when he turns up," she answered. Her face was deadpan, intending to give little away, and especially to prevent herself from saying *well, sort of* with regards to her plan. "And that reminds me, Maggie. The razor . . . it's not the one I think it is, is it? You told me you threw it away," Penny said with a look that said *don't lie to me*.

At first Maggie's lips barely moved, and then she whispered, "Sorry . . . I lied. I couldn't bring myself to throw it away and for some reason, and don't ask me why, I never took it out of my travel bag. As you know, we all got dressed up next door and it was in the side pocket . . . I'm so sorry, he must have found it."

"Well, what's done is done," said Penny with an air of resignation. "What matters now is that we stay calm and sort this out."

"What did you mean when you replied to June and said, 'Yes, of course I know it'. What did she say to you? It was said out of context, wasn't it?" James remarked, his military training in interrogation being aroused by Penny's unexpected curt response to something that June had said to her.

"Oh yes, that." She glanced up at the kitchen clock above the door conscious that ten minutes was now less than eight. "It's from Shakespeare; with my aunts, it's always bloody Shakespeare!" Penny replied. "Briefly what she said was, 'Cowards die many times before their deaths'. It's a metaphor. June was quoting a passage that was about dying inside if you run away from being brave and valiant. She was trying to say that neither she nor May would want it on their conscience that because of them Auner was taken away from Maggie." She paused for a moment, aware there was something else he wanted to know. "Well, I suppose I'd better tell you my plan, hadn't I?"

"Right, I'm on, as the saying goes. You know what to do. Fifteen minutes, and in the mean time I'll keep him distracted. That will give Oak plenty of time to get here," Penny said.

"Yes, that's all well and good, maid, but how will you know when the fifteen minutes are up?"

"I'm an actress, sweetheart, remember? Timing is in my blood," Penny whispered, and opened the front door to the cottage adjacent to hers. "Hello," she called clearly and calmly.

The alternative of rushing in panic-stricken and screeching like a wailing banshee would be, for the safe release of her two aunts, counter-productive, and Penny had realised she held an advantage over Sidney, aces up her bathrobe sleeve. And that was that she knew his two hostages better than anyone, *especially* Sidney! Any frailty in them was purely physical; their minds were still as sharp as pins, and it was their depth of knowledge of many Shakespearian sociopathic characters that would put him at a disadvantage. June knew the paranoia he was displaying could be used against him, and so did her niece!

Calling out "It's Penny!" and leaving the door ajar for Maggie, she walked cautiously into the hallway, peering into the lounge and then the kitchen as she made her way to the foot of the stairs. She paused, her eyes scanning upwards at the landing and into the weakening afternoon light from the north-facing window. There she saw her Aunt June gazing down at her and standing by the open door to her bedroom where Sidney obviously had May. She rested one hand on the hardwood balustrade in front of her and raised the forefinger of her other to her lips. June expressed a momentary flash of relief as they set eyes on each other, and then the acting began. For Penny, it was to remain silent while June spoke, and in a manner, accent and tone that Penny knew was in the character of someone who was definitely *not* her aunt: Dame June McCain.

"You're alone, why?" June called down the stairs. "Where's Maggie? She should be here and with the boy by now." Following her bluster, her arthritic fingers gestured like a disfigured duck's beak that it was now Penny's turn to wing it!

Spurred on by her aunt's seemingly agitated demeanour, Penny paced up the stairs with a reassuring wink at her aunt and stood in the doorway of the bedroom. The idea of ever coming face to face with the man, who was now her brother-in-law, either willingly or otherwise, had always been abhorrent to her. Just seeing his twisted, conceited leer and gaunt unshaven face made her flesh creep. She felt an ache like a fist in the pit of her stomach that was a cocktail of fear for the safety of her two aunts, and rage that Sidney had the gall and blind arrogance to attempt to get his son back, and on her wedding day of all days! In stark contrast to June's 'outburst', her ruse would be to show an outward impression of composure and compliance. And seeing May looking distressed with Sidney's arm around her neck, and holding the blade of the cut-throat razor against her skin, brought into sharp focus the need to negate his threatening demeanour and quickly.

Having been in the same bedroom only three days earlier, preparing it with Mavis for the elderly ladies' visit, she already knew it wasn't what one would describe as sizable. Its two single beds and small side cabinets were to her left and faced the outer wall and sash window, and Sidney and May stood to one side. On a clear day, the sun would drench the room as it rose in the east but now what light of the day remained, spilled in like a dull hew, greying the normally colourful floral wallpaper. With the wardrobe and dressing table taking up further floor space, moving about was a matter of measured steps, and any momentary rash idea on her part to physically take him on alone could have consequences that made her shudder.

To have any chance of placating the wretched man before Maggie and Oak arrived, she would have to keep her cool – and it would involve her having to swap places with May. The tiniest smile conveyed a kindly greeting to her niece, before the drawl and sinister voice of a man who cared little for niceties such as politeness broke the silence.

"Ah, at last I get to meet Samuel's new wife . . . So, are you going to answer that decrepit old woman shouting on the landing or do I have to hurt this one?" Penny barely had time to draw breath before he continued, but time enough to take an instant dislike to Sam being called Samuel, a name she knew he hated. "Where's my kid, I want him here now?"

"He'll be here shortly. He was asleep and you can't expect Maggie to drag him out of bed, so, in the meantime, let my aunt go. Please, I'm begging you."

"No. I want my fucking kid first!" he shouted. It was the predictable hostile response that Penny had expected. But there was something in his eyes that stirred Penny's suspicion. Had he got something more than just blood running through his veins, she wondered? Now there was an added reason to placate him, and by the only means left open to her: feminine cajoling; playing to his ego and having his hated brother's wife at his mercy.

Softening her gaze with an alluring pout, she moved towards him slowly, submissively, with a sway of her hips as if she was yielding to her master.

"Surely, you couldn't do better than having your brother's bride as your captive?" said Penny effortlessly, as though her words were carried on feathers to float in the air for Sidney to breath in and be intoxicated by. She could see by the spite now flaring in his eyes that the thought of having *her,* the wife of a man who stole his son, fed his insatiable self-serving desire to dominate and again win out over his brother for the prize of getting what he came for – Auner.

Drawing in a deep breath as if he were replenishing his zeal, Sidney's demeanour changed towards May from one of intimidating violence to disregard, and she became what Penny had hoped: surplus to requirements.

"Go over there and keep that mouth of yours shut," ordered Sidney, his eyes indicating the bed furthest away from them. "And you, stay where you are," he growled, peering past Penny at June who was about to join her sister. "You stay there by the door and look out for that bitch of a niece with my kid."

Penny now stood just inches from him, and her expression,

which moments before was appealing, now showed disdain. It wasn't necessary to continue with the seductive act now that her aunt was out of Sidney's reach. She had succeeded in her ruse, but at a cost she naively wasn't prepared for . . .

Sidney, with a sneer, surveyed his new bargaining chip and wasted little time in demonstrating his assertive narcissistic prowess over her.

He kept his thumb firmly pressed into the hook of the razor's veined blade to keep it open and deadly, thus continuing to intimidate. What changed was his tone of voice: it was now cold and concise as he set about spitefully reopening his brother's Pandora's box. He was intent on reviving Sam's recent, as well as distant, nightmarish past for the perverse pleasure of taunting Penny by breaking secrets, secrets that even if Penny was aware of them, he doubted that her aunts were.

"Did Samuel ever describe exactly how he came to have those scars across his body?" he asked.

Sidney detected her sharp intake of breath, a spur for him to continue to taunt her; but it wasn't a question that May felt could go unanswered.

"What's this awful man talking about, dear? What scars?"

"Hush, May, please. This has nothing to do with you," Penny said, shooting her a stern look, not wanting in any way to add fuel to Sidney's rekindling of Sam's past. But it was in vain.

"No on the contrary," Sidney said, his voice as cold as ice. "I think your aunts should know how an acquaintance of mine, many years ago, and using this same blade, attempted to disembowel him, slicing Samuel apart like a piece of meat, and how he cried like a baby."

"You . . . bastard!" came the snarl from Penny who, had it not been for the razor pressing the fleshy underside of her chin, wouldn't have restrained herself from slapping his face, a loss of self-discipline she would make an exception to.

"Now, now," tutted Sidney gleefully, observing, without conscience, the two elderly women bury their faces in their hands, muffling the sound of their revulsion.

Penny remained silent, unable to retaliate in Sam's defence as her head was tilted back and to one side by the pressure of the blade.

"Alas, according to Samuel," Sidney continued, "Rodrigo – the Barber as he liked to be known – is now dead, along with two other men . . . dead and burned Samuel informed me." Sidney then paused, lowering his blade; but he now used a different weapon to taunt her. It was another secret, and this time it was about her. "I don't imagine that Samuel thought you'd ever need to know this, but I think you do." Again, his eyes flared with spite. "You see, one of those other men who died once tried to kill you!"

"Me? What the hell are you talking about? No one's tried to kill me, you're lying!" cried Penny.

"Really, am I?" Sidney answered, posing his question with a smug grin. "Your car accident almost two years ago, remember? I sent a man to kill Samuel and he fucked up . . . he didn't have the sense to notice you were driving his car, not Samuel." Sidney watched with obvious pleasure as this information twisted Penny's face in horror as she relived the moment that almost killed her. Seeing her like that thrilled him. He had frightened her and they both knew it. Now, despite wanting to show restraint in her dealings with him, she bit back.

"Sam is right, you are deranged. I can see for myself why your own wife begged Maggie to take your son as far as she could away from you." With those bitter words and the mention of Auner, she was reminded that within minutes Maggie would, if she was on time, walk up the stairs; but Sidney hadn't yet finished with spewing the past. It was as though all thoughts of wanting his son back were temporarily pigeonholed by the sheer desire to destroy any resemblance of trust between new husband and wife.

He wanted to voice the secrets that he knew never needed to be told.

"I have a secret that your new husband is unaware of," he snarled. He paused briefly for a deep intake of air as if he was further inflating his ego and then continued. "Annie, your predecessor, his loyal and faithful wife, the woman who supposedly stood by him through thick and thin, put up with his womanising . . . well, what Samuel doesn't know is that for over twenty years, she was, in fact, cheating on *him*!"

He heard the forlorn and desperate sound of "No" escape Penny's lips, the utterance that he was seeking. "Oh yes. I bumped into Annie on a train heading for London many, many years ago. She was going to see an art collection and meet up with an old friend she'd known when she studied there. Out of devilment, I decided to follow her to a very plush hotel in Mayfair – far too expensive for her budget. So, I did some nosing about, and each time I heard she was going to London to visit art galleries, which was partly true, so did I. Maybe you've heard of her lover? He and his wife were well-known patrons of the Arts . . . Sir Malcombe Goodmann. I think by the time of his death he was made a lord. Annie and he would meet as regular as clockwork.

"Oh my god, Penny, that's Archie's father!" cried June.

"Yes, don't you think I know that," Penny replied, aware, like her aunts, that if it was true, it had the potential to destroy Sam's loving memories of his late wife and split a new family apart. Penny's angry breath pounded his face as he smiled a scornful smile back at her. "How do we know you're not lying just to hurt your brother? If you hate Sam as much as you seem to, you would have told him long ago, wouldn't you?"

"Yes, maybe it's time I should," he answered. "Maybe I'll tell Maggie first . . . By the way, where is she? She should be here by now with my kid."

"I told you, she can't just drag him out of bed. He's a small child and he's still suffering from what you put him through."

Her reply was a mixture of fantasy and pure acting, timed to perfection to nullify Sidney's ability to tell truth from fiction.

"If you're lying, I'll cut you, and don't think I won't," he snapped, and his words were carried on stale breath and spittle that came to rest on her still made up face, a face that just a short time ago was smiling with joy, celebrating her marriage. Now she found herself fighting for the survival of her family, an endeavour that hinged on a trait that, as an actor, she relied on – timing – an intuitive internal clock that, despite the erratic rhythm of her pounding heart, silently counted down to the time when Maggie would make her preplanned entrance. It would be a distraction, and Penny knew that if her timing was out, even by a second, if she didn't die, she would be scarred for life by the same blade that once tortured her darling husband, Sam.

"What I'd like to know," said Penny, as her subconscious clock continued to tick down, "is how do you expect to get away from here? There are security people everywhere."

"Ha!" Sidney scoffed. "The same way I got back into the country. I have people who owe me. Within hours we'll be a thousand miles from here and, apart from that bloody French woman recognising me earlier, it's all going to plan . . . my plan."

If there was ever an inappropriate time for Penny to smile to herself, it was then; but she couldn't help it. It was in recognition of 'that bloody French woman' who she knew was the wily Madame Renard, and her gift for not only forecasting the future, but forecasting the end . . . the end of Sidney. Madame Renard knew Penny had the means with which to make that forecast come true. The subduing factor to that smile was . . . could she see it through?

That question was about to be answered by Sidney's actions, and would raise screams of horror from May and June. Sidney had stopped talking. Sensing what she thought was his hand tampering with her, she flinched, and feeling a pull against her waist, glanced down to see that he had slipped the razor behind the tie of her bathrobe. Even before the blade had run its length, her robe gaped open exposing her naked body. With her breath now short and spiked with fear, she managed a feeble glance across at May who, spurred to her feet, and along with her sister, helplessly looked on as their niece, instigated by the coldness of the Satanized steel that was again placed at her throat, was cajoled to slip off her bathrobe.

"Now, we all have a secret that I know none of you would ever dare tell Samuel about," he boasted.

"You horrible, horrible man. You're disgusting. Leave her alone," May cried vehemently, in full theatrical voice that would have carried to the furthest corner of any auditorium.

Sidney, however, had become mesmerised by the blue lace-wedding garter on Penny's left thigh, bringing his spite to an even lower level.

"Take it off, I want it," he ordered.

"No," Penny hissed through clenched teeth.

"You'll take it off . . . or I will," he snarled, his desire emphasised by brushing her bare breasts and tummy with the blade as he lowered it towards her thigh.

With a shudder of fear, Penny briefly closed her eyes for a moment to compose herself, then opened them, and with an unflinching stare, focused straight back at him. She reached down for his wrist and with little resistance from Sidney moved his arm away from her body, and then with gasps of bewilderment from her aunts and a sick sigh of pleasure from Sidney, she stepped even closer to him, placing her free hand on his shoulder as if she wanted to steady herself while she removed the garter . . . and then she stopped, hearing that Sidney had, and to the second, run out of time.

"Oh at last, thank God you're here, hurry please," cried June who, from the doorway and with a frantic beckoning motion of her hand, could at last see Maggie quickly making her way up the stairs.

Lulled into self-belief that he was still in control, Sidney was slow to react as Maggie appeared in the doorway, but she was not with Auner as he expected. The one person Sidney feared more than his own brother followed her.

"Let her go, fella," Oak roared, his eyes steady and cold.

Sidney was now opened-mouthed and peering over Penny's shoulder at the big Canadian. Like her aunts, Oak could only spectate as their niece simultaneously, and with one hand still grasping Sidney's wrist and the other now clamping down on his shoulder, with all the might she could muster, brought her gartered thigh up and into his groin. He responded with a sharp yelp of pain that would prove to be his last. Penny then pulled from her hair Marie Antoinette's pin, loaned to her by Madame Renard and, with adrenaline- fuelled anger rushing through every sinew of her body, thrust it up into the nape of his neck and through into his brain. She drew back, watching his face pale in front of her, his eyes now fixed and dilated, eyes that if they were the windows to his soul were vacant and soulless. Then, like a pack of cards and with the voice of May ringing in his ears, "Bravo, dear! You, brave girl!" he crumpled at her feet and stared motionless up at the bedroom's sloping ceiling.

"Oh shit," Penny muttered. She held what remained of the French artefact in her hand, shocked that the pin had broken off from the pearl and was still embedded in Sidney's head. "Now I'm in trouble . . ."

"Here, dear, cover yourself up," came the rushed and kindly voice of June, doing her best to hide Penny's exposed body from the only male still standing. Penny, though, didn't show any concern that Oak had seen her like that. He was the one brother-in-law she knew would always be gentle and caring towards her, and above all discreet.

"What an utterly nasty piece of work, dear, nothing like his brother at all!" June declared.

"That's a bloody understatement, June," Penny replied, still gazing at Sidney as Maggie knelt beside him and placed two fingers on the side of his neck, checking for signs of life. "So . . . am I a murderess?" she asked, half-heartedly, as if she didn't care if she was.

"No, maid, you're not," Maggie replied looking up at her with a frown. "From what I can tell, you've screwed him up good and proper, but he's not dead. See . . . his pupils are still dilating and he's blinking. But by the looks of him, you've damaged the spinal nerves at the base of his brain. He can see and possibly hear us, but that's all. With that pin still stuck in his head, he's wasted!"

"Oh dear, so what do you think we should do with him now, we can't leave him like this?" May asked.

"You ladies are going to do nothing, he's my concern now," Oak said, his forceful reply leaving them in no doubt that whatever was to become of Sidney, it wouldn't involve them. "This never happened. Sidney was never here. Is that understood?"

With wordless nods the two aunts agreed. Their desire that Sidney's callous disclosures, especially concerning Sam's late wife should never be repeated, for them outweighed any pangs of humanity towards a man who they thought was clearly deranged. As for Penny, she read between the lines and understood why Oak insisted on taking it upon himself to deal with Sidney. Facing him, she slipped her hand into his large, reassuring palm. Now, for the first time, tears began to trickle down her face, not for what she had done, but knowing that Oak planned to revenge the death of his wife and Sam's sister Ruth and, rightly or wrongly, she felt like she knew Maggie did. It was finally time to put things right once and for all.

"Here, take this," said Maggie, reaching up to hand her uncle the cut-throat razor. "Penny was right, I shouldn't have kept it. I'm sorry, I should have realised . . . death follows it."

"I'll dispose of it, young lady, don't you worry. But you'd all better get your skates on, especially you," said Oak, looking pointedly at Penny. "Before I 'disappeared' to come here, Sam was talking about coming back to pick you up before your evening guests start to arrive."

"Oh bugger, we'd better clear off then," replied Maggie, rising to her feet. "I'll get James to run us back." Then she whispered in Oak's ear, "When James returns, he's got access to the perfect place to take Sidney."

"Wait a moment," said Penny, turning her back on Oak. "That bastard wanted this, so he can bloody well have it now." And with a slight wobble as she stood for a moment on one leg, she slipped her blue garter off and, with contempt in her eyes, placed it onto Sidney's limp wrist. "Here, take it to hell with you, you bastard!"

Despite the anger and tension Penny was feeling, she managed to have a wash and in double-quick time slipped back into her wedding gown. She then skilfully touched up her make-up in the back of the limousine as James drove her, Maggie and Auner back to the wedding reception. May and June felt that after such an unpleasant experience at the hands of Sidney, what they really needed most was a hot cup of sweet tea and a little belated peace and quiet before they rejoined the party.

Penny knew she would have to act as never before, now, as if nothing had happened. *The show must go on,* she thought to herself.

"Hello, husband . . . missed me?" she asked, sauntering up to Sam. She savoured the comforting sensation of his arm wrap around her waist, pulling her into him and kissing her freshly applied lipstick. They were standing in the plush lounge area of the marquee where most of the guests had congregated to relax to the music of a grand piano, accompanied by the mellow sound of the harpist. She'd found him talking to four of their friends, one of who had become a renowned Broadway playwright and whom they counted amongst their dearest of friends.

"Hi, there, Miss Penny. Enjoyed your rest?" said Aaron Ackkron. His boyish, excitable smile was always a pleasure to experience, especially when she knew it was directed at her. Aaron was the kindest of people who, despite towering over everyone with his giant frame, didn't have an aggressive bone in his body; not like the monstrous excuse of a man who, as she settled back into her role as a joyous bride, was on his way to meet his end.

"I doubt we can get this done before the light goes, fella," said Oak, aware that where they were heading, it was dangerous enough in daylight let alone in the dark.

"It's like old times, isn't it? Sort of déjà vu so to speak, us getting rid of lowlifes," James quipped, shutting the rear hatch of the Range Rover he had commandeered without Sam's knowledge, knowing the limo would never have made it where they planned to go. "Right," he continued, "I've already told all the security guys in the briefing this morning that for health and safety reasons guests should be kept well away from that area, so hopefully we should have a clear run.

"Ha!" Oak laughed, remembering Sam's last words to his brother.

"What's so funny?" asked James, as he watched Oak coiling up fifty feet of hemp rope that he had acquired from Sam's shed.

"I'll tell yer when we get there, fella," Oak replied with a smirk, throwing the coil onto the back seat and giving Sidney a brief glace as he lay motionless in the rear of the car.

"I'll drive. We'll take the long way round through the back lane so that we don't have to go through the village. All you need to do is open the gates for me," said James.

They set off on a route that he roughly calculated should take less than seven minutes, and hoped they wouldn't draw attention to themselves. He was mindful that freelance photographers were prowling about like hungry jackals ready to snap at anyone who was the vicinity of the wedding reception – which was less than two hundred yards from their intended destination.

"OK, Oak," said James. He kept his eyes firmly on the narrow country lane ahead, and as the car's headlamps were turned off, he slowed right down to a crawl. Now his army training took over, and he spoke in a calm, orderly tone, making sure that his instructions were fully understood. "Just down here on the right is a gap in the hedgerow, and there's a rough farm track that will take us up to a five-bar gate at the corner of the field. Before we drive in, you'll have to scout around to make sure it's all clear. If I were paparazzi this is where I'd be lurking, but be careful, there are brambles everywhere. You don't want to go back to the reception looking like you've been mauled by the beast of Dartmoor!"

"Sure thing, fella, you can leave this to me," said Oak. His self-assured smile as he climbed out of the vehicle was a testament that both were once again working as a team. "If there're any critters here, I'll flush them out."

As the shadows that had formed in the soft glow of twilight deepened with the onset of dusk, James waited on tender hooks for Oak to return. Having wound down his side window, he could pick out in the distance the muddled chatter of people's voices drifting over from the marquee, the lights of which beginning to glimmer. Even for a seasoned ex-soldier like James, waiting for the big Canadian to return made time run painfully slowly, particularly when murder was on the menu.

Then his patience was rewarded by a gravelly whisper from Oak, who had reappeared stealthily in the fading light and was standing at the driver's door. "All clear, fella. Someone's been here recently. Possibly to take pictures, like you said. But they're not here now."

Christ, it's getting dark now, thought James, who then, without the use of his headlamps and as quietly as he possibly could, reversed the car close to the eight-foot-high temporary roofless structure that surrounded Sidney's final resting place. As head of security, when Trudy handed over the padlock keys, he didn't think for one moment he'd have to use them for this clandestine purpose. It was second-time-lucky before he removed the padlock to the door, which was thankfully situated on the blind side, away from prying eyes. It gave them access to an area that measured no more than twenty feet square.

"I've only been here once before, with Trudy," said James, straining his eyes to pick out the shape of a galvanised cage, its steel bars three inches apart, that some weeks before had been erected over the gaping hole of the disused mineshaft. "I have to go on what Trudy told me," he continued, treading carefully, aware that like on the outside brambles were an added hazard. "I don't know how much you know about this place," James said then, "but they had to have this hoarding constructed for health and safety reasons before they got permission for the reception to be held here. Also, a colony of rare bats has taken up residence down there, so to protect them and to stop locals dumping their rubbish down it, they had to have this cage fitted over the shaft."

"So, how the blazes are we going to get Sidney between those bars?" Oak asked sounding baffled. "Cut him into bits?!"

"No, we don't," James replied, stopping short of giving a reason. He picked his way nearer to the cage that was set on what remained of a concrete outer plinth. Once, a mighty pump engine had loomed over it, enclosing an area of about twelve feet by fifteen. "It's here somewhere," he said, his hands searching over the bars; he spoke quietly so as not to disturb the bats. Like Oak, he knew that the night time was when they were most active, and the eerie sounds of unseen fluttering wings and the odour of ammonia from the stagnant air of the shaft, confirmed they were in the presence of mammals that could leave a nasty stain on their dress shirts. "Ah, here it is . . . give me a hand, would you?" asked James, who was once again fumbling to find the right key to open the padlock. "It's an access hatch, look . . . there's a space in it just big enough for the bats to come and go," his voice now strained as he and Oak lifted it up and over to one side with a metallic clang. "Apparently," he whispered, "there are those who, in the name of science, like to poke their heads down into places like this. Frigging mad if you ask me!"

"Jesus, fella, I thought you said there was no chance anyone would come here?" Even in the poor light, James couldn't miss seeing the whites of Oak's eyes widen with concern that the shaft may not be as secure as he thought.

"Trust me, its fine," answered James, giving Oak a reassuring pat on the back. "This shaft is over three hundred feet deep, and goes straight down to water – and God knows how deep from there. With all that bat shit in it, it's like a caustic soup . . . he'll be like paper mâché within days!"

"OK, fella, that's sounds good enough for me," said Oak, sounding reassured.

With their sight now accustomed to the dark, the two jacketless men, their cravats tucked out of the way into their shirts, made their way back to Sam's car and prepared to unload their human cargo.

"You won't need this where you're going," muttered James as he riffled through Sidney's pockets and finding his phone, slipped it into his own pocket.

"Why do you want that?" asked Oak.

"Insurance," replied James. "Someone somewhere will know Sidney was here. If they start nosing around, then we'll have an idea who they might be if they try and ring him. You can't be too careful, can you?"

"I can't see anyone worrying about this bag of shit, fella," Oak seethed.

"Ah, and what do we have here . . . pills?" said James, peering into a clear cellophane bag.

"Amphetamines, I expect," replied Oak. "They sure aren't

heart pills, coz he hasn't got one!" Penny said she thought he was on something. That would be typical of him. Taking drugs to pretend to be a man, the coward."

Then they heard it, a gargled moan like a child's first attempt to string a collection of fumbled words together; but it wasn't an infant, only the infantile murmuring of a man in his sixties whose damaged brain seemingly still had the capacity to fire off electrical impulses of consciousness and thoughts; and whatever those thoughts were, they were expressed through his eyes, which were now deranged with awareness of his surroundings and probable fate.

"Jeeez, you surprised me! Good, I'm pleased you're still with us," exclaimed Oak. "I wouldn't want you to miss the next bit," he added, his words so cold and menacing that they could have come from Sidney's own mouth.

With his left knee resting on the edge of the vehicle, Oak reached in, and with both hands grappled with Sidney's shirt collar, dragging him unceremoniously forward, his head dangling over the side like a limp fillet of fish. With saliva spluttering from the sagging orifice of his mouth, Sidney still managed to form a guttural amalgam of incoherent sounds.

"There's a plastic carrier bag in the driver's door. I'll get it and put it over his head, if you want?"

But James's suggestion was quickly turned down by Oak's terse response: "Hell, no, and have him miss seeing what's going to happen?" he said, as he continued to manhandle his brother-in-law, slinging him head first over his right shoulder like a butcher's carcass of meat. "Right, fella, let's get this over with. Bring the rope along, James."

Sidney was now laid stretched out on top of the barred cage, his head dangling into the bat-infested shaft; being disturbed, some of them flew out into the night sky, verbally protesting with screeches and chattering clicks.

"Sod it! That's all we need," James hissed. He looked up towards the night sky and at the bright shafts of light that were now cutting through the narrow gaps between the panels, illuminating the bats' supposedly private residence. "I forgot about the spotlights! They're directed at the artwork on this hoarding around us. We'd better get a move on," he hastily instructed, unfurling the rope as Oak tied one end around Sidney's ankles. "I know Sam wants to see it all lit up, and the last thing we need is him taking a closer look. He's sure to notice his car tucked around the back."

"Well, let's do it then," Oak replied. "Sidney's ready, aren't you, fella?" he said nonchalantly, ignoring further sounds of garbled choking.

Now taking the rope firmly in his right hand, he fed it behind his back to his left as James launched Sidney, pushing and cajoling his body inch by terminal inch so that his shoulders, followed by his torso and finally his tethered legs, dangled upside down into the dank nothingness. Oak took the strain, and although he was holding the full weight of a man, it seemed effortless to him. With the sound of rope rubbing against the steel cage, he fed it between his hands slowly, foot by foot, not wanting to disturb the other hanging occupants until he reached the rope's end, and then he stopped. He pondered for a moment and sighed, as if exhaling all possible thoughts of pity towards the man whose life now hung by the strength in his hands.

"You asked me earlier why I laughed," he said, peering through the muddied light at James. "Well, the last time Sam saw Sidney, he told him that if he ever set eyes on him again, he'd drop him down a hole so deep that to rescue him they'd have to dig a tunnel on the opposite side of the world to get to him. And here we are." And then, still without showing an inkling of emotion, he softened his grip on the rope and instantly, like a whip, it flashed away from him. He leant forward towards the cage, straining to listen for the inevitable but distant splash as Sidney reached his terminus. "Come on, fella, let's finish off here," said Oak and keeping his word to Maggie, he dropped the cut-throat razor into the abyss, too, another piece of Sam's torturous past. "It's about time I got you back to that niece of mine."

"Ha! You know, too, do you?" said James, now wondering who else knew about him and Maggie

"Bah! Instinct, fella. When you two are together, you're like dogs on heat! You're a good guy, James, one of the best. If Sam and my late wife Ruth were here now, like me, they'd thank you for what you've done for our family."

"Are we ready, ladies?" asked the relaxed and now contented Oak, his forearms taking May and June's arms as he proceeded to escort them back into the marquee after their extended rest.

Out of character for them, nothing was said or asked by the sisters when he and James returned to the cottage to collect them. For the two elderly ladies, too many secrets had been voiced that day . . . and new ones made . . . and neither of them wanted to dwell on what had taken place. Their only insistence was that both men remove their shirts and trousers for a quick sponge down and iron before they rejoined the festivities.

However, James slipped away once they arrived back at the venue, eager as head of security to do the rounds before meeting up with the others. Moments later he came across Penny, who was outside enjoying the warm evening. She was talking privately to Madame Renard on the patio, which was decked out with comfortable seating so the guests could sit and admire the illuminated artwork painted on the hoardings that surrounded the mine shaft, where less than an hour before he and Oak had been putting an end to Sidney. Beckoning James over to join them, Penny reached out for his hand as she listened to Madame Renard confirm that it was her – 'that bloody French woman' as Sidney had called her – who had alerted James to his presence. (She had recognised him when she and Mavis took an early morning stroll into the village for some freshly baked bread.)

Clasped in Penny's hand was the large pearl from the broken hairpin, now a gift from the perceptive matriarch. She had suggested that it could be incorporated into a piece of jewellery of her choosing, so that every time she wore it, it would remind her that there is nothing more important, as a wife and mother, than protecting the ones you love – your family.

It was the small hours of the morning before the celebrations finally came to an end. Penny and Sam had just hugged and kissed the last of their invited guests goodbye, apart from their inner circle of family plus one: Trudy, known to some as Miss Busy Knickers and The Ring Master to others. Either way, she was a dear and indispensable friend and they had affirmed their admiration for her masterly organisation of their truly beautiful wedding to everyone earlier in Sam's speech. It was the one and only time they would see her blush. Now they were ensconced in the lounge, and some were still nibbling away at slices of the magnificent five-tier wedding cake, a masterpiece of Monsieur Johnny's culinary skills.

Penny nipped off to the bathroom, returning minutes later arm in arm with James, who had been doing his security checks again, and she couldn't resist a little harmless banter with her new daughter.

"You really should be more careful, Mags," she said, shooting her a mischievous grin. "This is the second time I've found your man wandering around."

Hearing the spontaneous laughter around her and accepting that their relationship was now the worst kept secret, all Maggie could do was shrug and let out a little laugh herself.

"I told you, hun," said Maggie as she gently moved the sleeping Auner's legs so that James could sit next to them. "I should have known you can't have any secrets in this family!"

Then she realised how wrong she was, and that there still needed to be. With tender motherly love for the child who had been bestowed on her, she stroked Auner's peaceful face, hoping that his young memory would, in time, expunge all knowledge of his ordeal at the hands of Moses Jones and Button – a secret his family would always want to keep from him.

Then there were the two aunts, May and June, who with their half-brother Archie sitting between them, looked like three peas in a pod. They could only shudder at the thought of Archie ever finding out (although he knew Lord Malcombe wasn't in fact his biological father) that he had had a twenty-year affair with Sam's late wife Annie. Knowing Archie as they did, he would never be able to look his great friend in the eye again, aware that the one pillar of strength Sam hung onto after his brother Sidney betrayed him, and the death of his sister Ruth, was Annie. They dreaded that either man would ever find out the truth, so it was a secret the two sisters intended to take to their graves.

With a kindly peck on her cheek, Penny declined Estelle's offer to change places with her so that she could sit next to her new husband, as she had already decided where she wanted to sit – Oak's lap.

"Jesus, woman, how many weeks pregnant did you say you were?" he said, pretending to struggle, a grimace on his face as Penny fidgeted about getting comfortable.

"Look at her," said Sam, shaking his head in equally good-humoured disbelief. "The ink is hardly dry on our marriage license and she's cavorting with another man already!"

In spite of what she'd been through with Sidney at the cottage, and what she'd done to him, Penny couldn't, and didn't even want to, shake off the overwhelming sensation of euphoria. Like her aunts, she had been subjected to truths that Sam had previously kept from her, and secrets that were kept from him, all instigated by a man who was now dead. One reason she thought that she felt like that was, despite Sam's belief that the family had heard the last of Sidney, his existence was still akin to the sword of Damocles ready to fall at any time should Sidney appear – which had been proved by his appearance at the cottage. His demise cast no shadow of doubt in her soul that what Oak had done was right and had finally removed that threat. At the same time, he had revenged the death of his dearly missed wife, Ruth, another secret Sam must never know about, especially considering his brother's corpse lay rotting in a watery grave less than two hundred yards from where they were seated.

"Swapsy," said Penny, gesturing with a nod to Estelle that she did want to sit next to Sam after all.

Flicking off her shoes, she curled up next to him and resting her head on his shoulder, purred like the cat that got the cream.

Sam peered into his glass of single malt, now with a splash of water in it. He too pondered, but not of the past, but of the future. He had taken the long reach back and settled old scores, and, even though one man eluded him, he was content to let sleeping dogs lie. All he wanted now was to move on. A new future with Penny beckoned but, at the back of his mind, he knew the past was only in suspension, and that a name from his Pandora's box would once more be uttered, when one day a voice at the end of the phone, Peters Faber's voice, would say, "Sam, I've found Kazemi . . ."

Epilogue

Three Weeks Later

Sam stood in his garden staring up at the early morning sky trying to see what he was looking for and, although he knew it was a waste of time, he still persisted. Not even the aroma of his freshly ground coffee or the early morning chorus of birds could distract him. He let out a long and forlorn sigh. It was all so different from the day before, when Penny and he had shared pictures of their honeymoon in Canada with the locals in the Bal Maiden Arms. Later that evening they had tearfully watched as Emily was cleverly reincarnated by computer-generated imagery, dancing and skipping with her sister Clare, scattering rose petals as Penny walked down the aisle. Trudy had made their wish come true.

Shifting his gaze, he looked at the aerial photograph that had mysteriously appeared on his phone a few hours before. It wasn't just any run-of-the-mill picture. This one, although grainy and imperfect, was detailed enough for Sam to recognise his cottage, his home. It was then that he realised it had probably been sent by the same people he first became aware of after he had confronted Kazemi at the theatre, people who did their work in the shadows. It had been sent as a message, and they were prepared to use a spy satellite some seventy-four miles out in space to do so. It was a message that *said whatever you plan to do next, we're watching you, especially where sleeping dogs lie . . .*

To be continued . . .

About the Author

Patrick Jeremy Paterson was born in Marylebone, London, in 1955 and spent his formative years in a small fishing village on the breathtaking River Fowey in Cornwall. It was no wonder that with the saltiness of the sea air his constant companion, he joined the merchant navy. From cook to deckhand, quartermaster and first mate, these years were some of his happiest . . . and darkest . . . and provided the inspiration for many of the fictional characters in his books.

On leaving the sea, he and his wife spent the next thirty years building a successful window repair company, until Patrick retired to pursue his love of writing.

Connect with the Author

www.facebook.com/Anddontforgettheroses
anddontforgettheroses@yahoo.com
www.facebook.com/patrickj.paterson
https://twitter.com/patrickpaterso7
https://www.patersonbooks.com